SAVAGE
SINS OF THE BANNA

ERIN RUSSELL

By Erin Russell
Copyright © 2025 by Erin Russell
Cover by the author
Formatting by Dysfunktion Aesthetics
Editing by Heather Caryn Edits
Proofreading by The Blue Couch Edits

No part of this book may be reproduced or transmitted in any form or by any means, electronic or mechanical, including photocopying, recording or by an information storage and retrieval system—except by a reviewer who may quote brief passages in a review to be printed in a magazine or newspaper—without permission in writing from the publisher. No portion of this book may be reproduced in any form without written permission from the publisher or author, except as permitted by U.S. copyright law. This book is sold subject to the condition that it shall not, by way of trade or otherwise, be lent, resold, hired out, or otherwise circulated without the publisher's prior consent in any form of binding or cover other than that in which it is published and without a similar condition including this condition being imposed on the subsequent purchaser.

The text and artwork of this book were entirely created by humans. No generative AI was used.

Any references to historical events, real people, or real places are used fictitiously. Names, characters, and places are products of the author's imagination.

ISBN 979-8-9899256-8-1

Sins of the Banna is a dark mafia romance series and contains the kinds of themes and content you would expect from the genre. Nothing here is a blueprint for healthy relationships and includes a variety of poor life choices, sexual and otherwise.

You'll find the same kind of violence and toxicity you would in any other book about organized crime, as well as explicit sexual content that is only suitable for adult readers.
All relationships portrayed are between consenting adults.

Realistic descriptions of medical procedures
(with a glossary at the back for anyone who's interested)
A relationship that some people might consider forbidden
Themes of suicide & (non-sexual) childhood abuse

If you would like to read a detailed content warning that may contain spoilers, please check my website.

www.erinrussellauthor.com

I know a lot of dark romances have a very sexy dedication about being for all the people who really want to get railed by a ~~redacted~~.

Well, this book is a little weird for dark romance. So, in the spirit of that, it's dedicated to anyone who's ever fallen off a couch and puked on themselves in a moment of trash mental health self-destruction.

Yeah, you. You still deserve a banging sex life.

Y'know, after you shower and brush your teeth, and maybe take a nap.

May the soft top dom of your dreams tuck you neatly into bed every night and tell you what a good job you did.

Chapter One

Savage

When you think of the mafia, you probably think of glamor and violence. It's fast-talking New Yorkers wearing shiny suits and making deals over smoky backroom poker games. Or stony-faced Russians eliminating their competition with brutal efficiency. Pablo Escobar surrounded by tigers and cocaine.

They're all dropping the bodies of whoever gets in their way and looking sexy as fuck while they do it.

It's what TV and books have been shoving down our throats for decades. I can walk into any Target right now and find books with some doll-faced heroine being swept off her feet by a gorgeous Armani-clad mafia prince with a BDSM habit and a secret heart of gold.

Well, I'm the mafia prince of Oklahoma.

If that's not life kicking me in the balls, I don't know what is.

There is no glamor in what I do. There are drug deals, and constant infighting, and an endless fucking stream of enemies that my father expects me to eliminate. Violence is messy. Dead bodies fucking stink. Hacking them up is the kind of workout that would make an Olympian pass out from exhaustion, and I'm really fucking sick of it.

I quit. I know the tattoos that cover my neck and face are supposed to mean *blood in, blood out*; but for all the shitty things my father has done to me, I don't believe he'll kill me. Not if I do it right and go to him first. This job is eating me from the inside out, and if I keep going, I don't think there will be much left of me to keep doing his dirty work.

I'll kill anyone he wants. I'll do any dirty job; whatever he asks for. I'll fake my own fucking death. As long as he lets me go.

It's bad enough I'm already pulling a Tony Soprano and seeing a shrink in secret, because I need the meds to survive. If anyone found that out, I'd be a laughingstock. A vulnerable one. Let's not even contemplate how they'd react if they found out about any of my other embarrassing peccadillos.

Banna Lieutenants are supposed to be the cornerstones of our organization. We're a brotherhood. *Banna* means bond in Irish, or band, as in *band of brothers*. It's supposed to be unbreakable. Except I don't think our ancestors accounted for many of us living past the age of twenty-one and having enough time for our demons to hook their claws into us.

Ironically, I looked the word up once when I was a teenager, and it has a couple other meanings as well. One of which is "hostage".

"You alright, Savage?"

My second-in-command stares at me, probably because we've been sitting outside the courthouse for a couple of minutes, and I have yet to make any attempt to step out of the car.

Even my name sounds stupid. All the lieutenants are given these code names when they're promoted. They're supposed to sound bad-ass, I guess. Personally, I think that we probably just take too much meth. You know, for professional criminals who are supposed to be slick. It's a stupid name, and I'm stuck with it for life.

Not only because the Banna is my entire life, but because no one can pronounce my given name. Tadhg. Like 'tiger', without the -er. Not hard, but how many people in Oklahoma City can wrap their heads around it?

My ignorant father was born here. I'm pretty sure we have as much Chickasaw blood in our family as Irish, but the man loves to play the part, and he thinks using the old-country names makes us look more legit. It's the same reason his birth certificate reads 'Patrick', but he'll break a man's nose for calling him anything other than Pádraig. The older he gets, the more he clings to this weird vanity about it.

I think it's the fact that we murder anyone who gets in our way that keeps us in power. No one cares how *Irish* the Irish Mafia is but him, as long as we're still supplying the region with guns and drugs.

"I'm fine, Colm. Let's get this over with."

He nods gruffly, but he doesn't look convinced. His light eyes are still on me, but I can't tell if it's concern or suspicion he's trying to mask. With any of my brothers-in-arms, either is possible. And out of all of us, Colm has a reputation for being the most enigmatic. He's even-tempered, but also keeps everything close to the chest. In a gang of loud-mouths and violence junkies, he's always the voice of caution, only killing when he absolutely needs to.

His fingers tap out a rhythm on the back of the passenger seat, where he's twisted to look back at me. He has ink from his first knuckles up, just like me and all the other Banna soldiers. Except his face is bare, because he's not a lieutenant. Plus, the letters across his fingers spell out "KNOW HOPE", while mine say "SAVAGE", followed by the Banna snake.

Because nothing's cooler than having your own fake name tattooed across your hands.

"Let's get this over with," I repeat, reaching for the car door.

Today is the one rare day I'm actually wearing a suit. It's ridiculously uncomfortable. Normally, I wear clothes with enough give that I can fight in them. I have no idea how all those mobsters in the sixties were out there kicking each other's asses while wearing loafers; I swear to god. But today I have a court appearance I wasn't able to wiggle out of.

The DA has pulled me in to testify against our biggest rival: the Aryan Brotherhood. I'm not going to say shit, of course. We've been blood rivals with the Brotherhood for as long as anyone can remember and nothing is going to change that, so there's no point in getting the law involved. No one ever rats. I know it and she knows it, but I think she's throwing me on the stand anyway, hoping I'll cave at the last minute and, *"Do the right thing, Mr. Moynihan."*

As if I'm physically capable. Father beat that ability out of me a long, long time ago.

I'll go up there, swear in, say I saw nothing, and then move on with my life. The DA can rest easy knowing that justice will be served regardless of the verdict. Our way may be messier, but it's much more to the point. The Aryan Brotherhood doesn't get away with anything when they're in our territory.

I step out of the car with a sigh, buttoning up my jacket as I move toward the entrance. It's a drab, gray building that looks like it's more suited to issuing parking citations than staunch justice. But what do I know?

As I walk—Colm hot on my heels, also dressed in an ill-fitting suit—I rehearse what I'm going to say to Father tonight. How I'm going to plead with him for my freedom. I have to imply that it's a matter of life or death, which I'm beginning to feel like it is, without saying it outright. Letting him on to the truth of my mental state would be disastrous.

The man can scent weakness like a bloodhound, and he might be inclined to correct me. It's something he hasn't done since I grew taller than him and added about eighty more pounds of muscle to my frame, but the threat always exists. Lurking in the back of my mind and memories, even if it's not real.

I'll go up to him, stand strong, make my case for why I deserve to exit the organization with a little dignity, and then escape this exhausting life for good.

Fuck knows what I'm going to do after that, but that's a problem for Future Savage.

I'm so in my head that I hear the commotion thirty seconds after everyone else does.

I'm trained to be on high alert at all times. It's been instilled in me since I was a little boy protecting my stepbrother from Father's rages, long before my formal training began. For as long as I can remember, it was instinct. But protecting Micah was a worthy cause. Probably the only worthy cause I ever had.

Nowadays, all the misery that I've been drowning in has

left me sluggish, and saving my own hide isn't enough motivation to switch that instinct back on. This thirty-second delay is a prime example of that. As soon as I clock it, I realize it's probably about to cost me my life. I've become slow and vulnerable, and the Aryan Brotherhood must have sensed it.

I reach for my Glock, but it's not there. The courthouse. I had to leave it in the car for the metal detectors.

Fuck.

Four men with their faces covered in dirty bandanas charge up the steps. The courthouse security guards are moving at the speed that only fat courthouse rent-a-cops would. They look like they'd rather run for their lives than put themselves in between two groups of criminals about to battle it out on their doorstep.

The wall of sound hits me first. Then the acrid smell of blood and gunpowder fills my nose, and I find myself face down on the rough cement steps without any awareness of how I got there. My shoulder throbs and so does my stomach, so I must have been hit.

Each gasping breath of air I try to take is thick with dirt and dust. My lips graze the rough ground, and I wonder if the last sensation I'll experience in life is tasting the boot prints of everyone who's gone up and down these steps before me.

Fuck this. I wasn't even going to say anything. I was going to keep my mouth shut and then get out. And now I'm surrounded by nothing but yelling and bright, gripping pain. I see Colm at an awkward angle, but it looks like unlike me, he was still carrying when they attacked. He's firing at someone now, so maybe there's a chance of us getting out of here alive. Or at least him.

I hope Colm doesn't die. I don't have any friends in this business, but if I did, he might be it.

In a flash of clarity, I wish it had been Father here to go down with me instead of anyone else. He's the one who deserves this kind of undignified end.

Well, I deserve it too. After everything he's made me do.

Right before the world goes black, I have one final thought. I hope at least I don't have to see him when we both make it to Hell.

Chapter Two

Savage

There's so much noise when I wake up that my initial thought is *I wish I'd died.* My entire body throbs and my head feels like it's two sizes bigger than usual.

My father's voice filters through the din. My entire being has been cultivated to be attuned to him. His every mood and desire. Every shift in the wind. The cells of my body have always pointed toward him, like grass growing toward the sun.

But the Oklahoma sun. The kind that burns so fiercely in summer that the grass wilts and withers under its glare. It's no surprise my addled brain hears his bellow before I even open my eyes or make a conclusive deduction on whether I'm truly alive.

"If they want a war, we'll show those dumb Nazi fucks

what a real war looks like." His voice drips with vitriol and rage.

There's murmuring, like the sound of someone standing close and trying to calm him down.

Good luck.

"They. Shot. Tadhg," he spits. "He could have been killed. Look at him! He's still halfway to being a corpse."

Father calling me by my real name makes it clear how grave this is. He hasn't called me anything but Savage in years. I was already feeling shaky, gripped by pain and nausea, but the intensity of his reaction is unsettling me more deeply than anything else.

"Exactly," a quiet voice says. It's tense but rational. Maybe Colm, if he didn't die back at the courthouse. "He can't stay here. Look at him. It'll take weeks or even months for him to recover from this. If we stay here, he's leaving us vulnerable."

My eyes are open, I think. I recognize the vaulted ceiling of one of our safe houses, although I'm too dopey to figure out which one right now. Maybe one of the industrial storage facilities outside of the city. Then the world shimmers for a moment, and when it comes back into focus, Father's clammy hands are on my face.

It's such a shock. My gut reaction is to jerk away from his touch. I wouldn't usually lose control in front of him like this, but right now my brain feels like pain soup with nothing but raw animal instincts swimming around in it, desperately trying to keep my body operating.

I'm weak, so I don't make it far. Father frowns, which sets off warning bells in my head.

God, everything hurts so much. I should never have stayed with him. I should have run away the second I turned eighteen.

Maybe I could have found wherever Micah and his mom ended up when they fled my father's influence. They might have taken me in, and then I'd be a normal person instead of a sweaty, bullet-ridden criminal about to die on a warehouse floor, cradled in the arms of the person I hate the most in this world.

My world has always been painful, but when I had Micah, I also had a purpose. Protecting him from Father kept me focused. It made me feel useful, and I think it was the thing that let me cling to my humanity for much longer than Father probably wanted.

If he'd had total control, I would have come out of the womb with a gun in each hand and no moral compass to drag me down.

Father's disappointment was my fault, but protecting Micah from his wrath was my responsibility. It's not like his mother was ever going to do it. She shocked us all by eventually sobering up, coming to her senses, and sneaking out of our lives in the middle of the night.

I can understand why she needed to get away from *him*. But the childish part of me will never not be angry about the fact that she took Micah with her. Without him, my life was suddenly meaningless. The only thing I had left was keeping Father happy.

Which I devoted myself to, and look how well that worked out for me.

I think I moan. I want to roll over on my side because the pain is climbing up my ribs like a monster trying to reach my throat. The floor is cold. Concrete. It feels like pure relief on my overheated skin, but Father keeps pushing me back whenever I roll over.

"Stay still, Tadhg. You'll tear the wound worse. Those fuckers really got you." He's muttering to me, and I don't think he knows if I can hear him or not. At some point, my eyes closed again. "Don't worry, though. I'm going to tear their fucking world apart. I'll show them what happens when you fuck with the Banna."

I try to summon some kind of gratitude or fondness in response to his rage, but nothing happens. There's nothing but hollowness.

I genuinely don't give a fuck about the Aryan Brotherhood. I just want the pain to stop.

I just want to go back in time and slip out of my bedroom window so I can escape with Micah and his mom. I want to know what it's like to be a normal twenty-five-year-old who has girlfriends and goes to college or has a job and plays flag football on the weekend.

Someone who doesn't know the texture of a person's insides. And who hasn't missed their stepbrother like an amputated limb for twelve years.

Someone who isn't dying on a warehouse floor.

I hope they ended up somewhere nice. At least someone in this world escaped my father's reach.

My vision seems to thin and fray at the edges like worn-out film. Memories of my childhood superimpose themselves on top. I know it's probably a sign that I have a fever, which is bad, but I don't care. If I'm going to die, I'd rather die thinking about the past.

"Tadhg. Can you hear me, son?"

There's something hot and tight around my hand. I thought my eyes were open, but I must have closed them at some point, because when I try to blink, they open and the light is offensively bright.

"How do you feel?"

"Da?" I try to put his face in focus, but everything is blurry. My head hurts too much, and I close my eyes again.

"I told you." Colm's calm voice pierces the veil of my semi-consciousness again. "He's fucked up. He needs medical attention, and then we all need to get out of town until we can settle down this situation. Out of Oklahoma, if we can. You can't stay here either. Not with all the other…"

I'm not sure if he trails off or if I stop caring. Whatever.

Let the Aryan Brotherhood show up and finish me off. I can go back to my dreams of being a kid again. This is the shit that seems like a nightmare.

When I wake up the next time, I feel more conscious. But that also means the pain is sharper. My shoulder throbs, along with my side and one hip, and no part of my body wants to move. Which is why it sucks that a lot of hands are pulling at me.

I try to bat them away, but moving my arms only makes the pain worse, and someone quickly pins my arms to my sides.

Or maybe it's a blanket? I'm rocking from side to side like I'm being carried. Which is making me nauseous. There's no warning before I turn my head and vomit onto the floor, and someone near me shouts.

It's dark wherever we are, but I can smell rain. That intense petrichor smell that comes with hot summer storms and means that water is probably falling from the sky right now in thick sheets. If I concentrate, maybe I can hear it.

When the sound starts to pull me back into a dream-memory, I'm more than happy to go.

THE RAIN IS COMING DOWN IN SHEETS THAT ARE SO THICK, YOU can hardly see through them. I'm soaked to the bone and shivering because the air conditioning is blasting, making my wet t-shirt feel like an icy cage. The air is still thick with summer heat despite the storm, which is why the A/C is on. It wasn't accounting for the trash cans to get blown halfway down the block and for me to get soaked running after them.

Micah throws another blanket around my shoulders and rubs my arms while I shiver. He's twelve, only a year younger than me, but he's a full head shorter and his hands are small and delicate. Rubbing my arms isn't warming me up at all, but it is making me feel better.

Da would probably make fun of him if he saw Micah playing nursemaid like this, but luckily, he and Cheryl are asleep. Or passed out. I don't really care.

I rescued the cans so I don't get a hiding when he wakes up, and Micah can take care of me like he wants, with no one else around to tease him.

"You're an idiot," he says in the same long-suffering tone he almost always uses with me. "Trash cans are not worth getting pneumonia over."

"Yeah, but you know how mad he'd be. I'll be fine."

Micah watches me for a long time before he goes to grab another cheap fleece blanket. I keep shivering.

I'M SHIVERING. I THINK I'M IN THE BACK OF AN SUV. I

can tell that it's daytime, but I'm not sure how much time has passed since the shooting.

The sun is streaming in, and it's August, so it's probably hot as Satan's ball sack outside. But whoever's driving has the A/C going, and it's making the car seem like a walk-in freezer. I'm stretched across the back seat with a canvas jacket thrown over me, but it's useless. My skin is covered in cold sweat, making me stick to the tan leather seats so much there's a wet sucking sound when I try to shift position.

I want to ask them to turn it down, but my tongue feels too thick, and my throat is too dry.

Even swallowing takes so much effort, I'm ready to go back to sleep.

I touch my side where it hurts, and my fingers come away covered in dark, tacky blood. That's my confirmation it's time to go back to sleep.

Fuck consciousness.

I DON'T KNOW HOW MUCH TIME PASSES AFTER THAT. IT could be days. I get jostled and poked and prodded, but the pain gets worse and so does the shivering. I'm still bleeding, and it's getting harder to tell the difference between my dreams and when I'm awake.

The dreams about Micah are coming more frequently. He was the only one who ever took care of me, so it makes sense. I don't normally let myself think about him, but if I'm going to die, who cares?

Dream-Micah cleans up my wounds and wraps me in a warm blanket, and it's the first time I've felt relief since I found out I survived.

The next time I open my eyes, I know I'm really awake because everything hurts again. We've stopped moving at last. Thank fuck.

I feel more clearheaded than I have in days. My vision is almost normal. Except for the fact that dream-Micah is standing in front of me, in the middle of what might be the real world.

Also, he doesn't look like dream-Micah anymore. He looks like an adult version of the child that lives in my memories.

He still has the same concerned wrinkle between his eyes that he always used to, but his face is different. It's a man's face, with sharp cheekbones under those big doe eyes. His dark hair isn't long and messy anymore. Instead, it's shorter at the sides and longer on top, just long enough to fall into his face and curl into his eyes.

Nothing feels right. Nothing feels real. I reach out for him on instinct, and he frowns, but leans down and tangles his hand in mine. Exactly how we used to in the closet. His hand is warm, but much larger than it used to be. It's a man's hand, with a square palm and long fingers.

I still can't decide if he's real or if I'm dreaming, but I cling to him, anyway.

Micah comes closer until his face is hovering just over mine. His mouth tugs up on one side in an approximation of a smile, although he looks drawn and tired, with dark shadows under his eyes.

His eyes are the same as they always were, though. No matter if the rest of him is different. They're dark blue, like the color of river water when it's been raining, and the banks are about to burst.

"Hey, Tadhg," he says in a quiet voice. "Fancy seeing you here."

I try to smile at him, but my face isn't cooperating. Instead, I'm hit by a sudden wave of weakness. My chest feels concave, and that weakness is pulling the rest of me down with it. My eyes fill, and all the thoughts and feelings that I'm so careful to keep stuffed beneath the surface threaten to spill out.

What's happening to me?

Micah frowns, because he was always good at reading how I felt, even when I tried to hide it. I can see him do a million lightning-quick calculations before his eyes flick to the side with a nervous glance. To the side where Father is probably standing, my brain realizes as it slowly comes back to reality.

"I'm sure it hurts like a bitch, brother," he says. He's giving me an out for the single tear that's already slipped out of my eye and the others that are threatening to follow. His voice also sounds kind of fake. Not only like it's the adult version of his voice that I've never heard before, but like it's artificially deep, or something. "I'm going to get you fixed up. Promise. Close your eyes and try to stay still."

I do as he says because that makes everything seem so much simpler in that moment. I also don't want to risk catching a glimpse of my father's face.

But I don't let go of his hand, and he doesn't let go of mine. If this is a dream, it's a weird one, but I'll take it.

Chapter Three

Micah

When someone woke me up by pounding on my door at three in the afternoon, I thought it was a very aggressive Jehovah's Witness. Or maybe my landlord, because he sucks at giving me twenty-four hours' notice for repairs even though I've repeatedly reminded him I work nights.

I sleep during the day. Which means if you need me to be anywhere but unconscious in my bed in the afternoon, you need to give me notice.

I had stumbled to the door and pulled it open without looking, which was my first mistake. My second mistake was freezing as the blind-panic instincts of my childhood took over and the rest of me refused to believe what I was seeing.

Patrick Moynihan. Thug. Criminal. Domestic abuser.

Possibly some kind of mafia boss now, if the rumors are true.

Also, my former stepfather.

He and his goons had burst into my apartment with the decorum of a pack of rabid wolves, dragging what I initially thought was a corpse behind them, wrapped up in a ratty blanket.

When I realized the corpse was Tadhg and he was actually alive, if barely, it was the second time I froze in shock.

Fuck you, Mom, for bringing these people into my life all over again.

When she dragged me out of bed twelve years ago and told me we were making a run for it, I thought that was it. I was losing my brother forever as the price for escaping my stepfather. I didn't expect her to completely turn her life around, but I thought at least this chapter of our past was closed, with all the good and bad parts it contained.

Instead, I find out that Mom's been secretly in touch with Patrick fucking Moynihan, the bane of both our existences, for years. She and I still don't have the best relationship. When I can't get hold of her, I assume it means she's relapsing. Turns out, sometimes it also meant she'd been letting Patrick crawl his ass from Oklahoma to Missouri just to spend a "business trip" getting high with her here in Mission Flats. So, when he needed to go on the lam, he knew exactly who would be the easiest to exploit.

And when he showed up on her doorstep with Tadhg looking half dead, instead of making him take his son to a hospital, like a rational human being, my lovely mother said, "Micah's an ER nurse, he can help."

Now Patrick is pacing up and down, worrying a trail in the kitchen floor and arguing with one of his henchmen about something while I focus on not overhearing anything

I don't have to. The other three men, who all manage to look like carbon copies of one another despite having vastly different hair and clothes, are lounging around my home, taking up a disproportionate amount of space and sneering at my decor.

And poor Tadhg is on my couch, propped up as comfortably as I could arrange him, drifting in and out of consciousness.

I told her 400 miles wasn't far enough away from him. We should have moved to the moon.

We should have taken Tadhg with us like I begged her to, and said fuck the consequences.

Patrick stops his pacing abruptly to snap at me.

"Help him, boy! Why do you think your mother sent us here? She said you were a… nurse."

I don't miss the derision in his voice when he says 'nurse', because he doesn't bother to hide it. Of course, he's still the kind of old-school douchebag who would consider nursing a humiliating profession for a man.

Never mind that he'd probably faint at half the shit I see on my shifts, no matter how many people he's arranged to be murdered. There's a difference between seeing death from a distance and being elbow-deep while trying to stop it.

"Yeah, I'm a nurse. At a hospital. Where the drugs and medical supplies live. Do you think I steal stuff to keep at my house? Everyone I know would go to the hospital if they got hurt, and I'd lose my license if I got caught stealing."

I'm working very hard to keep an edge to my tone and not let my hands shake. I remember how good Patrick was at scenting fear, and I'm sure he's only gotten better at it as he's risen in power.

His henchmen can't be much safer, either. They're already eyeing me up and down like I'm a novelty. Of course, it doesn't help that I threw on the nearest clothes I could find before answering the door—fitted gray sweats and a baggy, cropped Eras Tour t-shirt. It's not quite short enough to be a full-on crop top, but everything about the cut of the clothes is not-heterosexual enough for these guys to clock it.

Just enough to make the atmosphere in the room even more uncomfortable than it was already.

I wasn't expecting to have to put my homophobe-guard up. At least, not more than your average day in rural Missouri, which is something I've gotten very good at managing.

"He needs IV antibiotics. He needs pain meds. He needs stitches, and potentially surgery. An X-ray would be great. And all I've got is a normal human first aid kit with basic wound care shit. If you really want him to live, you'd take him to the hospital."

Pat looks at me like I'm stupid. Maybe I am. I already know he'd let his son die rather than jeopardize his business. I may have only known him when I was a child, but I saw how little he cared about Tadhg in picture-perfect clarity back then. I'm sure it hasn't changed.

If Tadhg works for the same organization—like the tattoos crawling all over his skin say he does—then his father will be even more pragmatic about the situation. *A natural hazard of the job.*

Pat steps up to me, puffing out his chest and drawing himself up in a way I haven't witnessed in years, but is still deeply familiar.

He's a little slimmer now. Still muscular, but in a lean way, without the pudge. It makes his face seem more angular and hawkish, but his brown eyes are clear and his skin, although wrinkled, looks better. Maybe he stopped drinking so heavily. I'd say good for him, but really, I mean good for the people around him.

It always seemed like his tendency to violence was directly tied to the booze. The fact that he's immersed himself in organized crime since Mom and I left indicates otherwise, but maybe he's at least stopped beating on his family.

On Tadhg.

Tadhg, who has fucking grown. Which makes sense because it's been over a decade. But it's still startling to see. Even unconscious and bleeding out, the strength and power in his body is obvious.

I would take that as another sign Patrick doesn't lay hands on him anymore, but I'm not that naïve. Pat always held absolute control over my brother's emotions, and abuse like that—from the day you're born—isn't something you outgrow.

Also, there are other ways to abuse someone than with your fists. Even if Patrick stopped laying into his son; even if Tadhg didn't have to spend more nights hiding in closets after I left, it doesn't mean he isn't still hurting him every day. And knowing Tadhg like I used to, he's probably still convinced he deserves it.

I realize Patrick is staring me down, waiting for a reaction to his posturing. He's still intimidating, I'll give him that. The air of menace, the cold glare, the set jaw covered in gray stubble. The large snake tattoo on his neck that matches everyone else in the room except me.

It's all a vibe. A vibe designed to make me feel small if I let it.

"Are you saying you won't help him?" he hisses.

Internally, I'm at full fight-or-flight. But I'm very practiced at appearing calm in a crisis, so I don't think I'm letting anything show.

"Look, I wasn't expecting this, but I definitely don't want Tadhg to die. I'll help however I can. I'm just saying I don't know how much I can do. I think you need to take him to a hospital. If you're gonna keep refusing..." I sigh, running a hand through my messy bedhead and weighing exactly how much I'd be risking my nursing license here. As well as my brother's chances of survival.

His color is fucking terrible, and it's getting worse by the minute. A gray pallor is setting in, and he's shivering under the blanket. I touch his forehead, and he feels as feverish as I imagined. When I feel for a pulse, it's racing, like his breathing is, despite the fact that he's unconscious. I press my thumb into his nail bed, and the sluggish way his blood refills tells me all I need to know.

This is more than an infected wound. This is the start of sepsis. If Patrick keeps dithering over this, it'll be too late for Tadhg no matter what they decide.

Ugh. *Fine.* But I want the gods of medical ethics to know I'm only doing this because I basically owe Tadhg my life a thousand times over.

"If you can get your hands on some medical supplies—I don't want to know how—I can help him. But you need to get it here now. IV antibiotics, painkillers if you can, IV fluids, suture shit, and anything else you can get your grubby little paws on."

Patrick narrows his eyes at me, but I can see him make the conscious decision to let the disrespect slide. I'm young —if we're not talking in gay years—and because of my girlish figure, I look even younger. I've found that people will let you get away with a lot of shit when you're doe-eyed and boyish.

Hooray for twink privilege.

"Alright. But if he dies…" Patrick trails off, because the rest of the sentence is clear without him needing to say it out loud.

"Yeah, yeah, whatever. Consider me suitably terrified. Go get me what I need."

I turn to grab whatever medical supplies I do have in the apartment. My voice stays level, thank god, although there's a hint of a tremor to my hand that I'm trying to hide.

I really, really hope this doesn't end in my untimely, brutal dismemberment.

When I get back to Tadhg with my bag of mediocre wound care shit, Patrick is arguing with one of his men. The tall one with a dark buzz cut who stands out because he's the only conscious man in here not vibrating with a threatening, chaotic energy. I didn't know they hired people who weren't savage lunatics for this job, but apparently, I was wrong. I pretend I'm not listening while I set up to clean the wounds as much as I can, but I pick up the gist of the conversation.

"Where's that blond dumbcunt we recruited from the motorcycle club? Isn't that the point of hiring locals? So we could be set up to run a proper organization by the time we got here? I didn't drive all this way to grow fucking corn."

Patrick's voice gets louder and louder as he snaps at his underlings, but whichever one responds seems unintimidated.

"Yeah. Eamon. I'll call him. I'm sure he can sort something out. Give me a second."

After that, it's all murmuring interspersed with silences. Which gives me the time to focus on my long-lost stepbrother and assess his medical condition.

My professional medical opinion is that his condition sucks.

They only had him in boxers underneath the blanket, so once I pulled that away, it was easy to see the extent of his injuries. Each wound is covered by bandages that were hastily placed, and they're all so soaked through with blood and serosanguinous fluid they're practically peeling themselves off. He has tattoos everywhere. Mostly cheap-looking with the kind of dark, violent imagery and fake-Irish symbolism I expect from a gang like this, but they do nothing to hide how much damage there is.

I've got a plastic bag thrown down flat so I can toss everything onto it and easily clean it up later. The more bandages I peel off, the more dread sinks into my bones.

There are at least three entry wounds: one to the shoulder, one to the hip and one to the side that could easily have hit nothing or could have hit a bunch of organs that are slowly killing him. Without imaging, there's no way for me to know until it's too late. What's worse is that none of them are healing well. They're covered in tacky, congealed blood and scabbing that I wouldn't doubt is covering pockets of pus.

Tiny, bright-red little lines spiderweb away from each wound, confirming this shit is infected as fuck. Tadhg needs serious, real-person medicine, and he needs it yesterday. If his dad tries to pawn me off with a bottle of something oral, I don't know what I'm going to do. Without IV meds and fluids, my instincts right now are screaming at me that my brother doesn't stand a chance.

His eyes flicker open for the first time since I've been poking at him. They're hazel, with a ring around the iris that looks like liquid gold. When we were little, I thought they made him look like he was magical or something. Sometimes

I told myself he had magic powers, but he had to keep it a secret. He couldn't tell me until the time was right.

One day, if I was patient, he would use his powers to break us both out and take us to a different world, and we'd never see our shitty, neglectful parents again.

It's the same stupid shit all little kids dream about. But looking at his eyes, even though they're hazy with fever, transports me right back to that daydream for a minute. I'm so distracted I barely notice he's reached for me until I'm grabbing his hand back on instinct, like we used to when we were little. When things got really bad.

He blinks at me, and I can read the confusion on his face. It's obvious he doesn't know where the fuck he is and wasn't expecting to see me. The thought makes me smile, although nothing about this is funny.

"Hey, Tadhg," I say, his name rolling off my tongue like it still lives there. Like we haven't spent over a decade apart. "Fancy seeing you here."

I can see the moment he grasps that what he's looking at is real. Something in his face crumples, and his chest lifts with the kind of tension that I know means he's being slapped by a wave of emotion.

It doesn't help that we're being watched by Patrick and his parade of thugs. I'm sure Tadhg doesn't want any of them seeing him vulnerable like this, let alone daring to have a feeling. If this crew of losers doesn't scream *toxic masculinity*, I don't know what does.

"I'm sure it hurts like a bitch, brother," I say. Hopefully, that will pass off any reaction he has as pain, rather than the dreaded clutch of emotion that strikes fear into these men's fragile little hearts. "I'm going to get you fixed up. Promise. Try to stay still."

Relief filters down into his face, and relaxation takes him

just a moment before he closes his eyes and slips back into sleep.

I'm hit by my own wave of emotion. It's incredible how much I've missed him, even after all these years. But there's no time for that right now, so I pack it away along with all my other feelings.

At least I have the stuff to clean up his wounds and get a better look at how badly the infection has set in. While I pull together my supplies and make a start, I look up at Patrick. He's still hovering, completely useless for anything apart from increasing the level of tension in the room.

"Did you find something? Are supplies coming?"

He nods but doesn't elaborate. Great.

The smallest of the men—although that's not saying much, they're all unnecessarily beefy—looks even more bored and twitchy than the rest of them. He's around my height, maybe 5'10", but broad-shouldered and well-muscled, wearing a denim jacket with the sleeves ripped off to put all that muscle on display. Every inch of him is in constant movement, like he's anxious or possibly on uppers. His hair is shaved into a short mohawk that was probably dyed green a couple weeks ago, but now looks faded to a bleached-out dishwater color. His face—which has several shitty, faded tattoos, probably to hide the fact that he's even more baby-faced than I am—is making a constant series of expressions as he examines everything I own, picking things up and putting them down one after another without relent.

When his hands finally find a picture of me at Pride last year with my arms around a gorgeous man and both of us dressed in outfits that make it very clear where we were, he sneers.

"Are we really going to let Savage stay here?" he asks Patrick, while pointing to me. "What if he gets him *sick*?"

Jesus fucking Christ.

Patrick opens his mouth to answer, but I don't give him the chance. Without stopping what I'm doing, I snap at the mohawk-moron who keeps touching my things.

"You did not just spout that shit at me in my own home. No way. I'm a medical-fucking-professional and you all look like you crawled out of a meth den. I bet this is the cleanest place you've been in your entire life. You can't barge in here demanding help and serve me this homophobic bullshit at the same time."

The man who spoke looks taken aback by the fact that I actually replied, while Patrick's face seems to be contorting itself, trying to settle on whether he's angry or amused.

"You can't have it both ways. Either you get your free illegal medical care and figure out how to suppress your crippling homophobia for a while, or you get the fuck out and take Tadhg to the hospital. But he's febrile, tachypneic, and barely conscious. Which means he could be on the cusp of going septic, and you took so long getting here that it might be too late to save him, anyway. So, which is it? Hospital or secret medical care from the queer ex-stepson? I don't give a fuck as long as Tadhg gets help."

"Savage," is all Mohawk says to me, his expression a mixture of anger and haughty disgust.

"What?"

"His name is Savage. He's a lieutenant of the Banna, and you should show him some respect."

The man's voice drips with disdain, and he says the sentence with such conviction I think he genuinely doesn't realize how ridiculous he sounds.

I use all my self-control to stifle the urge to laugh. Tadhg is dying, my life has been hurled into chaos, and all they care about is their fabricated military-esque chain of command. As if they're not a bunch of redneck skinhead drug dealers playing dress-up.

And people like this say gay men are melodramatic.

"Yes. Savage. A completely appropriate and not-at-all ridiculous name. Well, he's my brother, and this is my apartment, so I think I'll call him whatever the fuck I want, but thanks for your input."

When the man takes a step toward me, fury written clearly in his eyes, I flinch. I can't help it. I've been trying to play it all cool, but I let myself go too far, clearly.

Tadhg isn't even my brother. Not really, not anymore. We were two kids who were stuck together in a shitty situation by circumstance and used to look out for each other, but there's no blood or real connection between us. The intense protectiveness I feel toward him is completely vestigial, and I don't even know if he would appreciate it, if he were conscious. It doesn't change the fact that I feel it just as deeply now as I always did, though. These men couldn't carve that out of me if they tried.

They're just all so ridiculous, I can't help but laugh at them, even if I'm still half-convinced they're going to murder me.

"Knock it off, Lucky." Patrick's voice cuts through the tension, and the man instantly takes a step back. "We're here to clean this mess up and save Savage, not make it worse. Micah is Cheryl's boy. He's not to be harmed without my permission."

How generous. Thanks, *Dad.*

Patrick is looking at the picture that sparked this little conversation with as much disgust as the others. I refuse to let it get to me, though.

I didn't work this hard to be out and proud to let some ghost from my past send me into a flurry of self-doubt.

Standing my ground is the only way to keep this powder keg from turning into a Chernobyl-scale disaster.

Inside, my organs are all curdling with fear. The remnants of all those nights spent cowering in a closet with Tadhg, hiding from Patrick, are too ingrained in me to let it go. But I can't let it show.

We're saved from any more awkward conversation by a knock at the door. I'm assuming it's the illegal medical supplies, and I desperately hope my neighbors haven't noticed the redneck mafia traipsing in and out of my place. My apartment has an outdoor entrance, and it's on a corner, so maybe I'm getting away with it, but still. I already deal with enough snide shit for bringing "too many" dates home.

I don't need to add criminals into the mix.

One of the random henchmen I can't keep track of opens the door—as if it's his place to let people into my home—and a tall, broad figure walks in carrying a jump bag. As soon as I get a look at who it is, my jaw hits the floor.

"Tristan?"

Green eyes narrow at me as he takes in the scene.

"Micah." He nods.

He's a county paramedic and a damn good one, while I'm an ER nurse at the only hospital with a trauma certification in the area. That means we interact a lot. I've known him for over a year, and while he's always come across as anarchic and kind of an adrenaline junkie, I chalked that up to being a first responder.

In a million years, I never would have pegged him for working with people like this. My afternoon just went from chaotic to absurd, and I really want to go back to bed.

Chapter Four

Micah

Tristan moves into the room slowly. I can tell from the way he holds himself that he's keeping track of where everyone else is and treating this whole situation like a threat.

I would do the same, but I'm pretty sure if these guys wanted to murder me, fighting my way out wouldn't be an option. Charm and subterfuge are the only things I have on my side right now.

"What the fuck are you doing hanging out with these people?" he asks me, as if I wasn't about to ask him the same thing.

I nod toward Tadhg.

"That's my brother. Well, stepbrother. Former stepbrother. It's complicated. He's… I don't know, but Patrick dragged him here and asked me to save him because they can't go to the hospital, and I owe Tadhg too much not to try."

Tristan nods. His expression is still severe, but he's softening bit by bit as the Banna members in the room continue to keep their distance. I look him in the eye.

"What the fuck are you doing here? Besides risking your entire career?"

He sighs deeply, and I can hear the frustration in it. "It's a long story that involves me making terrible choices for noble reasons. I swear. Now I have a debt to work off."

I'm dying of curiosity. Normally, like any good hospital worker, gossip is my bread and butter. Plus, I'm convinced Tristan is low-key dating someone for the first time since I've met him, and there has to be a juicy story there.

Now's not the time, though, because Tadhg is literally dying. I can pester him for details later.

I look around, feeling off-balance and grasping for what to do next. In the end, my brain tells me to focus on the medicine. I can't control the weird situation with Pat and his thugs. And I have no idea how to unpack the complicated emotions that Tadhg being here brings up.

Medicine I can do.

Leading Tristan over to the couch, I talk him through the situation. He snaps straight into business mode as well, kneeling on the floor and reaching out to feel for a heart rate and checking his capillary refill like I did before he starts decanting from his bag of tricks.

"It's been about two days since he was shot. Three wounds, as far as I can tell, and the infection is everywhere. He was alert for a few minutes, but I think he's starting to decompensate. Please tell me you have real medicine."

With a flourish, Tristan pulls some vials out of his bag.

"Fuck yeah. I've got ceftriaxone. The not-fucking-around antibiotic. We'll clear this right up."

He throws the vials at me one by one, and I scrabble to catch them while he reaches in and pulls out some other things, throwing me more vials and syringes, seemingly at random.

"Here, reconstitute these while I check his blood sugar."

I'm distracted for a minute, the vials clutched in my hands, because Tristan has so much shit. He puts a pulse ox on one of Tadhg's fingers to check his blood oxygen. Then he throws a blood pressure cuff down next to him. Bags of saline and supplies for an IV go next to that.

He pulls up Tadhg's closest hand, swiping a fingertip with a sterile wipe, poking it with a lancet, swiping one more time with the wipe and then squeezing until blood beads up. He taps the strip of a glucometer to it to check his glucose, and then taps it again with something else that looks almost identical.

My thoughts do a record scratch. Having a glucometer is one thing, because diabetic people all need one in their home, so you can buy them at a pharmacy. But beyond checking a blood sugar, we're getting into the kind of stuff normal people don't get to just own.

"Tristan, are you stealing equipment from your job? Where the fuck did you get a lactatometer?"

He gives me a flat look and shrugs. "Amazon."

What the fuck?

Both machines beep, so I'm distracted from more questions by looking at him for answers. The amount of lactate in Tadhg's blood is the quickest way to tell how sick he is; the higher it is, the longer his body has been degrading in its ability to cope with the trauma.

"Well, what are his values?"

"Fucked." Thanks for not mincing words, I guess. But the fact that he's not giving me actual numbers is freaking me out. "Here, dilute the cef in this."

He throws a bag of D5W at me, which tells me the infection in Tadhg's body is so bad it's causing his blood sugar to crash, and we need to increase it. None of this is comforting me.

My hands shake a little as I reconstitute the powder in the vials with saline and then start setting up the infusion. Tristan clocks it, because he notices everything. That's never happened to me at work before. I'm giving myself a pass because, technically, Tadhg is still my brother—kind of—and I don't want him to die. Also, this has been a weird fucking day.

Without giving me the chance to protest, Tristan places the IV in Tadhg himself. When Tadhg barely stirs for the process, Tristan grimaces and places a second IV in the other arm.

"What's the dose?" I ask him, assuming he does this shit all the time on the ambulance.

"I don't know. Look it up."

"What? You don't know? I thought you knew what you were doing?"

He rolls his eyes at me. "Yeah, because we do so many hours-long antibiotic infusions on the ride to the hospital. You double-check shitty intern doctor math all day long. This is just leaving out the intermediary step. It'll be fine."

"Jesus fucking Christ," I mutter under my breath, walking over to my wall of textbooks to try to find something helpful. While I'm flipping through a pharmacology book, something else occurs to me.

"Where did the drugs come from? Medical supplies are

one thing, but I know you're not getting IV antibiotics off Amazon. Please tell me you're not skimming from the ER."

"Hell no, I like my job."

Tristan glances up briefly from where he's pulled over my TV stand and jury-rigging it to serve as an IV pole, and then his eyes return to his work.

"When I got caught up with these fuckers"—the unmistakable tension in the room reminds me that they're listening to everything we say—"part of the deal was sourcing supplies for my illegal assistance. Some stuff I can buy, some stuff is expired supplies that I take from work because no one cares about it, but for the meds, I made a contact at a vet's office. I can't get anything controlled, obviously, but shit with no street value like antibiotics and potassium, that's all easy for her to pocket and sell to me under the table."

I swear my mouth is hanging open, and my hands have frozen on a random page of the book.

"Excuse me? You're putting animal drugs in my brother?"

Tristan laughs, still not interrupting his work as he turns to take a blood pressure.

"They're all the same, dude. We're all buying the same shit from the same pharmaceutical suppliers. Do you think big pharma is out there spending money on developing kitten-specific antibiotics? Hell no, they get our hand-me-downs and make it work. Unless it's a food animal that our corporate overlords actually care about. It's all the same stuff, but even more under-regulated than we are. Ergo, bootleg ceftriaxone. Oh, and I have pressers. You know, just in case he starts to circle the drain and we need to bring him back."

The expression that crosses his normally impassive face

makes me clench with fear, and I'm reminded again he never actually told me what the blood values were.

"Tristan, what was his lactate?"

"Don't worry about it. It doesn't change what we're going to do, so focus on what you can control. Now what's the dosage?"

I want to argue, but that tremor in my hands is getting worse as a deep sense of foreboding washes through me.

When I was little, I thought I was going to see Tadhg die a hundred times. Every time his dad got too angry, or Pat was gone and my mom got too high and neglectful. But I was a weak, helpless little kid back then, and as awful as it would have been, I think I would have forgiven myself, eventually. Or Pat would have killed me, too.

Getting him back, being stunned by how fucking relieved I feel about it, and letting him slip through my fingers... While saving people from shit like this is literally my job? That's not something I'm emotionally prepared to recover from.

That can't happen.

Tristan's right. I focus on the book in my hand until I can actually read the numbers. Once I have a dosage, I double-check a few online databases to make sure nothing dramatic has changed since I bought this book during my undergrad, and then I make the infusion.

Meanwhile, Tristan continues to move around like this is all second nature. He's turned my living room into a trauma bay, repurposing everything within reach into whatever he needs. He's taking manual vitals at regular intervals without needing to check the clock, and the lack of our usual monitoring equipment hasn't seemed to trip him up for a second.

I move fast in a crisis, but I still need a calculator sometimes. Like a normal human. Whatever he's doing is insane.

"Tristan, who the fuck are you? I've known you for two years as a county paramedic, and let's be real, this is not exactly the frontline of medicine out here. The last trauma patient you brought me got drunk and tried to fist-fight a deer. Then you walk in here like a professional fixer, ignoring my apartment full of mafia morons and triaging Tadhg in about fourteen seconds. Like… are you John fucking Wick? What is happening right now?"

"I think John Wick only killed people. He didn't put them back together."

Tristan's tone is completely dry, as if my outburst doesn't bother him, which annoys me even more. The short henchman that got in my face earlier—Lucky, I think Patrick called him—is growling at me in the background, probably about the 'mafia moron' comment, but I'm so far past caring.

"Tristan," I snap.

"Alright, alright, don't get your panties in a twist."

I put my hand over my mouth, coughing the word 'homophobia' loudly into it while making pointed eye contact with him until he relents and holds up his hands.

"Sorry. I'm sorry, I'm sorry, I swear all I do is apologize now. I've been trying to be a better person, but why does personal growth have to be so exhausting?" He sighs and turns back to what he was doing. "I had a shitty childhood. I grew up around people a lot like these guys. My charming, narcissistic con artist of a mother is actually waiting outside in the car right now. I dealt with that for a long time and afterwards I was a combat medic for a decade. This isn't my first time treating a gunshot wound with stolen supplies and a bunch of armed goons breathing down my neck."

There's a pause, and I'm not quite sure how to respond.

"That was a lot of information to take in," I say at last.

"I'm trying to be more open with my friends, or whatever. We're friends, right?"

Tristan peers at me, and I notice the barest glimpse of vulnerability in his normally bulletproof expression.

"Yeah." I shrug.

"Okay. Then let's save your brother. And you can fill me in on how you have a gangster brother I never knew about."

"Stepbrother. Former stepbrother, really. We were really close when we were little." I lower my voice, to make sure Patrick can't overhear us, despite the fact that he's now deep in conversation with the calm, buzz-cut guy. "Living with his dad was rough. Tadhg did a lot for me. He always protected me. Then my mom took me and we ran, and that was it. I never thought I'd see him again. It's weird."

I stare at Tadhg, thinking about the past, until I notice Tristan watching me with a sharp gaze.

"Shut up," I tell him, although I'm not sure why.

FORTY-FIVE MINUTES LATER, WE'VE DONE EVERYTHING WE could think of using Tristan's stolen goods. We're pumping Tadhg full of antibiotics and fluids, we're monitoring his vitals as well as we can, and we did a rough-and-ready flush, then debridement, of his wounds to remove the festering, necrotic tissue to get fresh blood flowing again.

Watching Tristan hacking away at an open wound very, very close to Tadhg's abdominal cavity, armed with only some sterile gloves and a small scalpel, is not something I had on my bucket list.

"I hate this," I say. I keep alternating between sitting on

the floor next to him so I can feel his pulse and getting up to pace out my nervous energy.

"I know."

"He needs so much more than this. He needs blood cultures. And rads or an ultrasound or something to make sure he's not bleeding internally. Oh, and a fucking doctor."

I glare at Tristan, even though he's my only ally here, because I know he won't take it personally. He remains as unperturbed as ever, of course.

"This is field medicine. We're throwing stuff at the wall to see what sticks. He's young, he's strong. He already seems to be improving. Hopefully, he'll wake up soon. In the meantime, we'll keep trying shit."

Tristan claps a hand on my shoulder before moving away to clean up some of the bloody debris surrounding us. I take one more second to mourn the loss of my security deposit and curse myself for renting a place with a ccream-colored carpet, before I turn my thoughts back to the matter at hand.

At least Patrick has given us a little space once he decided we weren't going to slit Tadhg's throat. He's in the kitchen with the others, helping themselves to my food. My apartment isn't large, but it's enough distance that I feel like I can finally breathe without being overheard.

Tristan is silent for a long time, like he's working himself up to saying something.

"You're normally the most calm person in a group of people who make their living by being calm in an emergency. I don't think I've ever seen you flustered. He means a lot to you, even after all these years?"

I don't say anything for a while.

"He saved me. Again and again and again. Patrick wasn't easy for anyone to live with, and I had all this"—I gesture to myself—"going on. I can't count how many times he took the brunt of Pat's temper to protect me, and he didn't owe me shit. We hadn't grown up together. We only lived together for a few years. He still did it every time. And I paid him back by sneaking out in the middle of the night with Mom and running away. I abandoned him like everybody else does. The least I can do is not let him go into organ failure on my couch."

I'm interrupted by a faint moan.

Finally.

He's waking up again. I drop to my knees, turning Tadhg's face toward me and looking at his eyes to get a read on how alert he is. As I peel back one eyelid with my thumb, he brings up a hand to weakly swat me away, which is an excellent sign.

There's a long moment where Tadhg blinks and tries to orient himself, but I don't say anything. Eventually, when I'm about to burst from impatience, hazel eyes gaze into mine with a surprising amount of lucidity.

"Tadhg?" I prompt, hoping he's not about to slip back into unconsciousness.

His brow furrows, and his eyes flick from side to side like he's taking in my face. I'm hovering close enough to probably fill his field of vision. He recognized me last time he woke up, but he was so disoriented it's possible he doesn't remember.

"Bambi?" he whispers, still staring at me with that confused expression.

Fuck. Tristan definitely heard that. I can practically feel him smirking behind me.

I can't help but huff a laugh, anyway. It's been so freaking long since I've heard that name. Tadhg always used to tease me when we were little. I had big eyes and long, skinny limbs that I hadn't grown into yet, and I was a frightened little kid who probably always looked like I was lost in a forest.

Tadhg pretended it was a mocking nickname. The kind of mean shit that older brothers are supposed to do to their little brothers. But it always felt secretly sweet to me. Especially because he insisted on really treating me like a fragile woodland creature that needed to be fiercely protected, to the detriment of his own safety.

Hearing it now makes my heart swell, even if it is a little embarrassing.

"Yeah," I whisper, reaching out again to place my palm against his face so I can feel if he's as clammy as before. "It's me. Do you remember what happened, or where you are?"

He blinks again, looking around and wincing.

"The courthouse. Those Aryan fucks shot me. Am I dead?" He whips his head to look at me with an alarmed face. "Are you—?"

"No one's dead." I shake my head, using my hand on his face to keep his focus on me so he doesn't spiral into a panic. "You were badly hurt. Patrick brought you to me to hide out, and I patched you up. Don't worry. We can figure out the rest later. Right now, you need to rest and heal. I'll take care of you."

He watches me with hooded eyes, and every muscle in his face relaxes like I just hit him with a shot of valium. He blinks once in slow motion and nods fractionally.

"Okay, Bambi. Whatever you say."

His words are starting to slur, but more like he's exhausted than dysphasic. He turns his face so it's even more cradled in my hand, with my hand trapped between him and the couch, and I don't have the heart to move it. I sit quietly for a minute while he closes his eyes again, and eventually his breathing evens out into a deep, healthy rhythm.

He's still fucked up, but it's a hell of a lot better than the unconscious, panting, and gray-skinned person they dragged in here a couple of hours ago.

Once I'm sure he's out, I gently slide my hand out and stand back up. I turn around to face Tristan, expecting him to rib the shit out of me for the stupid nickname.

Instead, he's watching me with his head cocked and an enigmatic expression on his face.

"What?"

His brow furrows and his mouth moves, but no sound comes out yet, like he wants to say something but can't quite figure out how to say it.

Unfortunately—or possibly fortunately—we're interrupted again when yet another person lets themselves into my apartment.

"Tristan!"

The woman who walks in immediately snaps at him, without bothering to introduce herself. She's attractive and well-dressed, maybe late thirties, but with a harsh quality to her face that sets off some of my internal alarms.

Is this who Tristan's been dating? He's kept things close to the chest, but she isn't even close to who I had guessed.

Tristan lets out a bone-deep sigh and looks at me.

"Speaking of the she-witch. See, I made the mistake of mentioning Satan's mistress, and now she's manifested from the ether. Micah, this is my mother. Please don't make eye contact or she'll steal your soul. Kaitlyn, this is Micah. Please don't infect him with your toxic personality. Also, I thought I told you to wait in the fucking car."

Kaitlyn rolls her eyes, like the barrage of insults that just slipped out of his mouth is nothing unusual for them. She puts one hand on her slender hip and throws long, chestnut, wavy hair over her shoulder with a dramatic huff before she speaks.

Now that he's said it, I see the resemblance. She has the same coloring as Tristan, as well as similar features. How the fuck is this woman old enough to be his mother? I wouldn't have guessed her as a day over forty, but I guess I was wrong.

"Are you done playing doctor? It's been over an hour, and we have pickups to do. Eamon's waiting on us."

Tristan snorts. "*You* have pickups to do. I am not a fucking gangster anymore and want nothing to do with it. I've fulfilled my obligation by patching up this one. The deal I made with Eamon was for illegal medical care only, so you can drop me home and do your fucking drug runs yourself. Use my car, I don't give a fuck. Just leave me out of it."

She sighs as deeply as he did when she walked in, but doesn't put up a fight. All she does is open the door and make another impatient face at him.

"I'll never understand how I raised a child with such delicate sensibilities. Fine, have your way. Leave your mother unprotected. But let's go, we're losing daylight."

Tristan shakes his head and turns to me with an apologetic grimace.

"Sorry. I'll leave my supplies, call me if he takes a turn for the worse or you need me to source something specific and I'll do what I can." He takes a long glance at all the men still loitering in my kitchen, surrounding Patrick like a flock of sheep. "Are you sure you're okay here with them?"

"Yeah, unfortunately, this is not my first rodeo dealing with Patrick. He's always been obsessed with my mom. He won't let them hurt me without reason, for her sake. At least as long as he stays sober. The homophobic snark I can handle."

Tristan looks sad, but I brush it off. I don't need his pity. I can deal.

"Oh, can you do me one favor?" I add. "Can you find out your mom's skincare routine for me? I'm dying to know how a woman who looks like that has a thirty-two-year-old son."

Tristan glares at me, but he doesn't say anything. He grabs a couple bits and pieces from his supplies, thrusting them into his pockets, but leaves the majority of it for me as he heads to the door. Right before he leaves, he turns to Patrick and the others with a cold smile.

"Gentlemen, always a pleasure. I'd love to stay, but my boyfriend is waiting for me. Let me know whenever you need my services again. In the meantime, I'll be at his place. It's the auto shop on Rt. 19 and he's the big burly mechanic you'll see flipping tires out back. We look forward to your next summons."

With that announcement, he grabs his mother roughly and heads out the door, closing it behind him. All the guys, who were previously looking some combination of bored and irritated, now have naked shock on their face.

Nothing upsets small-minded homophobes like queer men who don't fit into their teeny-tiny stereotype bubbles. I don't think it'll make a difference in how they treat me to know that some of their tough, manly local employees are also smoking pole, but I appreciate the gesture on Tristan's part.

Also, it means I totally called it on who he's been secretly dating.

Fuck yeah.

With one smug smile at the guys, I return to my seat on

the floor next to the couch. I hold Tadhg's wrist in my hand, taking a manual heart rate to compare to the reading on the pulse ox and make sure nothing's changed, and when I realize I have nothing else to do right now but wait, I decide to keep holding on. If Tadhg has no one else to watch out for him right now, the least I can do is make sure he has my full attention.

He deserves that much, at least.

Chapter Five

Savage

It's too dark. I can tell my eyes are open because they're dry as hell, but the world isn't coming into focus. Forcing myself to blink is unnaturally difficult, but I do it repeatedly until the blurry outlines form themselves into shapes.

I'm inside, and wherever it is doesn't look like a safe house. It looks like somewhere normal people live.

I shift to get a better look, but it only reminds me I'm injured. Pain screams up my left side from my hip to my shoulder, and then it seems to echo through my body like a bell being rung.

A whimper slips out of me, and my first thought is to look for Father, in case he can hear me. It's bad enough that I nearly got taken out by our mortal enemies. If he sees me whimpering and whining about it like a child, he might be tempted to finish the job himself.

Father hates displays of weakness and submission more than anything. He says it goes against everything we stand for. And right now, I feel weaker and more fragile than I knew was possible.

My entire body aches and weighs me so heavily into whatever rough fabric I'm lying on that I'm threatening to dissolve through to the floor. But it's heavy in an unstable way. Like those ships at the bottom of the ocean covered in rust and barnacles. They're still a thousand tons of dead weight but look like one well-placed hit could cause them to shatter.

There's a rustling noise somewhere, but I can't turn my head far enough to see. It sounds like someone moving toward me, which makes me tense defensively. Not that I would be able to fight even the most meager threat at this point. Why bother trying?

My stomach cramps painfully while the wound in my hip throbs, and I wonder if it would have been easier if the Aryans had just shot me in the head.

"Tadhg?"

I hear a voice but still can't make out a face. And I'm not sure who would be speaking, because no one's called me anything but Savage in years.

Unless... Did Father use my real name before? Or was that some kind of fever dream?

Everything hurts too much to care.

Warm, soft hands touch my face. I flinch back at first, but the grip is too strong and I'm being turned to look into a pair of big, dark blue eyes. As soon as I see Micah's face again, the other memories filter back, and I realize this isn't the first time I've woken up since they dragged me away from the courthouse.

The fog inside my head clears. We drove for a long time, while I gradually felt sicker and sicker. I must have had a fever, because everything I remember from the drive is distorted and unreal.

I was dreaming about me and Micah when we were kids, and I thought it might be a sign I was dying. Or already dead and had somehow snuck my way into something passing for a decent afterlife.

Then I woke up feeling mostly lucid, and Micah was here. All grown up and moving around me with a level of self-assured confidence I barely recognized.

Father was here too, along with Colm and the others. But now, everything's quiet.

Micah's eyes search my face as he touches me, pressing on my skin in different places like he's looking for something. At some point he must have turned on a lamp, because a soft orange light is casting deep shadows on his face. I don't know what to say, so I take a look at him while he's feeling my face, peeling back my eyelids, and pressing his fingers against my throat over my fluttering pulse, like a horse about to be sold at auction.

He's lost the softness in his face, although his eyes are still just as big and bright. His cheeks used to be round; now he has the kind of cheekbones you see on models or TikTok stars that look like they could cut glass, and his lips have that kind of permanent pout everybody wants as well. He looks beautiful, in a delicate, sophisticated sort of way. The total opposite of everything I'm used to looking at.

He looks grown up.

"You're really here?"

Those are the first words that actually make their way out of my mouth. They come out a little slurred, but I'm a lot more with it than I was any of the other times I woke up. Micah smiles a little, and I see the hint of a dimple that makes him look more like the boy in my memories.

Which makes me want to put a real smile on his face, but I don't know if I have that in me right now. I blink a few more times to snap my brain back to reality and then try to shuffle myself up into a seated position, but the pain stops me before I get anywhere.

"Stop that," Micah hisses, putting his hands on my shoulders to keep me in the same position. "You're lucky to be alive, you great big buffoon of a man. Do you have any idea how scared I was? Your scumbag father darkens my doorstep after all these years, only to put me in charge of saving you from whatever disaster he got you into. I swear to god, Tadhg, if you crawl back into my life now only to die on me, I will never forgive you. I will fucking hara-kiri myself and follow you to the afterlife so I can scold you forever. Do you understand?"

He's staring at me, and his big Bambi eyes are so wide and serious I can't look away. It's like a wall in my mind comes crashing down, and I remember exactly what it feels like to have someone in the world give a shit whether you live or die. Not because of what they need you for, but because they care about you.

I haven't had that since the day he left, and I think I forced myself to forget.

Now he's holding my face in his tender hands and looking at me like he wants me to live. The small, slithering thing inside my chest that had been steadily whispering to me how much better it might have been if I'd died is retreating in the face of all that warmth.

"Tadhg?"

His voice is soft and earnest, and the sound is so real and

close to me it makes my chest crumple like a soda can being stepped on.

My throat tightens, heat rushes to my face, and suddenly, every breath I take feels like it's a whole-body process, until I'm rocking forward, like I'm rolling on the ocean. My brain fills with static, and my thoughts are an indistinct jumble I can't pick through. The only things I'm able to focus on are the way my breaths are speeding up, rolling through my body one crashing wave at a time, and Micah's face.

I'm not really aware that I'm crying. Crying isn't something I'm supposed to do. Ever.

Of course, like everything else that Father expects me to be *'better than'*, it's something I do all the fucking time.

The familiar prickle around my eyes and wetness on my face tell me it's too late to stop it. Instead, I focus on trying to catch my breath, but I can't. I'm still rocking forward with it, so much it hurts my side every time I move.

Micah's eyes go wide for a moment, but his expression switches to something placid yet confident in an instant. I'd be impressed if I had the mental capacity for it. He takes in a breath and sighs, the words, "Oh, honey," escaping his lips like a prayer.

Of course, that doesn't help. The absurdity of it — someone calling *me*, Padraig Moynihan's pet butcher — *'honey'*, makes me want to laugh. But the laugh gets caught up in the rest of the squeezing and straining that's going on inside me, and it comes out just as choked as every other breath.

Micah's hands are still on my face. His eyes flick from side to side quickly, like he's trying to decide something. He's been able to fix everything else that was fucked up about me so far. Hell, maybe he can fix this too.

With only a little hesitation, Micah folds his legs up under him and lies next to me on the couch. It's a decent size and made of some dark blue fabric that matches his eyes, but I take up a lot of space. He's slender though, like he used to be, even if his personality gives off the impression of someone who takes up more space now. He manages to shimmy into an impossibly small sliver of space in between my body and the edge of the sofa, and before I know it, his cheek is resting on my shoulder.

If it were anyone else, it would be impossibly, unfathomably weird. But with Micah, all this does is activate a bunch of muscle-memory pathways in my brain I'd forgotten about.

He used to get so scared. He was a tiny slip of a thing, and Father's rage seemed like a monster that filled the whole house sometimes. Even if we were hidden, Micah would tremble and cry, so I would pull him close until he calmed down. I couldn't do a lot about the shitty situation we were both in, but if clinging to me made him less scared, I was happy to let him bury his face in my neck and clutch at my side until he stopped shaking.

So now, although I'm the one freaking out, my body does exactly what it used to without needing any input from me. He's on my uninjured side, so I'm able to lift my arm enough for him to slip underneath it. His cheek presses into my shoulder, and then the warmth of his palm finds my face again. His weight is draped against my body from top to bottom, and it's like a line of warmth and stillness I can anchor myself by.

My chest is still trying to turn itself inside out and my body is being taken along for the ride, but I focus on how calm Micah is. There's a solidity to him he didn't have before. He feels like something indestructible, while I feel like a 210 lb weight that's about to be blown away.

Like dandelion seeds in a frigid breeze.

I want to turn and wrap myself around him until I'm as solid as he is. But my left arm is fucking useless. Instead, all I can do is dig the fingers of my right hand into whatever part of him I can reach and cling to it. With his shirt fisted in my hand and my eyes closed, I stave off the impending embarrassment for the sake of getting my shit under control. My ragged, raspy breathing fills the room with sound.

At least now I know Father definitely isn't here anymore, or he would have knocked us both off this couch by now.

Achingly slowly, like a seedling opening its first leaves, the muscles in my chest unclench one by one. My breathing gradually evens out, although the shaking seems to have set up shop in my body and is refusing to leave.

The more relaxed the rest of me gets, the weirder the shaking feels. It's not like normal, hyperventilating trembling. It's more like electrical shocks. Like my body is jerking suddenly in small, unpredictable ways, and I can't control it.

Fuck it. I don't care anymore. It's not the first time my body has betrayed me; I'm sure it won't be the last.

I can't even die right.

I think I want to tear off my skin and crawl into the nearest corpse to see if that works out any better for me.

Micah uses his hand resting on my face to turn me to face him. He's barely two inches away. It's the weirdest here-but-not-here feeling, like I'm living in a memory and the present at the same time. Everything we're doing feels inherently normal and comforting because it's something we've done a million times before. But also, twelve years and a lifetime of changes are standing between those versions of us and who we are now.

I'm abruptly aware of how much older Micah looks, although I noticed it before. It's like the thought lurches into my brain. His face is smooth, but I can see a hint of stubble, like he hasn't had the chance to shave in a while. He smells good, like much fancier soap than any man I know would ever own. And his hair, which always used to be a mess, is styled now. Like the kind of messy curls you pay a lot of money for, because you want to tempt people to run their fingers through them.

Because my former little brother is an adult now. He's an adult with his own life, who probably has a job and goes on dates and has normal fucking sex and pays taxes and does all the other things that people who aren't scumbags do with their time.

Suddenly, it seems like I'm tainting him just by letting him touch me.

I'm the one who was too weak to escape Father's influence. I let him drag me down into the mud and turn me into exactly the kind of evil, disgusting piece of shit I always knew he would. And then, without my permission, he saved my life by dragging me all the way to Micah, so I could infect the only good person I know with this disgusting bullshit.

As much as I was jealous of him for getting out, he deserved it. I can't jeopardize that for him. I need to get away from him before I put him in danger. Or worse, he realizes exactly what I let Da turn me into.

"Get off," I say, my voice coming out in a rasp. Everywhere he's touching me feels like a brand. Like the poison is seeping out of my skin and burning into his. I need it to stop.

Micah looks at me with a confused frown on his face.

"What?"

"Get off!" I'm choking on the words. My body is flushing hot and cold, and I feel like my limbs are going to jerk so hard they might tear themselves apart. I need to escape. The panic makes my stomach churn; while my heart races and my vision starts to swim.

I realize this is more than just the despair that hit me a minute ago. There's something wrong with me. I'm not registering the pain of my wounds anymore; all I can feel is *wrong*. Like my body is screaming a warning at me.

Maybe it's telling me I'm dying. Or maybe my body agrees that I'm toxic, and I need to get away from Micah before he gets hurt. Whatever the feeling is, it's tearing through me like wildfire.

"Oh fuck," I think Micah mutters as he scrabbles to put his feet on the floor.

I'm relieved he's finally getting the fuck away from me. But then he turns and puts his hands on me, catching my shoulders when I do my best to pitch my broken, twitching body off the couch.

"Tadhg, stop! Stay still, you'll hurt yourself."

I need him to stop touching me. I think my skin is about to melt off my bones. The floor lurches underneath me, and I shove Micah away as well as I can before I nosedive into the floor.

The fall is barely a foot, but I land directly on my eye socket, so pain throbs through my face while the rest of my body crumples downward in slow motion. There's a tearing feeling in my hand, and then I'm pretty sure I see blood and maybe water spilling over me and onto the carpet.

Micah keeps touching me, pulling at me with his fucking

soft, warm hands, trying to move me to do I don't know what.

My stomach clenches again, this time hard enough to make me double over. I'm on my side on the floor, I think, and I curl myself up as tightly as I can with the left side of my body too injured to cooperate.

Blood is everywhere now. My face is wet with it, and the world smells like iron. And Micah won't leave.

My stomach heaves, and then I'm choking as something bitter fills my mouth. I can't breathe, and whenever I try, there's too much snot and vomit to get any air. I try to roll onto my back, but I'm too dizzy to tell which way is up, and my body is still jerking with those electric shocks that make it hard to move.

"Jesus fucking Christ."

Micah's voice is disembodied, floating around me. The world seems intangible, and all I can do is reach out and grab for something to hold on to.

My hands come up empty, because there's nothing to grab. I'm anchorless. But then a strong arm wraps around my waist and a hand grips me by the hair. Someone comes up behind me, as my body gets twisted against my will. The hand pulls on my hair until my neck stretches out long, and when my stomach heaves again to puke, this time thin, bright yellow liquid spills out of my mouth.

Air rushes in to replace it, and it's such a relief I feel myself sag. I blink a few times and take one deep, heaving breath after another, trying to reorient myself and chase away the blackness that was edging into my vision. My throat is screaming raw from where I think I inhaled some vomit, and the thought is so disgusting I almost puke again, but my stomach is empty when it lurches this time.

My hoarse breathing fills my ears, and my body is

shaking so hard I know I can't be holding myself up. Especially when I only have my right hand on the ground.

Awareness is coming back to me, bit by bit. I'm kneeling on the carpet. I can see a disgusting mess of blood and vomit underneath me, and my good arm is propping me up, seeping blood from the spot where I must have ripped out an IV, while my injured arm hangs limply.

Micah's holding me up, I realize. It's his arm around my chest and his hand in my hair. It's a weird sensation, but I also don't want him to let go. The moment I inhaled and choked on my own vomit was the most profound sense of terror I think I've ever felt, and this is not my first time almost dying. It was a visceral, whole-body sense of impending doom. And his hand in my hair—keeping me upright and not letting me collapse back into a scrunched-up ball of disaster-flesh—is the only thing keeping it from happening again.

I relax into his arms and breathe until the world makes more sense. A little at a time.

After a while, Micah must be tired, because he pulls us both down into a sitting position. He props himself up against the boxy couch and then leans my back against his chest. I'm nearly twice the width of him, but it doesn't matter. It still feels anchoring.

His hand moves to the center of my chest, his fingers splayed as I take one rattling breath after another. I can feel him breathing behind me, and gradually I fall into the same rhythm as him. Deep, slow breaths. Mine sounds wet and putrid.

His other hand, I realize, has slipped out of my hair at some point because I'm laying my head back against his shoulder. He holds my wrist for a while, maybe checking my pulse again, and then presses his fingers against the bleeding tear in the skin where the IV used to be.

We lie together in a communal trauma heap for a long time before either of us speaks.

"Just let me help you."

That's the thing Micah eventually says. He whispers it, because his face is still next to mine. And he tightens his grip on my chest as he says the words. I can't imagine what he thinks is the reason I freaked out and tried to yeet myself into fucking oblivion from his couch, but I'm sure it wasn't a pretty sight.

Either way, here he is. Still keeping me upright. Refusing to let me go.

I sigh and lean more of my weight into his body. I don't know what I'm supposed to do here, but I'm too tired now to work it out.

Micah

I knew I would have my hands full with Tadhg's injuries. And I was fully expecting Patrick and his goons to be a constant pain in my ass.

Reuniting with Tadhg once he woke up... That was something I was hoping would not be a big deal. Worst-case scenario, it was going to be a little awkward. Once the moron mafia packed up and left to plot their world takeover or whatever, I'd had a little peace and quiet to consider it.

I called out to work and then sat in the dark, monitoring my brother's vitals as they slowly strengthened, waiting for him to come back to me. And in the meantime, I tried to picture everything that might have happened to him in the past twelve years.

In everything that crossed my mind, I never expected him to react like he did. But now I feel stupid as hell.

Of course he's changed. Of course, he's been warped and twisted and controlled until he's a shadow of his shitty, abusive father, and nothing like the boy who used to protect me. His father is the only constant he's ever had in life, considering his mother overdosed on heroin when he was too young to remember, and I abandoned him before either of us had the chance to truly grow up.

Homophobia and toxic masculinity run deeper in Patrick than anything else. Based on the way his associates *watched* me, I'm assuming that's the standard he enforces across his crew.

I should never have laid down next to Tadhg like that. Something that was innocent and comforting when we were little kids carries different connotations now that we're adults. Even if I still think of him as a brother, we're not actually related. We were never even legally considered stepbrothers, because Mom and Pat didn't bother with a marriage license.

And now we're practically strangers. Strangers who laid next to each other on a single sofa.

It must have been enough to trigger his "no gay shit" reflex and make him nearly kill himself trying to scrabble away from me. Watching the color drain from his skin while he aspirated on his fucking vomit… That was an experience.

Knowing it was all because he was so desperate not to touch me? Yeah, that wasn't a high point of my existence.

Now, he's exhausted, lying still in my arms, and I can't tell if his initial reaction was a knee-jerk panic response and this is the real him, or if that was the real him and this is him being too exhausted to fight anymore.

I can put up with a lot. The way I move, the way I talk, everything about me screamed *queer* since before I was old enough to understand what it meant. Which isn't ideal for a child in the Bible Belt, even if things are better than they used to be. But I learned to embrace it, and to stand up for myself, and it ultimately made me stronger. If I had the choice to go back, I wouldn't change anything about myself.

I'd change the fucking world to make it less shitty, so other kids aren't forced to be that strong, but I wouldn't change a thing about me.

Tadhg continues to breathe, propped up against my chest. The rattle I hear tells me he definitely aspirated, but there's nothing I can do about it now. He's already getting all the antibiotics I have. If that's not enough, Tristan will have to come back with something else.

I just need him to calm down. He looked fucking terrified. First, terrified of me, then he had that look in his eye patients sometimes have right before they die.

A 'sense of impending doom' is a real medical symptom, and I've seen it in too many people's faces not to believe them when they say it. That was how Tadhg looked. Like his body was falling out from under him, and he was preparing to be detached from it.

But we're both still here.

In the dim light, I look down at the tattoos crawling all over his body. They're all violent. Knives. Guns. Skulls. A lot of symbols I vaguely recognize as gang signs, and some that I'm pretty sure are meant to represent things like the kills you've made.

I don't know what I'm going to do about this situation. If Patrick has genuinely turned my brother into a monster,

Tadhg might not be willing to let me take care of him once he's strong enough to put some distance between us. But now that he's here, I realize I still love him as much as I used to.

I'm going to try. Even if I have to tolerate some homophobic bullshit. His recovery is going to be slow, and they don't have anyone else to take care of him. If Patrick has spent the last decade being a devil on his shoulder, this is my chance to be an angel.

A very gay, exhausted angel.

Chapter Six

𝔅

Savage

I don't know how long we sit together. Long enough that the adrenaline drains out of the room. Quiet settles over us both, the only real noise being the harsh, rattling sound of my breathing.

Eventually, I feel more like myself. Or at least the numb, detached version of myself that I slip into after I have one of these little panic whatevers. The part of me that was concerned about infecting Micah with my toxins is walled off in a distant section of my mind, letting out occasional muffled screams, while the rest of me is too selfish and desperate for comfort to care about the consequences.

My head is resting on his shoulder, so it doesn't take much strength to turn to my left until I'm facing him. I'm too close to see his whole face, but it doesn't matter. He fills my field of vision, and the smell of whatever fruity soap he uses is wallpapering over the scent of vomit in my nostrils, so I'll take it.

"Why are you being nice to me, Bambi?" I ask. My voice is rougher than it was before my little couch-diving vomit adventure, so I sound even more like a cartoon villain. It's fitting.

Micah leans back a little to get a better look at me. I can feel the warmth rolling off his skin, and we're both sweaty from exertion. I think that if he pulled away from me right now, I might dissolve.

"Because you're still my brother, asshole."

I snort. He never did mince words, even if he used to be a lot more shy about it.

"You should kick me out," I mumble into the pale, sweaty skin of his shoulder.

"Yeah, well, you're not the boss of me. And neither is Patrick. You should be in a hospital, but he's made it clear that's not going to happen. Without legal medical care, I'm the next best thing. I don't trust him not to put you in a dog kennel and let you bleed to death. So, you're stuck here until you're healthy enough to fight me over it. Thankfully, your father seemed to be happy to have one less thing to worry about, so he didn't put up much of a fight when I offered to have you recover here."

A swirl of conflicting emotions hits me right in the breastbone, but I don't have the energy to deal with any of them right now, so I let the numbness shove them aside.

"He left?"

"Yeah, hun," he says, his voice going soft. His hand comes up and rests on the back of my head, right where he grabbed me by the hair earlier. It rests there, hovering like he wants to stroke my hair or something and is stopping himself.

I feel like a pathetic little kid, but I would give my left nut for him to stroke my hair right now, I swear. Where the fuck have my nuts gotten me, anyway? My skin is prickling with the screaming need to be touched in any kind of comfort, and I'm so desperate for it, but so unwilling to ask, the conflict makes my insides turn to sludge.

Micah's hand stays put, barely touching me, just resting on the back of my head like a tease of the kind of familial comfort I'm not allowed to have.

I try not to feel the disappointment that's tugging at the edge of my awareness when I think about the fact that Father isn't here anymore. Of course he left. Why would he hang around to watch me sleep off an injury?

I'm still a little shocked he went to so much effort to save me in the first place. It probably has more to do with asserting his dominance over the Aryans than actually protecting me, so it makes sense that he'd farm me out to Micah's care as soon as he could and then head back to take care of the Banna. They're his *real* family, after all.

That's what he's always told me. Well, he always told me that they're *my* real family and deserve my allegiance over anything else in life, even over the woman I end up marrying and the children I end up having, but the underlying message was always clear.

The joke's on him though, because he has no idea that I'm way too fucking broken to ever have children. It's his fault, of course, but I wouldn't want to give him the sick satisfaction of knowing that.

"And you don't mind having a fucking criminal bleeding and puking all over your floor?" I try not to sound vulnerable when I say it. I'm digging around in my chest for my normal tough-guy gangster voice, but it seems to have wilted away in the power of Micah's unflappable presence.

Because the truth is, now that Micah is next to me again, my entire existence is screaming that this is the way it was always meant to be. That he was the missing chunk from my life—the approximation of a family I've always secretly craved—and if I let him go one more time, I won't survive.

He laughs softly. "I mean, I could do with less vomiting in the future, but it's always better out than in. And you're not a random gangster, you're *you*. You always have a place here." There's a pause, and I can tell he's working out how to say something. "As long as you don't mind living in the same apartment as a homo."

It feels like all the air is sucked out of the room, although I'm not sure why. Micah is looking me straight in the eye, leaning back with an unwavering, confident expression. There's a grim set to his face, like he's aware that I might freak out or say horrible, terrible things to him, but there's no hesitation.

Once again, I'm overwhelmed by how fucking strong of a man he's grown into.

"I will not tolerate homophobia in this house. I know you live and work with Neanderthals, and they were all fucking rude while they were here, but I expect you to do better if you ever loved me. You don't have to like it, but you have to respect me enough to keep your mouth shut and be polite, or I'll find someplace else for you to stay. I still love you, brother, but I'm not undoing a lifetime's worth of work on getting comfortable with myself to let someone stay here who's going to chip away at that."

I couldn't describe how I'm feeling if you microwaved it directly from my consciousness. All I know is that whatever it is, it's strong. Overwhelming. I'm looking into Micah's river-blue eyes, and I can't believe how much he's changed.

The nervous, terrified kid has turned into this

formidable person who's telling me—someone who could normally bench press him—to take him as is or get out.

I can't even conceive of what it would be like to do that.

All of my inarticulate, unnamable emotion swells and swells inside me until I'm choking on it, and it starts leaking out of my eyes. I don't know why, because I'm not crying. I'm not making any noise. There are just tears slipping out of my eyes and wetting my cheeks in still silence.

It's weird and embarrassing, but that's been such a theme of the day that I think I've become numb to the feeling of it.

Micah cocks his head at me when he notices, his eyebrows quirking and his eyes boring into mine.

"Tadhg?"

I shake my head, trying to shake off the weird, fractured pieces of emotions that are causing the storm inside my head. The motion dislodges his hand from the back of my head, and I immediately miss it.

Clearing my throat, I try to sound normal when I answer him. I can't explain to him what's wrong. I can't even explain it to myself. I need him to stop looking at me and not ask any more questions than I'm prepared to answer right now, which is zero.

"I'm fine," I croak out. "It's fine. I wouldn't want you to be anything other than yourself."

For some reason, that last part makes that swirl of emotion rage instead of relax, and I make a choked sound that might have wanted to be a sob.

God, I'm such a disgusting mess of a human being. No wonder Da fucking hates me.

I swallow the noise down and don't make it again, and then force the most wooden, unbelievable smile onto my face.

"It's fine," I say again.

Micah keeps frowning and doesn't let his eyes drift away from my face. He tightens his grip on me a little bit and I can see him working out what to say, but eventually he seems to settle on not making me talk about it anymore, thank fuck.

"Okay, Tadhg," he says, reaching out to wipe away the wetness on my cheeks without acknowledging it out loud. Which only makes more tears slip out, obviously.

Jesus fucking Christ, Savage. Get it together.

I take in a deep breath through my nose, shake my head a little bit to try to shake loose all this bullshit, and then pull myself out of his grasp. I don't have the strength to fully move away from him, but his closeness is making the world feel too soft and delicate, it's making me soft and delicate. It's confusing me.

Once I get his soft, strong hands off me, I'll feel more like myself.

"Can you help me back onto the couch, please?"

Hopefully, this will change the subject forever and we can never talk about it again.

Micah

I'm so confused.

I was expecting disgust. Possibly anger, or disappointment, or whatever echo of Patrick's normal toxic behavior Tadhg is used to repeating when it comes to encountering homosexuals in the wild.

I was hoping he would be able to temper it because of his childhood affection for me, and I could gradually chip away at all that toxic masculinity until I eventually revealed the sweet, gentle brother I used to know.

I was *not* expecting tears.

Why the fuck did he cry? Was he so angry and disgusted, but too weak to do anything else about it in his wounded state? Or maybe he realized that I'm too different to ever fit into his life, and once he's better, he's going to leave and we'll never see each other again, and he was sad about it?

It's all weird and nonsensical.

And stupid. Obviously. There's no reason for my gayness to upset him at all, but I was never naïve enough to expect a neutral reaction. I was just hoping for a non-violent one.

I'll let it go for now, because he's had enough of a day already and he just woke up. But we'll be circling back to this eventually, I guarantee it. Patrick has had twelve years to plant toxic shit in my brother and I'm going to pull it all out, root and stem.

For now, I need to fix whatever he just fucked up about his physical health, though.

I help him get back onto the couch and more or less comfortable. I clean up the mess, and then give him a quick wipe down and look over his wounds. He seems sleepy and goes quiet as I work. His eyes are open, but he's barely responsive. Almost like he's dissociating.

It actually freaks me out, so I talk while I work. I talk to him about my job and try to reassure him that while the whole situation is awkward, me caring for him feels completely normal, so there's no reason for him to be self-conscious about it. I'm not sure how much it sinks in, but hopefully he takes the point. I let him know that I'll call in some favors and get my shifts covered for the next few days. I'll tell my department head I had a family emergency.

She's not going to like it, but it is what it is. I can't exactly leave him here alone when he's like this. Who knows what he'll do next.

Tadhg gradually becomes more and more tired until his eyelids are drooping, and I know he's not hearing a word I say. Luckily, he's so sleepy that when I remind him he probably needs to pee, because I've been pumping fluids into him after all the blood that he lost, he's too tired to make it super awkward. It only takes a second for me to convince him that there's no way in hell he's walking to the bathroom. Instead, I bring over a water jug with a wide opening for him to use as a urinal that I can throw away whenever this is over, then move to the kitchen to give him some privacy while he relieves himself.

It takes him a painfully long time to fumble with his blankets and boxers when he's this weak. If he were a patient, I would never let him piss unassisted at this point. Nobody has time for this, let's be honest.

But after the crisis we just got through, plus his awkward reaction to me coming out to him, I don't want to push any more than I have to. Activities that involve his naked cock—no matter that helping a sick person urinate is quite literally one of the least arousing activities you can participate in—would be opening up another can of worms, I'm sure.

Instead, I take over a wipe to quickly clean up any mess once he's done and then flush the contents down the toilet. At least there's no blood in his urine, thank fuck. If his kidneys were injured, we'd be way, way beyond the boundaries of my emergency couch medicine.

And Tadhg continues to slip closer and closer to sleep through all of this.

By the time I have him clean and another round of fluids and antibiotics running through his new IV, he's out cold. I'm guessing he'll sleep for a long time, given the amount of stress he put his body under in the last hour.

I take the time to clean up the apartment. The goons didn't leave too much of a mess, thank god, even if they ate a ton of my food. There's a small pile on the table of Tadhg's crap that they left for him, including a gun that I firmly refuse to touch.

Not that I can't. I'm an Oklahoma/Missouri boy, after all. But I don't believe that guns are good for the world, and just because I know how to use one doesn't mean I think that doing it is beneficial.

Hard pass.

I spend a long time on the phone arranging my time off work, which really means arguing with people. By the end of it, I've given up on subtlety. I'm straight-up telling people my brother has a life-threatening medical condition and needs me to take care of him.

None of them knew I had a brother, and I seriously doubt they're able to track down the kind of paper trail that would reveal his identity. I know Tadhg is lying low here, but we're a long way from the people looking for him and a handful of ER nurses in a middle-of-nowhere hospital in a different state aren't going to be the key to him getting caught.

He sleeps for so long, I'm able to get a full eight hours myself after I detach him from his empty IV bags once the infusion is done. Which feels unnatural because I'm more used to catnaps here and there, followed by the occasional binge-sleep during my days off to catch up.

Which, as a nurse, I'm aware you can't do. But buying into that *eight hours every single night* crap is quitter talk. Daywalker talk that doesn't apply to nightshifters, who are fueled by caffeine and willpower alone.

When I wake up, Tadhg is thankfully in exactly the same position I left him, sleeping peacefully. I'm able to shower, make myself some coffee, and tidy up a little more before he starts to stir.

Of course, once he opens his eyes, all hell has to break loose again. Because why could anything be easy about this week?

Chapter Seven

Savage

When I wake up this time, I feel more like a human. I remember pretty quickly what happened before, and Bambi is right there in the kitchen, moving with fluid grace as he hums to himself and fixes some food, confirming that it wasn't all a weird, contradictory dream.

I have an entire two minutes of peace before I start to feel... off.

There's a twitchiness inside me that becomes more and more apparent as I become more awake. But it's been such a shitty week, it takes me longer to recognize it than it normally would.

This isn't the twitchiness of panic setting in, or residual self-hatred taking itself out on my body because it has nowhere else to go. This is purely physical. This is my individual muscles jolting like they've each been touched by a battery at random intervals.

My fingers twitch, and then my hands, and then I connect all the dots.

My meds. This is what happens when I forget to take my meds for too long.

The last time this happened, I was stuck on a "simple" job that turned into a three-day operation. I couldn't go home, and I obviously couldn't tell anyone what was wrong because gangsters barely take medicine for physical illness. Taking mental health meds? Yeah, that's a death sentence in the eyes of my father and brethren, I'm sure.

That's the ultimate sign that I've cracked and am no longer one of them.

After I spent the last day of that job sweating, twitching, feeling dizzy, disoriented and paranoid—and ultimately snorting a little crank, which I fucking hate, to be able to power through—I got smart. I bought a little keychain fob thing that looks discreet, but unscrews and has a space to shove some extra pills.

None of the guys have noticed it yet, but I'm hoping if they do, they assume it's some kind of retro eighties coke spoon situation. That's kind of cool.

No, it's an emergency three-day stash of my motherfucking psych meds.

But is it here? Or am I completely, utterly fucked? It's been days since I've been shot, which means the withdrawal already has its claws in my body and I've just been too fucked up to notice.

Once again, because I'm a wreck of a human being, this realization is followed by a surge of panic taking over my body. My stomach lurches and adrenaline tingles in my fingers, my heart pounds and I'm dragging my broken body off the couch before I'm consciously aware of making the decision.

It hurts. I ache everywhere as well as the throbbing pain in the wounds themselves, but I feel a lot better than last time, and at least now I'm not connected to any fucking tubes like last time.

Micah

I know Tadhg's awake because there's an abrupt sound of things tumbling to the ground, and I'm immediately prepared for a repeat of what happened last time.

But I'm surprised by how he looks. He's wide-eyed and a little panicked, which isn't a shock at this point, but his color is good. His movement is somewhat coordinated, and he's not nearly as weak as he was before he knocked out around half a day ago.

It's clear that the antibiotics have finally had the chance to do their job. The infection is rolling back, his vitals are normalizing, and he's had enough fluids to replace the lost blood volume.

Which is all great news. If only he could keep from panicking long enough for me to tell him. I have no idea what he's been through in the last twelve years without me, but it must have been worse than whatever I was picturing. He's a mess. He's not just acting like someone who's been brainwashed into a life of violence, this is someone on full sensory red alert at all times.

I was a panicky kid in a scary home. I was wobbly and flighty, like a baby deer. Hence, Bambi.

Right now, Tadhg seems more like one of those old

bobcats that's been freed from an illegal backyard zoo. Equal parts angry and afraid, but too weak from spending a lifetime in its tiny, chain-link cage to do anything but throw itself against the wall in terror. Too traumatized to accept help, but also too mutilated to survive in the wild on its own.

I don't know why that's the image that my mind conjures. It's just the most accurate parallel I can think of as I watch him try to haul his trembling, fragile body onto the ground. I want to reach for him. I think he's trying to stand up, but if he keeps up all this jerky movement, he's going to tear his wound again and undo all the healing he just did.

But I also don't want to catch a fist, and I'm aware that he could be so blinded by panic right now that he might not even realize it's me. And I don't want to point out that he seems to be having some sort of extended panic reaction, because his ego has already taken a beating today and I don't trust its structural integrity right now, based on what I've seen.

Instead, I approach slowly with my hands outstretched. He's managed to get his feet under him, with one hand on the couch taking his weight while the injured one clumsily untangles the blanket from around him.

"Whoa," I say quietly, trying to get his attention. "What's up?"

His gaze is swiping from side to side like a searchlight, and I can see him totally focused on whatever it is that's gotten him moving. I gently wrap my hand around his free elbow and disentangle the last part of the blanket. He's dressed only in boxers and bandages, and between me holding one arm and the couch supporting the other, he's able to very shakily stand up for the first time since he was dragged into my apartment.

Fuck, he got tall. And jacked. Not like a gym bro with

perfectly articulated muscle definition, or enormous like a bodybuilder. But the kind of whole-body muscle and bulk that comes with usable power.

He just looks intimidating, broad-shouldered with thick arms and a strong chest. And he's covered in so many tattoos that his already tanned skin looks darker, with golden hair covering his chest and stomach and arms that's glinting in the low light. His dark, reddish-blond hair is cut into something that's like a cross between a mullet and a mohawk, a little longer on top and in the back, but shaved short on the sides. Which is redneck as hell, but he somehow manages to pull off. He looks like a hot NASCAR driver or something.

Except he's trembling and constantly on the verge of total collapse.

He's like the physical embodiment of traditional masculinity wrapped around the physical embodiment of a panic attack.

He stops moving, seeming lost for a second. I still don't think he's totally clocked my presence, so I use my free hand to take his face and tilt it down to face me. I'm not a tiny guy, by any stretch of the imagination. I'm average height and more lithe than muscular, but not really dainty enough or young enough to keep calling myself a twink for any reason other than denial. Yet I still have to physically pull his head down so his hazel eyes are pointed at mine.

"What's wrong, Tadhg?"

"I need my keys. Where's my shit?"

I give him a *what the fuck* look. That wasn't what I was expecting at all. If anything, I thought he would be panicking about getting to his dad and his stupid, brutal job.

My mind grasps for an answer. "Uh, someone left a gun

and some other shit on the table that they said belonged to you. It's over there. Just sit down and I'll go get it."

"No!" He lurches away from me, pulling his arm out of my grasp.

So, it's going to be another one of those days, I see.

With a hand pressed against the wound on his hip, which is definitely bleeding again, he takes one staggering step after the other toward the table. He manages to make the walk across my living room look like the fucking Iditarod, but I know if I touch him again, he'll only hurt himself worse.

Instead, I watch, and I wait.

Like a drunk toddler, he collapses against my shitty Ikea high-top, but he gets there. The pile of stuff barely has anything in it, but he manages to make rifling through it look unnecessarily dramatic until he comes up with his keys clutched in his hand.

He's already looking a lot paler than a few minutes ago. When he turns to look at me, I give him the same calm, only slightly condescending raised eyebrows look that all nurses use when their patient is being a pain in the ass.

"Okay. Can I get you back to the couch now, please? Before you topple over?"

His eyes dart from side to side for a second, like a little kid about to get scolded. But then he relents. Without too much grumbling, he lets me take his elbow again, and this time he really leans his ridiculous, bulky body into me while we traverse the great living room passage one more time.

Tadhg falls back onto the threadbare, sweat-soaked cushions with a loud exhale, and gives me an inscrutable look, even while he's still trying to catch his breath from the exertion.

"Could you get me some water?" His tone is suspiciously

polite, and I don't know what he's going to do as soon as my back is turned to acquiesce.

I glare at him. "That depends. Are you going to exit the couch area while I do, or can we take a break from interpretive dance for the rest of the day? My back and knees aren't what they used to be, asshole. I don't need to be dragging you off the floor anymore if you collapse and tear your wound open. And I definitely don't feel like doing surgery in my apartment to stuff your intestines back in when they fall out of the hole it'll make. That sounds tedious AF. These hands were not intended to accordion fold your small intestine back into your abdominal cavity, brother."

My tone is light, but I hold his gaze so he knows I'm not totally fucking around. I half expect him to piss and moan about it, or pull a big tough gangster act and try to intimidate me, even though it wouldn't have a chance in hell of working.

He doesn't do either, though. Instead, he does something that fucking floors me.

Tadhg smiles at me.

A real smile, too. Slightly unhinged, but what about either of us isn't?

"Sure, Bambi."

It's all he says, but he keeps smiling, and his voice is soft, so I'll call it a win.

Still suspicious, I slowly turn and head to the kitchen to grab him some water. I keep my ear trained on him behind me, and while I hear some rustling, there's nothing disastrous. When I turn around with the cup in my hand, he's still on the couch, his eyes trained on me like a loyal dog waiting for me to return.

I hand him the cup. Some bright-blue plastic promotional tumbler I got at a job fair after graduation because I don't trust him with anything heavy right now. His hand still shakes as he takes it, but he's more or less okay as he brings it to his face and takes a sip, only sputtering a little when he tilts his head back to swallow.

He hands it back to me and I put it on the coffee table within his reach. For some reason, the whole exchange feels surreal. Everything about him is designed to be as thuggish as possible. His body, his aggressive tattoos, his ridiculous fucking name. There's a snake on his neck, for fuck's sake. I think I can see a large knife outlined under the shaved part on the left side of his head.

But he's looking up at me with big, round eyes and a grateful expression. When there's no aggression or terror on his face, you can notice his actual features, which are just as pretty as they used to be.

I think he always hated how he looked. His face is just as masculine as the rest of him, with a perfect jawline covered in something between stubble and a beard. But he also has thick, dark eyelashes that most people would murder for, a straight nose, full lips and the kind of symmetry that makes everything just work.

It's the perfect blend of "pretty" features on a conventionally handsome face. Fuck, he's prettier than I am, even though I'm definitely the feminine looking-one of the two of us. Which I'm sure makes him crazy, and lowkey always has. He'd rather look like his thug father, so he covers it all up with the stubble and scars. There's a nasty one cutting through his eyebrow on the right side, and a series of numbers and small symbols tattooed by his hairline on the left.

It's all designed to make him look crustier, but it's not enough. He still has the porcelain-doll perfection of the face he was born with, even under all those manufactured flaws he's carved into it.

"Happy now?" I ask, while he continues to watch me in silence, wearing a fond expression that's so unexpected it's kind of eating away at my heart. "I can't call out from work forever, so I need you to cooperate if you want your recovery to ever have an end date. So, are you gonna be a good boy?"

He doesn't reply. He just hits me with a *what-the-fuck* look of his own.

I didn't mean it like that, but the words rolled off my tongue out of habit and I'm reminded again that me and Tadhg live in very, very different worlds now.

He'd probably strangle someone else for calling him a *good boy*. Well, it's good to know I still have brother privileges after all this time.

Barely half an hour later, his eyelids grow heavy again and he falls into the most restful-looking sleep he's had since he got here.

Chapter Eight

Micah

For the next two days, we have minimal drama. I don't know who's more surprised, me or Tadhg, but I'll take what I can get.

It feels bizarrely peaceful.

It's easier than it should be to fall back into old habits and patterns. He lets me take care of him without as much grumbling as I expected, but almost immediately we bicker the same way we used to as kids. He teases me a little, even if there's a hesitance to him. And I let him get away with it because it's nice to see him do anything other than go from one intense freak out to the next.

Slowly, the terrible circumstances of our reunion feel farther and farther away, replaced by the constant magnetized pull to stay in each other's orbits we always used to have. Which should feel weird but doesn't. Almost right away, it doesn't matter that time has passed. We're in a brand-new version of our own bubble, where we're the only two real people in the world, and nothing else matters.

I should probably be more concerned about how unhealthy that is and always was, or how readily my mind slips back into it. I don't have the energy to worry, though.

What's important is that he's here and getting better. He can get up and walk around unassisted, even if he's slow and needs to lean on the furniture most of the time. He's eating solid food and keeping it down, and I was able to pull his IV. The infection in his wounds is continuing to recede, and there have been no signs of any catastrophic organ damage I wasn't previously aware of.

I tentatively allow myself to hope for the best. I let myself be lulled into feeling like this is just a normal, long-lost brotherly reunion, and not the sign of impending chaos in our lives.

Last night, while he was heavy-lidded and ready to drift off into another of his near-catatonic sleeps, he even thanked me for taking such good care of him. His big, meaty paw squeezed my hand, and my heart seemed to squeeze itself at the same time.

I don't know what I would have done if he hadn't survived.

This is all movement in the right direction. And that Tadhg isn't fighting me on any of it is giving me the confidence to finally ask the question I've been dying to ask.

He's sitting on the couch, his arm thrown casually over the back of it in a way that makes his bicep look unfairly juicy. I'm trying not to be jealous. Not that I have any interest in looking like him; I'm very happy with my body. But it must be nice to walk around looking like a human weapon of mass destruction.

His leg on the injured side is stretched out, propped up on the cheap chipboard table so he doesn't put pressure on the wounds, while his other leg is bent so he's half-sitting, half-reclining. I think he feels better not having to lounge around like an invalid.

It's all the same to me, obviously, but if I've learned anything in the past few days, it's that his pride is as robust as a spun-glass spiderweb.

Which isn't his fault. Anyone would be fucked up by our violent, miserable childhood. Especially if it was followed by a life of crime and violence that you never wanted to be a part of. And that's exactly what I need to ask him about, even if I'm worried that broaching the topic is going to set back all the progress we've made and potentially trigger another one of his panic attacks. The ones that neither of us is allowed to acknowledge exist, obviously.

Straight men are such delicate beasts.

I shimmy into the narrow wedge of the couch that Tadhg isn't occupying, and he turns his head to take me in with a lazy half-smile. He's a little glassy-eyed, because Tristan came by two days ago with a handful of street-sourced Percocets that his mother, of all people, acquired.

Which I *hate* giving to Tadhg and am rationing as tightly as I can. But they're at least stamped and branded so the chances of being laced with fentanyl are relatively low. I'm monitoring him around the clock, and Tristan had the common sense to bring me an emergency dose of Narcan with the pills. Just in case.

And I'm not leaving the stash anywhere he can get his grubby paws on them. Because I love my brother—even if that's a little weird after all this time—and the level of instability I've seen from him in the past three days has made it clear he doesn't belong around anything with the potential to harm himself or others.

I even stole the bullets from his gun when he was sleeping. Hopefully, he hasn't noticed and won't need it until he's feeling more stable. Or ever, if I have my way.

"What's up, Bambi?" he says to me, only a hint of a slur to his voice.

"Can we talk?"

His eyes darken at that. He cocks his head, and a veil of focus immediately comes over his face. He doesn't say anything, just watches me intently, waiting for me to say whatever is on my mind.

Which I wish I'd formulated more clearly in my head beforehand, because now that I have to wing it, I feel like it's going to come out wrong.

"What happened?"

Yeah, that's really clear. *Good job* me.

Tadhg cocks his head even more and squints at me. "Do you mean what happened during the shooting?"

"God, no." I shudder. I can fill in the blanks on that and definitely don't need a more vivid picture than what my brain is already making up. "I mean, what happened with you to end up here? We always... You always swore we were going to run away once we were old enough. You never wanted to be like him. I know it was shitty of me to leave you alone—"

"You deserved to get out, Bambi." His voice is barely a whisper, and he's not looking me in the eye. But I can tell he's serious when he interrupts me.

"I know, but so did you. I always believed you would, with or without me. So, what happened? Why did you stay? Does he have something he can hold over you? I just want to help, if I can. I feel like I owe you that much."

Tadhg laughs and looks across the room; his head turned as far away from me as possible. There's no humor in his laughter, and every muscle in his body seems tense, despite the fact that he's barely moving.

"You don't owe me anything, Micah."

For some reason, the fact that he uses my real name stings a little.

I lean over him, resting one hand gently on his good thigh for balance and using the other to turn his face so he's looking at me. He lets me move him, but his eyes continue to dart around the room, belying how anxious he is, even if the rest of his body isn't showing it.

Looking into his eyes, I keep my voice calm and even, and don't let him wiggle his way out of this question.

"I don't want to fight about it, Tadhg. We both deserved a million times better than what we were born with. But I always hoped you got out. I'm just asking what happened. Maybe I can help."

He stares at me. His mouth moves like he's about to start speaking, the beginnings of a half dozen words hanging on his lips, which are finally pink and smooth again after days of being pallid and split from sickness.

There are tears shimmering in his eyes, but like always, I pretend not to notice them. I can see his breath catching. I'm convinced that if I stay as still as possible, holding his chin so he can't escape from me, eventually he'll crack and tell me the truth.

He has to know that there's at least one person in the fucking world who's on his side and thinks that he deserves good things. I'll convince him of that if it kills me.

Right when I feel the energy in the room turning like he's about to speak, there's a pounding at the door.

Fuck these fucking selfish, violent people. Fuck their

insistence on showing up uninvited. I know it's more mafia morons without even having to look, based solely on how they knock like they're the big bad wolf trying to get in.

I'm about to get up and let the idiots in. Tadhg's reaction to the sudden interruption, however, is something to behold.

It's instantaneous.

Gone is my brother—vulnerable and weirdly shy—sitting in front of me. In a heartbeat, he's replaced by something cold, violent and utterly still. I can see him listening to the sound, the wheels in his head turning while he calculates I-don't-know-what before ultimately sliding off the couch.

He's still injured, but it's a more controlled and graceful movement than he's managed so far. He doesn't say anything, but he looks at me with the same stern, protective look he used to get in our closet-hiding days and points toward my bedroom.

Fuck that, though. I'm not leaving him. Besides, it's definitely his fucking friends. Or maybe my super. Or a million other possibilities that aren't here to murder us, despite whatever his jacked-up nervous system is telling him right now.

As a silent compromise, I stay put and don't follow him to the door. He has his gun in his hand, pulled from somewhere on his person despite the fact that he's barefoot and dressed in sweatpants. I cringe inwardly at the fact that he doesn't know I stole the bullets, but I'm still convinced he won't need them.

His thick, callused fingers wrap around the grip of the Glock like they're a second skin, and he pads over to the door to look through the peephole. There's tension in every inch of him, his muscles straining in his attempt to be as quiet as possible. I can only imagine how much pain and energy this must be taking in his state.

As soon as he sees who's on the other side, he blows out a giant breath. The gun gets lowered, which eases my nerves, although not put away entirely. Without saying anything to me, Tadhg unlocks the door, unhooks the chain and then opens the door just wide enough for a person to slip inside.

The first one to enter is named Colm, I think. He was helping Patrick when they were all here arguing over Tadhg's dying body, and out of all of them, he was the only one who seemed remotely calm. He was also the only one who looked at me like a human instead of either looking right through me as if I were the help, or looking at me like I was something disgusting, like the mohawk-moron that Patrick called Lucky.

And speak of the devil. After Colm comes Lucky, with the bleached, faded, disheveled mohawk, still carrying himself with the same twitchy, reckless energy that he had before. Of course, as soon as he sets foot inside, his eyes land on me and his face morphs into an expression of undisguised disdain. I think he even flexes his arms, uncovered by the raggedy cut off denim jacket he's wearing, like he's trying to intimidate me.

Sure, pal. Try all you like. I've faced much scarier homophobes than you. Your insecurity is screaming at me so loud I could hear it from the fucking moon.

And then the last person to enter my home is someone who wasn't here before. He's tall, blond, and leanly muscled, like a coyote that hasn't had enough meals. He has that weird predatory energy to him, too. His eyes roam over the space, taking everything in, and all my warning bells are immediately set off.

My blood curdles like milk as he steps further into my space; a predator on the prowl.

I've spent my short but action-packed nursing career learning to read people quickly, and I've spent a lifetime learning how to pick bigots and homophobes out of a crowd, and then determine from their body language which ones were all talk, and which ones would throw down and really hurt me.

And which ones would say all the vicious things, then try to drag you behind a bar to fuck you into submission. Because it's somehow not gay if the sex is vicious and cruel, even though you're still taking pleasure in another man's body. The fact that you're taking it instead of being given somehow makes it a trophy or a hunt.

Because queer love is disgusting, but hunting "weaker" people for sport is their birthright, no matter where your dick ends up.

I've met a few men like that before, especially when I was younger and less cautious about the bar scene. But if there's any gift Patrick gave me, it's a finely honed radar for violence in men. I've always been able to avoid them in the past. I've made a point of it, even though it shouldn't be mine or anyone else's responsibility to not "allow" themselves to be in a position to be brutalized.

So why is one of them suddenly standing in my living room?

I don't know how I know. I just do. Every internal alarm I have is screeching, and the way he's helping himself to the space, walking around and casually touching everything on the shelves like the dark shadow of a curious child, is only confirming it.

Tadhg and the other two are murmuring to each other, and I was so distracted by my own thoughts I didn't really hear what they said. Not that they wanted me to. Or acknowledged that I was here.

I watched my mom get treated like this for years. This gangster-wife bullshit, where she's a shadow until they want a beer or a fuck or a scapegoat for their misplaced anger. And somehow, by agreeing to take care of Tadhg, I've ended up falling into that same space in their tiny chauvinistic brains.

When Lucky walks into the kitchen, opens the fridge and grabs a beer, I bristle with irritation. When he twists off the cap, sniffs it and makes a face—probably because it's a decent IPA that I have left over from a date, and he's never drunk anything that didn't taste like ditchwater—I feel my jaw clench. Then he jumps up on my counter, happy as anything, and takes a giant swig.

"Can I fucking help you? Or are you just here to touch all my shit without permission?"

Lucky's eyebrows perk, but he stays seated and keeps drinking my beer. Blond guy comes closer though, licking his lips and looking at me lasciviously without seeming to give a fuck that the others can see him.

Colm ignores my outburst, turning to Tadhg to point in blond-guy's direction.

"This is Eamon. He's the local guy we put in charge of setting up. He's been helping out your father while you've been recovering."

Eamon takes another step toward me instead of looking at them.

"No one told me that the famous Savage has a *sister*," he says, his tone dripping with intent.

I'm fucking pissed. I'm not surprised, and I've been prepared to hear all sorts of shit out of their mouths for as long as I have to deal with these assholes, but for whatever reason, this guy is rubbing me all the wrong ways.

He's creepy, he's invasive, and he's staring at me like I'm

a piece of meat, right in front of all his homophobic little friends. The vibe in here is rapey AF.

I'm about to lay into him, but before I get the chance, there's a blur of motion in front of me.

Savage

I have that fucker's throat in my grip before I know what's happening. I've felt completely off-kilter for the past few days. Longer, if I'm being honest. Years. A lifetime.

But this is something I was trained to do. Bashing in someone's skull isn't something I've ever enjoyed or actually *wanted* to do, but in this case, I can make an exception.

How dare he look at Micah like that? In his own fucking home?

I'll squeeze him until his eyeballs pop out of his skull and then scoop his brain out of the empty holes with a melon baller, loving every minute of it.

The fucking audacity of this piece of shit.

I squeeze hard, already feeling cartilage being crushed beneath my strength. There's pain screaming from my side and I'm so much weaker than normal, otherwise I would have snapped his spine by now, but I'm not in a rush. I lean my body weight into him, pinning his body between me and the wall. We're about the same height, but I've got more bulk than him and, more importantly, his colossal arrogance has left him unprotected.

Clearly, someone thinks he's king shit big dick around here, and is about to learn that is not the case. Even though I only said the words in my head, I still punctuate them with a growl as I tighten my fingers even more around his throat.

His face is turning an absolutely delicious shade of purple, and there's serotonin in my body for the first time in months.

I feel light and buzzy, like my blood has been replaced by champagne. I could do this forever. Fuck the pain.

My ears are ringing. I'm so high on adrenaline and the sheer, raw pleasure of destruction. Which is why it takes me a while to notice the yelling. But eventually, the ringing becomes hollow and then echoes out, replaced by the flat, intrusive sounds of the real world.

Everyone is yelling. Lucky is screaming like a lunatic, grabbing uselessly at my shoulders. Colm has his hands wrapped around mine and is trying to peel my fingers back from the fucker's throat while giving me firm commands to release him in the same tone you would use with a disobedient guard dog. And beyond that, I can hear Bambi yelling at me to stop.

That's what catches my attention. I'm distracted momentarily, which makes me weaken my grip enough for Colm to get my fingers off the man's neck and allows Lucky to haul me back a half foot.

I barely bite back a scream, because Lucky wrapped his arms all the way around my torso to do it, and it pulled on every wound I have. The pain is so sharp and abrupt; I feel like I'm going to puke. My breath stutters, and all the fight drains out of me abruptly as I'm struggling to stand upright and breathe. I feel like I got punched in the chest, it's so hard to get my lungs to expand, and my stomach is still churning, threatening to erupt at any second.

Then Micah's not yelling at me. He's barreling into Lucky, telling him to keep his hands off me and creating a blessed bubble of space around me while I catch my breath. I'm distracted from the pain for a moment by how impressed I am, watching my slender little brother body-slam that fucking idiotic bulldog like it's nothing.

To protect me.

There are spots swimming in front of my eyes, but they're clearing. Oxygen is getting into my lungs slowly, and the ripping pain is receding, although I know that I've fucked up and done damage to my wounds. Eventually, I'm able to stand fully upright again and look at the other men in the room.

Colm is looking at me with a shocked expression. Lucky looks pissed, and the blond fucker, Eamon, is still struggling to catch his breath, worse off than I am.

"Savage, are you fucking high? What the fuck?" Colm, usually rational and measured, looks at me with disbelief.

I wipe my face, which is now a mess of spit and sweat.

"He's lucky he's still breathing. Get him out of here. If I hear one more shitty word out of his mouth again, I'll stake him to an anthill, naked and covered in honey. I don't care who he is."

Lucky's eyes look like they're about to pop out of his head. I have a well-earned reputation for extreme violence in my organization. It's what Father wanted from me. He bred me for it. I hate it, but it has its uses. And even if I've been slacking lately because of all my… other stuff. I have enough of a history for everyone to know I'm not joking.

Colm frowns, because he's probably the only one who can get away with calling me out on something other than Father.

"I think that would be an overreaction, and we both know it. And so would your da. We came to talk business, but obviously you're still fucked up on painkillers."

The mention of Father brings me a little closer to reality, and I'm immediately grateful that Colm is putting a PR spin on this incident barely three minutes after it happened, using the painkillers as an excuse.

I really didn't think through what Father's reaction would be. I don't know who this dude is or how important to the organization he is. I just reacted. He looked at Micah like that, and I snapped. It's a habit that's too ingrained in me to get rid of.

"We'll come back tomorrow, Sav. And maybe you'll be a little dried out by then, eh?" Colm gives me a meaningful look with one eyebrow raised. Lucky's gaze is darting between us, like he's trying to pick up on everything that's not being said.

I don't say anything. I can't compromise now, or I'll look weak. I just stand there, watching them with a grim expression while they file out of Bambi's apartment and pretending it isn't still overwhelmingly painful to breathe.

When they're gone, I sag. I need to sit down before I collapse.

"Jesus, Tadhg."

Micah reaches for me, but I flinch away from his touch. Goddammit. Being near him is too strange. There are too many conflicting parts of myself that are being forced to interact, and it's making me feel weird and weak.

He looks surprised and hurt when I won't let him touch me, but I don't have the energy to explain. Instead, I drag my aching body back to the couch by myself. I slip my gun out of my sweatpants pocket where I had very uncomfortably stashed it when the guys walked in and toss it on the coffee table.

Then I lie back, throwing my arm over my eyes to create the illusion of darkness, well aware that Micah is studying me in silence through all of this.

I don't know what to do. He makes me weak. Before

they showed up, I was actually considering giving him an honest answer to his question, for fuck's sake. And wouldn't that just be a disaster?

If I told Micah that I wanted to leave the Banna and any of the others found out, it would put not just mine, but his life at risk as well.

It was stupid of me. And selfish. Like everything else I do.

I need to get away from him before I do anything else reckless and pull him into more of my mess.

I want him to come over and force me to accept his affection. The small, sad, desperate part of me that can't bear to keep doing this is screaming at him to come and touch me, tell me that everything's going to be alright and maybe I can get out just like he did, and join him here in his normal fucking life.

But the rest of me knows better. There's no out for me. The violence is rooted so deeply within me that even if I did physically leave, I would still be a walking powder keg of brutality. What just happened only proves that.

I need to get away. Being here is only confusing both of us and putting him at risk. As soon as I can walk more than ten steps without losing my breath, I'll find a new place to hide out from the Aryans. Or maybe I'll pick up and run. I don't care anymore. As long as I can take my brutal, pathetic self away from him and keep him safe.

Chapter Nine

B

Micah

The funk that Tadhg fell into after the incident with his asshole 'coworkers' has been concerning to say the least. He doesn't want to talk to me any more than he has to. Any opening I saw to talk about his life has been completely shuttered, and we suddenly feel like two strangers sharing an apartment.

At first, he just slept. He'd been sleeping like the dead, which worked for me because his body still has a lot of healing to do. But the past two or three days, I don't think he's been sleeping at all. He's trying to hide it from me, but I can tell.

He's jittery and on edge. His hands twitch a little, and he's constantly consumed by some sort of dark, introspective cloud that he refuses to let either of us acknowledge.

I'd be worried about withdrawal, but I've been so

careful with all the meds I've doled out, and he's had the lowest possible doses of painkillers. Unless he had something he was hiding from me. But I know the signs of every street drug there is, and nothing about his behavior before gave me an indication that he was under the influence.

It doesn't make sense. But it's got my stomach twisted in knots with worry. The more his body heals, the worse his mental state seems to get, and the farther out of reach my brother is. If he heals much more, he won't *need* to be here anymore, and I may lose him for good.

Unacceptable.

What's also not helping is that I'm completely out of PTO, as well as the good graces of my department head. I have to go back to work, which means leaving Tadhg unattended to do god-knows-what. Even if it's just stewing in his own abstract misery, it's not a good idea.

But I'm out of options. Not only has my PTO dwindled to nothing, there's a bad flu going around the hospital, which has left them in a staffing nightmare, needing emergency coverage. When I get off the phone call where I was just informed it's time to get my ass back to work tonight or find a new job, I walk out of my bedroom to let him know. But instead of finding him sprawled on the couch in a semi-catatonic daze, or sitting up and staring at the wall, fidgeting and anxious, he's… dressed?

Sort of. He's trying. And there's another fucking mafia moron in my living room.

At least this time it's Colm, who is the only one of them who doesn't give me the ick. They turn and stare at me as if I'm the one invading their space, and I'm stuck watching Tadhg attempt to get a plain black t-shirt over his head with fumbling fingers.

Colm doesn't help him, and I want to offer, but I know it

wouldn't go down well. He might if we were alone, but definitely not in front of the other Banna. Instead, we both have to stand there as Tadhg swallows down his grunts of pain and tries to stretch out muscles that are still repairing themselves.

Lifting his arms over his head must be agony. He's already white as a sheet and sweating, but I know nothing I say will stop him.

"Going somewhere?"

I try not to sound too much like an angry sitcom housewife when I say it, but I don't know how much I succeed.

Tadhg grunts in my direction, refusing to meet my eye when the t-shirt finally slides down over his face. When he doesn't respond, Colm is the one to break the long, awkward silence.

"There's a meeting. I'm driving him. Should be back in a couple of hours."

His tone is just as gruff as the rest of them, but at least he looks me in the eye when he speaks to me.

I don't know what to do. If I make Tadhg feel like I'm henpecking him in front of his men, he'll withdraw even further. But there's no way he should be up and moving around right now. Especially in a situation where he will be unwilling to show any 'weakness'.

"Tadhg, can you help me for a second before you leave?" I'm scrambling. "I need to steal your strength for something before I go to work."

To make my point, I raise my hand and wiggle my fingers. I'm actually a fuck-ton stronger than I look because I haul people around for a living, but I have long, elegant-looking fingers, so you wouldn't guess it at first sight.

Colm takes the hint, thank fuck.

"I'll be outside."

It's all he says before disappearing through the front door like a ghost. Is this what it's like to have a bodyguard?

Not wasting any time, I hurry over to Tadhg and speak to him in a harsh whisper.

"You cannot do anything strenuous. Do you understand me? You're healing, but you could still really fuck yourself up if you re-injure yourself. You shouldn't be going to this at all, but I know telling you not to would be a waste of oxygen, so I'll tell you this instead: sit as much as you can. No sudden movements. Absolutely no lifting, bending or twisting. And if you're not in this apartment when I get back from my shift in the morning, I will call the fucking cops."

Tadhg raises his eyebrows at me but stays silent.

"I'm not kidding. I'll do it. I'm not letting Patrick undo all my hard work by having you spend the night digging graves or beating people up or whatever the fuck you do for him."

My brother snorts, and it's the closest thing to mirth I've seen from him in days.

He watches me in silence for a moment that stretches out like syrup until something in his hard eyes softens.

"Okay, Bambi. I'll be back."

Then he lets out a heavy sigh and ruffles my hair like a child, before turning away from me to follow Colm out the door.

I'm not sure I believe him.

𝔖𝔞𝔳𝔞𝔤𝔢

My head is already throbbing when we get into the car,

and it feels like there's two inches of plexiglass in between me and the rest of the world.

And inside that plexiglass, I'm like a rat in a cage, buzzing so hard on anxiety I'm ready to chew off my own arm. I swear it wasn't this bad last time I ran out of my meds. It felt like I had the flu: I was dizzy, nauseous and foggy-headed, as well as being kind of wound up.

This time is so much worse. Maybe because I've been on this one for a while, after going through fourteen different rounds of trying endless medications until my shrink eventually settled on one that she said gave me appropriate "coverage", whatever that means. They all have their own horror-show side effects, but at least with this one I've been able to get up, get dressed and get through my shitty day-to-day life.

Now that it's been taken away, I feel like my skin went with it. I'm raw and exposed to the world; one giant nerve throbbing out in the open. Which completely contradicts the plexiglass imagery, but my brain is throwing these metaphors at me faster than I can process them. When I don't really give a fuck about the poetry of the situation.

All I want is to feel fucking *normal*.

Wasn't that the point of all this in the first place? I risk my life by sneaking out to see the shrink and I fuck up my already fucked-up body with the meds so I can feel like a normal human being. Not so I can continue to eke out a meager existence until the second I skip a few days of pills and then feel like the universe is falling apart.

But here I am. Red raw, itching out of my own hollow human shell, trapped in between reality and my own twisted perception of it, and now I have to go see my father and pretend I give a fuck about Banna business.

I miss sleeping most of all. The best thing about the

amitriptyline was how I slept like the dead, which is not something I'd ever experienced before. No nightmares, no fidgeting, no staring into the shadows of the room. It was such a relief after a lifetime of nights spent in terror that I was willing to accept the drug strangling whatever enthusiasm my dick had left for life, which was hardly a lot to begin with.

Maybe it's a sign that I'm already half-checked out of this plane of existence, but I'd rather sleep well than fuck well. No question. Anyone who says otherwise has no idea what it feels like to never be safe in your own home.

When Colm turns the engine off, the sudden silence in the car makes me jump so hard it startles him. Which makes sense, because who jumps at silence?

This guy, that's who. This fucking walking wreck of a human being.

He looks at me, not bothering to hide the empathy and curiosity on his face.

"Do you want me to tell your father you're still too injured? You got shot three times. I think the guys will understand if you need more than a week to sleep it off."

I pull my normal bullish, aggressive expression onto my face to hide whatever reality might be leaking through my crumbling mask.

"No. I'm fine. Let's just get this over with. I fucking hate the countryside. This whole place smells like cow shit."

I'm saying it mostly for something to say, but it's also true. The Banna headquarters, which were the local motorcycle club headquarters until we took over, is out in the middle of nowhere. It's a huge converted farmhouse sitting off a rural route that runs in between two nothing towns, where hopefully even the Aryan Brotherhood won't be able to find us.

And there's plenty of land, which means plenty of space to store whatever guns, drugs or anything else Father is planning on shuffling through this place.

We get out of the car, and I concentrate on not flinching as the pain sears every time I try to bend or flex at the waist. At least Colm picked me up in an Escalade, so I don't have to climb out of some low riding sedan or something. I might hurl if I had to bend that much.

Our feet get sucked into the mud with every step we take toward the main house. How are farms always muddy, even when it hasn't rained? They're steeped in misery, that's how. The house is rundown and shabby, which is most likely deliberate. No one wants to attract more attention than they have to.

Everything seems normal until we get a little closer, and I hear the strangest noises. It's almost like children crying? Or screaming? But not quite. Like some hell-dimension version of it. I see chain-link cages running along one wall of the main building and blink my eyes until the double-vision that's been plaguing me rolls back.

I don't think I'm hallucinating, but what the fuck? They can't possibly be keeping kids in cages. Not even my father would do something like that, and I know firsthand how little he cares about kids' welfare.

Colm catches my wide-eyed stare and makes a face like he stepped in something disgusting.

"I know. The fucking things stink and make a constant racket. But our deal for the property included the former club president's old lady getting to stay here. She keeps her mouth shut and the place clean, so it's a fair deal, but no one said anything about the side business she runs out of the house and how much fucking screaming we'd have to put up with. Padraig is already about to lose it, I swear. That woman of his — Cheryl — is the only reason he hasn't set the little shits on fire."

I'm sure my mouth is hanging open, but it feels like Colm and I are operating in two slightly different realities.

"But why are they in cages in the first place?"

I don't know what else to ask. We're moving at an excruciatingly slow pace toward the house, and this weird situation isn't helping me concentrate on putting one foot in front of the other. I still can't let him help me when the others could come out and see at any minute. I need to present a strong front.

Colm cocks his head at me, his brow furrowed.

"Where else would she put them?"

"I thought we didn't associate with people who sell kids? That's Father's only rule. What the fuck? And in *cages*?"

Colm's feet stutter to a stop and he turns to look at me, flabbergasted. Then he laughs. A hearty laugh that I've rarely heard from his mouth. He can barely talk, he's laughing so hard.

"Jesus H Christ, Sav. No! They're fucking foxes. Little yappy screaming fox things. She breeds them and sells them on Facebook as exotic pets or whatever. You know how people love that shit. Although, why anyone would want a wild animal in their home is beyond me. Humans are already enough to deal with."

His laughter fades as he stops walking again and looks at me more closely.

"You thought that sound was kids screaming?"

"I—"

I don't know what to say. Yes?

The connection between my physical senses and my brain has been fried until it feels like beef jerky, and only a sliver of information is getting through.

Help me, please God, don't make me see Father like this. I just want to go back to Micah and sleep until everything makes sense again.

Instead, I shrug. "It's weird screaming. How the fuck am I supposed to know what a fox sounds like?"

I shove him for emphasis, which makes me feel more normal for about a third of a second, until more pain tears through my side, quickly followed by a wave of nausea. It's so bad I have to stop for a minute, taking a few rough breaths in through my gritted teeth while Colm watches me with a deliberately blank face.

After a minute, his fingers touch the small of my back. Just slightly, to get me moving forward, but discreetly enough that I don't think anyone else would notice if they were watching.

"Come on, Sav. Padraig's waiting. Let's get this over with and then I'll take you back, okay?"

One more deep breath in and out, and the nausea fades enough for me to straighten up, taking another step forward. I've gotten too used to lounging around Micah's apartment wearing sweatpants and the soft cotton undershirts he Amazoned for me. Now I'm wearing the clothes Colm brought, which are just normal jeans and a t-shirt, but everything feels too tight.

The denim is rough and scratchy against my skin, everything presses in too hard over my wounds, and the whole thing is so tight I feel like it's about to strangle the breath from my lungs.

There are too many emotions warring inside of me right now to pick any of them out, which is fine, because I have no use for any of them, anyway. All I need to do is get through today without melting into a puddle in front of Father and the others.

Colm and I stay silent for the rest of the walk. I can feel his concern, but I appreciate that he doesn't say anything. We've worked together for a long enough time that he's seen me in many of my less-controlled moments and knows what I'm really capable of. And what I'm capable of powering through.

Today is just another day on the endless, interminable trail of days that will ultimately lead to my death.

Which will be the only day in history when Father and I both get what we want.

When we get inside, everyone is sitting around a large, scarred table that fills up the main room. Father is sitting at the head of it, as expected, and the sight of him makes my entire body flush hot and cold with adrenaline. My muscles tense in preparation for... something, and the last few brain cells I had working to keep me moving seem to blue screen before diving into whatever sewer drain sits at the bottom of my shitty, desiccated frontal lobe.

When everyone sees me, they clap. A few of them stand up to pat me on the shoulder or something equally masculine, each one rocking my body forward in a way that makes my wounds throb and my stomach churn. Once again, I feel like I'm watching it all through plexiglass. I think I'm making the right noises and facial expressions in response, but I'm too braindead to know for sure.

What little mental energy I have left is trained on Father, whose attention is trained on me in return. He's watching me from his seat. His eyes are focused, but his expression is neutral in a way that always makes me nervous, and my body continues to sing with the urge to flee this fucking situation. Just run. Arms and legs flailing like a Muppet. I don't care, just fucking run until he can't see me anymore.

Even if it ends with me bleeding out in a ditch in the woods.

With both hands, I mentally reach inside myself, take hold of my frayed, withered focus and yank at it until the words people are saying start to sound like words I can comprehend.

"—called everyone here, now that Savage is back on his feet, to decide what to do about the Aryans. If we want to answer this contract with a contract of our own, with an all-out war, or bide our time until we can see just how much strength they're willing to devote to this little passion project."

Contract?

I swallow around the lump of sand in my throat and make sure my face is contorted in its usual mask of anger and disgust.

"What contract?"

My voice comes out raspy, because it's still fucked up from all the nasty vomit I inhaled days ago. I'm okay with that though, because it fits with the image I'm trying to present of someone you don't want to fuck with.

Father looks at me, his eyes scanning my face for longer than they need to, until I wonder just what it is he's looking for. I really need to sit down, but the chairs are all full and I'd rather open a fucking vein than ask someone to give up their seat for me like a cripple.

My knees start to buckle under Father's discerning gaze, so I lock them and swallow back another wave of nausea.

"Our informant tells us that the courthouse attack wasn't about your testimony, which makes sense. Everyone knew you weren't going to say shit. It was just a convenient time that they knew where to find you. It turns out there's a contract taken out on you for something else, but they couldn't rustle up much more information than that."

"Oh."

It sounds stupid, but I can't think of what else to say. The list of people who would like to see me dead now includes Father, myself, and every member of the Aryan Brotherhood.

Yippee.

Of course, Father has never said it outright. I'm just inferring from context.

"We're not going to let that happen," he says, like it's a given, which it definitely isn't. "But there's a larger question of what to do in the meantime. Our forces are still splintered. We've only just established ourselves here, and it would take a long time to pick up and head back to Oklahoma, as much as I'm already sick of this goddamn hick town. It isn't a good time to be getting into an all-out war with them over one minor attack."

On your son, but sure. Whatever.

"At the very least," Colm interjects in a level voice, "Sav needs to stay out of it. He's still too injured to defend himself, and if he starts messing around with Banna business, all he's going to do is draw more attention to our new location."

On instinct, I bristle at the implication that I'm weak. Of course it's true, but it didn't need to be said out loud.

Not when I can see Eamon, his throat purple and yellow from the bruises I left him, eying me like I'm a human obstacle to his ascension in the chain of command.

Standing is making me feel lightheaded. I need to get out of here. Father is still watching me as well, and my pulse is racing.

"I can do whatever you need, Father. I'm healing."

The words come out of my mouth like it's muscle memory.

Some of the guys are looking at me, some at Father. But what's worse is that *some* of them, including a few I don't recognize who must be locals, are looking to Eamon. That condescending fuck.

These are my men, and they're looking at him like he's some kind of authority figure whose example they're going to follow. After the way he spoke about Micah, he's lucky he still has a fucking jaw.

The next time it happens, I'll remove it from his face and see how many funny jokes he can spit without it.

The image of that blond fuck walking around without his lower jaw, tendrils of raw flesh hanging down, trying desperately to make his shitty, homophobic comments all while eying Micah like a piece of meat, makes me laugh.

No, not laugh, fucking *giggle*. I'm too on edge. I'm too full of adrenaline and my sanity is officially on a razor wire that's tethered between my consciousness and the rest of the universe, with me dangling underneath, trying to talk myself out of letting go.

"I mean, you could also just fucking hand me over. If that's what you want, Father. Drive me out to the woods, bring the Aryans to meet you, put me on my knees, and watch them put two bullets in my head so we can all be fucking done with this. Amirite?"

I look around, a smile on my face for the first time in days. It's such a simple solution. It would save everybody all this trouble.

But nobody agrees with me. A couple guys are smiling like it's a joke. Colm's gaze is burning into me with naked concern. Eamon looks fucking smug, of all things, and Father is watching me with calculating intensity. But no one is getting that it's an easy out.

"Seriously! Let's say fuck the war. Give me to them and move on with our lives. Well, your lives. Who wants to have more of these fucking meetings, anyway?"

The distant sound of foxes screaming is still a horrific backdrop to my thoughts. I gesture for emphasis, but it makes me lose my balance, and I stagger, catching myself on the back of someone's chair in front of me. Colm takes a step toward me, but I wave him off.

"What's the fucking point in a war? I'm half-dead anyway, as you can see. Let's fucking *go*. Come on, Father. If you call them now, we can have all this over with before dinner. I'm fucking..."

My words trail off, and I realize I'm slurring a little. Maybe they'll think I'm drunk instead of so incredibly deep in withdrawal and my own insane train of thought that the world kind of looks upside-down right now.

"What?" I ask, because they're still staring at me in silence.

The silence that fills the room is thicker and more impenetrable than the imaginary plexiglass from before.

"Father?" I ask, hating how small my voice sounds.

"I think it's clear that your injuries need more time to heal, Savage. You're no use to us like this and you're only putting yourself and us in more danger. Go back to your brother's and rest up. Stay off the grid and stay the hell away from anything to do with Banna business. When you're feeling better, we can make a plan of attack."

Father's tone doesn't leave room for argument, as usual. I can't help but feel chastised, but I'm not sure why.

"Colm, take him back to Micah."

Eamon snorts. "Enjoy playing happy housewife with the little queer, *Savage*." He somehow makes my name sound like an insult.

Rage filters through my incoherent view of the world, but when it tries to grip my body, I'm already too exhausted to do anything about it. Instead, I turn toward him and make a point of looking down at where he's seated at the table.

"Sure. I'm on vacation. Enjoy picking up my workload while I run a train through the local talent."

The words feel gross and performative even as I'm saying them, but I have to say something. Preferably something that makes me seem more normal in front of the men I just accidentally unhinged and displayed my psychotic mind to. And if I tell him how I really feel—that he needs to take Micah's name out of his mouth before I relieve him of his tongue—I think the guys might take it the wrong way.

Fucking random girls is normal. It's what normal guys do. They're telling me to lie low and pretend to be a normal, small-town man, which is kind of what I always dreamed of, anyway. I can do that.

Maybe.

I turn around and head for the door before he has the chance to answer, forcing myself to walk upright no matter how much my body screams at me for it.

As soon as I get through the front door, I double over and puke into the wilted grass in front of one of the fox cages. I vomit water, then bile, then I dry-heave until I realize that Colm's hands are the only thing holding me up.

My abdomen hurts so much I wouldn't be surprised if I looked down and saw my intestines hanging out, so I don't let myself look.

"Come on Sav, let's get out of here," he says in a hushed tone.

He half-drags, half-escorts me back to the Escalade. By the time we get there, the dark spots at the edge of my vision have traveled into the center, and I'm pretty sure I pass out before he has the chance to put me inside.

Chapter Ten

Micah

Of course my first night back at work is a full moon. On a Friday night. In my shitty, small-town ER.

I don't know what I did in a past life to deserve this, because I definitely didn't earn this kind of punishment in my lifetime. I'm not perfect, but I do my best. My karma can't be this bad.

"Micah—new patients in beds four, six, and eight are yours when you get to them," the charge nurse, Rebecca, yells at me as I hustle past with an armful of supplies. I'm on my way to a trauma bay to help with an emergent paracentesis because they don't have enough hands. It's not my patient, but there's only one tech for the entire unit tonight, which means all the nurses are doing their own tech work as well as helping each other where they can. Just physically transferring patients to inpatient and back is keeping our girl wrapped up all night, so for everything else, we're on our own.

Which sucks, because I already have the maximum amount of patients they can legally assign to me. But it is what it is. We'll only get through it by helping each other.

The House Supervisor wasn't exaggerating when she told me we were short-staffed tonight. Wait times are so long I'd almost think it was worth people driving all the way to the city, if I didn't know it's probably just as busy there.

Every linens cart is bare, I'm late for all my vitals, and if one more person asks me to get them a cup of coffee and a turkey sandwich, I'm going to scream.

I'd rather deal with a fucking code.

Not really, but it's close.

The only upside is that all this hustle leaves me no time to worry about Tadhg. He still wasn't back by the time I left for my shift, which wasn't a surprise, but does nothing for the worry slowly eating a hole in my chest. I'm beginning to wonder how slim the chances are that he'll come back at all.

If he collapses or has a medical emergency during their "meeting"—or whatever dark, violent shit they're doing—will they bring him to me here? Or will they let him rot until I get home, uncaring about whether he lives or dies, just like before.

I'd always thought I made my peace with the anger I held for Patrick. I'd folded it into a small, containable thing that lived buried deep inside me and rarely put up a fuss.

But right now, that anger is a living, breathing beast. It's kicking inside me, scratching and clawing at my insides, demanding to be heard. Because everything he ever did to me paled in comparison to how he treated Tadhg, and it looks like in the past twelve years, it's only gotten worse.

I swear, if my brother re-injures himself in some chauvinistic display of faux-fortitude because his piece-of-shit father is watching him, I will murder someone.

I should probably be more concerned about the risk that this situation is putting me in. Both legally and physically. But it's overshadowed by my concern and possibly tinged with the guilt that I never checked on Tadhg after Mom took me away from them both. I was too young when that happened, sure. But I've been an adult for a long time and there was nothing to stop me reaching out to him except my own fear and shame.

The man has clearly been living in a vacuum of affection for his entire life. I don't think I've ever seen someone so desperately in need of a little *tenderness*. I'm sure he'd lose his shit if I phrased it that way to him, but it's the truth.

"Micah!" a voice interrupts my dark musings, and when I look up, I see Tristan leaning over the patient I was on my way to help with. "Is that the centesis kit?"

"Yeah." I hustle toward him, shoving the sterile supplies in his hands so he can set up for the procedure. I see one of the ER docs hustling over, iPad in hand, which means Tristan and I have a few minutes to get things ready for them while they talk to the patient and get consent.

Rushing a sterile procedure isn't ideal, but sometimes these things have to happen in the ER, and this can't wait. The patient has so much extra fluid sitting in his abdomen he can barely breathe. With two people assisting, the doctor should be able to relieve the pressure and finish his intake swiftly.

Tristan and I move together well. Normally, he's handing a patient off to me instead of working on one at the same time, but I think our minds work in a similar way, so it's easy to see what needs to be done and fill the gap without a lot of over-communication. By the time the consent form is signed, the patient is as prepped as can be.

Doc grabs the ultrasound, picks a good spot and gets ready to shove the world's longest needle in there. The patient's wife cringes at the sight of it, but Tristan and I are inured. I distract her and get her to sit in a nearby chair, while Tristan helps the doc collect some samples of the fluid.

"Are you technically allowed to be helping with this?" I ask him when I turn around, which only gets me an eye roll in return, while the doctor studiously ignores our conversation. Tristan doesn't answer because he has a small gauze pack between his teeth while his hands are full, which is also against protocol, even if it's still in the plastic wrapper.

You can take the Army medic out of the field, but you can never take the field medicine out of the medic…

He lets me take the gauze out of his mouth and open it for the doctor while managing to give me another derisive look.

"As if you guys don't need the help. If the state of Missouri asks, I'm eating lunch right now."

Thankfully, it doesn't take long before we have several containers full of neon yellow belly liquid and a much thinner patient. The doctor withdraws the needle and hastily puts a Band-Aid over the incision, tosses his sharps in the bin, and then hustles out to get to the next situation.

Tristan lets out a long, deep exhale as we both look at the mess the doc left us.

"I haven't seen you all week. Does this mean you-know-who is doing better?"

He looks around us and keeps his voice low. I appreciate him trying not to spread the news of my long-lost stepbrother around the hospital, even if I technically did let the department head and HR know when I begged them for more time off. I could still live without the gossip.

"Kind of." I shrug. "He's mobile, which is a plus, but that's the least of my worries, at this point. The stuff he's involved with is…"

I look at Tristan, his cool green eyes taking mine in. I don't need to say it because he knows what I mean.

Tristan nods. "Yep. Well, there are ways to get out of that. If that's what he wants."

Sighing, I chew my bottom lip for a second before I answer. I don't know what the fuck he wants, at this point. I just know what he *needs*.

"Yeah, well, I'm not in charge here. We'll see. I gotta go, I have a stack of patients waiting."

I turn to go, but Tristan doesn't stop talking.

"Don't be afraid to suggest it. Even if it pisses him off. Sometimes people are looking for a way out even when they won't admit it out loud. I speak from experience."

Turning back to look at him, I narrow my eyes, but he just shrugs and gives me a blank face, refusing to elaborate. The gossip in me is dying to know more about his whole deal, but I don't have the time to pull it out of him. Later.

The hallway is lined with Welch Allyns, the vitals machines on wheels that automatically send all the info to a patient's electronic chart. I grab one, punch in my login information and then roll the thing across to Tristan more aggressively than I need to.

"If you're going to be here working illegally, at least make yourself useful. All the patients on this row need vitals," I say, pointing at the bays that contain my patients, as well as the two that Rebecca took, even though charge nurses aren't technically supposed to take patients.

But what are you gonna do?

Tristan grumbles, because swooping in to help out with procedures is a lot sexier than helping with grunt work, which is what we really need. But he does it anyway.

I'll take the help. And I'll take his advice about Tadhg on board. Later. When I can think about anything other than how to survive the world's shittiest swing shift.

I THINK MY BRIEF RESPITE FROM WORK MADE ME GO SOFT. Every part of my body aches. I can feel my bones and joints, as if they just want to announce their existence with pain, and walking from my car to the door of my apartment makes my pulse pound in my swollen feet with every step.

Definitely got weak. I need a shower, I need to peel off these disgusting scrubs and compression socks, and I need to sleep.

Once I make sure Tadhg is all right. Or even here.

My swing finished at midnight, but it was so chaotic trying to give report to the oncoming nurses on the patients I had to transfer over that I didn't get out of there until after one. Which means it's now past 1:30am and there's absolutely no reason that Tadhg shouldn't be back from a meeting he left for this afternoon.

The apartment is still and quiet when I unlock the door. It swings open silently, and nothing moves inside. No lights are on, and there's nothing moving except the ceiling fan in the living room that I think I left on earlier.

When my eyes hit the couch and he's not there, my stomach drops.

God, what did Patrick do?

But it does look disturbed, and when I see a dark streak

on the carpet that might be blood, everything in my body curdles with fear.

I should probably hit the lights, but I'm too distracted and there's enough light streaming in the kitchen windows from the parking lot halogens that I can see everything.

"Tadhg!"

A rustling sound is all I get in return, but I follow it to the kitchen, terrified of what I'm going to find.

Whatever it is, I can't help but think it's my fault. I was the only person who should have known better than to leave him alone, and what did I do? I abandoned him to his father's clutches. Again.

Tadhg is in the farthest corner of the kitchen. The little island blocked him from my view when I first stepped inside, but as soon as I move deeper into the apartment, I can see him. He's huddled in the corner, sitting on the ground with his legs bent in front of him, even though it probably hurts to put pressure on his abdomen like that.

It looks like he tried to get undressed at some point, because his t-shirt is discarded next to him, but the pants are only unbuttoned and slid halfway down his ass, black boxers showing but no further. His shoes and socks are kicked off, and the way his borrowed jeans are pulled down makes the legs swallow up his bare feet so they're only half sticking out.

It makes him look child-like, in a weird way. Like he's being swallowed whole by these clothes that Colm brought him. Like they were drowning him, even though they're technically his size.

But that's a weird thought. There's a lot of strike-through on his bandage where the wound at his hip has started bleeding again, but the one on his arm looks relatively clean.

I take this all in over the course of a few seconds, mostly out of instinct. Assessing and calculating a patient's condition comes with the gig.

Unfortunately, I'm flustered enough by the fact that it's Tadhg, so it takes me longer than I'd like to get to his face.

He looks... Vacant. No. Hollow.

Like someone scooped out all the things that make him my brother and left this damaged husk behind. His eyes are open, but they're not looking at me, and his body is still. If it weren't for the barest rise and fall of his chest, he'd hardly look alive.

The only part of him that's actively participating in existence are the fingers of his right hand, which are curled around his gun.

It's resting on his knee, but he's clinging to it with a level of commitment that makes me deeply uneasy.

Once I see him, I push down my own panic to keep my movements smooth and slow. I don't want to startle him or make things worse, whatever's going on. A little at a time, I move deeper into the kitchen before sinking to my knees in front of him, joining him on the shitty, cheap linoleum.

"Tadhg?" I speak softly this time, reaching out to put one hand on the knee that doesn't have a weapon resting on it.

He blinks before turning his head slightly to look at me, but everything about the movement is syrup-slow. Like he's moving through a vat of molasses, and getting his face to re-angle a few degrees is the hardest thing he's had to do all day.

"What happened?"

He licks his lips, and I can hear how tacky his mouth is, like he hasn't opened it or swallowed in a long time. His lips part like he's about to speak and his head cocks to the side, but whatever thought is trying to circle to the top of his consciousness gets stuck somewhere and can't break through.

When the words fail to form, he ends up sighing instead, and I can see his fingers rubbing over the metal of the gun in his hand, his thumb flicking the safety off and on like a nervous habit.

"I'm tired."

It's all he says, in the end, and his voice sounds gravelly and hoarse.

"Okay. Can I help you get back to the couch and you can try to get some sleep?" My tone is carefully neutral, but he's shaking his head before I even finish.

"I can't sleep. I hate the fucking couch. I couldn't just… lie there. Anymore." He blinks again, slowly, and licks his lips. "I'm too tired."

The words are all disjointed, and his pauses are unnatural, but he's not slurring his words. His pupils look normal. He doesn't seem impaired, just so fucking deep in a depressive episode that he can barely bring himself to speak.

Of course, I'd rather not be fucking guessing when it comes to my brother's safety, but if I couldn't get him to the hospital for a life-threatening gunshot wound, I think my chances of getting him there for a mental health episode are pretty much null.

"Can you give me the gun, Tadhg?"

His eyes narrow, and his expression sharpens as soon as the words leave my mouth.

"No." He can't really get away from me in this position, but he shrinks back into the cabinets he's leaning against, and I can see his fingers tighten around the grip, even in the low light. "You shouldn't touch it. It's too dangerous."

As much as I appreciate the sudden jolt of liveliness that

seems to have injected into him, I'd feel a lot better if he would give me the weapon he's been sitting here caressing.

I mentally weigh the pros and cons of calling Tristan for backup. On the one hand, he's bigger than me and more able to wrestle Tadhg into submission if it's needed. He also might have a sedative in his magic bag of tricks. But on the other hand, bringing a stranger into this situation is very likely to escalate it, which is not what I need right now.

I decide to use it as a last resort, keeping my eyes trained on Tadhg.

"Tadhg, why are you holding it?"

I know the answer, but I want to see if he'll say the words out loud. At first, he just looks at me, but then he lets out a cold, bitter laugh.

"I don't even know, Bambi. I don't know what the fuck I'm doing. But it seemed like a good idea at the time."

He shakes his head, and at least a little life has seeped back into his body with this conversation, his muscles loosening as he talks to me. But when he raises his gun hand to his head and uses the muzzle to scratch at his temple absentmindedly, it takes all my self-control not to try to snatch it from him.

He's staring at the wall, his eyes glazed over, and the muzzle is still resting against the side of his head like an afterthought.

"Tadhg." I sharpen my voice, a little command sinking into it. "Look at me."

Wide, round eyes snap to mine in the dark. I don't reach for the gun, because I don't think he'll let me take it, but I don't think I can go another minute without touching more than his knee. I reach forward so slowly it makes me ache, and take a firm grip of his jaw, forcing him to keep his attention on me.

"What's happening here?" Again, I use my stern, bossy voice on him. It's normally something I reserve for my patients or my hookups, but he seems to respond best to clear commands when he's fucked up like this. And given what I know about his life, it makes sense, in a twisted sort of way.

With the gun still resting against his head, Tadhg's face shifts through the most harrowing series of expressions I've ever seen. And this is far from the first time I've borne witness to someone on the brink of suicide.

Because that's what this is, I finally admit. Tadhg is in so much fucking pain from whatever his father and his violent life has been putting him through that he'd rather consider putting a bullet in his mouth than asking me for help.

Than letting me love him. Even if I wasn't there for him before, I'm here now.

His eyes are bloodshot, but there are no tears. He looks dry, at a bone-deep level. Like all the life has been sucked out of him.

"I'm so fucking tired, Bambi," he whispers into the small space between us, his voice weighed down by more heartbreak and exhaustion than I know how to comprehend.

Then his face twists, and I can see the skin on his hand get pale and bloodless as he squeezes the grip so tightly. He doesn't squeeze the trigger, but his finger is next to it, resting there like it's waiting for something.

And his hand isn't shaking. His hands have been shaking for a fucking week, and this is the first time they're steady. Tadhg slow-blinks again a couple of times, and I can see his chest rise and fall as his breaths come faster and faster.

I don't know what to do. I feel like anything I do right now could set him off, and it could all be over.

I still have one hand on his face though, and the other on

his knee, and he's not pushing me away. He's holding my gaze and I feel like he wants me to help, he's just so broken he doesn't know how to ask.

Well, I can ask.

"Please don't," I whisper to him. When he doesn't flinch at the sound, it gives me a little confidence. I lean in more closely, squeezing his jaw in my fingers so he can't look away. "Please, Tadhg. Don't leave me. Stay with me."

When the urge hits, I don't question it. I use my grip on his knee to part his legs and then slowly, carefully squeeze between them. Normally, I would be careful of his injuries, but there are more dangerous things at play right now.

I have to let go of him for a second to get myself situated, but it's only briefly and then I'm sitting in his lap, straddling him so that our faces are only inches apart. I still don't reach for the gun, but I wrap both my hands around his neck and interlock my fingers at the back, so I'm enveloping him as well as I possibly can with my smaller body.

I don't let him look away. He's watching me do all this, unmoving, the gun still held to his temple but without his finger slipping to the trigger.

"Please don't."

Finally, a hint of wetness swells in his eyes, pulled from some reservoir deep within his body. His lower lip trembles, making him look so much like a child, and I rub my thumbs gently across his cheekbones, over and over, to hold his attention.

"Please don't, Tadhg."

There's a tremor in his hand, finally, and it falls a fraction of an inch away from his head.

Taking a risk, I let go of his neck at the same time as I lean my forehead into his. If he wants to shoot himself, he'll have to shoot me too, and I know he never would. My left hand wraps itself around his, which is wrapped in turn around the gun, and together we bring it to down to the floor at an excruciatingly slow pace.

Once it's on the ground, I can feel him unclench his fingers, one by one. It feels like it physically hurts, but he does it. Until eventually the gun is lying there, untouched, and I have my brother's hand cradled in mine.

I bring it back up until both our hands are between our chests. I'm trying my best to breathe steadily, when somewhere along the way, Tadhg's chest started to heave like he's on the verge of having another panic attack.

I've kept myself so tightly controlled this whole time, but as soon as the gun is gone, it feels like something inside me snaps, and a sob escapes me.

That was too close. I won't let this happen again. I forbid it.

My sob triggers something in Tadhg, and he finally starts to cry. It's quiet, but I can tell. My forehead is still leaning against his, but I can see his eyes squeezed shut and feel how his rapid, shuddery breathing racks his body.

"Just let me take care of you, okay?" I finally ask in a thick voice.

He doesn't answer, but I feel him nod against me, even though his eyes are still closed.

I take a deep breath and prepare to lean back and give him a little room, but he doesn't let me. His left hand snakes out and grabs my scrub top, fisting it and holding me so tightly I couldn't go anywhere, no matter how hard I tried.

That's when I know it's sunk in. That he means it.

Still, I say it one more time, so he knows I really mean it, too.

"Just let me take care of you."

Chapter Eleven

Savage

All that manic, jittery energy from before is gone. My normal destructive urges, the ones that are directed both outward and inward, are gone.

The only thing that's left is an endless expanse of numb exhaustion.

And Micah.

Micah with his calm, commanding voice telling me what to do.

Tadhg, don't let your father bully you.

Tadhg, you don't have to be a worthless, violent sack of shit if you would just put some effort in.

Tadhg, don't spray your brains all over my linoleum, please. I really don't want to clean it up.

He hasn't actually said any of those things, but the implication is there. I hear it.

When Colm dragged my sorry ass inside after the meeting, he'd tried to hang out with me for a while, but I'd told him to get lost. I made some excuse about needing to rest.

As if he couldn't tell I hadn't slept properly for days. Maybe that's what's getting to me. I always feel shitty, but it could be the lack of sleep that's specifically making me feel like the world ripped my skin off and keeps slow-dripping acid on every soft, exposed piece of flesh that it can find.

I just wanted it to stop.

I just needed to sleep.

I don't know what I was thinking before. There was no plan. No real conscious thought. I just knew I couldn't spend another goddamn minute on that couch where I've been for so many hours—staring at the ceiling, cursing my own existence and feeling like I'm losing it.

The kitchen wasn't necessarily the better option, but I didn't want to get blood on Bambi's bougie, clean-smelling sheets. The cold, hard linoleum on my bare skin grounds me in the same way as the bite of metal against my skin did before Micah took the gun out of my hand.

"Come on, hun. Let's get you up," Micah says as he stands up, grabbing my hands to pull me with him.

He has the usual tone of command that always sneaks into his voice, which might be because of his job or might be because he's fucking bossy. But something trips me up.

"Why are you calling me 'hun'?" My voice sounds like I swallowed glass.

Micah lets out a little nervous laugh-exhale.

"It's a nurse thing. Or a healthcare thing, in general. I don't know, it's just what we call people. It's familiar, without being too familiar, and helps when you can't remember their name. I promise it's not an affront to your masculinity, if that's what you're worried about. I say it to everyone."

That's the part that seems to bug me more than anything. How generic it feels. But I'm absolutely not fucking saying that out loud. I narrow my eyes at him, but take the hand he offers anyway and do my best to stand up without making a pained sound. He steadies me, helping me move after I pull my pants back up, and I hate how pathetic I must look. Apart from the fact that the wound on my hip is burning like hellfire, my legs are about as stable as a baby antelope's, and as soon as I'm upright, a wave of dizziness hits me.

My vision snows, and the only thing that keeps me upright is Micah looping his arms around my chest in a practiced movement.

"Whoa," he says as he leans us both back against the counter. "What the fuck did they do to you?"

"Nothing."

It's true. They did absolutely nothing to me. In fact, they told me to go home and get more rest. Lie low. Everything I should have wanted to hear, considering before all this started, I was about to beg Father for my freedom from the Banna in the first place.

So why the fuck did him halfway giving it to me, unprompted, make me spiral so hard I nearly ended up eating a bullet?

That seems like it might be a later question, I realize, as my stomach flips and my knees threaten to buckle.

"Come on, *bro*."

There's a teasing lilt to Micah's voice as he says it, which I kind of like. I'm glad I didn't scare him too badly, even if I did make him cry for a second there. Which was enough to make me regret ever coming home to him in the first place.

If this ever happens again, it can't be in his house. I've figured out that much, at least.

I don't have the energy to decide if it's going to happen again. Giving up on it happening today sapped the last tiny reservoir of strength that I had in me, and left me bled dry. All I can do now is let Micah pull me around and pose me like a doll.

Fuck, I bet he would have loved to have a doll when we were kids. If only we'd had that kind of childhood. He would have done its hair and outfits half the time, and spent the other half the time doing extravagant, fake surgeries.

The thought makes me giggle, picturing baby Micah wandering around dragging a Barbie after him, and my father laughing fondly, in this weird fantasy reality that I've created. Real-world Micah looks at me funny when I laugh, but he doesn't say anything.

He'd laugh too if he could see what's in my head.

Instead, he pulls me around and tells me he's going to get me cleaned up. He doesn't make me shower, thank fuck, because I don't think I could stand for that long. And he also doesn't make me sit back on the godforsaken couch.

He leads me into his bedroom and makes me sit on the edge of his mattress. The dark sheets are rumpled because he never makes his bed, but they're clean and the whole room smells like fabric softener and whatever citrusy fucking aftershave he uses.

It smells like a nice person lives here. Homey.

He tugs my jeans the rest of the way off me, which is such a relief because I couldn't do it earlier, even though it felt like the damn things were trying to squeeze the life out of me. It leaves me in just my underwear, but I'm well past caring about that. There's no room for modesty when you've spent as much time as I have crying, vomiting and generally falling apart on your stepbrother's living room floor.

And the kitchen floor now, I guess.

...yay me?

Variety is the spice of my abject fucking misery?

Micah gets a wet washcloth and gives me a general scrub down with it, trying to swipe away as much of the sweat and whatever withdrawal poison I've been excreting from my pores. Then he disappears for a minute and comes back with gauze and a pink liquid, which he uses to clean up my wounds before prodding at them for longer than has to be necessary.

Ultimately, he ends up rebandaging them. He doesn't say anything during this, apart from asking me to move around this way and that and hold my limbs out of the way. Every time he touches me, it's gentle but firm, and I don't have to do anything other than what he tells me.

It's nice. He's in control. He just keeps talking in that calm, I'm-the-boss voice and I kind of want to let Micah be in charge of me for the rest of my existence.

That wouldn't be so bad, I think. He'd make me shower and eat real food, and he probably wouldn't let me murder anyone hardly at all.

The next time he disappears, he comes back with some of those buttery soft sweatpants that he bought me and a clean white undershirt. He wrestles them on me one by one, and when he's done, I look like someone that you might let sleep in a real home. Everything that's touching me is so soft, it lulls me into a sense of security that has all the rancid, disjointed thoughts from earlier walled up in a distant part of my brain.

I'm sure they'll break out and hunt me down later, but

right now I'm tired. I know I won't sleep, but at least I'm exhausted enough not to care.

A knock at the door startles me, but it's like my body is half-powered down and doesn't have the wherewithal to respond. So, I feel the startle internally, but I don't actually move in response. Instead, my face turns slowly in the direction of the front door, despite the fact that I can't actually see it from Micah's bedroom.

"It's fine," Micah says, taking hold of my face and forcing me to look at him in that way that always calms me down. "It's Tristan. He's dropping off meds I asked him for that I think will help. He's not coming in. I'm going to go to the door to get it, and then I'm coming right back. Got it?"

I nod, feeling stupid and tongue-tied. This shouldn't be a stressful experience.

There's only someone at the door. I've literally tortured people to death without batting an eye. The discordance between these two things is tripping me up, but all those other parts of my life feel far away right now, and the life that Micah's wrapped around me is down-soft and I don't want anyone else to step inside this fragile cage.

"I'll be right back."

He looks at me sharply one more time before stepping away. I hear murmured voices drifting down the hallway, but they're not loud enough for me to make out the words. Which is fine. I don't want to hear what they're saying about me, anyway.

I'm already aware of how pathetic I am. I don't need to hear them confirm it.

I just need to sleep.

The thought kicks around my consciousness as I lie back on Micah's soft, detergent-scented bed. But I know I won't. I'll lie on his couch all night, staring at that fucking ceiling fan while my brain twists itself into knots until I feel like the world is upside down, just like every other night since I ran out of my stupid meds.

There's no point in even trying, but I'm out of other options. Father won't let me work. Neither him nor Micah will let me off myself. And I really don't have the energy to run.

I'll just lie here until Micah comes back and he'll tell me what to do. That's something I can handle.

Micah

"Thank you-thank you-thank you," I whisper as I open the door.

Tristan stares at me, waiting to see if I'm going to let him come in. I weigh the benefits and ultimately decide it's better to risk him seeing Tadhg than my neighbors seeing what I'm about to give him. This is Mission Flats, but still.

Why invite trouble?

Tristan walks inside, looking as ragged as I feel after an exhausting shift and then being pulled out of bed by my 911 favor.

"Don't move."

I leave him in the doorway, with the door closed so at least my neighbors can't see if any of them are awake and spying, then dart into the kitchen. I don't even want to touch the fucking thing, my stomach flipping when I pick it up.

I have no idea if Tadhg even replaced the bullets that I stole when Colm first dropped this off with the rest of his stuff. I don't want to know.

Frankly, I feel like how close I came to losing him isn't really contingent on that. If he'd made up his mind, a lack of bullets wouldn't have stopped him.

I held him back this time, but I can't take any more chances. I don't know if I can stop him again, but I can at least remove anything from the house that makes it easier for him to make a terrible split-second decision.

"Here, take this. Hide it somewhere for me, please."

Tristan's eyes widen in a shocked expression that I'm not used to seeing on him. He's generally a take-everything-in-stride kind of guy. But I guess he knows the significance of what I'm handing him.

"Micah, does this belong to the Banna? This is a big deal. I can't steal this." He holds up his hand, refusing to even touch it.

"You didn't steal it. I stole it, and you're holding on to it for me. I'll give it back to him when I can trust him, but I need it to be out of this apartment for a little while. You have no idea how bad things got tonight, Tristan. I'm really scared."

I don't know when my voice started to crack in my hysterical little whisper-ramble, but it was somewhere in there. And the sympathy that seeps into Tristan's expression makes my stomach churn even more.

"Fine," he sighs. "But if I get murdered over it, you're going to have to answer to Ford."

I can't help but smile a little, despite the circumstances. I've been waiting for the tea on his secret boyfriend forever, and all the life-and-death family shenanigans have really derailed my gossip game.

"Mm, the super-secret burly boyfriend. Yes. Tell me, Tristan, how long have you been waxing the mechanic's tail pipe?"

The snort that he lets out is incredibly undignified, and it feels nice to have the mood lightened for a second, even if it's only by one percent. Today has been a lot.

"I don't know, a couple months. Why, you jealous?"

My face scrunches up. "I do just fine for myself, thank you. When I'm not caught up in this shit."

"I'm sure you do, sassy pants. Now, are you going to tell me why you wanted a sedative?"

"I just gave you his gun and told you I can't have it in the house. I'm sure you can put the rest of the pieces together."

"Are you in danger?" Tristan looks at me intently, his brow furrowed in concern.

I shake my head. "He would never hurt me. No matter how... *off* he gets. It's not like that. Obviously, I can't say the same thing about the rest of them, but we're both powerless in that respect. All we can do is hope for the best. Tadhg I can at least help."

Tristan sighs, and it's a bone-deep sound.

"Okay, well, I'm sorry but this is all I have," he says as he hands me a few one milliliter amber vials.

I turn them over to look at the label. "What the fuck? Are you seriously telling me you can't find anyone to sell you normal sedatives in this drug-addicted town?"

"I told you, I'm doing this shit to pay off my debt so I can live my life. Not so I can lose my career when I get busted for buying street xannies from some undercover cop. If you wanna go out there and risk your own license, be my guest. Otherwise, you can take whatever weird expired shit I'm able to pocket or get from my veterinary contact. Besides, it'll definitely put him to sleep."

"Yeah, and give him an abscess in the process." I keep turning the vials over in my hand, wondering if this is worth it. "This is gross. I don't even like using promethazine when it's not expired. It literally fucking burns the tissue where you inject it."

"Well, it's non-addictive, it'll send him to sleep and most importantly, it's not controlled, so it won't send either of us to prison for the rest of our lives. You've got to pick your battles here, kid."

"Fine." I sigh again but stash the vials and then some syringes that he hands me in my scrubs. "Thank you," I add as an afterthought, because he doesn't actually have to help me with this and he's doing me a huge solid.

"You're welcome." Tristan stares at me for a minute while he tucks the gun in his waistband and then makes sure his shirt is covering it. "Call me if you need me, okay? I know we weren't exactly besties before, but this is a weird situation. There's not a lot of people you can ask for help, and I'm one of them, so don't hesitate to reach out. I'd rather get inconvenienced once or twice than get a call here when I'm on shift and find something I don't wanna find, you hear me?"

I nod. "Same to you. Now go home and snuggle your man." I only met him once, briefly, but he was like 6'5" and stacked. I bet he snuggles the shit out of Tristan, the little hussy.

He just laughs and opens the door, leaving as quietly as he came.

It doesn't take me long to look up a dosage for the medication on my phone and then pull up a dose for Tadhg. Mentally, I'm cursing and second-guessing myself the entire time. This isn't a good medication. It's basically a jacked-up version of Benadryl, but the risk of doing damage to your tissue when you inject it, especially when you inject it into a muscle like I'm about to, is pretty substantial.

It seems risky. But on the other hand... Tadhg is already full of damaged tissue and that can heal. He can't heal from a hole in the head.

He hasn't been sleeping. I've suspected it for a while, but now I'm sure. The thing I don't understand is why, though. It's like a switch was flipped. He slept so well for a while, and then suddenly he became erratic, irritable and always seemed like he was just half a step out of sync with the world around him.

I'm sure he knows more about what's going on with him than he's telling me, and his stupid fucking macho pride is threatening to be the death of him. Maybe if I can just get him to rest, lower the cortisol in his body a little and let him take a breath, he'll be more rational. Then I can talk him into telling me the truth, so we can find a solution.

Whatever it is, I know I can help him. And a hell of a lot more effectively than I'm doing right now.

One look at his face when I walk back into the room confirms it. He sits up immediately, like I'm calling him to attention, even though his movements are sluggish. He needs to rest, and he can't be left alone. He's too high-risk right now. His skin is chalky, looking pallid in contrast to all his dark tattoos. The clothes I bought for him seem to hang off him, even though he's barely been here long enough to lose weight, and the expression he's giving me is lifeless.

At least he's looking at me.

"How do you feel?" Stupid question, but always worth asking to see what answer will float to the surface.

He shrugs, and his gaze flits to the ground.

My stepbrother sits on the edge of the mattress, his shoulders slumped and his body seeming to weigh him down into the ground. I move forward, the medication in my pocket for now, and stand between his knees. So far, I've figured out that the best way to get his attention when he's dissociating or out of it is to get into his personal space. Touch him, talk to him, put myself in his field of vision.

He didn't get nearly enough affectionate touch when we were children, and I can't imagine that's changed. It's time to start filling that void ASAP.

Once I'm bracketed in between his legs, I let my hands rest gently on his shoulders. I think it's a positive sign that he doesn't startle or flinch away from the touch, but who knows? He could just be that numb. I rub his shoulders and down over his arms, trying to bring a little life back into this cold flesh.

It only takes a minute before I feel him shiver under my palms, and he tilts his face to look up at me.

"Bambi?" His voice is so small. I don't think even he knows what he's asking for, but whatever it is, I want to give it to him.

My heart thuds against my chest so hard I feel like tiny fissures are forming in my ribs, trying to hold it in. The depth of affection I still hold for him, even after all this time and distance, threatens to overwhelm me. I don't know why.

Maybe it's what we went through. It's hard to suffer that much pain with another person and ever get over the bond that you forge. I don't know. Either way, my body is screaming to wrap myself around him and squeeze him tight until he's safe. Safe from his father, from himself, from everyone in the whole goddamn world.

I cup his cheeks, like I did in the kitchen before, and sweep my thumbs across them in a way that makes him shiver again. His eyes turn unfocused, but he's still watching me like I hold the answers to the universe in my hands.

Maybe I do.

"I have a medication. I'm going to give you an injection

and it's going to help you sleep, and then I think you're going to feel better. And you're going to share the bed with me, because you need real sleep, and I worry that the couch is making things worse. So, it's going to be a shot, drink a glass of water, and then sleep for as long as your body wants you to. None of this is up for discussion, got it?"

Tadhg nods. His eyes are heavy-lidded, and I don't think he would have the energy to argue with me even if he wanted to.

Once I have him on board, the rest is easy. I decide to do the injection in his quad, because it's a large volume and his legs are ridiculously sized. He barely even flinches, even though I'm sure it must fucking burn.

After that, he eats three saltines that I feed him in little pieces and drinks the glass of water I hold to his face. I plan to refill it and leave it next to him, but at the last minute, I swerve and leave a reusable bottle instead of the glass. Not that I realistically think he'll wake up and immediately start smashing anything that could become sharp and harmful, but it's more of a habit.

Once my danger-eyes are turned on, I see the threat in all the household objects.

I get him tucked in, and it barely takes fifteen minutes before he's asleep. Thank fucking Krishna, Jesus, Troye Sivan, whoever. I don't care. I'm just glad he's asleep.

Once I'm confident I can get away for a minute, I do a quick round up of everything else in the apartment that seems too dangerous to leave, throw it all in a backpack and then take it downstairs to stash in the trunk of my car. When I get back, he's still sleeping in the position I left him in, an expression of twisted pain on his face even in his slumber, but at least it's something.

As soon as everything is done, my own exhaustion hits

me like a brick wall. I yawn my way through showering and changing and then crawl into bed next to Tadhg.

It's been over a decade since I shared a bed with my stepbrother. He's more than doubled in size since then, and it's weird to feel his immense presence next to me on the mattress. Especially when I'm generally not a sleepover kind of guy anyway. My dates tend to be *get some and get out*, especially because of my wacky work schedule.

Which is how I like it. It normally bothers me listening to another person breathe all night. But right now, the sound of him breathing is like a balm. I wouldn't be able to sleep anywhere else. I need to be here so I can be sure he's safe.

If no one else in the freaking universe is going to watch out for this man, then I can't let him out of my sight.

Savage

Waking up before I went on the meds always felt like a sudden kick of adrenaline—a *who-what-where* arousal of fight or flight that had me go from resting to awake in a few seconds, taking in my surroundings with my heart screeching to keep up.

It was exhausting. That was one of my favorite things about the meds. One of the things that made it worth all the shitty side effects, that I was finally able to get some sleep and wake up in a way that didn't feel like I'd been dumped into a bucket of ice water.

But this is something I've never experienced. This feels like clawing my way to the top of a swimming pool with a tarp tangled around my ankles. I swear I almost wake up—

my eyes slitting open and my awareness scratching at the surface before diving back down—five or six times before I wake up for real.

When I do, Micah is next to me. I don't know why, but that immediately soothes the thrum of anxiety already threatening to take hold of my chest.

It's nighttime. Dark, at least, but it's hard to tell with all the blackout curtains and shit he has in his apartment. He's lying next to me in lounge clothes that make him look like something out of a catalog for modern, trendy, overpriced homewares, scrolling on an iPad.

"I didn't know you had glasses."

Micah jumps a little, inhaling and making an "O" with his mouth as he turns toward me. He blinks once before snatching the glasses off his face, and I swear I can see his cheeks coloring in the light coming from the iPad screen. They have thick, dark rims. Classic nerd glasses, and they suit him.

He looks less like a real nerd and more like a porn star wearing prop glasses. *Nerd gets railed by the football team after practice.* That kind of thing.

My mind feels completely scrambled. I wonder how much I've slept to feel this out of it.

"Yeah, well, I only wear them if I'm reading in bed," he says, but I've already forgotten the question.

When I don't reply, Micah shifts, sitting up further in the bed and turning until his entire body is oriented toward me. I feel like I should do the same, but my limbs are still too leaden and just the thought of it is exhausting.

At least my mind feels sleep-muddled, not the way it did before, though. I take one deep breath after another, carefully probing at the corners of my consciousness like I'm taking inventory, and it seems like the various wheels and cogs are much more lined up and in their places than they have been the last few days.

Finally.

"How do you feel?" Micah's voice interrupts my thoughts.

I shrug. I don't know how to answer him when he says that.

"Mmm."

But he doesn't prod any further. Instead, he reaches out and turns me to face him, manhandling me the way he's started doing more and more often. His strong, deft fingers touch me over, peeling down my eyelids and smoothing over my skin until I feel like a horse at the market.

"Can I help you?"

That makes him smile—genuinely smile—and he looks so beatific I can't help but smile at him. I'm not sure how long it's been since we had a moment of peace like this between us, but I instantly feel fifty pounds lighter.

Yesterday seems far away. Like it was a different version of myself that did those things, not the body I'm in right now. Even though that version of myself is realistically the one that takes the wheel more often than not.

Maybe here, with Micah's soft sheets and nice dishes and medications for everything instead of toughing it out, I can keep being this person instead. I like this version much better.

Maybe this really is my chance at a do-over, and I'm about to experience what it's like to be a normal person.

Savage, the normal guy. Doing what normal people do.

Whatever the fuck that is.

Chapter Twelve

Savage

It's been one week since The Incident™. I'm finally over the hump of my medication withdrawal, thank fuck, but that doesn't change the fact that Micah has permanently installed me in his bedroom instead of the couch.

He claims it's to support my "healing", and it was a mistake to leave me out there in the first place. But if he meant physical healing, then I feel like he'd be taking the couch instead of sleeping in here with me. He wants me here so he can spy on me and make sure I'm not rummaging through the kitchen knives or something.

If he thinks I haven't noticed the sudden absence of sharp things and overdosey things inside his apartment, he's underestimating me. I'm a wreck, but I'm not an idiot. He's watching me every minute of every day that he's not at work, like I'm a block of C4 with a really, really long fuse that we're both waiting to finally go off.

But it's whatever. I hate feeling like I'm being babied, but I don't hate the company. It's making me realize that I've been lonely basically since the day he left me the first time, so having his warm, solid, confident presence around is settling something turbulent inside me. Day by day, hour by hour, the knot in my gut untwists. Like every time he hands me a bowl of pasta or a fucking peanut butter and jelly sandwich, I one-up in the "normal" column and get another inch away from the murderous, violent version of myself I hate so much.

He can babysit me all he wants, if it makes him feel better.

As well as being farther from the precipice of insanity, I'm also back to being mostly a functional person physically. I don't think I'll be lifting dead bodies anytime soon, but that's fine by me. At least I can get up and walk around without looking like a plague victim on the verge of collapse.

The downside to all this is that I'm fucking *bored*. Not only am I functional again, but all the twitchy, anxious energy I had that pushed me to take the damned meds in the first place is back in force. It's like an itch in the back of my brain that I can't scratch, constantly telling me that I need to be up and moving, that I should be on the lookout for some kind of threat, but it refuses to give me any additional information.

It has me checking the perimeter of Micah's shoebox apartment twenty times a day, which is worse than useless and only makes me feel more like a prisoner.

My dick is waking up as well, which is another crisis that I don't have the energy to deal with. I've fought a life-long battle with that motherfucker. It never works when I need it to, and then it perks up at the most inconvenient possible moments.

After more than a decade of feeling hollow and betrayed whenever my cock wilted on the spot while I was trying to use the fucker, I didn't mind the side effect of the meds making it worse. It already felt numb and useless half the time anyway; what's wrong with escalating that to all the time? I was already having to fabricate my sex life for the sake of my reputation.

I'd rather make up lies for the rest of the Banna, then have it get back to them from some girl that I soft-cocked halfway through sex, had a panic attack and kicked her out. That shit is more humiliating than anything else my trash brain and broken body can throw at me.

Except now I'm waking up with boners every morning. Thank fuck Micah is working swing and nightshift, so we're mostly on an opposite sleep schedule. It's bad enough having to talk myself down from the ledge of trying to jerk off, because I *know* it won't work, and I'll just be disappointed again. I don't want Micah to see me going through the stages of grief every morning and asking me what's wrong, when I'd rather put a rifle in my mouth than tell him the truth.

That I'm not just an evil man, I'm a useless one as well.

My dad always told me I was a worthless piece of shit, and it turned out he was right. He's an asshole, but he probably knows me better than anyone else. He's the only one that sees through my mask of *Savage, the mafia enforcer*, and sees the weak, scared kid that he loved to beat on. It's only for the sake of his reputation that he doesn't let the men know the truth about me, I'm sure.

Which is why I won't ask him for help with my other problem: money. Micah's asleep, after getting home from his shift sometime in the wee hours. So, I'm out in his kitchen, making myself breakfast with his food, wearing clothes he bought me, all with money he makes at a job that I can now see runs him fucking ragged.

The guilt creeping in about being a leech on my little brother is threatening to drown me. I can't access my legal bank accounts, because I'm off the grid. All my cash stashes are back in Oklahoma. And normally I would be getting cash for work, but I've been benched.

I can't go to my father for a fucking hand out. I'd rather turn myself over to the Aryans. But I also can't keep stealing Micah's money forever, considering he works himself to the bone for it and I've been nothing but a burden since the day I showed up on his doorstep.

Shoving a piece of burned toast in my face, I decide to do something about it. Once upon a time, I was a person in the world. I've never had a real job, but I did do things other than lie around all day convalescing and despondently staring at the wall like a crated dog waiting for its owner to come home.

I've already showered, so it doesn't take me long to dig out the jeans that Colm brought me to go to the meeting where I lowkey threatened to off myself and got excused from duty indefinitely. Like a dumbass.

Pulling them on felt like a prison the first time. It was this stiff, harsh contrast to all the soft fabrics and gentle touches that Micah had been surrounding me with. But this time it feels better, like I'm taking action on something. When I walk out of the front door, Micah's keys in my hand and a scribbled note left on the kitchen counter, I feel more like myself—the better side of myself—than I have in years.

I still have to move slowly, because I'm stiff where I'm healing, but it's not enough that anyone would notice unless they were looking. When people I walk past stare at me, it's for the normal reasons. The tattoos, my build, the permanently angry set of my face—they all scream *criminal*. They're scared of me. Which is a hell of a lot better than pity.

Micah drives a white VW Jetta, which is not only a stupid car to have in the first place but also makes me feel ridiculous crouching down and folding myself in half to get inside. He may be a lot slimmer and a few inches shorter than me, but he's not that small. I have no idea how he drives this thing every day without feeling like he's wearing it.

Hopefully, the rest of the Banna are too busy doing real work to notice me driving around town in a girly-ass car. If it gets back to Father, not only will it remind him that I exist and potentially make him want something from me, but it's also bound to trigger his *no gay shit* internal barometer.

I'm too tired to catch a beating today. I just want to find a way to make some money under the table that doesn't require me to maim, mangle or dismember anyone.

After two hours of driving, I've gotten used to the Jetta. I've even found a tolerable radio station to listen to, and I haven't seen anyone I recognize that might report me back to Father. But I've learned a few things about this area: it's pretty, it's fucking empty, and there are absolutely no jobs.

Micah lives in a medium-sized town called Mission Flats, but it only took me a couple minutes to figure out that all the jobs here were real. Every business here is part of a chain, and corporate offices need social security numbers, which is not something I can do.

So, I go through the smaller towns in the surrounding area, looking for anything ramshackle that might need help. There's a town called Mishicot that seems like an overgrown trailer park, and as soon as I see someone batch cooking meth on their bicycle, I know the chances of there being work are fucking slim.

Another town is Possum Hollow, which is a dumb, hick fucking name. I ask in a couple of places: feed stores, small farms, even a mechanic outside of town where I get side-eyed and the silent treatment, but no one's hiring.

By the time afternoon hits, I'm exhausted. I haven't been out of the house and moving around this much since the meeting, I've had zero fucking success, and by now, Micah is probably awake and potentially pissed I took his matchbox racer without asking.

Not ready to go back a complete failure, I look for a bar or something. I just want a little more time to feel like a competent adult out in the world, not being supervised or cared for. And I haven't had a beer in weeks.

It doesn't take long to find one. One that looks classy enough—by the standards of the area, at least—that I'm not likely to run into any of my guys. It describes itself as a "bar & lounge" on the sign, there are no motorcycles in the parking lot, and I can't see a single person wearing a cut. No motorcycle club affiliation isn't necessarily a mark of quality, but a beer's a beer and I just don't want to run into fucking Eamon or my father.

Once I've parked in the gravel lot, I walk across to the entrance. It's kind of... cute. That would be the best way to describe it, not that that's a word I use very often. The Feral Possum. There's a little logo with the fucking rodents on it, and a bunch of cartoons on their little A-frame advertising drinks specials outside.

I wonder if Micah drinks here. It seems like the kind of place where nice people might hang out.

When I see a rainbow flag in the window though, I

143

freeze. It's a small flag, relatively discreet, and even more evidence that this might be Micah's kind of place. But could potentially be a problem if I got caught here.

I take a peek through the door though, and it looks *normal*. No more flags, nothing that looks like I would picture a gay bar looking, not that I have any idea. I decide to shove my concerns to the back of my brain for the sake of getting out of the fall afternoon sun and getting something cold to drink.

Inside, it's exactly like every other bar I've been in, except a little cleaner with a slightly nicer clientele. I definitely stand out because of my tattoos, but not to the point that people are pointing and staring.

It'll do. I take a seat at the bar, drumming my fingers on the wood and shoving down the unease crawling through my gut for some reason I can't put my finger on. It doesn't take long for the bartender to notice me, because it's still early and the place is mostly empty. He wanders over, a polite customer service smile on his face, and puts a cardboard coaster with the possum logo on it in front of me.

"What can I get you?"

If anyone stands out in here, it's him over me. I may look a little on the thuggish side, but he's not dressed like any bartender I've seen in real life. He's wearing clothes like he walked out of a cologne ad—pressed slacks, a white shirt and a fucking waistcoat. His hair and dark beard are meticulously styled, and everything about him looks way too expensive to belong in a town like this.

I get distracted by it, so it takes me a second to answer, and when I realize I was staring, I stammer a little because I feel like a dumbass.

So much for reclaiming my confident former self.

"Draft of whatever is fine," I say, lowering my eyes and trying to remember how to be around normal people.

He just nods, ignoring my awkwardness. "Lager?"

"Yeah, sure."

We go through the rest of the exchange in silence, him pouring me a draft and me handing over some cash that I also took from Micah, like the leech that I am. But the first sip tastes like cold, hard relief, and I immediately know that coming here was a good idea.

I can face Micah and my failures in an hour. They'll still be there.

It's slow, so the bartender isn't very busy. He mostly cleans and fiddles with the little tubs of things behind the bar, or chats with the woman who seems to be working with him. He doesn't strike up a conversation with me, but that's not surprising. Nothing about my appearance was designed to be inviting.

I'm halfway through my beer and feeling more light-headed than I should, because apparently a couple weeks of near-death and medication purging have turned me into a lightweight. It also makes me relaxed enough to loosen my tongue.

I gesture to the bartender, and he moves toward me, his expression placid and calm in that way only deeply confident, emotionally stable people can really master. It makes me a little jealous.

"Is this a gay bar?"

They weren't the words that I intended to come out of my mouth, but they're the ones my brain shoved out before anything else could get there.

The man's expression becomes guarded, and I can see him taking me in, like I just crossed the line from customer to potential threat.

"No, but we're welcoming to everyone, and I like to make sure people know that. There aren't always places around here where people can be themselves, and this is a safe space for that. Is that a problem?" His tone is measured and even.

I shake my head. "No. My, uh. My brother's gay. I was just asking."

That makes him look a little shocked, his eyes widening slightly, and I see him give me another once-over subtly before he leans back.

"Okay. Well, he's more than welcome here. Along with anyone else who isn't going to be an idiot and cause trouble."

Pointed, but sure.

"Is there any chance you're hiring?" I spit out, because my brain to mouth filter has been nullified by half a fucking beer, apparently.

He cocks his head at me. "Your brother needs a job?"

"Not him." I shake my head, looking down at my beer and then up again. "Me. I'm looking for work, and I'm having trouble finding anything."

He pauses for longer than is socially acceptable, like he's turning something over in his mind. Eventually his eyes narrow, and he moves closer before he responds in a quiet voice.

"I thought you already had a job," he says, tapping his neck in the same spot that my Banna tattoo sits.

Ahh. So, he's less innocent than the waistcoat and fancy cologne made me assume.

The trouble is, it's impossible to explain my situation to anyone, let alone when I can't actually say anything.

"I..." I trail off and look around, even though I know there's no one near us. My throat feels tight for some reason.

When I look back at him, there's this kind of weird empathy on his face. Not like pity, which I fucking hate, but like he gets what I'm about to say. "Not right now. I'm on sabbatical, I guess. I just want a real job, but I can't do paperwork or anything like that. I can work, I swear. I don't cause trouble. I just need something... normal. Please."

He nods, and that empathetic, understanding expression stays on his face.

"Well, I already know you're not a cop, so I can do under the table. The pay is shit but if you want to be a barback for me, I could use the help. It's easy. Safe."

The last word hits me like a kick in the gut, and I blink a couple of times before I know how to answer him.

"Yeah. Yeah, uh, thank you. That would be great."

"I'm Gunnar," he says, offering me his hand to shake.

I take it, and he squeezes it, reaching out to cover it with his other for a second, like I've seen grandfathers and shit do on TV.

"I can't have trouble here," he says, holding my gaze. "But I know what it's like to need a little help sometimes. If you just need to get distance from something. If you show up and behave yourself, I'm happy to help as much as I can."

Well, shit. I don't know what to say to that, and the man is still holding my hand while he looks me in the eye, making my nerves crawl into my throat and seal it shut.

I cough a little, pulling my hand back to safety.

"Yeah. Thanks." It's stupid, but it's all I know to say. I tell myself I don't know what else he's trying to imply, and the pressure behind my eyes is exhaustion from being out all day for the first time.

Nothing else.

Chapter Thirteen

Micah

He's laughing. My brother, who had a gun in his hand barely a week ago, is laughing. At a gay fucking movie.

I knew it was a risk putting on *The Birdcage*, but he's been on this super intense kick of doing "normal" things for the past few days. So, I've been trying to accommodate him. We cook food and watch TV—he's never even heard of *Love Island*—and go for walks in the evening to stop him getting an embolism from sitting around all day. Also because his jittery energy was really starting to grate my nerves.

It's all lulled me into a false sense of normalcy, and I decided to push the boat out by making him watch the godfather of all gay movies. Maybe as a test to see how much of his father's homophobia has seeped into him over the years and how much of it is just surface-deep.

And he's *laughing*.

Tadhg is leaning back on the couch, one foot up on the coffee table and a bowl of popcorn in his lap, giggling like a dumbass at the constant barrage of slapstick slip-and-fall drag jokes on the TV. If it weren't for all the muscles and the super violent tattoos, you'd never think he's killed people.

I mean, I don't actually know that he's killed people. But I would assume. Not only is it common sense, given his line of work, but the amount of raw anguish he seems to contain goes way past just our childhood trauma.

You'd also never think any of the drama we've had for the past couple of weeks had happened, but I'm okay with that.

I'm not naive enough to think it's going to stay this way. Issues like Tadhg's don't just go away, even if he's doing much better. And Patrick will eventually show up to drag him back to work. We can only drag out the excuse of his "recovery" for so long.

When I saw how proud he was after he got that job the other day... I'd do anything to protect that. He acted like it was no big deal. And it is a shitty job, but still. I like that bar, and I think that crowd will be a good influence on him. I could tell he was pleased with himself, even if he was trying not to show it.

I have no idea how I'm going to pull him out of Patrick's clutches for good so he can continue to laugh and eat sandwiches and whatever other normal shit he wants to do, but I'm here for it. I'm here for all of it.

I catch Tadhg looking at me out of the corner of my eye. His attention stays on me instead of the screen for a beat too long, then he reaches out to poke me with the foot he has kicked up nonchalantly on the couch beside me.

"Yes?" I have to control my face so I don't fucking beam

at him when I turn to look. He's just so relaxed. It's filling my cold, dead little nightshift-worker heart with warmth.

"Do you ever do that?"

"What?" He's still looking at me, his expression more serious than I was expecting.

"That," he says, tossing his head in the direction of the TV, where Nathan Lane is in full, glorious drag. Ah.

I give him a smile that I try very hard not to make patronizing.

"No, it's not really my thing. Besides, I'm absolutely horrendous at makeup. I must have skipped that class at orientation. I nailed the dick-sucking final though, and that's the important one."

Tadhg looks at me for a minute, his eyes slightly wide, and I can practically see him trying to work through my answer. I'm a little worried I've gone too far but also pissed at myself for worrying about it when I told myself I wasn't going to make myself smaller or straighter for anyone's comfort.

But then it doesn't matter, because a smile breaks out on his face again and he lets out a deep, throaty chuckle.

"Sure, Bambi. You do you, I guess."

He's smiling at me like I'm the ridiculous one in this conversation, but I'll take him thinking I'm kinda silly over him being homophobic any day.

In fact, the whole conversation is so unexpectedly chill, it gives me the confidence to broach a topic I've been sitting on for a couple days. I have a friend from nursing school who does travel nursing, so I hardly ever get to see him. But we've been on and off fuckbuddies since school, and we normally hook up whenever he's in town, unless one of us—him, let's be realistic—is in a relationship.

He's here now, and I've been blowing him off because I

was worried about Tadhg. But I would really like to see him if I could manage it without causing problems. Not only is he my friend, but all this drama and stress has me pent up as fuck, and I can think of nothing better than taking it out on Scott.

It's a shame we're incompatible romantically because he's everything I like in bed. Right now that's all I need though. Just something to take the edge off. I've had too many life and death experiences in the past two weeks and no fucking orgasms. I've even been too stressed to jerk off in the shower, and I think it's starting to get to me.

"Speaking of sucking dick," I say, instantly regretting it when Tadhg cuts his gaze back to me with a wary expression. "I'm gonna go on a date tonight. If that's cool."

I swear I can see the color drain from Tadhg's face. I know sometimes it's a lot different to be accepting of gayness when it's a concept versus actually in your face, but it's not like he's being asked to participate, for fuck's sake. Or even watch. I'm just stepping out for the evening.

"A *date?*" I don't miss the way his tone immediately shifts from playful to intense.

Watching his face, I can't tell what exactly about this is bothering him, but the whole mood of the room just changed. He pulls his outstretched leg back and puts it on the floor, sitting up and leaning forward to rest his elbows on his knees. There's tension in all the muscles of his arms and back, so much that I can see the definition through the soft cotton t-shirt he's wearing.

When he suddenly straightens his back and turns back to face me again, his expression is cold.

"No. Absolutely not. It's not safe."

I swear my eyes double in size and I wonder if I'm hearing things.

"Um... There seems to be a miscommunication here. Tadhg, I was asking if you're going to be alright to be home alone for a few hours. I wasn't asking for your *permission.*"

He fists his hands and relaxes them over and over a few times, flicking his gaze between me and the ground. I can practically see the anxiety crawling into him, and normally I would prioritize making him feel more relaxed, but not when he's treating me like a child.

"Who is he? How do you know him? Where would you go? There's no way this is safe. He could do anything to you. Or worse, the Aryan Brotherhood could come looking for me and find you instead, and I won't be there to protect you. This is un-fucking-acceptable, Bambi. I said no."

There was a waver of uncertainty in his voice at first, but by the end of his little speech, he's completely solid and sounds so much like Patrick during one of his commanding rants that it's making me feel a little nauseous.

Part of me realizes that this is a regurgitated reaction from spending too much time with his father. But I can't control my own anger. He's so fucking out of pocket here, and I can't even think of why.

"Look, I'm sorry I won't be at your beck and call for the evening, but I don't see what your problem is. I go to work without you, and no one attacks me there. You sound completely paranoid right now." I look at him more closely and try to see beneath the hard outer shell to figure out what's causing all this anger. Is it homophobia? Or something else entirely that I'm missing?

I take a deep breath in and let it out, forcing myself to relax, despite the anger that's wrestling for control of my brain right now.

"What's wrong, Tadhg? Why is this bothering you so much?" I ask softly.

For a split second, his face twitches and I think he might tell me the truth. But then the hint of vulnerability is gone.

Tadhg stands, his fists clenched and his shoulders up around his ears. He turns to face me, pointing at me and looming over me in a way that's more intimidating than I want to admit.

Not only does it give me flashbacks to my childhood with Patrick, but it reminds me of something I'd forgotten. That this isn't just my stepbrother. This is my brother in the shell of an angry, violent criminal, and I need to keep working to dig him out.

But I'm also not going to roll over and tolerate whatever bullshit toxic behavior he wants to throw at me. Not in my own home. Not when I've been cleaning up his piss and puke and kissing his booboos and holding him while he fell apart for a few weeks. I deserve a little more respect than this.

"It's bothering me that I'm working hard to keep you safe, and you're willing to throw it all away just so you can get laid. I heard that gay guys were loose, but I didn't realize my own brother was this much of a desperate slut. Can't you go a couple weeks without spreading your legs, or is some loser's dick worth dying over?"

His hand is shaking as he points it at me, and a flush of rage is climbing up his neck. But any chance I had at containing my own anger went out the window when he called me a slut.

Springing from the couch, I shove him with both hands a lot harder than I should. I'm smaller than him, but I still make him rock back a few steps.

It doesn't make me feel any better.

"How dare you call me names in my house. Do you have any idea how much I've sacrificed to take care of you? And you want to stand here throwing homophobic shit at me? You sound just like your father, by the way. I never thought I'd see the day you turned into that piece of shit."

Tadhg crosses his arms, I think, to try to conceal how much his hands are shaking, and his face is going through a barrage of emotions. It was a shitty thing to say. But all my empathy is walled off behind my anger, along with how much he hurt me with the things he said.

"I said 'no'. That's final, Micah. You're not going to slut around on my watch. Have a little self-respect and learn to get off your knees. I forbid it."

My mouth is hanging open so wide I could catch flies. The bottom-shaming here is just the tip of the iceberg, but it's catching my attention for whatever reason.

Of course he assumes I'm a bottom. Just like he asked me if I did drag. Because even if he hasn't been sitting here calling me slurs all week, he still thinks less of me for who I am. He still assumes that I'm girly and weak and submissive, and that all of those things are inherently bad.

He can take every single one of those thoughts and throw them in the trash, obviously. But I don't have the wherewithal to explain that to him right now. I'm too pissed, and I'm letting myself embrace the anger because it's the only thing holding back the stinging pressure behind my eyes.

Cocking my hip, I sink into a much sassier, camp persona, because fuck him.

"You know, I was going to be nice and go back to his place to fuck, even though he stays with his mom when he's in town, and it would mean we'd have to be quiet. But if you want to act like a spoiled brat, then you can put up with me bringing my big gay date back here and having as much loud, faggy sex as I want all over *my* apartment. If you don't want to hear it, I suggest you find somewhere else to be. Or you can stay here and fuck yourself. Be my guest. But I'm not dealing with your shit until you check your fucking attitude, Tadhg. Fuck you."

I don't let myself look at him while I grab my shit, including a change of clothes and my phone charger. I can change at Scott's house; he's seen me look worse. It was barely even going to be a date until Tadhg decided to start World War III over it like a brat.

I slam the door behind me without caring about my neighbors.

It hurts. My chest feels knotted, and my stomach is churning, and every inch of me feels hot.

Maybe I shouldn't have left him like that. He's fragile right now, even if he's acting like a dick. But everything he was saying brought back too many fucked-up memories and I need a little space to process it.

In the wake of everything that's happened, I've only been dealing with the soft, broken side of Tadhg. I'd let myself forget about the angry version of him, but apparently it's back.

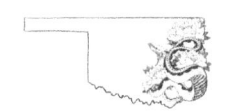

An hour later, the adrenaline has left my system. I'm tired in the wake of it, but I have a cocktail in front of me and Scott is smiling warmly at me across the small high-top table.

Of course we couldn't go to The Feral Possum, because who knows if he's there now. Instead, we're in some bougie wine bar in Mission Flats that is a little too pretentious for my taste, but at least I know there's no chance I'll run into anyone with a snake tattoo on their neck for the next couple of hours.

"Are you okay, Micah? Have you been working too much?"

He raises a dark eyebrow at me while he gives me an evaluating look. Scott is a sweetheart, and I do miss him when he's not around, even if I have no interest in anything more than a friends-with-benefits situation.

Not to mention, he's 6'1" and has that thick, ex-athlete body type that I'm hopelessly thirsty for. Ortho nurses, man. I can't help myself. They're all so square-jawed and deliciously brawny, who wouldn't want to put them on their knees for you?

"I'm fine," I say with a sigh, rubbing a hand over my face. "I just… Did I ever tell you I used to have a stepbrother?"

Scott cocks his head, which I take as a no. I jump in and give him an extremely abridged version of the story, including our childhood trauma and the fight we had in the apartment just now, but leaving out anything to do with Tadhg's criminal affiliations or the fact that he came to me with a fucking gunshot wound.

I give him a vague explanation about Tadhg being on sabbatical from work and needing a place to crash temporarily, which Scott politely accepts without digging deeper. The fact that he was a giant asshole tonight is the real point of my story, anyway.

"Wow," he says when I finish. "That's definitely an extreme reaction. It kind of seems like he was jealous. Is he really protective of you or something? Or possessive?"

The words hit me at a weird angle. I hadn't really looked at it that way. I just assumed Tadhg was channeling his father and using me as a dumping ground for all that irrational rage and vitriol.

"I don't think so. I mean, we literally hadn't seen each other since we were kids. He's just an angry person. Like I said, his dad was such a dick, and who knows what he's had to put up with since I left."

I fall silent for a second, taking a sip of my drink as an old, buried memory floats to the surface.

"You know how I'm dyslexic?"

Scott smirks. "Yes, I remember finding some very creative, practical ways to study anatomy together in school, thank you."

I snort, but brush past the memory. "Well, it got a lot better once my mom was sober and I was in a decent school and had the support, et cetera. But when we were still in Oklahoma with Patrick and Tadhg, it was bad. I hated reading and it made me super anxious, but I loved books. Especially because watching TV or doing anything that made a lot of noise was risky because you never knew what would set Pat off."

Scott gives me a sympathetic look that peeves me, but I ignore it and power through.

"So, Tadhg used to read to me a lot when we were kids. We'd squirrel ourselves away somewhere, even in a closet or something with a flashlight if Patrick was on a rampage, and he'd read to me in a quiet voice. *Narnia*, *Lord of the Rings*, shit like that. I actually don't know where the books came from. Looking back, I think he might have stolen them from school for me."

The thought makes me almost laugh, but the sadness washing over the whole thing makes me swallow it.

"Well, one day Patrick caught us. And it was bad. He was shit-faced and pissed about something else, he stumbled on us reading together under a blanket. Ripped the book out of Tadhg's hand and tore it in half. Started yelling, called us little f-slurs, all that horrible shit."

I keep my voice down so no one overhears me and gets offended, because even second-hand, it's an unpleasant collection of words. I can already feel myself shutting down emotionally, becoming detached the way you have to when you want to recount a story like this.

"Anyway. Just like all the other times Pat was pissed, Tadhg took the heat for me, because you're right, he was protective. He was a little older and a lot bigger, and it was his dad, so I think he felt like he owed it to me or something. So, he says it's all his fault and Patrick ends up dragging him off to do fuck knows what. Awful shit, I'm sure. Like an hour later, Tadhg comes back to our room. He's covered in bruises and looks like he's been crying, but he isn't crying. His face is like… stone. Totally blank. And Patrick stands in the doorway and watches while Tadhg goes through the room, pulling out every book from their hiding places and ripping them all to shreds in front of me."

I can practically see it. It was a million years ago, but now that I'm thinking about it, it feels so fresh. Maybe because the anger that Tadhg held then is so identical to the anger I saw in him today.

"It was awful. I was crying, so he starts yelling at me, saying all the same shit his dad says to him. 'F' this and 'F' that. He was so angry. It was just… rage. We were always close, and having him turn on me like that, even though I understood it was because Patrick was making him do it; that hurt so much more than anything Patrick ever did to me. That night I was so scared I couldn't sleep, and Tadhg crawled into bed with me and apologized a million times. But it was never the same after that."

Shrugging, I look at Scott for the first time since I started telling the story, and he has a weird expression on his face.

"What?"

He frowns but doesn't answer for a long time.

"I'm sorry, Micah. That's a really sad story. I can see why today would be upsetting for you."

A laugh slips out of me, but it sounds forced. "I'm not upset. It's fine, really. I'm just pissed he thinks he can get away with acting like such a jackass after I've been bending over backward to take care of him. He'll apologize once the moment passes, is my point. It'll be fine."

Scott still looks concerned, but I don't want to talk about this anymore. I change the subject and ask him about work.

I'm determined not to think about Tadhg or Patrick or any of the rest of it until I get home. Just like I'm determined to get laid, and fuck Tadhg and whatever he thinks. He can have a front row seat for all I care. Maybe he'll learn a few things.

I refuse to spend any more time feeling shitty about myself, especially not because of him.

Chapter Fourteen

Savage

When Micah leaves, it's like he takes all the air in the room with him. My body gives me a split second to decide between raging out or hyperventilating, and it feels like all I've done recently is have meltdowns, so there's really no choice.

I flip the coffee table immediately. Popcorn scatters everywhere and a glass shatters, making me feel a fraction more stable. But it's not enough.

Pacing up and down the living room, I try to wrestle the anger throbbing in my chest into submission before I do any real damage to Micah's living room.

I just don't understand why he'd be so willful. All I'm doing is trying to protect him, and he throws it in my face? How am I supposed to let him go out doing fuck knows what with some stranger, without knowing if he's going to be safe?

It's intolerable. Just the thought of someone touching Micah—*hurting* him—makes me want to rip my skin off strip by strip. After I've ripped off theirs, obviously.

And the fact that he doesn't understand that and listen to me makes it all worse. I'm here, watching out for him, and he doesn't give a shit. All he cares about is his dick. Telling me I'm like my father was a cheap shot, and he said it to hurt me.

Well, he doesn't know who he's fucking with. Just because he's my Bambi doesn't mean I'm going to let him get away with treating me like shit when I'm the only one looking out for him.

If he thinks he's bringing his date back here to get off, let's see how well he does when I bring a date home first. There's only one bed in this apartment and I'll be fucking someone in it before I let my little brother get bent over just to prove a stupid point to me.

I told the guys I was going to be spending my sabbatical fucking my way through the local girls, after all. It was a lie at the time, but now my dick's working again. As much as it ever was. I can power through one night. Maintain my reputation with the Banna and show Micah what he gets for being a slut.

My head feels jumbled; all my thoughts racing so fast, I can barely pick out each individual one. Distantly, I think a part of myself is screaming that this is a bad idea. But I refuse to listen.

I'm too angry. Rage is quivering through me, and it's not leaving space for any other thoughts or emotions.

Punishing Micah for what he said and what he's about to do is the only solution.

The dumbass left his car here as well, presumably because he plans to get shitfaced on this date and leave himself even more vulnerable to danger. At least it gives me a way out. Grabbing his keys, I head to the parking lot, and the only thing I can think about is getting a girl back here as quickly as possible so I can finally make Micah pay.

IT'S MORE CROWDED THAN I EXPECTED. I DON'T KNOW why I came to The Feral Possum, but it's basically the only place I know around here, and I would still prefer not to run into any of the Banna if I can avoid it. Even if I'm doing something that they'd approve of, for once.

"Sav?" Gunnar looks up at me from behind the bar when I walk in, because the man seems to notice everything immediately.

I went with *Sav* when he asked me my name the first time. I shouldn't spread the name Savage around if I can help it, in case it gets to the wrong ears. Plus, it sounds dumb as fuck to anyone who doesn't know the Banna or isn't already afraid of me.

I could use my real name, and it was on the tip of my tongue, but... Micah's the only one who calls me that.

Sav was a good compromise. It could be short for lots of shit, probably.

"You know you're not working tonight," he continues.

"Yeah, I just came for a drink. If that's cool."

I don't know when I turned into this simpering, uncertain thing, but I hate it. I take a deep breath, stand up tall and roll my shoulders back, and then look at Gunnar with an expression that fits Savage the fucking gangster, not

Tadhg the loser who has temper tantrums about fights with his stepbrother.

Gunnar gives me a slow, steady once-over, just like he did when we met. I get the feeling that he can see the shift in my demeanor and isn't impressed, which makes me feel like even more of a dumbass than I did before.

I already hate this and want to go home.

"Is everything okay?"

I can tell by his tone he knows he's not getting an answer, but it was nice of him to ask anyway. He's a nice guy. This is a nice place, full of normal people. I really don't belong here, but it'll do for what I need to get done.

"Can I get a beer?" I ask instead of responding to his question.

Gunnar just nods, pulling me a draft and leaving it in front of me. He doesn't linger, which is good because I can't handle someone that observant right now. I already feel like all my thoughts and feelings and rationality have jumped the track; I don't need the most stable, reasonable man in Possum Hollow standing next to me as some sort of demonic juxtaposition to really hammer home how fucked I am.

My fingers drum on the bar without me being totally aware of it, and my heart is already hammering in my chest.

Picking up girls should be easy for me. I'm tall. I'm hot. A lot of girls, especially the kind of girls you can pick up in bars, love an alpha male type. But for me, it's always been layered in all this stress about what's gonna happen when I finally get her naked and whether my worthless dick is going to cooperate this time, or if this will be the time word gets back to my father about yet another one of my failings.

It puts me too in my head. I think I'm good at disguising it, but still. Except right now it's even worse, because I can't focus on anything except where Micah might be right now and whether or not he's safe.

Well, half of me is worried about him being safe, the other half is still so fucking furious about how he shoved his attitude in my face that I'll do anything to one up him.

Including getting over my distaste for what's about to happen.

A few minutes later though, a girl with a nice face and a low-cut shirt catches my eye from across the bar, and I swallow down all that distaste to focus on what really matters. Showing Micah who's in charge here.

THE GIRL IS WRITHING AND MOANING UNDERNEATH ME, but I can tell she's not into it. The fact that she's faking it is only making things harder for me.

We're in Bambi's bed. It only took me a couple hours to pick someone up, and either his date is going well or he's in the process of being fucking murdered, because he still isn't back. Maybe he was all talk, and they decided to go back to the other guy's house after all.

The thought distracts me. Which is annoying as hell, because this girl is a find. She's got dark hair, big, pretty eyes that look even bigger with all the eyeliner she's wearing, and a tight little body that fits easily in my hands. I could tell she was into me as soon as we locked eyes back at the bar, and she made it explicitly clear that she was also looking for a no-strings hookup. In theory, I was more than happy to oblige. But now that we're here, everything's falling apart.

She keeps pulling me into kisses, which is distracting

and frankly not why we're here. Kissing has never been something I enjoyed. Putting your mouth on someone else's mouth is just kind of weird. I always feel like it seems like I'm about to eat them.

We finally got down to business, but now I'm on top of her and I'm already crawling into my own head. Maybe I shouldn't have made her come before we started fucking. I thought it would be polite, but instead it's making it harder to keep her interest. I've got one hand working her clit, the other propping me up and I'm pounding into her, but the slightly glazed look in her eye and the hint of fakeness to her noises is making me want to flee the situation, and my dick is getting the message.

It's always ready to bounce at a moment's notice. The second something feels off, it's like all the blood abandons ship. I can feel the telltale start of *nothingness* that normally precedes it giving up on me, and I put all my concentration into keeping myself in the moment.

The tight, wet heat of her around me. How good it feels to touch someone's bare skin. The rhythmic pumping, in and out.

I bury my face in her neck, trying to make the world narrow in so I can focus, but she's wearing a super sweet perfume. It clashes with the lingering scent of Micah's fancy, citrusy aftershave and makes things even worse.

The girl—Chelsea, thank fuck I remember her name—is giving an A+ for effort performance though. She digs her fingernails into my back, scraping them down hard enough to send pain radiating through me and jolt some life back into my sex drive.

"Oh yeah, that's it, right there, fuck me harder, Daddy!" she moans in a cheesy porno voice.

Oh fuck. I appreciate that she's trying, but not the Daddy shit. I can't handle it.

To distract her, I pull out, quickly manhandling her until she's on her stomach and then thrusting back in. I can tell she's the kind of girl who likes to be thrown around a little, and I don't really give a fuck at this point, but at least she's little enough it's not putting too much of a strain on my injury site.

I ignore the lingering soreness, focusing on the way she arches her back and pushes her ass toward me.

Digging my fingers into her hip, I stare at where my cock is tunneling into her and try to let all the sensations get through to me. I chase away every lingering anxiety in my brain and reach for that teasing trail of arousal that's curling somewhere inside of me. It's a slippery fucker, but I can grab onto it. I know I can. I just have to concentrate.

"Yeah, Daddy, harder!"

Fuck, Chelsea, shut up. I'm trying to concentrate.

The door to the apartment slams open, making me jump so hard I break rhythm for a second. Great. Just what I need: more distractions.

When I came up with this plan—in a moment of short-sighted anger, I'll admit—I was having glorious, epic sex that was going to show him who the real man here was. Not this shitshow of borderline wilting erections and Chelsea running her mouth.

At least I know he's not dead, I guess.

But based on the sounds drifting in from the living room, not only did he not get murdered, his date is going a hell of a lot better than mine is. I can hear the thuds of clothes and shoes being kicked off, and it never occurred to me that he wouldn't even try to use the bedroom. He wasn't even fazed by the mess I left in the living room, apparently.

Mother of fuck, I'm going to have to listen to my little brother get railed against the kitchen counter. This was a terrible fucking plan.

If he starts calling his date 'Daddy', my dick will probably crawl so far into my body it'll never come back out.

"Sav?" Chelsea's voice shocks me out of my thoughts. I realize I've slowed down to the point that I was only kind of moving. She's still bent over in front of me, but now she looks annoyed, instead of the fake horny face she had before. I'm still mostly hard though, which is a fucking miracle, so I'm determined to try for an orgasm. It's the only thing other than Bambi's drugs that might get me to sleep tonight.

I'm not giving up.

Outside my bedroom, I can hear furniture being pushed aside, things being knocked over and some breathy groans. I can hear fucking everything through these thin walls, but they're obviously too caught up in each other to hear us.

A curl of panic starts in my chest. I hate this, and I have no idea why. I just want it all to stop and things to go back to normal. But I'm too far in to back out now.

I'm Savage fucking Moynihan. I can't pussy out of this situation, or I'll never be able to look myself in the face again.

"Yeah, take it," I growl at her, cringing a little at my own cheesiness. But when I grab a hank of her hair and tug, she moans like she means it. I'll never get why some girls like getting roughed up like that. It must hurt, right? But whatever works for you.

I start fucking her again in earnest, trying to block out the sounds from my stepbrother and his date.

But when I hear Micah's voice, it's not saying any of the things that I was expecting from him.

"That's it, bitch. Get on your knees for me. Open that pretty mouth like a good little slut."

Bambi?

I swear my brain goes offline. I was emotionally preparing myself to try and listen to some guy grunting away on top of him like I'm doing to the very patient Chelsea right now, not... whatever the fuck that was.

I can feel the heat under my skin, crawling down my neck and over my chest. My gut twists a little, maybe with embarrassment at my assumption. I try to ignore it and focus on the task at hand.

Chelsea. Her wet pussy, clenching around me. My stiff cock.

"That's it, bitch. Keep that wet mouth open for me. Stay still while I fuck your pretty face," Micah says, his voice sounding like it's completely surrounding me, even from the other room.

Chelsea's pussy is making wet sounds as I thrust into her, but I can barely hear them over the sudden sounds of choking and gagging coming from outside. Micah is keeping up his litany of dirty talk, with a surprising level of control to his voice, all while the guy sucking his dick sounds like he's getting it rammed halfway down his throat.

Finally, I feel the first hint of an orgasm building low in my belly. My balls rise up and my cock is throbbing, and I refuse to let this opportunity pass, so I fuck her as hard as I can, still pulling on her hair. Chelsea wails in either fake or real pleasure, but I ignore it.

"That's it. Are you going to beg for me to come on your face, like a good slut?" Micah asks.

God, I can feel it getting close. I'm almost there. I can't lose it now, not after all this time. Ignore them all.

"Please, Sir," the dude says in a voice like gravel,

sounding like he's crying as he talks. "Please come on my face. Please," he sobs one final time, making it clear he's totally released any sense of dignity in exchange for… whatever it is my little brother is doing for him.

"Good slut," Micah says. I can finally hear him lose the edge of control to his voice, and then there's a gasp as I'm assuming he comes all over the man with the surprisingly deep voice who must be kneeling in front of him. Probably with his mouth hanging open, too. If he acts like the desperate slut Micah's treating him as.

"Fuck!" I choke on the word as my own orgasm catches me by surprise. It's been so long to get here that it hits me like a freight train when it finally arrives. My cock flexes as I empty myself into the condom, buried balls deep in her. I hold Chelsea down because it's coming in waves. Every muscle in my body is tense and there are more choked sounds coming out of my mouth as I ride it out.

My orgasm must last longer than Micah's, because they're quiet outside by the time I finally collapse on top of Chelsea in a sweaty, breathless heap.

As soon as I do, I feel like it's too much, and I need her to be as far away from me as possible. Anyone touching me right now feels like too much.

"Sorry about my brother," I grunt, hoping she doesn't make a scene.

"Yeah." Chelsea shrugs as she lets my dick slip out of her. I wince, oversensitive as fuck, but she's been really patient tonight so I can't exactly expect more out of her. "That was definitely something."

She doesn't look pissed though, only tired. There's a little awkwardness, but it's not terrible and I'm mostly too blissed out on oxytocin to care. She grabs her stuff and gets dressed, barely blinking before she slips out of the room to show herself out.

Normally chicks say something like, "*We should do this again sometime,*" but she doesn't. I don't blame her.

I wouldn't want to fuck me again either.

I hope she interrupts Micah and his cum-dumpster's afterglow on the way out. My orgasm high lasted about four seconds, and I'm already back to rage. It pumps through me, my pulse still racing from the activity and every injury on my body screaming at me that that was a mistake.

The familiar feeling of self-loathing washes over me. I have the urge to go out there and drag Micah's date out by his hair so this day can finally be over, but part of me knows that would ultimately make things worse.

Instead, I'm left hovering by the door. I get rid of the condom, but beyond that, I have no idea what the next step in my grand fucking plan for revenge is supposed to be.

Chapter Fifteen

Micah

I'm leaning against the kitchen counter, trying to catch my breath and watching Scott wipe the cum off his face when a random, half-dressed girl emerges from my bedroom and makes a beeline for the door.

"Um, hello?" I say, because I'm an idiot.

She freezes and looks at us both. There's an edge of horror in her expression, and there's no way she didn't hear everything that just went down in here. I'm not ashamed, per se, because that was some phenomenally hot sex. But I would like to know who the fuck she is and why she's in my house.

"Sorry."

She mumbles the word and rushes past us, discomfort rolling off her in waves as she practically flings the door open and bounds through it. She doesn't even stop to put her shoes on, she just grabs them.

Now that's a bad end to a date. Which is what I'm assuming she is. Because my brother is a piece of shit.

"That little fucking brat," I mutter under my breath, mostly to myself. Scott is busy trying to cover his junk with his hands and also not to combust with self-consciousness, if the color of his face is anything to go by. "Tadhg!"

I don't get a response, but I'm not sure I was expecting one. Scott looks completely bewildered as I grab my briefs and tug them on, not bothering with anything else before storming toward the bedroom. He can get dressed or not as he pleases, I really don't care.

"Tadhg Jonah Moynihan, you show your fucking face!"

I'm about to wrench open the door when he does it for me, almost making me fall through the opening. And there he stands—my stepbrother, ladies and gentlemen—bare-ass naked, covered in tattoos from head to toe, and wearing a smug, self-satisfied smirk that I absolutely see right through.

I've seen him naked or mostly naked many times since he's been here because of how injured he's been, but it's so different in this context. The smell of sex is lingering in the air, and I swear he's still half-hard from whatever he just did with that girl. I don't appreciate the scene he's trying to make, or the amount of discomfort that grips me because of it.

"Sorry, I was napping," he says. "Can I help you with something, Bambi?"

The teasing tone to his voice is so artificial and undercut with cruelty. I know he's trying to make a point here, and I know it's not a kind one. I just don't know what it is that he's getting at.

"Don't 'Bambi' me, and put your penis away, asshole.

Why are there random women running out of my apartment half-dressed?"

Tadhg makes a nonchalant face. "I don't know, *Micah*, why are you face-fucking dudes in the kitchen when you know I'm home? To prove a point? Some kind of big gay point?"

"The point is that it's *my* apartment. It's my life, my fuck-buddy, my dick, and you have no right to tell me what to do with any of it!"

The temptation to shove him is overwhelming, even though I'm not normally a violent person. But I know it would be like shoving a brick wall.

Instead, he begins to crowd me. The few inches of height he has on me, along with the mountain of muscle, suddenly seem much more apparent as he looms over me. The whole time he's been here, he's mostly been lying down and broken. But right now, this is him drawn up to his most intimidating self.

And it's working, despite the fact that he's still naked and smells like cum and drug-store perfume.

One of his hands comes to rest on my chest, and he walks me backward until I hit the hallway wall. With his face barely an inch from mine and an intensity simmering between us that I wasn't expecting, he finally speaks.

"I'm trying to keep you safe. And instead of letting me, you're shoving your fucked-up sex life in my face."

The skin of his chest and neck is flushed with anger now. We're right back to where we started; his obsession with keeping me safe. But there's nothing to keep me safe from here. I don't understand what wire is crossed in his brain, but whatever it is, he seems to be latching onto it with his whole heart.

Despite the digs he's making, this doesn't feel like homophobia so much as Tadhg just being... off. And as pissed as I am at him for acting like a petulant teenager, my adult-brain is still capable of seeing that this isn't rational behavior.

Fuck, he isn't really doing better, is he?

I bring my hand to rest on his, still over my racing heart, and hold it softly. I search his eyes for a hint of what's going on in his head, but I come up empty. There's just a storm of emotion there, but nothing I can piece together.

"What do you need to keep me safe from, Tadhg?" I ask softly.

He blinks, his face twitching like the question threw him off. But before he can answer, a voice interrupts us from a few feet away.

"Are you alright, Micah?"

I glance to my right, and see that Scott is now fully dressed and looking at me and Tadhg with the wary incredulity we deserve.

Tadhg, of course, tenses at the interruption. He turns to face Scott, eyeing him up and down and instinctively putting my body a little behind his. It's clear that he doesn't like whatever he sees, because he practically bristles with hostility toward Scott. He brings one hand to loosely cover his naked, now-flaccid dick, but still puffs out his chest and stands tall, like Scott needs to go through him to get to me.

"He's fine. You can go. Your services have been fulfilled, clearly."

Scott's eyes nearly pop out of his head, and I don't blame him. I slap Tadhg on the arm and shove him out of my way.

"Jesus, Tadhg, don't be fucking rude. Scott's my friend. You're the one making a scene. For the love of god, will you go put some pants on."

Scott is still staring between us, bug-eyed, but Tadhg

only stiffens, standing there like he's some kind of fucking sentry.

Looking up at his stony face, I try very hard not to raise my voice but fail a little.

"Pants! Now!"

With a slow exhale, he finally turns and disappears back into the room, but not without casting one more unnecessarily aggressive glare at Scott.

Scott, bless him, who looks at me and mouths *what the fuck?* in silence. I know his family is pretty normal; this is probably a lot for him.

"Sorry, he's having a bad week." Understatement, but it's not like I can give him details. Scott points at his own abdomen where Tadhg's gunshot wound is, because he just saw the whole thing and it's pretty obvious what it is to anyone who's seen one before. His eyebrows are raised, but I just shake my head. I need him to take the hint and not ask more questions about this.

"Look, I need to deal with him, can I call you later?"

He looks between me and the wall that Tadhg is standing behind one more time.

"Dude, are you sure you're going to be okay alone?"

I huff. We're going around in circles, and I also really fucking hate being treated like I can't take care of myself. "I told you, it's fine. He's my brother. Stepbrother. Whatever, the point is, I've got it. I will text you later."

Scott holds my gaze for a few more beats, but then he finally breaks it. He moves toward me to say goodbye, but of course that's when Tadhg reappears from the bedroom. He's in low-slung jeans that make him look even more ripped than he did naked, and of course no shirt, and he immediately places himself between me and Scott with a growl.

A literal growl. I'm surprised he doesn't snap his teeth at the man.

This is exhausting.

I mime texting and mouth *later*, before waving Scott away without saying anything. Reluctantly, he turns, but it's clear he thinks there's a good chance Tadhg is going to murder me in my sleep or something.

People from normal, happy families will never understand.

As soon as the door clicks behind him, I slap Tadhg on the arm again, making him turn to face me.

"Why are you acting fucking feral?"

"Why are you acting like a little bitch?" he hisses back.

Lord, give me patience.

I reach deep into the wellspring of tolerance that I normally save for patients who are acting out because they're detoxing or in incredible amounts of pain, and don't let this escalate into a childish pissing match.

"Just come fucking sit down with me, okay?"

He sulks, still like a teenager, but follows along with heavy movements as I grab him by the arm and drag him to the couch. On the way, I snag my sweater from where I tossed it on the living room floor when I came in—still ignoring that it's a disaster from Tadhg obviously having a hissy fit at some point, because he's such an adult—and pull it over my head, because it's getting cold in nothing but my underwear. I sit at one end, practically throwing him on the other, where he falls like a sack of potatoes. His face looks drawn, but there's a nervousness to him underneath all the over-the-top give-a-fuck attitude.

I pull my legs up and tuck them into my body, wrapping my arms around myself and sinking into the warmth of the oversized knit sweater.

"I need you to talk to me, Tadhg. What's going on with you? You're acting irrational and erratic; you seem really upset and I can't totally figure out what you're upset about… Can you just explain it to me? I know you're a man and men aren't supposed to use their words or whatever, but it's just you and me here, and no one else has to know if you emote. Just spill. What's going on?"

The silence that follows is fucking painful. I'm chatty by nature, and not filling it is almost impossible. But I know I have to let him come to me.

He fidgets, running his fingers over the fabric of his jeans and worrying at his bottom lip in a way that makes him look so much younger than the tattoos and the muscles and the attitude normally do.

Because he is young, really. We both are. But he was never allowed to be, so he never got to learn how to grow up the way I did. That's the difference.

"I don't know what you want me to say, Bambi. I'm fine. I was just mad that you weren't listening to me," he grumbles without looking at me.

I'm impressed. There are some feeling words in there somewhere.

"But *why* were you so worried about me in the first place? All I wanted was to go to dinner with my friend. And you were acting like it was super dangerous. What was going on in your head?"

He looks at me then, his brow furrowed, before going back to studying his hands.

"I-I don't know. It was just wrong. It wasn't safe. It wasn't right. My gut was telling me. And you weren't listening."

I'm trying to pick apart what he just said, and something about it makes me cock my head.

"Wait, did you feel like it wasn't *safe* for me to go, or that it was *wrong* for me to go? Because those are two different things."

"I—" He looks at me sharply, and then away. I can see a cavalcade of emotions working their way across his face, and tension quickly sets up shop in his neck and shoulders.

Despite his sudden shift in mood, there's no warning before he stands. I think he's about to pace angrily in front of the couch for a minute, so I stay put, but instead, he walks straight to the nearest wall and punches it.

He hits the wall three times with short, sharp jabs, each one hard enough to fill the space with sound and make me jump. Adrenaline is already flooding my bloodstream while my brain is struggling to catch up to what the fuck just happened. But before I can open my mouth to say something, Tadhg follows his initial punches by smacking his fucking forehead against the wall with a dull thud, hard enough that it's definitely going to have done some damage.

"Jesus, fuck," I mutter, springing off the couch on instinct and reaching up to grab his face before he can do it again.

I get one hand on his forehead, and it stops him hitting the wall again. As soon as my hands are on him, he seems to go limp. Utterly limp, like a ragdoll. His body is heavy, and his movements are sluggish as he lets me manhandle him back to sit on the couch.

The whole thing couldn't have lasted more than ninety seconds, but it's taken all the energy out of both of us. Tadhg is staring off into the distance as he sits slumped in his seat, and I'm frantically trying to make sense of what just happened.

I've never enjoyed the whole men-punching-walls thing. As a teenager, I saw it a lot, and it normally seemed like guys either acting out because they were wasted, didn't have a good handle on their anger, or were trying to impress girls with their "manliness". Mostly the latter.

Every single time, they just looked stupid.

But this didn't come across as an act of aggression so much as an act of desperation, or self-harm, and it has me just as worried as all of the other self-destructive things Tadhg's thrown himself into since he got here.

When he doesn't look at me or make any attempt to speak, I decide to get closer. I need him to snap out of this sudden malaise because it's freaking me out even more than the anger.

I crawl into his lap, folding myself up small as if I'm still a little kid and inserting myself into the warm space in front of his chest. He still doesn't move, so I drag his heavy arms until they're wrapped around me, and then put my face close to his neck. I can feel his pulse racing under his skin, and it's reassuring that it's still there, I guess.

"That wasn't an answer, Tadhg," I say, once we've both had a chance to settle.

He almost laughs. I swear. I can feel it. But it's like he's too numb.

"I don't feel right, Bambi. My head's fucked up."

The words are quiet, and they pull out of him like molasses.

"Do you normally feel like this, or is it just since you got shot?"

He tenses under me, and the silence that I get in response makes me feel like he's hiding something from me. But we are so far past fucking around time. He lost his right to privacy several fucking incidents ago. He's still shirtless, so it's not difficult for me to reach out and pinch his nipple

—really fucking hard—to try to shock a little sense into him.

"I swear to god, if you lie to me right now, things are about to get so ugly, Tadhg. This is your last chance to tell me what the fuck is going on with you before I lose my shit."

He takes a deep breath, and my whole body rises and falls from where I'm resting on his broad chest. Eventually, after a few false starts, he speaks.

"Things used to be… bad. But then I went on meds and that helped. But I didn't have the meds with me when they brought me here and I couldn't tell them, because Father would fucking kill me if he knew I was seeing a shrink. Ever since I ran out, it's been like it was before the meds, but worse. Just up and down, with my thoughts all fucking jumbled and everything twisted up."

He lets out a shaky exhale when he's finished, and my mind works overtime to process all that information.

Stupid, stupid man.

Depending on what meds he was on, ending them cold like that could have killed him. It basically almost did.

I focus very hard on keeping the anger and resentment out of my voice, because I'm really angry at the fucking universe for doing this to him, not him. Although I'm maybe a little angry at him… I can't stop the way my fingers dig into his skin wherever I can cling to him.

"Why didn't you tell me? I could have helped you. Stopping psych meds all of a sudden is dangerous. No wonder it seemed like you were going through some kind of withdrawal."

I feel him shrug, and turn his face even further away from mine, even though I'm still buried in his neck instead of forcing him to look me in the eye.

"You know I can't talk about that stuff," he mumbles.

"Don't give me that shit. This is me, not your shitty dad. You can talk to *me* about this stuff. No one else, but me. I could have helped."

An unexpected wave of emotion hits me while I'm speaking, and my voice actually cracks on the word 'helped'. I feel Tadhg stiffen underneath me again, before he puts the actual effort into wrapping his arms around me instead of letting them lie on top of me like two pieces of driftwood.

He hugs me into his chest, and we both sit in silence for a few minutes. I sniff, because my throat feels tight and there's a swirl of guilt and anger and a bunch of other emotions I don't really want to feel fighting for attention inside me.

"Okay," I say at last. "New deal. I won't go out with Scott again. Or anyone else, while you're still getting straightened out. I'll be here as much as I can, and we're going to figure out the best way to get you feeling better. Whether that is—getting meds off books or what."

He sighs. "You don't have to do that. I'm sorry I was pissy before. You shouldn't have to put your life on hold because of my shit. I'm fine. I felt like I was sick for a while, but that's all over. I'm over the withdrawal or whatever it was. I'm back to normal now, I guess. I think I'd just forgotten how it felt before I was on them."

I don't even hesitate before reaching out and pinching his nipple again, even harder than the last time. This time he actually yelps in pain, leaning back and looking me in the eye for the first time since this excruciating conversation started.

"Will you stop that?"

"Not until you stop being ridiculous. You are not fine. It's been what, a week? Two? People normally take months to taper off psych meds a little bit at a time, because you are trying to literally change the way your brain chemistry functions. And you just fucked around in there, slapped yourself on the hood and said 'good enough' before driving off. Absolutely not. Your brain is physiologically a disaster zone, and this will take time to fix. No wonder you're all over the place."

I hold his gaze with mine, trying to make him physically feel how serious I am about this. I don't even know why I'm so serious about this, but it feels more important than anything else I've ever done in my life.

"I am going to help you, and you are going to let me. End of discussion."

Tadhg blinks at me a few times and then his body softens under mine. "Alright, Bambi. Whatever you say."

Chapter Sixteen

Micah

I'm still not a hundred percent clear what's going on in my brother's head right now, but it's obviously a mess. I think our fight last night was a come-to-Jesus moment for him, though.

After we talked it out—more or less—he limited himself to slumped posture and short, muttered answers. But it was more like he was wrung out than being obstinate. He'd gotten a little drunk while he was out trawling for someone to bring home and shove in my face, and once I realized, I spent some time feeding and watering him before he eventually collapsed into bed like a wet rag.

I also made a mental note to scold him about drinking and driving later, but it was obvious it wouldn't have sunk in at that moment.

Since then, he's mostly slept. All night and a decent

portion of the day, only waking up to take a shower, eat some more food that I shoved in front of him and then crawling back into bed.

He's just exhausted. Between the physical toll of his injuries and the broken brain chemistry that his body is trying to fix, it makes sense. That doesn't mean it isn't hard to watch, though.

I'd stayed up last night, trying to keep my sleep schedule something close to organized, and then slept during the day. Tadhg hadn't even twitched when I slipped into bed next to him. He'd continued to snooze away, and I had laid there for too long watching the steady rise and fall of his chest, and the soft expression he wears in sleep when he's not having nightmares.

I feel like I should be more put out by the amount of space he's taking up in my life. Even if I'm happy to do it, it should feel like an imposition to give up more than half my bed to his oversized body, and spend all my time worrying about his mood swings. It doesn't, though, which is almost more worrying.

I like having him close, where I can reach out and touch him. It's like I constantly need to confirm that he's still there and in one piece. Getting him back has unlocked all the weird anxieties I used to have about him when we lived together. The ones I'd shoved deep, deep down when me and Mom ran away, and assumed I'd never have to examine again.

Instead, they're all shoved right in my face now. Front and center. All my constant gnawing concerns about his well-being, combined with my concerns over just *how* concerned I am. Because if there's one thing I've always been with Tadhg, it's over-attached.

I can't help it. As soon as my mom walked me into that

house, I was afraid. I could sense what kind of man Patrick was before I was even old enough to really understand what I was frightened of.

But with just as much conviction, I knew that Tadhg would protect me. And he took one look at me and seemed to know the same thing. It was set in stone, right from the start, and as kids, neither of us ever questioned it.

It feels like now it's my turn to protect him, and I'm terrified I'm going to miss something and fuck it up.

He deserves better.

I'm getting ready for my shift tonight when Tadhg finally emerges from his third sleep of the day. He looks a little like a zombie. There's a deep pillow crease running down his left cheek, his tawny hair is sticking up in every direction and curlier than he usually lets it get—I will never understand why some straight guys have a thing against having curly hair, as if it's innate effeminate or something instead of hot as fucking hell—and he's got an eye crusty that I'm dying to reach out and clean for him.

He's a mess. But he's my mess.

"Sleeping Beauty finally rises, I see," I say, before filling the apartment with the sound of my NutriBullet as I make a smoothie for the road.

Thank fuck, Tadhg wipes that crust away before it drives me insane. He's rubbing his eye with his fist in a gesture that's endearingly juvenile but looks so out of place with the rest of him.

I swear, he's mostly naked in this apartment more than he's clothed. Right now is no exception, because he's stumbled out of bed in nothing but a pair of black boxer briefs that I accidentally bought a size too small, and his canned-ham thighs are straining to bust out of them.

I'll never totally get used to it. I mean, I've seen a lot of hot guys naked. My tastes specifically mean that I've seen a lot of hot, masc, muscular men on their knees for me, begging for my cock.

Something about Tadhg is different. He's masculine, sure. But between the muscles, the tattoos and the sheer size of him, there's a certain lethality to his body that always seems to hammer home for me just what he's been doing with it since we last knew each other.

The men I fuck build their muscles in the gym, and then I like to make them cry and have messy orgasms. Tadhg spends his time building muscle by lifting dead bodies or kilos of cocaine or god knows what else. Honestly, a good weeping orgasm on his knees would probably do the man wonders, but that's not my place and it's certainly not something he's ready to emotionally cope with.

"You going to work, Bambi?" he asks when the blender finally stops whirring.

"Yep." Okay, I've been thinking about asking him this all day, and I think I just need to do it. Rip off the Band-Aid, and if he has a hissy fit about it, so be it. "And I was thinking that you could come with me?"

Tadhg doesn't say anything, but he does freeze, standing in the middle of the living room, his hand unmoving where he was just scratching his stomach a moment before.

"What for?"

I start to move toward him, but when he instinctively flinches away, I think better of it and stay in the kitchen.

"Maybe we could get some bloodwork done and check if your electrolytes are fucked up from your detox. Maybe we could get your prescription transferred to a pharmacy here and get a refill. I know you couldn't go for the gunshot because of the paper trail, but this is different. No one's going to care about some random guy coming into the

ER for a medication detox issue. No one's checking RX fills."

I can tell before he even speaks that it's going to be a hard *'no'*. His face immediately turns to stone, and it's like my sweet brother has been swallowed whole by the mafia monster that his father created in his place.

"Are you insane?" he spits. "Do you have any idea how dangerous that is? I might as well walk up to the Aryan Brotherhood—wait, I might as well walk *you* up to the Aryan Brotherhood with a bag over both our heads and beg them to kill us. Fuck no. My name is not going on any fucking paperwork, and my face is not going anywhere like that where someone might recognize it. All it takes is one nurse, one pharmacy tech, one person in the waiting room who has a connection and overhears the wrong thing and then they know where I am. Not to mention the shitstorm that would follow if my father heard."

He's bristling, standing tall as he leans into this growly, aggressive side of his personality that I hate so much.

I'm not going to push it. He sounds beyond paranoid, but I know that fighting him on it isn't the answer. I'll think of something. Maybe I can get the meds prescribed to myself through one of those online services or something.

It should probably be a cause for concern that I don't even hesitate before planning to commit what is technically medical fraud, but I don't care. The second he pointed a gun at his own head, my ethics went out the window. I could give a fuck, to be honest. It's actually a little scary how few fucks I give about right or wrong at this point.

Before I get the chance to backtrack though, Tadhg spins on his heel and heads toward the bathroom, muttering something about going to work.

He's barely started this new job at the Feral Possum, but

so far it seems good for him. He comes home when I'm still at work, so I don't get to see the immediate aftermath, but the next day, he always seems more calm than usual. It's Friday night, so they're bound to be just as busy as the ER will be tonight.

Hopefully, it'll distract him from whatever anger I just stirred up in him like a hornet's nest. At least Gunnar will be there to attempt to keep him out of trouble. I don't know the owner well, but every interaction I've had with him has been very chill, and he seems uniquely suited to keeping mouthy assholes in line.

I take a deep breath in and out, the condensation under my fingers making me aware that I'm still clutching my smoothie.

It'll be fine. He'll go to work, I'll go to work, we'll both be run off our feet, and we can revisit this topic tomorrow in the light of day.

And this weird pang of *something* that I get because I have to leave him? The feeling that's creeping into my awareness more and more with each passing day, but I can't possibly name or begin to understand? Yeah, that's a stone that's going to remain unturned.

Savage

Considering we're off a rural highway in the middle of nowhere, this place is packed.

I'm grateful for it. I need the noise and bustle to distract me. It couldn't have come at a better time. I need to turn my brain off and do nothing more mentally or emotionally challenging than running a commercial dishwasher for a few hours.

This is heaven.

"Sav, we need more garnish!" Gunnar calls from somewhere in the middle of the bar. The bar itself is a square in the middle of an open space, with one opening that allows staff in and out. Most days, the building seems huge, and patrons can linger in various corners. But right now, there are enough people—and enough rowdy people—that it's an overwhelming cacophony of noise and pheromones.

The floor is sticky. Every time I lift up the bar runner to try to wipe it down, it smells like stale lime juice, no matter how often I clean it. The whole place is thick with *humanity*.

As long as everyone has a drink in their hand and no one's causing trouble, I guess it doesn't really matter.

I dip into the little kitchen in the back, finding the fridge completely bare. I guess I underestimated how much to prep when I got here. Grabbing a sharp, curved knife from the block, I pull out a tub of mixed citrus and start slicing it as quickly as I can without making too much of a mess or sacrificing a finger.

I've never really cooked before, but I'm no stranger to fileting things. Gunnar told me I learned quickly when he first taught me how to do this prep, while giving me one of those sidelong glances of his that tells me he probably knows what I've done with knives other than cut up fruit, but we both know we're never going to talk about it.

It's peaceful, despite the noise. My blade hits the board over and over, and the limes and oranges fall into easy, matching slices. Something about the task gives me this sense of completion that I've never really had before, but it soothes me deep down in some part of me that's been ignored for too long.

I start the task. I finish the task. I have a little tub of fucking lime slices to show for it. And nobody got hurt in the process.

Fucking glorious.

People don't appreciate the purity of these things, I swear.

As soon as I'm done, I dip back out to the floor and into the bar, reloading the little black containers at each bartender's station. Gunnar nods at me, while the other one —Kasia, a woman in her late twenties or thirties who dresses like the nineties never ended—gives me the friendliest smile I've gotten out of her since I started.

I feel good. I feel normal. These normal people seem to accept me, at least, so that's a start.

I'm ducking out to go grab more longnecks for the fridges when I see something that makes my feet forget how to work, though.

Eamon.

What the fuck is he doing in a queer-ish bar? And not just here, but there's a kid next to him in their corner booth, and there's a lot less fucking space between them than I'd think anyone that worked for my father would allow.

His eyes flick up and he notices me. And instead of looking like he's been caught in the act, that fucker smiles. An unctuous smile that makes me shiver with disgust. Eamon reaches out to wrap one arm around his companion, who looks like he's barely old enough to drink, and then leans in and ostentatiously nibbles on the kid's ear while maintaining eye contact with me.

Who the fuck does he think he is? My father is going to eviscerate him.

It's a weird clash to have the Banna in here. I rub at the sudden tightness over my chest, realizing how much I'd been fooling myself into thinking I could keep playing pretend like this.

Even the kid has a Banna tattoo on his neck, I notice, when he tilts his head to give Eamon better access. His eyes are heavy-lidded, like he's been drinking for a while, although I'm sure I would have noticed if they'd been here for long.

I'm not sure entirely why, but my feet move before I can think it through. I devour the distance between us and plant both hands on the table, leaning over them in a movement that would set most men to quaking in their boots.

The kid looks wide-eyed and scared, but he's also so fucked up the fear is sluggish in coming to the surface. He shrinks away from me, but also doesn't get any closer to Eamon, the way you would expect.

Eamon, of course, just stares at me with the same self-satisfied smirk he always wears.

The prick.

I hate that he's here. It feels like tiny fissures are already forming in the world around me, and red-raw hands are reaching through them to snatch me back to a reality I'd successfully been hiding from. I knew I couldn't hide forever, but I thought I had at least a little more time. Instead, here he is, with his smug face to remind me that this is all temporary.

I don't belong here any more than he does, and eventually Father will drag us both home.

"What the fuck are you doing here? Are you following me?"

Eamon lets out a dry chuckle that chafes every inch of me and takes a dainty sip of his beer before he replies.

"Self-involved much? I know you think the world revolves around you, *Your Highness*, but some of us actually have a life outside of work. We like it here, don't we, Tobias?"

Tobias nods almost imperceptibly, his eyes never leaving my face and every muscle in his body poised to flee, despite how intoxicated he is.

"Does my father know you're here? Either of you? Wearing this on your neck"—I tap my own tattoo—"while fucking... snuggling?"

I keep expecting Eamon to falter and realize how much shit he's in, but nothing's getting through that impenetrable shell. Instead, his smirk turns into a full-on grin. He even leans over the table to get closer to me, and somehow, despite the fact that I'm looming over him, it's as if he's the one who has the upper hand all of a sudden.

"Your father," he starts to speak, but even as he does so, I can see his hand sliding up Tobias' back to rest possessively on the back of his neck. I can also see the way the kid is trying very hard not to flinch at the movement, which hits my own memories in a painful way I'd rather not acknowledge right now. I stuff all that down in my brain and focus on keeping myself as menacing as possible. "He respects me, because I'm a real man. And real men take what they want. Tobias here is a good little worker for us. He's excellent at crawling into small spaces undetected, which comes in handy in our line of work. He does his job."

Eamon's hand shifts from the boy's neck up to his dark, messy hair. It's long enough for him to grab a fistful, and he does it suddenly enough that it makes Tobias gasp as Eamon yanks his head back and bares his throat to both of us. I can see the muscles work as he swallows, and it's clear how hard he's working to keep himself still, letting himself be jerked around.

"It's also his job to keep his superiors happy. I saw something I wanted, and I took it." Eamon tightens his punishing grip. "Now it's mine. Padraig understands that. It's not about fucking rainbows or any of that bullshit," he continues, waving his free hand at our surroundings. "It's about ownership."

My eyes narrow. I can't believe that my father would buy this bullshit. I mean, I don't buy *his* homophobic bullshit, because honestly who cares who people fuck, but he's stuck to his guns on it as long as I've been alive. The thought that I might have been wrong about that… that I might have misinterpreted what he meant or who he fucking hates and why… it makes numbness spread through my limbs so quickly they threaten to drag me to the ground.

I guess it doesn't really matter if he hates fags or not. He's always hated *me*, and I never did shit. Right?

Eamon's voice continuing to drone on knocks me out of my painful reverie.

"Maybe one day I'll own your baby brother, too. He looks like he'd put up a fight. I like that."

I don't think. I'm across the table, glasses knocked onto the floor and my hands around Eamon's neck before I know what's happened.

Tobias immediately skitters away, and noise erupts around us as people notice what's going down. My fingers are tightening, feeling the seductive give of Eamon's flesh beneath my grip. But he's still grinning at me. So wide, I think he'd be laughing at me if he had enough breath.

He's not even fighting back, which makes it even more frustrating. Blackness is tinting the edges of my vision like I'm the one who's getting choked, and he's basically laughing at me.

After a few more seconds, the sounds of my name being

shouted from across the room finally break through my dim awareness. Then there are hands on me, pulling me off him.

It's Gunnar. He gets in my face, tossing me off Eamon with more strength than I would have suspected and then walking me toward the back with both hands planted on my chest. I'm still roiling with anger, but I let him. I feel too ragged to focus on anything right now, even killing that piece of shit.

It feels like I blink and then I'm back in the little kitchen. My spine is pressed into the cold metal door of the walk-in, and Gunnar's hands are still on my chest, pinning me there. I was expecting him to yell at me, but he's not.

He's talking. Repeating the same things over and over again, while my brain struggles to catch up.

"Take a deep breath. In through your nose, out through your mouth. Think. Breathe."

Over and over and over.

I must not have been breathing right, because when I do connect his words to my brain and then down to my chest, it aches to fill my lungs with oxygen.

But I do it. And then again. All while he holds me steady. His presence is much more calming than I would have expected anyone to manage in this situation, but something about his sharp gaze on me makes me feel like I'm rooted to the spot, and I have the chance to catch my breath.

When I finally feel under control, Gunnar seems to sense that and leans back, releasing me from his grasp.

He blows out a breath as well, running his hand through his hair. It's disheveled for the first time since I've met him, and I can see how he's already trying to comb it back into place with his fingers.

"Look, Sav, I hate that piece of shit, too," he says,

making my eyes widen. I wasn't aware that he knew Eamon, but okay. I guess I'm still the new guy here. "But that can't happen here. I can't have bar fights here at all, and especially not ones that might draw the attention of *his* boss."

He emphasizes the word "his" too much. As if we aren't both fully aware that it's my boss, too. Gunnar probably doesn't know that said boss is also my father, but it's enough.

"He'll get what's coming to him eventually. But not here."

Gunnar's repeating himself, but it makes sense that he's not sure how much of what he says is sinking in. After a few more beats, I let out another long breath and scrub a hand over my face, feeling all the lingering tension and anger drip dry out of me and soak into the floor runner.

"I'm sorry." They're the only words I manage to force out of my mouth right now, but they're a start.

Gunnar studies me for a minute, then gives me a sharp nod.

"Stay here."

Of course, I don't. I trail after him, watching from the edge of the employee area as he heads back on the floor. Kasia appears to have gotten most people settled. It's not like this town is a stranger to bar fights, and no one was really hurt.

I'm too far away to hear what gets said, but I see Gunnar get in Eamon's face and speak to him in tightly controlled anger.

They're about the same height, and both of them are towering over poor Tobias, who is pulled into Eamon's side in a death grip. He looks like he wants to be anywhere else, but he's still spaced out enough that I'm beginning to think he's had more than just alcohol tonight.

After a few clipped sentences are exchanged, Eamon shrugs and heads for the door, Tobias trailing behind him. But before he crosses the threshold, he turns and points his fingers at Gunnar like he's holding a pistol and gives him a wicked smirk.

Gunnar just rolls his eyes and reaches out for Tobias. It's a split second, but he grabs the kid and whispers something in his ear. Whatever it is, it's enough to make the boy's eyes go wide before Eamon drags him out the door, and he casts one long look at Gunnar over his shoulder as they disappear into the parking lot.

This whole situation is a shitshow and I'm suddenly exhausted.

When Gunnar walks back in, I'm not even surprised that he tells me to leave. I am surprised that he doesn't fire me, but that's probably coming later when he thinks I'm less homicidal. I'm kept penned in the kitchen by Kasia—who already hasn't taken a shine to me, and spends the whole time watching me with a wary expression that I probably deserve—until everyone's sure that Eamon has cleared the premises, and then I'm dispatched with orders to go straight home and accrue no trouble on my way there.

It's a weird feeling. I'm pretty sure all I've done since I showed up is bring problems for these people, but they still speak to me like I'm a real person. I don't know how to handle it.

I don't know how to handle any of this, really, but what else is new? Figuring out what the fuck is wrong with me seems like a tomorrow problem. Right now, I just want to shower until I forget that Eamon exists and then sleep until Micah comes home.

Chapter Seventeen

Savage

I can't get the images of the fight out of my head. The proprietary way Eamon handled Tobias, even though the boy clearly didn't enjoy it. The way he seemed completely fearless when it came to my father finding out he's fucking another man...

"I saw something I wanted, and I took it. Now it's mine. Padraig respects that."

I've spent my entire life being sure about the things my father hates and the things he needs me to be, and somehow Eamon managed to turn that idea on its head with just a few words. I've invested all this energy into being the kind of man my father wants me to be...

And it was what? All a waste?

I just want to know how every single motherfucker I

meet, including that smug, obsequious little shit, seems to have the kind of commanding, dominant energy that my father respects. Apart from me. What fucking gene did I not get that lets you act like you're in control of every situation?

Even Micah has it. And I know that Father is disgusted by the fact that he's gay, even though he never said as much out loud, but it's not like he ever did anything about it. He's always seemed content to keep Micah at arm's length, both when we were kids and recently, while taking his anger and his vitriol out on me.

I'd always assumed it was out of some kind of deference to Micah's mother, but maybe I was wrong. Maybe Father sees Micah's dominance and it earns him the few flakes of respect he needs to remain unbeaten. While I can do every single fucking thing right on paper, but he still manages to see right through me to my soft, constantly crumbling inner core.

And that's why I disgust him.

Which makes everything I've ever done for him a waste. Because I can control how I talk and act and who I fuck, but I can't dig that fucking weakness out of me, no matter how hard I try.

And I've tried.

I turn up the heat on the water sluicing over my body, hoping it can burn these thoughts out of me, but it doesn't work. Nothing works.

Micah was so different when I overheard him with his little *friend* the other day. It was a shock. I've always known he has this competent, controlled side of him. He's been amazing at taking care of me, obviously, while I've brought him nothing but chaos and misery. But seeing how that translated to his sex life wasn't something I ever wanted, but it was fucking eye-opening.

"Stay still while I fuck your pretty face."

"Good slut."

God, it's nothing I ever would have imagined coming out of his mouth. And once I saw the dude he was saying that shit to, that made it even more wild. That guy was big. He was basically my size. He had showy gym muscles, and I could have severed his esophagus with a spoon if I'd needed to, but still.

He seemed so masculine, but just a few minutes before I saw him, he'd been on his knees, begging my brother for more and crying to the sounds of 'good slut'.

I can't wrap my head around it.

If only I could figure out how to mainline that kind of dominance into myself, I think it would fix all my problems. I'm so jealous that even thinking about it is making me get hard. I pause to lean against the wall of the shower and focus on the sensations.

The water beating down on me, so hot that my skin prickles and tingles everywhere it lands.

The pressure and heat stiffening my cock at the thought of being that kind of dominant person in bed.

What it must be like. Putting someone on their knees. Having them look up at you with total desperation, tears on their face, coming undone for you.

I know all of Micah's expressions pretty well by this point, and I can clearly imagine the salacious, self-satisfied little smirk he probably wears while he pounds into that guy's mouth. While he lets all those filthy words slip out of him, praising him and teasing him and degrading him all in the same sentence.

How he probably makes the man shiver and want to touch himself, but forces him to wait for permission.

The tile is unforgiving where I'm leaning my forehead

against it, but I don't care. I'm too distracted by the feeling of a full, aching erection that I didn't have to fucking fight for. For the first time in months. Maybe longer.

I don't think. I reach down and wrap my hand around my length, stroking myself firmly before my body has the chance to realize what it's doing and call for a retreat. Every thought in my head turns into white noise at the pleasure of it, and then the world is reduced down to this: my tight grip, all that friction building something, and the sound of my panting breaths filling the room.

Panting like a slut.

The thought invades my mind from fuck-knows-where, but I'm too distracted to linger on it. It all feels too good.

Everything assaults me at once. The things that I'll never embody but Micah does: dominance, confidence, control. The way he made a man who could tower over him kneel and love him for it. There isn't even space in my brain for jealousy right now, because the images of it are all too vivid.

Even though I didn't actually see anything, because I was in the other room fucking that girl. And even though I should probably be thinking about her right now, as I fuck my own fist and moan into the emptiness of the bathroom.

But I don't. I want to know what it is about Micah that made that man kneel. I want to know how it felt, and if it was as incredible as it sounded.

I want to know how hard he came.

I want to know if my brother called him a 'good slut' while he spilled his cum all over the kitchen floor.

There's a telling pulse in my gut, and then I feel my cock flex. My orgasm hits me out of nowhere, almost like it did the other day, and before I know it, I'm painting the tile with so much cum I can't believe it was all trapped inside me.

My pulse is racing, and my heartbeat is too loud echoing in my ears. My chest heaves, but the steam is thick in the air and I can't seem to catch my breath.

I don't know what just happened. It wasn't right, I'm sure. Anyone who I told would say it was fucked up. But it didn't feel fucked up.

A sudden wave of hot anguish hits me, and I screw up my face for a second before I swallow it down. I will not cry over this.

It's bad enough that I act like a fucking pussy all the time. I'm not going to compound the humiliation by getting fucking weepy about it.

I consciously reach out and find the numbness that's always waiting at the periphery of my awareness. Grabbing on to it with both hands, I pull it over my body like a blanket and let it settle in.

No thoughts. No feelings. No idea what the fuck that was.

All I need to do is finish my shower and go to sleep. I can figure the rest of it out some other time. Or maybe never. Actually, *never* sounds perfect.

INSTEAD OF BEING WOKEN UP BY THE FEELING OF Micah's weight shifting the mattress, it's a pounding at the door.

My body goes from zero to sixty in an instant. I'm up and thrumming with adrenaline, heading to the door to see who the threat is. I clock that it's still dark out, and I couldn't have been asleep for more than a couple of hours.

Thankfully, Micah has a peephole. Because it is a threat at the door, but of all the threats in my life, it's not the worst. Colm, Lucky, and Eamon, all dressed like they're about to go rob a liquor store.

Which, to be fair, is possible.

I should be more cautious, but sleep is still dragging at my limbs and the small amount of distance I've gotten from my old life has made it seem that much less real, so without any other checks, I open the door and let them in.

They all pile into Bambi's apartment like they belong there, which immediately makes me chafe. But I don't say anything. If they're here as a group, it's because Father sent them. I know Colm can't stand Lucky and wouldn't be hanging out with him for fun, and I'd be fucking stunned to discover anyone in this world voluntarily spends their time with Eamon.

It was crystal clear from our interaction today that even his little boy toy is there against his will. Which sucks. If I were the hero type, maybe I could do something about it.

Unfortunately for Tobias, I'm sure I'm just another villain in his story. It's my birthright, same as the rest of these losers.

"What do you need?" I ask, rubbing sleep from my eye as I close the door behind them as softly as I can. We don't need to cause any more fuss for Micah's neighbors than we already have this past month.

Colm gives me an appraising look. His eyes run up and down my body—mostly exposed because I stumbled out here in just my boxer briefs—and I get the feeling he's looking for physical weaknesses.

"You look good. Better, Sav," he says while clapping me on the shoulder in that warm, masculine way some guys just master without meaning to.

"I don't know about you, Colm, but I'm not here for a lap dance. We've got work to do."

Eamon's voice is like a cheese grater to my fucking nerves. I force myself to look him in the eye, and I can't help but smile a little when I notice the bruises already forming on his throat from when I attacked him earlier.

With a faux-innocent expression, I gesture toward them. "What happened to you?"

If I was hoping to catch him off-guard, that was stupid. The smug shit always has something to say for himself.

"Just some bitch," he tells me, a glint in his eye and a wicked smile playing on his lips. "She didn't like the way I was fucking her. But don't worry, she'll get what's coming to her."

Anger curdles in my stomach, and I have to shove down the urge to strangle him all over again. Colm is looking between us with a wary expression that tells me he's reading between the lines here more than I'd like, but thankfully, Lucky breaks the tension.

"Come on, Savage! We caught one. It's finally time for a little fucking violence, after being cooped up in this shithole town for weeks."

He punches me on the arm harder than he needs to. When I look at him, he's practically bouncing on the balls of his feet in excitement, like a little kid on Christmas morning.

"Wait, caught one of who?"

"The Aryans! The motherfucking Aryans! Come on, let's go torture some information out of him."

He's already tugging at my arm, like I don't need to get dressed first. Eamon is still smirking at me, but Colm is the only one who seems to be taking this seriously, so I study his face.

"Your father gave orders. We need to extract some information from him, and you're still the best. He told us to come get you and then go work the guy over."

Something inside me sinks right through the floor. I think it was that teeny-tiny piece of hope that I'd allowed myself to have that maybe Father had forgotten about me. Or that maybe I wasn't worth anything to him anymore. That I could just drift away into nothingness, and I wouldn't have to deal with this anymore.

Of course not.

My thoughts flicker to Micah. What would he say if he knew what I was about to do? If he knew that not only was I a violent piece of shit, but also that I specifically excelled in this truly dark side of an already dark business?

"You good to do this, Sav? We can tell Padraig that you're still—"

"I'm fine." I cut Colm off, partly because I know my father won't take no for an answer if he's sending them here specifically to get me, and partly because Eamon is already looking at me gleefully, like this is exactly what he wanted to happen. "Let's just go."

In my head, I tell myself I want to get them out of the apartment as quickly as possible so there's no chance of Eamon and Micah crossing paths. But deep down, I know that's an excuse. Micah won't be home for hours. If I wanted to take a stand against my father, now would be the time to start.

Instead, I say yes, the way I always do. Because I'm weak, and the thought of fighting him is worse than bearing the shame of giving in.

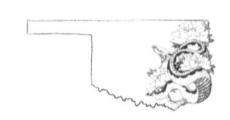

It didn't take long for me to get dressed and into Colm's Escalade with the others. In fact, the whole thing happened so quickly, it sort of feels like I blinked and ended up standing in a barn, on some satellite property we apparently own outside of town.

I don't have any of my old clothes here, just what Micah's bought me. And he's bought me *normal* people clothes. So I'm in jeans and a soft gray t-shirt made of some stretchy material that's snug across my chest and shoulders, making the sleeves ride up. Nothing else. It makes me feel kind of naked.

I'm standing in front of a man who's been stripped, beaten and suspended by his wrists from a rafter, but I'm the one who feels naked because I'm about to torture someone while wearing work boots and dark wash denim that my little brother bought me at Target. I'm not sure how that manages to be ridiculous and make sense at the same time, but my brain thinks it does.

We haven't even started, and I already feel floaty and disconnected from the room around me. God, how was I ever good at this?

Or maybe it's how easily I disconnect from reality that allows me to be good at it. Maybe you can't be good at torturing people if your mind stays present.

Well, Lucky and Eamon both look completely present and eager to get on with the show. Eamon is standing behind me, arms crossed over his chest to make himself look bigger, his usual self-satisfied smile on his face, happy to look like an extra in a mob movie.

Lucky is bouncing around, picking up all the different tools that they have laid out and waving them in the guy's face, accompanied by a string of bloodthirsty expletives and descriptions of what I'm about to do to him. He looks like a kid in a candy store, as usual. He doesn't even seem high. His eyes are bright and clear, his mohawk is perfectly coiffed and his entire being seems dedicated to scaring the shit out of this man for the fun of it.

Colm, as usual, stands to the side and watches with an indecipherable expression on his face.

I guess it's time to get this show on the road.

The man looks pissed. His face is covered in dried, tacky blood from a gash on his forehead. I'm assuming that's how they took him. He has shaggy, chin-length brown hair that's also matted with dried blood, and his body is almost as covered with tattoos as mine.

I don't know what all of them mean, but I know enough. He's mid-ranking—high enough that it's going to cause problems when he turns up missing—and he's definitely a member of the same branch of the Brotherhood that wants me dead.

"What information do we even need from him?" I ask Colm, my voice already hollow and echoey in my ears.

"Everything we can get. Where they're based around here. How many of them there are. What they're running, if it's more drugs and guns—"

He's still talking, but the sound of his voice is swallowed up by my blood rushing in my ears.

I think I would hate this less if it weren't all so fucking pointless. I'm not afraid to get my hands dirty. But I know exactly what level of debauched, gut-churning violence the next few hours are about to contain, and I know exactly how useless it all is.

The Brotherhood hate us, and we hate them, because we're rivals. We're all fucking criminals, who will continue to squabble over control of our shitty little trades in drugs and illegal weapons.

Sure, they're targeting me now, but tomorrow it'll be someone else. We kill this guy, then they kill one of ours in retribution—although please, God, if you exist, let it be Eamon—and so on and so on.

The demand for drugs and guns isn't exactly going anywhere. And it's not like there's not enough to go around: this country is *fucked up*.

All the rest of it feels like a lot of posturing at the end of the day. My father loves to brag about my skills in this particular arena. Information extraction. I think he likes the clout it brings him more than he likes any of the information I've ever actually tortured out of someone.

What a waste of energy.

With exhaustion nipping at my heels, fighting for dominance with my mounting anxiety, I turn my attention to the task at hand. I let the guys do the talking. I wasn't listening to Colm when he gave me the highlights, anyway. All I need to do is work.

The man makes it through all the nails on his right hand being pulled before he starts to scream. When I clip a battery to his testicles to start hitting him with low-level electric shocks, he starts to whimper.

But still, he doesn't talk. Clearly, someone here really drank the Kool-Aid.

I have a headache from all the screaming and the acrid stench of burning pubic hair. When I turn away for a few seconds to rub at my temples, Lucky loses his temper. I'm in my own protective mental bubble, so it takes longer than it should for the havoc to penetrate my consciousness.

When it does, I realize he's pummeling the guy's face, blood gushing from the prisoner's nose and down his chest, screaming at him for information, while the other two try to drag him away and yell at me to help.

My feeling of exhaustion only intensifies.

I need this to be over.

Steeling myself, I pull out a blade. It's time to get messy, so we can finally all move on with our lives.

The rest happens in a blur.

Blood. More screaming that turns to wet, choked gurgles. My muscles burning with exertion. A dull throb in my wound, where it still hasn't totally healed and isn't used to this. The constant chatter of Lucky's ridiculous running commentary in the background.

And then it's done.

We've gotten what we could from him, and if he's not dead, he's about to be. I'm moving like a zombie, shuffling around the barn to gather up my shit. My limbs are all sticky with his blood.

"Sav." Colm's face appears in front of mine, looking at me intently like he's been trying to get my attention for a while. "Do you want to go? Eamon volunteered to ditch the body."

I shrug. Whatever.

"Are you good?"

"I'm fine. I need a shower. Let's head out."

My voice sounds like a stranger's, but I don't have the energy to care.

Lucky and I pile into Colm's car while Eamon stays behind to clean up. I should really find a place to wash off here before I track evidence all over the car, but it's not going to happen. It's cold, in the early hours of the morning, and the idea of standing under a garden hose outside this barn is already making me shiver violently enough to have Colm looking at me and turning off the A/C.

It's not like anyone's going to be investigating this guy's death, anyway. No one cares when a criminal goes missing, and the people who do care are already fully aware of who is responsible.

They'll come for us soon enough. I just hope I have time to take a shower first and wash off the stench of his death.

Chapter Eighteen

Micah

This shift has been brutal. Not only is it unseasonably busy in the ER, but I've been a space cadet the whole fucking night. Dropping shit, misplacing shit, and taking ten times as long as usual to do basic math because I can't fucking concentrate.

Tadhg. He's all I can think about, as per usual. Which is starting to concern me all on its own. I realize that not only did we have a weird childhood, we've also been shoved into a situation where there is no guidebook on how to have healthy boundaries. Either way, even if there were, we'd be failing.

We were codependent little kids, and apparently, we've fallen directly into being codependent adults, as if there isn't a decade of emptiness sitting between us.

All I can focus on is getting him better. In my entire

career, I've never struggled to put my patients first until this moment. Stowing my shit and doing my job is my literal expertise.

But no. My brain is just *Tadhg, Tadhg, Tadhg*, on repeat, as if he can't function without me around to babysit him.

I put out some feelers for getting off-books psych meds from doctors that I'm friendly with earlier, and was immediately shut down. Which is a relief, to be honest. I'm glad that's not a thing that's happening here. I'm also glad I gave myself enough conversational wiggle room to not get reported for it.

After that, I operate on instinct, pushing through hour after hour, trying not to fuck up too badly and just make it until I can go home and see for myself that he's still okay.

He's not okay, though. I know it. He needs help. Between his father's abuse, his life of crime and his misadventures with medication withdrawal, he has the emotional regulation of a soup spoon.

How am I supposed to keep him from flying off the handle and doing something he can't come back from?

Relief washes through me when I see Tristan toward the end of my shift. He's riding a gurney, looking like he's basically holding the patient together with his bodyweight, which isn't a good sign and means I have a lot more work to do before the night is over.

But he's my only connection for less-than-legal drugs. And I'm quickly coming to understand that when it comes to my brother's safety, everything else takes a fucking backseat in importance.

I'll take the gnarly patient if it means I have a chance at getting Tristan to help me with my psych med issue.

It takes four of us, plus Tristan's EMT partner Cade, to lift the patient into the bed while Tristan extricates himself from whatever he was doing. I'm closest to him, so he grabs me and switches out our hands where he was holding off a sluggish bleeder.

From the pallid color of the man's skin, I'd say he's about running on empty, blood-wise. Who knows how long he was left for dead before whoever found him called 911.

It doesn't take long for a gowned-up trauma doc to take my place. There's hustle and bustle around us, and it looks like even though he's pretty bashed up, each wound is individually superficial enough and non-surgical that they're going to try to do a patch job here in the ER while we take care of evidence collection, before transferring him to ICU.

Of course, because I was the first qualified ER nurse to touch him, that means I'm the one assigned to forensics. So instead of clocking out in a few minutes like I was supposed to, I'm now stuck removing every item of clothing—which are weirdly clean, as if he was dressed after being beaten—and cataloging every single injury, from head to toe, in excruciating detail, for the legal record. And then waiting to talk to the cops, who I am historically not a fan of.

It's an important part of my job, obviously. But today's just not the day for it. Not to mention all the Nazi symbols tattooed on this guy's body are automatically making it harder for me to feel sympathetic.

Not that he deserved this. He's torn apart. If I didn't know better, I'd think he was attacked by a wild animal. But it's pretty obvious he was in the life, so he knew what he was risking.

Fuck. I'm very hardened to death and violence, but if this is the kind of thing that Tadhg has been around all his life, no wonder he's messed up. This is fucking savage. It's hard to wrap your head around how it's possible for one human being to do this to another, no matter how many times you see something this awful.

When I finally get home, it feels like I've been gone for days instead of hours. There's a stillness over the apartment that I used to find peaceful, but ever since Tadhg moved in, I've come to find it unsettling. Hopefully, it means he's just fast asleep after working hard all night.

I'm sure the bar was busy as well. I can only cross my fingers that he stayed out of trouble.

I toe off my sneakers at the door and throw my keys somewhere. It wasn't a particularly fluid-filled shift, but I still feel like every inch of my scrubs are sticking to me. At this point, I think a hot shower is needed just to cleanse my soul.

Cold morning light slips around the edges of my blackout curtains, casting the living room in dim shades of gray. It's dark enough that I don't see the footprint until I'm almost on top of it, but as soon as I do, there's no mistaking it.

Blood.

A bloody boot print, right in the middle of my carpet.

My chest clenches as a thousand scenarios run through my mind. If it were a couple of weeks ago, I would have run. Nothing would have been worth risking the chance of finding an intruder in my home, and running is always the safest course of action.

But not anymore. Because if there is an intruder, it's probably someone who came for Tadhg, and I can't leave him here alone. And if he's the only one here, then that blood is his, and it's possible that all my frantic worrying about his mental health has been for nothing, and I'm already too late.

Either way, my feet carry me deeper into the apartment before I have the chance to think any better of it.

I don't try to pick up a weapon. If there's someone in here, I'm not winning in a fight against them. Just like when Patrick first showed up, I have to rely on my wits, my charm, and sheer fucking luck to get me through whatever's coming next.

The bloody footprints disappear behind the bathroom door. I can't even decide what I want to find the least.

I just need him to be alive. Whatever else is happening, I can deal with. As long as he's still alive.

Please.

I take one shaky breath before I twist the handle and open the door. It gives easily and inside isn't exactly any of the scenarios I was mentally preparing myself for.

Tadhg is there. He's covered in blood, and it's immediately obvious that he's the one who left the trail of prints. There's no one else here. And although he's covered in blood, he's also standing over the sink, and I can't see anything that immediately looks like a wound.

His back is bowed, his head lowered, and I don't think he's noticed that I opened the door. I don't want to startle him more than I have to, so I keep my distance and say his name softly a few times.

Finally, as I get louder each time, one of them snaps through whatever is pulling his focus. He jerks away from the sink, looking at me in the mirror for a second before whirling around to take me in.

"Bambi?"

His head whips from side to side, like he's forgotten

where he is. I take a step toward him, one hand outstretched, treating him like the wild animal he's embodying right now.

"Shh, it's okay. It's me. There's no one else here. What happened?"

That was dumb. He's clearly not in question-answering mode, but my brain is kicking up a million of them and I couldn't stop that one from spilling out.

"You shouldn't be here," he says, his voice hoarse and barely louder than a whisper.

"What? No, Tadhg, look at me."

Feeling more confident he's not about to snap, I take hold of his arms, maneuvering him until he's fully facing me, and then I grab his face to keep his focus. There's dried blood flaking over his cheek and chin, but that's not important right now.

"Are. You. Hurt?"

He just snorts and shakes his head, moving my hands with him. When I stay stuck to him, waiting for more information, he reaches up and knocks my hands away with more force than I was expecting.

"You shouldn't touch me."

He won't meet my eyes as he says it. Everything he says sounds so hollow and numb. I feel like I'm not even talking to my brother right now but some shadow-version of him. Even more than when he first came to me and was out of his head with feverish delirium.

"Ok," I say quietly, more to myself than to him. "Ok. Let's get you cleaned up."

Because I'm not stupid, and I don't know exactly what happened to him, but I can put together the shape of it.

I reach for his shirt to peel it off him, but he flinches away. We don't have time to go through all the rounds of his self-loathing right now, though. I move in closer, trapping him against the sink with my body and holding his gaze with mine.

My fingers find the hem of his shirt and I pull it upward. If he wants me to leave him alone, he's going to have to hurt me, and I know that's where he draws the line.

He seems to realize the same thing, because he goes limp in my hands. He stands there, hanging from invisible strings, and lets me strip him down.

When I have his bloody shirt in my hands, it occurs to me that I need to put this somewhere. Preferably somewhere that's not going to transfer evidence all over my apartment. Just in case whoever was bleeding all over my stepbrother wasn't a willing participant…

There are garbage bags under the sink, and I'm able to kick open the cabinet door and fish them out with my foot, without getting my bloody fingerprints anywhere. I upend the roll, spreading the plastic all over the floor around us to catch as much debris as possible, before tearing one off to put his clothes into.

Tadhg continues to comply as I take his soiled clothes off piece by piece and toss them into the bag. I'll find somewhere to burn them later, I guess. I also make a mental note of everywhere that needs to be deep cleaned once we're done here.

As I'm doing this, my brain pulls up the images of a couple hours ago, when I was doing the exact same thing for my patient. Pulling off each item of clothing and carefully bagging it to protect the contents.

Although in that case, it was to preserve everything inside, while right now I'm already knee-deep in my plan to destroy evidence on Tadhg's behalf.

The thought brings me up short. What are the chances

that someone ends up brutally beaten and tortured—in an area where that's not exactly an everyday occurrence—and then Tadhg shows up covered in blood immediately after?

I don't want to think about the miniscule chances that the two things are not connected. Because I saw what *someone* did to that man. And it's a level of violence I would never want to see from someone I love.

Those are later thoughts, though. Right now, I have evidence to destroy.

Medical ethics are well and truly in my rearview mirror, apparently.

Once Tadhg is stripped, I hustle him toward the big cubicle shower and turn it on as hot as I think he can stand. This shower is huge and never runs out of hot water. It was the reason I took this apartment, and until today, it was my favorite thing about it. I have a feeling that's about to change though, after these new memories get attached to it.

I strip off my own scrubs and throw them in the garbage bag, because it's possible that there's traces of blood on them from coming in contact with him. Which I could also have gotten at the hospital, but why invite more trouble than I have to?

Once I'm down to my briefs and everything Tadhg touched is in the bag, I tie it shut, wrap it in another bag, scrape up all the others that were on the ground to toss them in there and seal the whole thing again. I'll deal with it later.

I glance over to check on Tadhg, but of course, he hasn't moved since I left him. He's standing in the shower, half under the spray and half out, staring at the ground like he's completely dissociated.

Fucking shitballs, this is not good.

I've seen him in a lot of terrible states since he showed

up, but it hasn't stopped each one of them from feeling like another string of barbed wire wrapped around my heart, squeezing it tighter.

I just want him to be okay. Which isn't going to happen if he keeps going on murder adventures while I'm at work.

Or if he ends up in prison.

With a sigh, I step into the shower with him. The only times he moves are when I move him, so it's clear he needs a little extra support right now in the form of babying. That's fine. When he was injured and unconscious, I bathed him just like any other patient.

To be fair, I wouldn't normally join a patient in the shower, but I need to shower the blood off as well. My underwear is still on, and if he can gather the wherewithal to be annoyed about me coddling him, frankly, I'll be thrilled.

Right now, he doesn't look capable of being annoyed about anything.

Standing next to him, I grab his arms and maneuver us until we're both under the spray, more or less. I'm not getting a lot of it, but it still feels like heaven on my sticky skin, after the day I've had. I tip his head back, letting the water run through his hair.

It's grown out a little at the back, long enough to curl around his neck. The water runs pink for a while, but I work my hand through his hair a couple of times, letting him sink into the contact, and eventually the blood fades away and the water turns clear.

When I tip his head back down, he blinks the water out of his eyes and looks at me properly. For the first time in a few minutes, I feel like he's actually seeing me.

"No." He speaks in a whisper, but when he goes on, his

voice rises to turn into a plaintive sort of whine. "No, no, no, don't touch me, please."

I'm torn. I don't want to hurt him. I don't want to force affection on him that he doesn't want. But I know in my fucking gut, that this reaction isn't about what he wants. It's about what he thinks I deserve, or some other shit.

Like he's tainted.

His hands come up, batting at mine with all the strength of a wet kitten. The weakness in his movements is what convinces me.

He needs me not to give up on him. He needs me not to run.

"Everything's fine, Tadhg. I'm not going anywhere. You're fine."

He keeps struggling though, so I wrap my arms around him and squeeze, which is more difficult than I expected. He's fucking thick.

As soon as I squeeze, he starts to thrash. It's like holding on to him has given him permission to lose his shit. Which is what I wanted, I guess.

He's still saying "no" and "please" and making noises like he wants to cry but can't quite get there, and jerking so hard one of us slips and we both end up on the shower floor. With the water still pelting down into us, Tadhg pulls away from me until his back hits the tile wall, but I don't let him go that easily.

I follow. And like I usually do when he's crawling out of his skin, I climb into his lap to settle him. It's worked before, and I think it'll work now. Getting in his face, making it clear I'm not leaving him no matter how determined he is to give up on himself, weighing him down physically with the force of how much I'm not fucking leaving him… That's the best I've got.

My legs are straddling his hips, and he's splayed out under me with his head resting against the shower wall. Shower water and blood and tears are all mingled on his face now, and they cover an expression of unbearable anguish that I never want to see him wear again.

So he can feel me even more, I grab his face and hold it close to mine.

"It's fine," I whisper, over and over. "You're okay. It's okay. I'm here. Everything's going to be fine. I'm not going anywhere."

It's all just babbled nonsense, but I need to get through to him.

And I do. He pulls himself together enough to sigh and look me in the eyes after a few minutes. But when he speaks, the voice that comes out of his mouth is completely devoid of emotion.

"You shouldn't be here. I'm not worth it."

It only makes me grip him tighter, my fingers digging into his cheeks hard enough that it probably hurts.

"You're worth it to me."

I lean forward, kissing him on the forehead. And he's fucking trapped between me and the shower wall now, so he can't duck away from me.

When I lean back and look at him again, his eyes are shining with unspoken emotion and hurt, so I do it again. I don't know what to say. I just need him to understand that it doesn't matter if he thinks he's worthless right now, I'll care enough about him for the both of us.

"You're worth it," I whisper, kissing him on one cheek. "You're worth it. I promise, Tadhg, you're worth everything. You don't deserve this. I'm not going anywhere, because you're fucking worth it."

I kiss him on the other cheek, and maybe my words

penetrate his thick skull, because he leans into it a little this time. His mouth is open, and his breath is coming in heavy pants, like just thinking about this is putting his body through a marathon's worth of stress.

"You're fucking worth it," I say one more time, leaning in to kiss him again.

But this time, he leans into it even more, his features soft and his body sinking into my hold. I catch the corner of his mouth, instead of his cheek, and feel the barest pressure of him kissing me back.

I don't know what comes over me. It's like I spend so much time trying to figure out how to pour my affection into this man when he'll let me. And now he's finally letting me in. A mix of awe and euphoria hit me, and I'm so desperate to capture the feeling before it flickers out of existence again.

I turn my face the barest fraction of an inch and kiss his mouth, and he kisses me back. It's small. Just lips pressed together. But it feels monumental.

It feels like him opening himself up to me, and I'm desperate for more.

When his lips part to take another raspy breath, I don't let myself think before I capture his mouth again. With water running down both our faces, I kiss him, and he allows himself to be kissed.

His fingers tighten where before they were just resting on my sides. Like he's pulling me in closer instead of pushing me away. I respond by opening my mouth on instinct, and he tentatively brushes my tongue with his.

I can't help the pleased noise that slips out of me. That wasn't supposed to be what this is about, but it feels like everything shifted in an instant.

Before I can process what's happening, we're kissing like

two people starving for each other. Tadhg's hands are everywhere, touching me, gripping me tighter to him, and I'm pressing myself closer on instinct where I'm riding his hips.

It feels like I'm losing my mind, but I don't want to stop. It feels right. But I also don't want Tadhg to realize what's happening and freak out more. Then I feel him getting hard beneath me, and if I wasn't sure how into this he was before, I am now.

He's stiff, rubbing up behind my balls and into the crease of my ass and letting out needy little moans every time we break apart. I can't stop myself from grabbing onto his hair to pull him back for better access, and the noise he makes at that is practically a purr.

I hesitate. Just for a second, because we really should talk about this. I've looked at him as a brother all my life, even though we're not actually related, by blood or the law. He was my protector. And now I have my tongue down his throat.

At a time when he's really fucking vulnerable, to boot.

But it's that vulnerability that convinces me not to say anything. Because as soon as I open my mouth, doubt flickers across his face and I can see him retreating back to that place of self-loathing that he's made his home.

I don't want him to doubt how much I care about him. Not for a second. And I don't want to give his father's shitty voice the chance to break into his inner monologue, if he's finally letting himself have something he wants. I can't let him question it. I'm not fucking questioning it, either. I just want us both to *feel*.

We can go slow. I'll let him lead, as much as I'm capable of doing that. But I won't make him voice it, or listen to me break it down. Not until he's less... raw.

I swoop in, tightening my grip in his hair hard enough to

sting and taking ownership of his mouth for a few more minutes. His hard-on does not flag in the slightest, and soon he's rutting up against me, panting and moaning in between kisses, grabbing at my hips like he's trying to find friction.

This time, I break our kiss because I need oxygen. The shower water isn't helping me find it, but I think we need it. The curtain of water feels like a barrier between us and the real world, and Tadhg needs that right now to be able to let himself go and ask for what he really wants.

When I look him in the eyes, he seems lost. But hungry. And whenever I try to pull back, even a fraction, he holds me tighter. Like he's desperate to keep me close.

His hips grind up into mine again, even as he searches my face for some kind of reaction. His mouth is open, still panting softly, and I can see that no words are coming to him any time soon.

He looks almost innocent. Which doesn't make sense, considering I came in here to wash off the blood of a man he beat, or tortured, or *somethinged*, but still. In this particular way, I guess he is innocent.

And scared.

I can't let him doubt me.

"You're so good, Tadhg," I whisper, running my thumb along his swollen lower lip, collecting all the water droplets that have gathered there. "You're so good and you don't even know it."

He shudders in my arms, and I can see the words taking hold of him in a way I haven't been able to before.

He grinds up into me again. Not hard, just instinctive. Needy. Desperate, almost.

It lights a fire in me.

I'd burn the world down for him on a random Tuesday as it is, but it doesn't help that right now he's flicking every kink switch I have about getting a big, strong man looking vulnerable and submissive on his knees for me.

The part of my brain that had Tadhg categorized as "brother" is officially offline. The rest of me—who eats guys like him for breakfast—takes one look at him and sees a needy slut.

There has to be a middle ground. As long as I don't let him get in his head.

"You're *my* good boy, Tadhg." Another shudder. "Does my good boy need to come?"

His breath stutters. He hesitates, like he's not sure if this is a trick.

"It's okay. It's okay, you can come. You can have anything you want. You have me. I'm not going anywhere."

Slowly, he nods, holding my gaze the entire time.

When his hips buck up again, it's more deliberate. I shuffle back, getting my knees on the ground and giving him more space to move. Tadhg follows, like always, still holding me close, until we're both on our knees, pressed together from sternum to pelvis, his hard, aching cock sliding against the declivity of my hip.

His movements are a little hesitant, so I kiss him again as a distraction. It works, and soon he's grinding against my hip steadily, working himself against my skin.

In between kisses, I continue to whisper, telling him how good he is and how much he deserves this. He never speaks, but he continues to clutch me to him like he never wants to let me go.

When I move my hands down to palm his ass, I can feel the muscles work as he ruts into me. I want to let him continue controlling the movements, which is why I don't try to escalate this into anything more. But I can't help myself when I reach between us and stroke my fingertips over the leaking head of his cock just once.

He fucking whimpers. He whimpers like a good, needy boy, and I kiss him again as a reward.

"That's it, Tadhg. You're doing so well. Make a mess all over me, go on. You deserve this."

When he stiffens, he holds me so tight to him I can barely breath. I feel every movement of his cock as it pulses and twitches, spilling warmth between our bodies. I feel the way his chest heaves and his body continues to shudder as it works itself through the orgasm, and I hold him tight through it all.

I've been hard for fuck knows how long, but I ignore it. I can take care of that later. This isn't about me.

This is about Tadhg finally letting himself go, even if it's just for a second. And if I have any say in what happens next, it won't be the end of it. This is just the fucking beginning.

Chapter Nineteen

Savage

I can't breathe. This isn't a new feeling for me, but the circumstances definitely are. My chest is heaving while my body tries to find anything to latch onto so it can straighten itself out after the most dizzying orgasm I've ever had. I'm distracted, so it takes me a minute to notice that Micah is still looking at me like I'm a bomb, and he's trying to figure out if he cut the right color wire.

I'm also trembling, but I don't know whether to blame that on the orgasm, the fact that my mind is blown into a thousand disparate pieces, or the shower water that's finally beginning to run cold.

"Come on," Micah says, his voice more gentle than I've ever heard it, and his thumb tracing a soft trail over my cheek the way he's taken to doing so often. "Let's get cleaned up."

"But you—" My voice is raspy with disuse, and I trail off, looking down at his crotch. He came into the shower in boxer briefs, I'm guessing to preserve what few barriers were left between us, although I clearly shot that all to hell. But they're soaked through, and the dark fabric is clinging to every inch of him. I can see the outline of his cock as clearly as if he were naked, and my eyes trip over it for a second before getting trapped there.

It's thick and long. Thicker *and* longer than mine, which is devoutly average, and looks even more huge and disproportionate on his slender body. I can see the way the fabric traces the flared head, and I can see how hard he is. How he's straining upward, trapped between the wet material and his stomach, thick and practically pulsing with arousal.

Which is good? I'm glad that he's not disgusted by whatever we just did, and only tolerating it to make me feel better because I'm such a hair-trigger disaster he's worried that one false move will set me off on a trail of self-destruction. But I'm also trying not to think about what it is we actually just did, because it seems so monumental and perspective-shifting that accepting it into my brain all at once will make me snap.

I let myself glance at the edges of it. Darting, fleeting glimmers of this new reality dancing at the periphery of my awareness. Nothing more than that until my chest has stopped heaving and I'm not still thrumming with the afterglow of that orgasm.

Micah should come, right? He should get to come, too. He's hard. He deserves it, after everything he does to take care of me, all the way up to coaxing said orgasm out of me with whispered filthy but loving words and electric touches. By letting me hump his hip like a desperate animal until I spilled myself all over my little brother.

No, not brother. Stepbrother. Former stepbrother. Fuck. I don't even know how to think of him anymore.

Mine.

My Bambi.

The thought makes me tremble harder, flushing with adrenaline at the realization that I would do anything and everything to protect this man. Even from myself. I think he mistakes it for distress, though, because he wraps his arms around me and pulls me into a tight hug under the now freezing water.

I slip a clumsy hand between us and grab his shaft through his underwear, pulling a sound out of him that's more breathy and... *feminine* than I've ever heard him make. I love seeing this soft, vulnerable side of him, which is different from all the vulnerable sides I've seen before, and my normally worthless dick is already trying to rally in response.

What is happening to me? And why don't I hate it?

I move my hand down his length once, pulling another delicious noise out of him before he pushes back from me.

"It's okay, Tadhg." He's a little breathless but composed. "I don't need that right now. Let's get out of this water and take a breath."

My heart stutters, and my brain feels like it's flattening and twisting, trying to figure out the hidden meaning behind his words. He doesn't want it? Or he just needs a minute? The specter of rejection is looming so large over both of us, and I hate how my fragile, fucked-up mind is just waiting for it to swoop in and crush me.

I don't say anything, but I think I manage a nod. My mouth is still hanging open as I breathe heavily, and droplets of water keep gathering on my bottom lip before dripping to the floor.

Micah hesitates, studying my face for a moment. It's weird to see him look unsure. He was a nervous kid, and I was used to him being unsure about everything. But here, in this reality, he's always in charge of the situation. His hesitance seems out of place, and I want to wipe it off his face.

But he doesn't give me the chance, because he seems to come to some decision before leaning in and kissing me again. Just like before, his kiss is firm and demanding, making me open up to him immediately in a way that makes my stomach bottom out like an elevator in freefall.

Everything in me clenches in anticipation, but he doesn't push it any farther.

The little voice demanding over and over again to know why I don't hate this is getting quieter, drowned out by the white noise of pleasure and adrenaline that seem to take over whenever he touches me like this.

He breaks the kiss eventually with a contented little hum, and I already want to find a way to get him to make that noise again. Something about it makes me vibrate with satisfaction.

"Come on," he repeats, more serious this time.

He takes my hand in his, which feels a little silly because my hand is bigger but he still manages to make me feel enveloped. Then he stands and turns off the water, pulling me to stand with him. Once I'm in the open air, I realize just how cold I've gotten, and my trembling turns to full on shivering.

Micah smiles at me fondly when he hears me hiss in a sharp breath between teeth that are on the verge of chattering. My body is a floodplain of adrenaline right now, which isn't helping, but he's shivering, too. Without a word, he pulls us both out and wraps me in not one but two towels before doing the same for himself.

Once there's a towel around his waist, he shucks off his sodden underwear. I caught enough of a glimpse to see that his erection had deflated, which isn't surprising, given the cold. But it does make me feel a pang of something. Guilt, maybe.

Or more like I missed a moment that I didn't want to miss. Which is yet another thought that my brain—now frayed tissue-paper thin—can't truly wrap itself around.

We both take a second to roughly towel off before heading down the hallway. I follow Micah into the bedroom, and he throws some of my clothes at me before getting dressed himself.

It's all soft things. Sweats and cotton t-shirts. Once we're clothed, Micah runs a towel over his hair one more time before throwing back the covers on the bed and pushing me unceremoniously toward it.

I don't know if he's expecting me to object, or freak out, or what. But so far I'm successfully keeping all the freaked-out parts of me walled up somewhere else, and the part of me that's in control is mostly just dazed.

I climb into bed, and the sweet relief that courses through me makes me realize just how exhausted I really was. Not that I did much to earn that exhaustion. Torture is what my body is built for, it's hardly a marathon. But all the weepy, self-indulgent equivocating afterwards seems to really have taken it out of me.

I cast that thought aside with another mental shrug and ignore my ever-growing *later* pile of problems.

Instead of climbing in with me, like I expected, Micah turns away. And it makes all that dulled panic and uncertainty rise right back up inside me. I jolt up, catching his wrist and holding him more tightly than I probably should, because he turns to look at me with wide eyes.

His mouth makes a small, shocked 'o' for a second, before his brain seems to piece it all together. Then everything about him softens all at once. His eyes crinkle at the side, and he leans over the bed to put his face only inches in front of mine.

"I'm coming back," he says in a conspiratorial whisper, sort of like we did when we were kids. "I'm just getting you some water and something to eat."

I don't know what to say to that. The truth is, it makes the trembling from before start up again, but this time deep, deep inside my chest in a place no one can see. The place that has always been dry and dusty because I haven't exactly lived a life where someone was cutting the crusts off my sandwiches or bringing me glasses of water.

Instead of speaking, I grunt my acquiescence, and it makes Micah give me another small smile. I uncurl my fingers from his wrist one by one, and before I know it, I'm alone in the room.

I hate it. It lets my mind drift toward all the walls inside me and the places they're bulging, where fissures are beginning to form from holding back too much with too little for too long.

Numbness washes over me, because it's easier than anything else, and I don't know how much time passes until Micah comes back. When he looks at me this time, it's with a little frown instead of that warm expression. I'm lying down, I realize. He sits on the mattress next to me and puts a plate down on the bedside table along with his obnoxiously oversized Hydroflask thing, then his fingers gently brush some hair away from my forehead.

"Can you sit up for me for a minute to eat something?" he asks, which is a lot easier than the other things he might have, like *Are you okay?* Or *What did we just do?*

With a groan, I pull myself up into a sitting position. Micah looks pleased and sits cross-legged on the mattress opposite me, reaching back and then depositing the plate between us.

It really is sandwiches. Not with the crusts cut off, because that would be ridiculous, but still. There's a little pile of peanut butter and jelly sandwiches on the plate, all cut diagonally in half. Like something you would see at a kid's birthday party.

Micah grabs one and starts eating it completely cavalierly, before nudging the plate toward me. I pick one up, but I'm slow to bring it to my mouth. It feels weird in my hand.

I suddenly worry that I didn't get all the blood out from under my nails. When I look at my hand, it seems too big and too rough and scarred to be holding something like this. But the way Micah is watching me intensely as he chews his own sandwich tells me I won't get away with not eating it.

When I take a bite, the sweet and salty flavors explode on my tongue in that way they do when you haven't eaten in way too long, and your mouth forgot what food tastes like. Like when you're so fucking thirsty that when you finally get to drink, water suddenly tastes like the most delicious elixir on the planet.

Micah nods slightly, still watching me, and his approval makes this all go down easier. Even if it shouldn't. I shouldn't need that from him, but it helps anyway.

In silence, we work our way through all the sandwiches and then pass the ridiculous flask of water between us until it's empty and Micah finally seems satisfied.

Then he finally lets me lie down again. Just when I feel so tired my body might punch through into another dimension of existence. Like I'm floating in a land that's parallel to this one, but where the air is viscous, and every movement is weighed down by extra gravity.

We lie on our sides, not touching, but looking at each other. Daylight filters in around the edges of Micah's blackout curtains. It's only a little, so we can still barely see each other, but you can tell from the color that the sun is already high in the sky outside and it's probably getting hot. I need to close my eyes, but I can't.

Instead, I watch the little dust motes floating in the air between us, caught in each tiny spear of sunlight that's broken through. I watch the way Micah blinks slowly and watches me back, his mind obviously humming with a thousand things he hasn't said yet but wants to.

Eventually, when neither of us has moved or closed our eyes, Micah reaches out to me. He cups my cheek for what feels like the thousandth time since I got here.

I hate it. I hate the way it makes me feel soft and fragile and like something that needs his protection. I hate it, but that doesn't stop me from nuzzling into his palm like a needy animal, taking in a deep, shuddering breath as the warmth of his skin manages to calm something in me that I didn't know was in distress.

"We can talk about all this later, yeah?" Micah whispers to me across the darkness.

"Yeah, Bambi. Of course."

"Just get some sleep for me. Please."

The *please* crumples something inside of me, just like it always does. I reach out and grab him by the waist, dragging his body across the foot and a half of mattress that's in between us.

Instead of objecting or stiffening, Micah just sighs. His body is soft and supple under my hands, and he lets me arrange him next to me, pressed against me everywhere. He slots one of his legs between mine and then slides his arms around my shoulders until my face is pressed against his neck. I keep my arms around his waist, exactly where they belong, and for a second, I cling to him so tightly that I don't know if he can breathe.

This is it. This is better. I don't know what the fuck any of it means, but not letting go is the only thing that makes me feel like I'm not unspooling at some distant corner of the universe, so I'm going to roll with that for as long as he'll let me and deal with the consequences later.

Micah

I don't know what time it is when we wake up, except that it's truly nighttime. Nothing but darkness sits on the other side of those curtains, and the room is so black I can only make out the vague outline of Tadhg's face, still only inches away from mine.

Thank god I had the foresight to call out for my shift while I was making those sandwiches before. I knew I wasn't going to be able to leave him until we'd at least had one conversation about what is happening between us.

The House Supervisor was pissed, and that's putting it mildly. I'm clearly on thin ice. But I'm not very replaceable in a rural area like this, so I feel like I can keep pushing a little more before I'm at risk of losing my job.

And if I have to pick between losing my job or potentially losing my brother, I'm picking Tadhg, every time.

Brother.

I shouldn't say that, even in the privacy of my own mind. We always threw the word around pretty casually, even after we'd been apart for so long. 'Stepbrother' seems clumsy, and we were so fucking close for the brief time that we were family, I never really thought it mattered what people thought about how we were related.

The only important thing to me back then was that we belonged to each other. We were the only family we could rely on. The only ones in each other's corner.

Now, after all this time, I still feel like we belong to each other. But I guess my child's brain couldn't comprehend that it was maybe meant to be in a different way—a different kind of family—and it's taken my adult brain a really long time to catch up.

He's fucking beautiful. I've always known that.

Even with his cheap tattoos and his redneck haircut that's one step away from being a mullet, he's still stunning to look at. Light golden skin with just a few freckles. Those fucking eyes with matching shades of gold in them. The kind of strong jaw and straight nose I always associated with what Patrick called "real men", but also with that gorgeous, pouty mouth.

If I'm being truly honest with myself. If I really dig deep into my inner bank of denial… Maybe I've projected a little of what I used to love about Tadhg onto the kinds of men that I fuck. There are maybe a few similarities there. If I really, really let myself think about it.

His entire body is like a wonderland of curves and muscle, so pretty and perfect he could have been made in a lab. But like a real person, not a Ken doll.

Well, a little like a Ken doll. But one with golden body hair in all the right places and little scars and imperfections and points of softness where the human body is supposed to be soft.

He's my Ken doll. And while my rational self is

screaming to figure out the ramifications of this huge, paradigm-altering shift in our relationship, the basic bitch part of myself just wants to take him out of the box and play with him.

No. Not until he wants to.

If he ever wants to.

I can't push him. He doesn't like to make decisions, I know, but in this case, he's going to have to lead a little or I'll feel like I'm dragging him into some toxic dynamic for my own twisted pleasure because I've just uncovered the world's most deeply buried subconscious lifelong crush.

"You're thinking very hard."

His voice interrupts me, and when I peer further into the darkness, I realize his eyes are open and he's watching me with that vulpine, calculating expression he sometimes gets.

"Mmm." I reach out to touch his cheek, and he immediately presses into it, like he always does, which soothes some of my worry. "I was thinking about what happened."

Tadhg stiffens. "Yeah?"

"I know this is a big question, but are you okay with it?"

I can just about make out the line of his Adam's apple bobbing as he swallows, but then he nods, the movement taking my hand with it.

"It was good. Are *you* okay with it?"

I bite my lip. I don't know whether I should be honest about how freaking okay with it I am. How seeing him rubbing one out against my hip unleashed something hungry in me, and I'm currently sporting raging fucking morning wood that's reaching out toward his body like a heat-seeking missile.

"Yeah. The more I think about it, the more I think maybe I wanted it for longer than I realized."

Tadhg's eyebrows raise, but I can faintly hear his breath quickening in the quiet room.

"Really?"

I nod. "Have you ever done anything with a man before?" It's the million-dollar question, and I don't know how he'll react, but I have to ask. I'm not asking him to label his sexuality, because I know what his dad is like and how this must be hard for him. But everything I know about him told me he liked girls. I want to know how much is shifting for him right now.

His face clouds, and he pulls fractionally away from my hand.

"Can we not talk about that right now? I don't... I just. It's not important. I liked it. It was good. I don't want to think about anything..."

Outside of this room, where the consequences live.

That's the unspoken end of his sentence.

"Sure."

He huffs a little, wiggling in the sleep-warm sheets like he's not comfortable. Then, just like he did last night, he reaches out and grabs me. Without a second's hesitation, he drags me across the sheets and into his broad chest, pressing us together.

Only this time, it's so abrupt that I don't have the chance to hide my erection, so he gets a stiff fucking jab of hard dick right into his abdomen.

Tadhg makes this breathy little gasping sound that is so precious I want him to make it a million more times, and I file it away in my mind as a memory I will take to my grave.

He hesitates, then his big hands reach down to cup my ass and roll my hips toward him, rubbing my cock against his stomach. This time it's my turn to gasp in surprise.

"You really liked it?" he asks me in a breathy whisper,

continuing to squeeze my ass and keep my hips rocking fluidly against him.

"I think it's pretty clear how much I liked it," I whisper back, wrapping my arms around his shoulders so I can put my mouth next to his ear.

Tadhg keeps us rocking in silence for a few more minutes. I can feel him getting hard as well, his length bulging the front of his sweats and rubbing against me with every movement. Eventually, he rolls onto his back so I'm straddling him again, and I take advantage of the moment to bring our faces together and kiss him.

I don't care about morning breath. I don't care about anything. I feel like I could kiss him like this every day for the rest of eternity and never get sick of it.

He's perfectly soft and pliant beneath me, responsive to my every touch, letting me fuck my tongue into his mouth and giving it back as good as he gets, all while letting out those breathy little moans and masculine grunts that are all going to be the death of me.

I can feel his body start to get tense with frustration as he seeks out more—more contact, more friction, more something.

But I swore I wouldn't let this go too fast until I knew he was really okay.

No matter how much I'd love to roll him over right now and fuck him until he screams and cries and forgets he ever thought of me as a brother, or a weak little child, or anything other than the man turning him inside out with pleasure.

"Fuck," he whispers when I break our lips apart for a second.

I don't think he means anything. He's already lust-glazed

and staring at me with blown pupils, waiting for me to tell him what to do next. Like the most perfect little…

None of that.

Not yet.

I shuffle down his body until I'm sitting between his spread legs instead of straddling them. Tadhg watches me intently the whole time, trying to make my features out in the dark, so I reach over and turn on a very soft side light I have for just this purpose. It bathes him in a cool glow, and the faint shadows it casts over him only make the curves and dips of his body look even more tantalizing.

When I bring my hand to his crotch, I rub my palm from the base of his cock all the way up with gentle pressure, over the fabric, but it's enough to make him gasp and writhe.

So needy.

Then I grab his hand and bring it down to where mine just was.

"Pull yourself out and show me how you like to be touched."

Tadhg looks at me for a minute while the words sink in. His brow furrows, but then he seems to understand. Instead of pulling himself out, though, he pushes down his sweats and boxer-briefs in one movement, pulling up one leg at a time to get rid of them entirely and managing to do it more gracefully than he should be able to.

Then he arches his back and reaches behind him, taking hold of the collar of his t-shirt and tugging it over his head. It gets thrown to the floor in the same direction as the pants.

In barely a few seconds, he went from fully dressed to completely naked and spread out in front of me like a fucking snack. I know I've seen him naked plenty of times since he's been injured, but normally with a clinical eye. Or when he's having a meltdown.

This is the first time when there's nothing else hovering over us, and I'm free to let my eyes rove over every inch of him, all the way down to his leaking erection.

As soon as I look at his cock, he fists it and starts to jerk himself. He doesn't fuck around. The movement is hard and fast, and soon he's panting, his hips jerking off the bed a little with each movement, his eyes flicking between meeting mine and looking at the tent in my own pants.

I stroke my length a few times over the fabric as well, to show him I'm in this with him. I just want to give him the chance to be in control.

"That's it. Fuck, you look pretty. You're like a perfect doll, made just for me. You know that, right?"

The words spill out of my mouth before I have the chance to think them through. I mean them, though.

Tadhg is breathing hard, still jerking himself roughly. His eyes are wide, and he's writhing but there's also an uncertainty to his expression that I don't like. I put my hands on his thighs, tracing the muscles there in little patterns with my fingernails and trying to control the pulsing arousal that's building in me at how fucking hot this is.

"That's it, doll," I whisper, because his hand is moving faster and I think he must be close to coming.

But then that uncertain expression becomes closer to panicked. His gaze leaves mine, and I hear him mutter, "*No, no, no, no,*" under his breath.

Before I can say anything, Tadhg shifts to lean up a little, and his movements get even faster. Too fast, and his grip is so hard it seems like it must hurt. I'm looking at it, which is when it hits me what's happening.

His cock is soft in his hand, and he's tugging at himself frantically, as if he's trying to summon back the wilted erection with sheer willpower and friction. But his clenched fist looks too tight, and the expression on his face is so fucking far from the pleasured one I saw just a minute ago.

"Tadhg, stop," I say, leaning forward to grab his wrist. "Stop, stop, stop, you'll hurt yourself."

I'm babbling, but he's barely paying attention to me. He seems to have sunk into a half-panicked place in his mind. Gently, I pull at his wrist until he lets himself go, and then I climb into his lap and take his face in my hands until he's looking at me.

He's breathing heavily, looking at me with wide eyes. It's a totally disproportionate amount of panic for something that's happened to every guy at some point in their life, but I feel like I can see the bigger picture here.

When you have so much panic being penned in by such thin, shaky walls for so long, it only takes the smallest cracks to let it all gush out.

"Shhh. It's okay." I repeat myself for a minute while he catches his breath, and then I capture his mouth in a kiss to distract him even more.

He kisses me back with so much fervor it's like he's trying to climb inside of me. I only break the kiss once I can feel him settle beneath me. I can also feel a hint of his erection returning and putting pressure on the underside of my thigh, but we're not paying attention to that right now.

"What happened?"

He shakes his head, not looking at me.

"Did you not want to do it?" I can't stop myself from tracing his bottom lip with my thumb as I ask him. I need the truth, but I really hope the answer isn't that I've already pushed him too far when that's the last thing I wanted to do.

"No," he says, his voice rough. "I wanted to. Really. It just happens sometimes." His eyes dart to meet mine, and then he glances down again. "A lot. It happens a lot," he says in a hushed tone.

"Oh." I can't think of anything else to say while I absorb that information. "Do you want to stop?"

He immediately shakes his head and then kisses me again with the same frenetic desperation as before.

I pull back, though, because we're getting off-track. I can't help but smile a little as I do. "Okay, okay, I get the picture. We'll keep going, but promise you'll tell me if you want to stop, okay? I won't be mad."

Tadhg nods, looking at me with the same mixture of hunger and apprehension in his eyes as before. "I just can't always... I can't—"

"Shh," I interrupt, wiggling a little on his lap for emphasis. "Look, I know you're used to being *the man* or whatever heteronormative bullshit, but you don't actually have to be a big swinging dick to have a good time in bed. There are lots of things people can do, regardless of what junk they have and how it works. And I think that you"—I slide back off his lap and push him until he's lying down again, with me kneeling between his legs, still fully clothed while he's naked and needy underneath me—"are secretly dying for the chance to be someone's little pillow princess."

Tadhg's eyebrows raise, but he doesn't say anything. He lets me keep talking, shivering and arching his back as I run my fingernails down his sides as I do.

"So why don't we try that for a while. And let your poor dick have some rest."

"What do you mean?" He asks like he doesn't want to know the answer.

"Do you trust me?"

He nods, and it's the most sure I've seen him look about anything in a while.

"Then lie back, relax, and let me take care of everything, doll. All you have to do is tell me if you hate it, and I'll stop. Otherwise, feel free to react however you want. Personally, I hope you're a screamer."

Even in the low light, I can see the blush that crawls up his chest and neck, all the way to his hairline, and it does a lot toward bringing back my own hard-on that flagged while we were talking.

I smile at him briefly, because how could I not? He's such a good boy, and he doesn't even know it.

Well, I guess it's time for him to find out.

Chapter Twenty

Savage

The way Micah is looking down at me—long shadows cast on his face by the little bedside lamp—is predatory. Which should probably make me nervous, but instead it just brings back a trickle of the arousal that fled me so abruptly before.

I don't know what happened. Everything felt amazing. I loved the way he was watching me, and the unabashed way he had started the whole thing. I was worried he was going to force me into several mind-bending conversations about what this all means, but instead he let us go with the flow.

It was perfect. Until the stray thought crossed my mind about what would happen if my boner fled the scene. Which made me nervous. Which triggered an immediate cascade of sensations marked by panic and the curling, quivering shame that led to me wanting nothing more than to crawl away and hide so he couldn't see my soft, useless cock.

But Micah didn't freak out, like I expected. I've had girls have different reactions, and even though most of them at least try to be nice, they're normally at best super uncomfortable, and at worst offended. Micah seemed to get it.

Although maybe that wasn't so much because he isn't a girl, and more because he's *him*. He knows me already, inside and out, and isn't some random stranger I dragged home.

And now he's looking at me like I didn't just ruin everything by being pathetic, and he still wants to do whatever it is—this new thing between us is.

Do you trust me?

He's the only person I trust. I don't even trust myself, but I trust him.

Micah leans over and fucks with a drawer for a minute, pulls out something I can't really make out, and then quickly drapes his body over mine. I try not to look. I don't want to know what he's doing. If I know, I'll think about what it all means, and then my brain will win.

I just want to feel. And to make him feel.

Micah kisses me again, just as deeply as before. His hips are in between my legs, and for some reason the fact that he's fully dressed while I'm completely bare-ass naked isn't making me feel exposed and vulnerable. It feels right.

Like I'm spread out for him to take whatever he wants. Which sounds fucked up when I articulate it in my head. But the thought of him *taking* gives me a deep sense of peace that I've barely even glimpsed in my previous life.

His kiss is heady and insistent. His hands run up and down my sides, and he grinds his hips into me a little as I let myself wrap my thighs around him and squeeze. We rut together like that until I'm breathless, and if he's trying to overwhelm me with sensation, he's succeeding.

Then he fucks with whatever he got out of the drawer again, his body still over me but his hands elsewhere, before leaning in to kiss me one more time.

He breaks away, his gaze intently boring into me.

"Just remember to trust me, doll. You deserve good things," he whispers.

I furrow my brow as I try to work out what he means, but I don't have time for thinking then because Micah's fingers are roaming. He hitches one of my legs up higher around his waist before trailing cold, wet fingertips over the crease of my ass and finding my hole.

My breath stutters, because this is probably the most alien sensation I've ever experienced, but I focus on shoving all the big thoughts out of my head and letting him do whatever he's going to do. And fuck me, he does. Micah doesn't hesitate. He watches me intently the whole time, but I think something in him recognizes that the more space he gives me to freak out, the more likely it is that it'll happen.

I trust him.

Micah's fingers circle my hole briefly before pressing into it. Again, I feel like he's trying to overwhelm me with sensation so I can't think, and it's working. I can't think. All I can do is adjust to the vibrating need for *more* that's already kicking up in my chest, even while my nerve endings deal with the insane combination of *pleasure-pain-weird* that he's causing.

He gets one finger into me swiftly, making me gasp. It sends a tingling through my body everywhere, and I don't know if that's adrenaline or desperation or what, but I don't hate it.

Micah fucks me with that finger for a while as he goes

back to kissing me—big, messy, open-mouthed kisses that seem to hit me in every nerve-ending as well. Then he presses in a second finger. It burns as I adjust, but I'm used to pain. I can handle pain. It's pure and simple. What I can't handle is the confusing waves of something like pleasure that this is also bringing with it.

But not like the pleasure I've felt before. This is different. I'm used to pleasure that's sharp and focused, but slippery. It lives in a point in your body, and you have to grab onto it with both hands before it wiggles away and escapes.

This is a low thrumming glow that's setting up residence in every inch of my skin, spreading from where he's touching me outwards. It's making me tingle and quiver and look at the world in a hazy sort of way. Like I'm high or something. Not like after an orgasm, when you just feel relief. But like actual, genuine pleasure.

Then he touches something inside of me, and the hazy tingle turns electric. My legs jerk and my cock, which was interested, but still at half-mast, fills out. It's like a lightning bolt of something rolls through me, and Micah keeps doing it over and over until I'm writhing on the sheets and rocking my hips to try to keep his fingers as deep inside me as possible.

I don't think about what I look like. I don't think about what it means. I think about the fact that this is Micah, and this feels better than any way I've ever been touched.

"That's it, doll," he whispers. "Fuck, I thought you might be responsive, but this is something else." He reaches up with his other hand to brush some hair away from my sweaty forehead, and I can't help it when a whine slips out of me as his fingers stroke what must be my prostate again and again. "You're so fucking sensitive. Does that feel good?"

My thighs are fully quaking now, and my stomach is twisted in knots while my chest heaves. I don't think I can talk, but I lick my parched lips and look him in the eye when I nod.

"Perfect." His voice is practically a purr, and he's looking at me with this weird kind of warmth I've never seen before. "You're doing so well for me." He moves his free hand down my body, stopping briefly to pinch my nipple and rub at it gently, which also makes me fucking gasp with a sensation I've never experienced. "Such a good boy, Tadhg."

His words are surrounding me, filling me with just as much hazy pleasure as the way his gentle finger-fucking is lighting up my insides.

Micah leans down to cover me with his body, bracing himself on his other arm and finally slipping a third finger inside of me. I spread my legs as wide as I can and grab at his waist, trying to hold him as close to me as possible. To get him inside of me.

I don't understand what's happening. I don't know when everything changed. But if I let my brain shut down and just feel—the way he wants me to—then it all makes a lot more sense.

I'm making the most humiliating noises that have ever come out of my mouth, breathy and desperate, choked out in time with him fucking his fingers into me, but I can't help it. And every time he touches that spot, my whole body quivers.

Micah is breathing as heavily as I am, and he's grinding his hips down over where his hand breaches me, holding me so close that to someone else it would look like he was actually fucking me.

"You're so good," he whispers in my ear. "So perfect.

Just like this, spread out underneath me, getting fucked. A perfect fucking pussy."

The words hit me in the same spot as his fingers, and I feel my dick throb, desperate for release. Micah just keeps pumping into me at the same pace, though. He licks a long stripe up my neck before he continues to whisper the same things in my ear over and over again.

Gorgeous.
So fucking sensitive.
I knew you would be.
I knew you needed this.
My perfect doll.
I'll never make you fuck anybody ever again, you were meant to spread your legs for me.
Such a perfect little cunt.

My breath hitches, and everything in my body tightens. I need release more than I need fucking oxygen.

"Bambi," I say on an exhale, my voice barely-there but still so desperate. "Bambi, please."

He kisses me again, grinding his hips against me at the same time like before, my aching dick rubbing against his stomach where his shirt has rucked up.

Micah breaks the kiss but doesn't move his mouth away, so close that his lips brush mine when he speaks, his forehead resting against mine.

"You can do it, doll," he says, his hand moving faster as he fucks into me, still managing to hit that same spot over and over until white-out pleasure is threatening to burn through me. "Come for me. Be a good girl and come for me."

My body clenches around his hand, trapping him inside me, as I finally pull an orgasm from somewhere deep, deep inside me. It seems to hit me in slow motion, taking a lifetime to crest, but when it finally does, I can't even breathe. I think I can feel my cock pulsing cum over my bare stomach, but I don't care. The full-body sensation gripping me is so much *more* than whatever shitty, anxiety-ridden climax I've clawed my way to before.

It also takes forever to ebb. Like the tide going out, it seems to tug and flow out of my body a little at a time. I'm strung bow-tight, still clenching around Micah's fingers and gripping onto his sweaty, stretched-out t-shirt for dear life for what feels like hours. It's probably only seconds, but who cares.

My world just lurched off its axis.

When the last of the pleasure finally spills out of my body, I let out a trembling exhale and force my muscles to relax. Micah is watching me with a smile that I could only describe as *proud*, even though that seems weird in this context, and still holding me close.

I hiss when he slides his fingers out of me and have a brief moment of panic at the weird, dysfunctional emptiness it leaves behind. But then I shake it away and focus on the warmth in his gaze.

"Look at you," he says, with a weird hitch to his voice.

I don't know what to say. I don't know if I can form words now, anyway. Instead, a mewling noise slips out of me. His eyebrows raise, but then he chuckles.

He's careful to keep one hand rubbing gently up and down my flank while he leans away and clumsily wipes his fingers on a wet wipe he pulled from somewhere. As if I need a point of contact with him or I might float away.

Or maybe he needs the point of contact. I don't know. I'm buzzing too much right now to care.

Then he leans back over me and kisses me with the same hunger as before.

It only takes a second of me squeezing my thighs around his hips to remember that once again, he's still hard, because I'm fucking selfish. I break the kiss. I'm not sure what I'm supposed to do here, but I want to do something.

I reach for his crotch again, and he freezes. His hand comes to grab mine, and he looks at me with a tense expression.

"You don't have to."

I huff and find my voice. "I want to. Let me make you feel good, Bambi. Please."

Again, please is always the magic word. He softens and lets go of my hand. Then, as if he had to think about it, he rolls onto his back. Like he's giving me free rein.

I don't know what to do. But I know what I want.

I want to taste him.

I've never wanted to put my mouth on someone's junk in my life. I honestly thought it was something we were all just doing to each other out of politeness or obligation. But right now, with Micah staring at me through half-lidded eyes and his erection straining through the fabric of his sweats, I want nothing more than to know what his release tastes like on my tongue.

I know it would be the culmination of all this *something* that's been building and building around us since last night.

There's no sense in hesitating. I unceremoniously tug down his pants, freeing his cock abruptly enough that it slaps against his stomach. It's swollen and blush-red at the tip, with a long string of glistening precum drawn between the slit and the spot on his stomach it just touched.

I crawl forward and situate myself between his legs. He's watching me with a certain hesitance, but I don't let any of that in. Instead, I wrap my fingers around the base of his cock—way too long and thick for his lithe little body—and then slide the tip into my mouth.

I shove as much of it as I can in there. My mouth waters immediately, and I'm choking and gagging, but I don't quit. Because Micah—my Micah—is coming undone, cursing up a storm, his back bowing off the bed, his hands flying down to thread his fingers through my hair as he hisses *"Jesus fucking Christ, Tadhg"* and then moans.

There's not going to be any finesse here, so I just go for it. I'm relentless. I bob up and down on his dick, running my tongue along any part of it I can reach, tasting as much of him as I can. I let it hit the back of my throat over and over, filling the room with the sounds of my gagging and making Micah pull my hair and gasp every time.

"Fuck," he hisses. "I'm almost—"

But he's not almost, he's there. Barely a few minutes after I started my savage assault on his dick, it throbs in my mouth—which is a bizarre sensation that I don't totally hate—and then I'm choking on his cum as well as his cockhead.

It's a mess. There's spit and cum everywhere. I'm sure I'm bright red and there are tears running down my face, and I'm still a little shaky from whatever fucking ass-magic he pulled on me a few minutes ago.

But I don't care. Because not just seeing him come undone, but actually feeling it—under my hands, under my body, in my mouth—was incredible.

He's breathing hard, his hips still jerking a little and his hands still tugging at my hair.

"Mother fucking Mary, Tadhg. What the fuck?" he breathes before letting go of my hair and collapsing backwards on the bed.

I don't even try to hide the smile that takes over my face. That was one of the most satisfying things I've ever done.

Even if I know I have a complicated knot of feelings and circumstances to unknot about it later. Right now, I just want to bask in the good.

"Come here, doll," he says, making grabby hands at me until I move further up the bed. "Who's my good little cocksucker?" he murmurs before pulling me unceremoniously over his body with more strength than I give him credit for and immediately shoves his tongue in my disgusting, messy mouth.

There are fluids *everywhere*. Neither of us gives a fuck.

Everything feels too good right now to care.

We kiss for a long time like that—sticky and debauched. Until Micah finally grabs the meat of my ass and jiggles it so playfully that I can't help but smile, his face smiling back at me from only a few inches away.

I've never had this before. This weird bubble of something. Like we're the only two people in the world that exist.

Although that's not completely true, I guess.

"What?" he asks, reading the shift of my thoughts on my face.

"I was thinking about how this feels. It's like the rest of the world is some unreachable distance away, and the only thing that matters is us." Heat crawls up my cheeks, because I didn't intend for that to come out with quite so much brutal honesty, but it's too late to take it back now. "But that's probably what normal people feel when they're sleeping with someone, right? Except, the only thing it reminded me of is what it was like when we were kids, and we would be able to hide away together. The times when we knew Da was out and your mom was gone or in a good mood and we could just exist together for a while. That felt like this." *Safe.* But I can't bring myself to voice. "And I can't figure out if that's... fucked up or not, I guess."

Micah's lips part on the start of a vowel, but no sound comes out. He watches me for a moment, his eyes flicking back and forth to take in the different parts of my face like he's searching for something I'm not saying.

Then his hand cups my cheek, and his thumb strokes over the arch of my cheekbone, and I don't even bother to pretend I'm not pushing into the contact with a soft sigh.

His words are measured and careful when he finally replies.

"I think there are a lot of different kinds of intimacy, and some of them include sex and some of them don't." There's a pause, and it's weighty enough I know I'm not going to like whatever he says next. "It makes sense that when you have a fundamentally fucked-up relationship with intimacy and relationships—family relationships as well as sexual ones— it's normal for those lines to feel... blurred. Or confusing."

I wince, unable to stop myself. I already knew he saw me as a walking disaster because how could he not? But it still hurts to hear him say it.

"So, you think my dad beat the shit out of me instead of loving me and it fucked up my head so much I turned into some kind of incestuous freak?"

Micah's eyes widen for a second, then he huffs and rolls them—hard.

"So dramatic," he mutters under his breath before grabbing my face with his other hand and wiggling even closer to me on the bed. "No. Is that what I said? Because I think that's really fucking far from what I said, Tadhg."

His tone is snappy, but he pauses to take a deep breath, and I can see the way his eyes soften. There's tension running through every inch of me, but it still doesn't stop me from reaching for him, wrapping my hands around his warm, tight waist in the way I'm quickly becoming addicted to. I can't get my fingers all the way around him—he's slim but not that small—but I can hold enough of him that it feels anchoring.

"And I was talking about myself, as well as you," he continues. "We had shitty parents. It fucks you up. That's not rocket science. We were hurled together when we were little kids and had no one else to rely on, and it makes sense that we became a little codependent. It wasn't sexual, because we were kids, but I think in hindsight it also wasn't as familial as we maybe thought it was. It was just intense. Because it was all the intimacy we had going around. And now it's shifted. It's not *incestuous.*" He huffs again. "We're still not—nor have we ever been—actually related. And you're not a freak. You're damaged. So am I. It doesn't mean we don't deserve to figure our shit out and be happy."

The thought buoys something inside me, but it's tremulous and I know that if I look at it too long, it'll crumble under the inspection. So instead, I close the few inches between us and wrap my arms all the way around him, burying my face in his warm, solid chest and closing my eyes.

His hands come to my head on instinct, fingers threading through my hair and scratching gently at my scalp. I want to purr like a cat in a perfect sun spot, but I control myself.

"Honestly, Tadhg, I thought you'd be freaking out about the gay thing more than the stepbrother thing," Micah adds, and I *hatehatehate* the piece of wall that starts chipping away at in my mind.

I have no intention of dignifying it with a response, so I growl instead and concentrate on the important thing—planting wet, open-mouthed kisses over every piece of skin I can find on Micah's abdomen. He shucked his shirt at some point during our post-sex make out session, so I have plenty to work with, and I'm enthusiastic about exploring it all and turning the volume on my brain down to zero.

My cock is on board with this plan. I can already feel it thickening a little, and this is hands down more response than I've gotten from that little motherfucker since I went through puberty.

It figures that my cock would only be interested in whatever was the most inconvenient, weird situation I could put myself in. I couldn't get turned on by normal shit, of course not...

Thinking of this—of him—as 'not normal' is a kneejerk reflex, but something about it doesn't sit right with me. Even in the solitude of my own thoughts, it feels out of place. Like a crooked seam, or a shirt tag that's impossibly itchy.

That's another thing I can circle back to come to terms with *never*.

Micah lets out a breathless little giggle when I hit a particularly sensitive spot just above his hip bone. I can feel him getting hard too, but instead of escalating, he grabs at the broad expanse of my naked back and tugs like he's pulling me toward him.

"Come on, big guy. We should probably eat something and drink water and brush our teeth and all the other shit functional people do. Even if it is the middle of the night. We can go back to bed after we've peopled for a little while."

I groan but let him move me however he wants. I like how it feels.

Thirty minutes later, we're cleaned up, half-dressed and sitting in the living room with plates of eggs and sausages that I cooked, while Micah watched me as if this was some sort of a miracle.

"See, I'm not a completely incompetent person," I say around a mouthful of food, once we've started eating.

"Yes, dear." Micah pats me on the head as he says it, and I'm still a little offended by how clearly he doesn't believe me when I say I *can* function outside of the realm of gangster bullshit, but as soon as I started eating, I realized how fucking hungry I was and that became the priority.

I'm sitting on the floor in front of him, and he's got a leg slung over each of my shoulders, so at least he can't really see the way I inhale my food. I don't really know why I sat on the floor when we came in here. Micah didn't comment on it though. He just hooked his legs over me like a suit of armor, bracketing me in between him and the couch, and then used one hand to keep doing that absent scratching thing he keeps doing to my hair while he eats with the other.

My food disappears quickly, and the fullness lulls me into a hazy space of contentment. My mind drifts, and I let myself lean back against him while he picks at his meal. We don't really talk, but we don't need to. We talked a lot already, and I'm sure he's going to make us talk about all the other shit later.

Right now, it's nice to just *be*.

I'm so unnaturally calm that when someone knocks on the door, it takes four or five seconds for my body to react. But as soon as it snaps into focus, I fucking react.

It's the middle of the night. We're only awake because of how jacked the past twenty-four hours have been and the fact that we both work nights. No one could possibly be at the door right now for a normal reason.

I jump up, knocking my plate on the floor but deciding to worry about that later. Turning to Micah, I signal to him to go lock himself in the bedroom, but he rolls his eyes at me. Which was cute before, but it's so fucking far from cute right now.

Instead of listening to me, he runs his hands soothingly down my bare arms and makes a shushing noise, like I'm a child. It makes me bristle, and I feel myself rising up to my full height on instinct.

His eyes narrow, and I get a weird thrill of premonition that I'm going to pay for this later. But unlike every other time in my life when I've felt that way, this is something that I might actually enjoy.

But now's not the time. I shake the thought from my head and scramble for pants and a shirt, because we were both lounging around in boxers in the warm apartment. Micah follows me to the bedroom and also pulls on some clothes, but at a ridiculously slow pace.

"Calm down," he whispers. "It's probably just Tristan. He works nights, too. And I asked him to look into getting you some meds."

I freeze, one leg in some dirty jeans and one leg still bare. The implications of that are too much to process in this moment and fracture through my mind, a mixture of anxiety that Micah included more people in my shameful—and potentially lethal, if Father finds out and loses his shit—secret, but also warm that he would care enough to try and fix something that's patently unfixable.

"Stay here," I hiss before shoving my other leg into the jeans and zipping them up, following them with a t-shirt. It must be his, because it's way too fucking tight, but there's more pounding coming from the door, so I don't have time to find one of mine. At least I remember to snag my gun from where I left it in the bathroom before everything changed. Not my actual gun, of course, which has mysteriously disappeared, with Micah insisting he doesn't know anything about it. But *a* gun.

Of course, he trails me to the door. I put a hand on his chest, keeping him at arm's length as I look through the peephole and praying he's right, and it's his friend. I would even take Colm. Colm, by himself, would have the decency to not see whatever weird state the apartment and my face are probably in.

Jesus fucking Christ, do either of us have hickeys?

My stomach bottoms out, and I don't let myself think about that anymore because I have to open the door, no matter who is on the other side.

It's dark outside, so it takes me a minute for my eyes to come into focus. And another minute for my brain to catch up with what they're seeing. I'm standing frozen for long enough that Micah pushes me to the side and looks for himself, letting out a little gasp of shock before he recovers himself.

I don't know what expression I'm wearing, but I must look terrible, because he holds my gaze for just a second and mouths the word *breathe*.

Then he nods once, stiffly, like everything might be okay, and muscles me out of the way to open the door, adopting the stance I recognize as his no-bullshit posture.

"What the fuck do you want, Patrick?"

There's a faint growl from the other side of the door, and my stomach would bottom out if it had anywhere else to go.

"Let me in, boy, before I knock this door down. It took you long enough to answer, what the fuck were you doing?"

The door creaks open slowly, like something out of a horror movie, and Micah is forced to move back to accommodate it.

"It's 2am. Most people are asleep. I repeat, what do you want?"

Micah's arms are crossed over his chest and his chin is tilted up, but there's a very faint tremble to his voice that hopefully only I notice.

Then my father slips through the doorway, his eyes immediately locking on me and taking me in from head to toe. It's like being scanned by a Terminator. I don't know what he sees when he looks at me and I never have, but I have no doubt it's not good.

His face is completely neutral as he closes the door behind him and crosses his own arms.

"Ah. Savage, there you are. Just who I was looking for."

I swallow hard, because I don't know what else to say. Words left me a long time ago, and every inch of my skin that's visible to him feels like it's screaming loud enough to be heard over any words that might come out of my mouth, anyway.

The silence is awkward, and Micah keeps looking between us like he wants to diffuse it but doesn't know how. Finally, it's Father that speaks.

"Shall we?" He points to the couch where I was sitting —no, *snuggling*—with Micah just a few minutes ago, and my stomach turns.

"Sure." The sound squeezes through frozen vocal cords. "Sorry. Hello, Father. Please, come in."

Chapter Twenty-One

Micah

The tension in the room immediately ratchets up to something close to unbearable as soon as Patrick steps inside. Tadhg is watching him, keeping his body just out of arm's reach—out of habit, I assume—but with all of his focus trained on his father. His shoulders are back and his chest out, and I swear he's standing taller than normal.

Most people wouldn't be able to see through the act. I can, though. I can practically see the way his pulse is racing by the fluttering of his throat, and I know his eyes are just a little wider than they should be.

"How can we help you?" he asks his father, voice unnervingly level.

Once the door is shut behind him, Patrick swings his head from side to side to take us both in. I'm carefully standing on the opposite side of him to Tadhg. I'm pretty sure the thought that his precious little killing machine was bending over and taking it from any man would never occur to Patrick, even if he walked into the room *in medias res*. That's in an entirely different stratosphere from the things he considers possible.

However, I'm also sure it's the only thing that my brother—*shit, must stop thinking that, EX-stepbrother, maybe kinda sorta future boyfriend?*—is thinking about right now is what we just did. He's probably convinced Patrick can smell it on him. I do a quick visual scan of him and the apartment, and there's nothing screaming 'sex' that I can see. We just have to get through this conversation without anyone starting a fight or having a meltdown, and everything will be fine.

Tell that to my hands, though. While Tadhg's body is rock steady, honed from years of practice suppressing his fear and discomfort, I'm already a little shaky. I shove them in my pockets so Patrick doesn't notice.

The longer I spent time away from the man, the more he became the bogeyman in my mind. Something terrifying, but not a real threat, because he no longer existed in the safe, normal-ish life Mom and I built for ourselves here.

"I suppose it doesn't matter if he hears," Patrick says with a shrug, reminding me of what I'm supposed to be focusing on.

I can't stop myself from rolling my eyes at him, which he definitely sees. His eyes narrow in return, but he doesn't move otherwise. It takes all my self-control not to flinch away.

Well, I've never really been interested in playing happy housewife, but right now I think I can make an exception.

"Can I get you a beer, Patrick?" I force as much pleasantness into my voice as I can through half-frozen vocal cords.

He leans back a little, quirking his eyebrows at me, but then nods once without a word. It's a relief when I get to slip a little farther out of his circle of influence, although I keep my gaze trained on Tadhg the whole time. Obviously, it takes me longer than humanly possible to grab everyone a beer from my kitchen, which is about six feet away from where they take a seat on the couch.

They start muttering between themselves immediately. Tadhg is sitting on the couch in a mirror image of his father's posture now—legs spread wide with his elbows on his knees, taking up a disproportionate amount of space. It seems so unlike the tender version of him I've been getting to know that it makes my stomach churn for a second.

Their voices are low, but I hear a few snippets of what's being said. Enough to pick up that Tadhg's blissful vacation from his work appears to be over. It hits me all at once that we'd both been fooling ourselves into thinking we could keep doing what we were doing and he'd just... drift away from the Banna in peace.

Fuck.

As I walk back, three open longnecks dangling between the fingers of my left hand, I must be too quiet, because Patrick keeps talking as if I'm out of earshot.

"—no way that body should have ended up in the hospital. Anyone could have taken care of it. And Colm told me Eamon *volunteered* to do it. I don't trust that shifty little queer, and he clearly has his eye on your job. Did you leave evidence on that Nazi fuck when you offed him?"

Tadhg can see me out of the corner of his eye, but he's careful not to look at me.

"Everything's fine, Father. I can take care of it," he says, more loudly than he needs to.

I take the opportunity to make some shuffling noises before I approach and put the beers in front of everyone.

Patrick takes his, doing a double-take as if he'd already forgotten I was there. In fact, he looks pretty ragged. He's not getting any younger, I guess, and running this kind of operation has to take a toll on you in the long run.

Good. I hope he has a heart attack, and we can escape this situation painlessly.

"Well. I want him out. He's a piece of shit, and I don't like the way he parades around that recruit he's sticking it to, as if it's something to be proud of. The kid doesn't even look like his balls have dropped yet. And if Eamon's dicking around acting like a fag and a pervert, it reflects on all of us." Patrick takes a sip of his beer and then looks at me out of the corner of his eye. "No offense."

"Now why would that possibly be considered offensive?" I drawl, making Tadhg's grip on his bottle tighten, but we all mutually seem to drop the issue before it gets out of hand.

Patrick shifts topic. He keeps ignoring me and talking to Tadhg—or *Savage*, like they all call him. And fuck, I'm really coming to hate when people call him that, especially his own goddamn father, as if Tadhg isn't dehumanized enough already. Patrick doesn't seem bothered by the fact that I'm sitting here, but he's also speaking in some kind of shorthand, so I only understand bits and pieces of what they're talking about.

Not that I care. I would never turn him in for anything, because it would inevitably come back on Tadhg. That's not my game plan here.

But what is my game plan?

What's realistically possible? That I keep looking the other way over all this shit until I eventually get in too deep and lose my nursing license over something? Or see the wrong thing, and Patrick kills me and my mom in retribution?

The thought makes me shudder. I'm still not close with my mom because there's a lot of trauma-water under that bridge, but I don't want her to die because of where I stuck my dick. Or where she let Patrick stick his.

Goddamn. Like mother, like son, I guess.

My mind is a runaway train, careening over rickety tracks, powered by all the thoughts I've refused to acknowledge until now. I don't even realize it's showing on my face until I catch Tadhg looking at me from the corner of his eye with a frown.

His fingers twitch, like an aborted attempt to reach for me. That's the thing that makes my heart crack open and start leaking black ooze all over the floor.

Because as impossible as it seems to help him escape this stupid shitty life he's trapped in, it seems even more impossible to abandon him in it.

"Okay. Thank you, Father."

I don't know what Tadhg is thanking him for, but his tone has a note of finality. I put down my untouched beer and stand up when they do.

We all go through the motions of saying goodbye, even though I'm in a daze, still lost in my own thoughts. Patrick turns toward me at the door for a moment, and I almost think he's going to hurt me. The scared child inside of me shrinks away, which pisses me off. I think I end up giving him a look that's half-defiance, half-discomfort.

Whatever it is, he looks awkward for a second. Who

knows? Maybe he was going to pat me on the head or something, like a pet.

Instead, he nods at Tadhg one more time before disappearing back into the night, leaving a gaping chasm of anxiety behind him.

𝔖𝔞𝔳𝔞𝔤𝔢

The air in the room is stifling, even after Father leaves. Micah and I orbit each other at a distance. Neither of us seems willing to go far, but we're also unwilling to reach for each other either.

I'm not sure what any of this means. Half my brain is slipping right back into work mode, calculating what to do next.

Eamon volunteered to dispose of the body and it turned up at a hospital, when I'm the person most likely to have evidence trace back to. Eamon clearly wants my job. If he did this on purpose, it means he isn't above fucking over the Banna to be king of the ashes.

None of this surprises me, because I wouldn't put anything out of reach for him, but it is a problem.

Eamon is a problem. One which Father will expect me to eliminate.

Normally, I wouldn't bat an eye. For once, I'd actually enjoy being sent on this particular murder mission. But while I had thought Micah was able to ignore the gaping stretch of time between now and when we last saw each other, including everything he probably knows I did in between, things are different now. I feel more dependent on him by the minute.

How can I expect him to keep looking at me and touching me the way he did last night if he's forced to confront just how disgusting I really am? How much has to happen before he starts to look at me with fear?

The thought sends a shiver running through me.

When I glance around to find Micah, he's farther away from me than I'd thought. He's in the kitchen, leaning against the counter, still holding a beer that I don't think he's really drinking and staring into space.

Even from this distance, my fingers are itching to reach for him. I've always had the urge to keep him close, and unlocking all the new ways of touching each other is only making the feeling more intense. But the expression on his face is melancholy. I can't tell if he'd even want me to touch him right now, and the thought of his rejection is even worse than just keeping my distance.

I must stare at him too long, though. Eventually he looks up at me, giving me a wan smile and finally taking a sip of his beer. It's only when he tosses his head at me that I obey and cross the distance to the kitchen.

Once I'm standing next to him, I still resist the urge to reach out and touch. But being closer means I can see him more clearly. Including the fact that his hands are shaking. Personally, I've dissolved into a pile of uselessness on the floor here more times than I can count, but seeing Micah unnerved is unnatural. At least, seeing the confident, adult version of him like this.

"What's wrong?" I ask.

Micah shakes his head and gives me a pissy look. "Nothing. I'm being dumb."

But the shaking doesn't stop.

"He's not going to hurt you."

Now that earns me a really pissy look.

"You know that's not true. He could hurt either of us any time he wants. He could make you do anything he wants, no matter how fucked up it is, and then at the last minute tell you 'congratulations, you finally won your freedom' before shooting you in the head like we're all living in an HBO series. He's capable of anything and the only thing he cares about is his own power."

I blink for a second, because that's a vivid and unnerving image.

"Honestly, Bambi, I don't think he's that clever."

Micah snorts, but there's no humor in it. "Yeah, well. Every scenario I play out keeps ending the same way. And I don't like it."

Sighing, I have to shut my eyes for a second because I can't look at him while I say this. "Do you want me to leave? I know—I know everything keeps changing with us. But I don't want to fuck up your life and put you in danger. I can go. Try to get out, maybe come back one day when I think it's safe."

Micah's eyes are wide, and his lips are parted when I finally look at him again.

"Don't you fucking dare," he breathes. Then—finally— his hands are on me. Gentle arms circle my waist and pull me closer to him until we're chest to chest, just like before. "Whatever half-assed plans you have about nobly sacrificing yourself or making up your own HBO drama can also get flushed down the fucking toilet, Tadhg. I'll make a plan. *We'll* make a plan. I just need a minute to think."

Then he lets out a long, shuddering exhale before shoving his face into my chest. I hug him back, holding him closer to me. It feels weird and not weird at the same time. Like our dynamic is constantly shifting. I always used to be the rescuer, now it's him, but then he acts like this, and I feel like we're little kids again. He's that small, fragile thing that I'm desperate to protect.

Am I the strong one or the weak one? Are we family or sexual?

Or are all of those words meaningless, and I'm wasting my time trying to decide?

I try to ignore the cascade of questions in my head and focus on the feel and smell of him while he gradually settles into my arms.

"Do you wanna sleep?" I ask, once we've been awkwardly huddled here for a while.

Micah takes another deep breath before leaning back. He keeps a tight hold of me but creates enough space so he can look me in the eye. There's a spark of something there, and I'm trying to place his expression when he leans in and kisses me.

Not like family.

Like someone desperate. It goes on and on until there are exactly zero thoughts left in my head other than how warm he is and how everything tastes like the two of us mingled together. When he breaks away, I chase his lips for more without thinking, my cock half-hard again and pressed against his thigh.

"What was that for?" I try not to sound too breathy when I ask, but I don't think that I'm successful.

Micah hesitates for a few seconds, which is also unlike him and makes me tilt my head to get a better look at him while I wait for an answer.

"Tadhg, can I fuck you?"

That is not what I was expecting.

Is this... Does this make me something? Something different than what I already am?

Fuck it. It's not like I didn't hate myself before. Maybe whatever this turns me into will be better.

I nod, because I can't find my words right now.

"Are you sure?" His hands are steady now as he reaches for my face in that way I've already come to love. "We can wait, if you're not ready. Or if you never want to. It's all okay."

"Do it. I want to." I choke the words out, filled with an overwhelming need that I can't possibly give voice to. Father showing up has made me more aware than ever that whatever is happening between us, it won't last. I'm not that lucky. I don't have time to nurse my fears and inhibitions. If I want to experience Micah before I die, I'll never know when my last chance might be, so it might as well be tonight. "Please, Bambi. Do it."

"Do you wanna talk about it first?"

I shake my head, which makes Micah frown, but apparently, he's also too tired and emotional to do more talking right now.

A tentative but irrepressible smile begins to spread across my face, because I know that no matter what, I'll get to have this at least once. As soon as he sees it, it spreads to his as well. And even though we don't move from our position, it feels like something *shifts*. Like all that tension from before is retreating, following Father on his way out of the apartment and sealing us back up in the same bubble we were building before he showed up.

Chapter Twenty-Two

Micah

I need this. But it's more than that, I think he needs this, too. It's irresponsible, and maybe I'm fooling myself. How well can I really know him when we've spent so much time apart?

But every inch of me is rooted in the belief that whenever Tadhg seems like he's about to float away, out of my reach, the best way to bring him back to Earth is by overwhelming him with the intensity of how much I want him. He scared me when he offered to leave. I wouldn't put it past him.

Even though he kept a calm, detached demeanor while he said the words, I could see his anxiety crawling just beneath the surface. He doesn't want to run from me, but he'll do it if he thinks I'm in danger. And I wouldn't put it past that reactionary brain of his to get too worked up over something small and then steal away in the middle of the night.

I do not want to have to track him down. I'm not built for those specific kinds of shenanigans. And I would absolutely stick out in a biker bar.

This is a much better alternative. Maybe it's too soon to crank the sex lever all the way up to eleven, but it feels right. I want to use any tool I have to burn away the threats of reality that are creeping in to haunt us. I want to devour him. To tear him apart, limb by limb, and then rebuild him so he's marked with me, inside and out.

I'll show him that he absolutely, incontrovertibly belongs to me, and anyone who wants to take him away will have to pry him out of my cold, dead hands.

Including his own self-sabotaging brain.

Savage

The floor is cold and unforgiving under my knees. My shoulders strain with my hands tied behind my back with some fancy silk rope that Bambi produced from somewhere, and it's taking constant micro-adjustments of all my muscles to keep myself from falling over. It's just uncomfortable enough to keep me in a state of constant red alert, and I can already feel the adrenaline flushing through me in a way that feels almost cleansing.

The edges of the world feel softer and at the center of everything is Micah in sharp, high-def focus. He's towering over me, looking ten feet tall from this angle and making me feel impossibly small and weak.

He puts one foot on my shoulder and looks down at me

with a dark expression. My body is threatening to rebel; every inch of me having been conditioned to escape this exact situation at all costs.

"I like you all trussed up and presented for me, doll, I can't lie." His voice seems deep and booming from overhead. "What do you say? Do you want me to fuck you?"

I do. I really do. Despite all the conflicting feelings this situation is giving me, I can already feel my hole clenching around nothing, wishing he would cut the theatrics and get inside me where he belongs. I only had a taste of it before, but I know I need more. I need *him*.

My cock is hard and straining, desperate to come from the way he's been edging me off and on for god knows how long already, a steady stream of precum making my balls and thighs a slick, warm mess.

I nod, looking up at him with pleading eyes.

"Use your words, doll."

"Fuck me, please, Micah." I hate how desperate my voice sounds, but there's no denying my desperation now. This should all feel difficult. This should feel anathema to everything I've ever been or pretended to be for the life I've lived until this point.

Instead, kneeling in front of Micah, begging to be used for the first time... it feels like slipping into the most comfortable skin I have.

It feels real.

We've spent maybe hours working up to this, as he slowly gave me more and more of himself with teasing, gentle touches. I was surprised to only feel a flicker of nervousness at the beginning before my body was all in. Something about surrounding myself with him makes all the bigger questions about what it means and who I'm supposed to be completely irrelevant, until it's just *"yes"* and *"more"* and *"please"* and *"yours"*.

He *talks* slowly at me, still looking like he has all the patience in the world despite the obvious bulge in his own pants, and reaches down to gently swipe the hair back from my sweaty forehead. I try not to lean into the touch like a needy creature, but I don't think I succeed.

"That's not what I want you to tell me, and you know it. I don't fuck brats or boys who think they're tough shit. I want to fuck that perfect, slutty hole of yours and remind you who you belong to."

My stomach twists. He leans over me, his shadow falling across my face, and for a split-second the image intersects with a sense-memory of how Dad used to do the same thing, leaning over me whenever he came to drag me out of the closet that Micah and I would hide from him in.

The two conflicting images twist and warp inside me, making my pulse skyrocket and my body tremble like it can't decide whether it wants to get fucked or flee. Neither can my brain, for that matter.

It feels like the world is suddenly underwater, and I have to drag my eyeballs up to look at Micah when his voice eventually penetrates the watery haze surrounding me.

His forehead is creased, and the hunger in his eyes has been replaced with that sharp analytical expression I always think of as his medicine face. Where I can tell he's calculating something. The hand that was just touching my hair moves down, even more slowly and gently than before, and takes hold of my chin while his thumb sweeps oh-so-lightly over my cheekbone, making me shiver in its wake.

Please don't ask me what's wrong.

I know he can sense something shifted, because a fine tremor has taken over every part of my body apart from my dick, which is still hard and needy and desperate to finally be allowed to come.

Finally, he speaks, his words so soft they graze against the surface of my mind like feathers falling from overhead.

"Tell me what you are, doll."

I tremble harder. The shame and confusion fight for dominance, but the desire to sink boneless into his arms is there as well.

"I'm—" My shaky voice cracks, and I have to clear my throat. "I'm a slutty hole."

Tadhg Moynihan, the Savage of the Brotherhood, bound and naked and hard on his knees, admitting to being nothing more than his stepbrother's slutty hole to use and discard.

Micah shakes his head, his frown deepening as his grip on my chin gets more firm.

"That's not what I said, doll. I said you're a *perfect* slutty hole. Not just that, you're *my* perfect slutty hole, and I'm always going to take care of you."

As he talks, he crouches in front of me so he isn't looming so large, and something inside me unkinks, letting my breath come a little easier. Micah slips his thumb from my chin up to my bottom lip, pressing into it, then sinking past it into my mouth. The warm, firm pad of his thumb glides over my tongue, and I wrap my lips around him and suck on instinct.

My eyes fall closed on their own, and I sink into the sensation. I'm still trembling, but that flash of fear is retreating, being overtaken by my sheer need.

I'm his. I'm *perfect*. The thought is confusing, but if I allow myself not to question it, it fills me with an easy warmth.

The fingers of his other hand find my nipple, tugging

and twisting hard enough to remind me how desperate I am for release. Fresh pre-cum slides down my shaft as he pulls hard on my nipple, stretching it out, then finally releases it so the blood floods back in like a slap.

He moves on to groping my pec, working and squeezing the muscle there while I continue to suckle on his thumb.

"Such perfect tits," he murmurs, and I melt a little under the praise.

He pulls his thumb out of my mouth, and I chase it with a whine, but it's quickly replaced by his two fingers. They aren't gentle this time, immediately pushing far back into my mouth, making me gag and my mouth water. He watches me with unashamed desire as I choke and spit runs down my chin.

"That's it, doll. Get them nice and wet for me," he murmurs as he finger-fucks my throat.

Still abusing my tits with his other hand, Micah withdraws the fingers. I'm desperate for him to finally touch my aching cock, but he denies me my release. Instead, he shuffles closer until he's straddling my thighs, his clothed body practically wrapped around my naked and bound one.

"I'll always take care of you," he whispers in my ear, his breath hot, as his fingers find my crease. Wet with my saliva, he drags them over it. My gut clenches, breath catching, and I feel like my spine is being twisted from inside. My body wants to pretzel itself in some way, it can't figure out what to do with all the sensations I'm getting.

Pleasure-pain is still throbbing out from my nipple as he abuses it, while my cock waves proudly in the air, so close to his stomach I can practically picture him leaning forward enough to graze it. I feel like just a hint of friction is all I need. My balls are heavy and tight, close to my body, more desperate to unload than I've ever been in my life, even though I came just a few hours ago.

I don't realize tears are running down my face until he shushes me.

His slick fingers rub over my hole again. Every inch of me feels like a live wire and I'm shaking worse than before, my body racked with shivers as he cages me in. My hole clenches, desperate for him to push in, but he keeps teasing me with fluttery touches.

I feel like I could choke on the desperation rising in my throat. Guttural, animal noises are being wrung from me, something between a moan and a sob.

"That's it, doll. All you have to do is kneel. You're already perfect for me, just as you are. You don't need to do anything but let me take care of you like you deserve."

Something about the honeyed voice he's using seems to carry those words directly into my soul. Without warning, he pushes his fingers into me, with an aching stretch and a pressure building at the base of my spine. He keeps shushing me while he moves his hands—one fucking me while the other twists my nipple—and everything in my body finally locks up.

This time, I do sob—a single, full body sob that bends me over at the waist—and as my muscles clench and strain, the pleasure builds as well and my cock finally unleashes everything that it's been holding back.

Cum spills out like someone opened a floodgate. My entire body is stiff and shaking as I soak my lap, my cock flexing in the air.

The feeling is such a profound release, that single sob trails off into a pathetic kind of wail.

Micah makes more gentle shushing sounds and holds me closer to him. When I feel him grab my throbbing cock I jump, overstimulated, but then he jerks me hard and fast and drags the trailing end of the orgasm out for even longer. Even when I'm spent and his rough hand hurts, he continues while I writhe in his grip, but something about it feels like another form of release.

After being so needy for so long, everything is overwhelming and I never want it to stop: both pleasure and pain.

When the feeling tips firmly into pain, my cock red raw and throbbing sensitively, I start to sob in earnest. I realize I'm saying the word "please" over and over, in between clumsily mouthing at his mouth, and Micah gradually slows his hand.

"No!" I wail. "Don't stop."

"Shh, that's enough now, doll," he says, holding me close. The fight goes out of me, a little at a time, and I sag into my restraints, letting Micah hold me up.

My mind drifts while he unties me. I don't know how much time passes, only that my wrists throb a little while he rubs the sensation back into them. When I'm eventually free, he rolls me over onto my front. I feel untethered for a brief moment of panic until he drapes his body over mine. He took his clothes off at some point, and it's all warm skin on skin.

I feel content as wet fingers slowly push into my hole, stretching me until I'm ready. He's gentle at first, but once his cock sinks into me, he presses my face into the tile and snaps his hips hard enough to jolt my body forward an inch.

At some point through all this I got hard again. Or it's possible I'm so desperate from the edging that it never really went down. Either way, my hard cock smears precum across the tile while Micah tries his best to fuck me through it.

"This pussy was made for my cock," he whispers. "I want to keep you tied up all the time. Breed you so much you're dripping with my cum twenty-four hours a day, sopping wet with it. I want people to smell me on you."

He digs his fingers hard enough into my pecs—tits—to leave bruises and then twist my nipple again until he pulls a scream out of me, joining the slapping sound of flesh on flesh as he drills into me.

"You're my little slut, right, doll?"

I sob out a sound close enough to a yes, desperate for him to fill me up.

"That's right, baby. My beautiful, perfect breeding bitch."

With that, he pulls out. Instead of me partially on my side, he pushes me so I'm completely prone, my face smashed into the tile, and spreads my legs as wide as they can go. My hard dick is trapped beneath my body, and I feel more exposed than ever before.

Kneeling between my spread thighs, Micah takes a minute to admire the view. His fingers drag over my slick crack first, spreading my cheeks, then both of his thumbs slip into my stretched and sloppy hole to tug it as wide as he can. I squirm, the sensation on the perfect knife-edge of that pleasure-pain that he gives me so well, and then I hear the sound of him spitting and feel wetness landing *inside* me.

Something about that feels like a more profound sense of ownership than anything that's happened until this point. I shiver and go even more boneless in his hands than before.

"Perfect," he whispers again, tugging one more time at my rim to see me gaping open for him.

There's a sharp crack that splits the air, and a second later I feel the pain of where he brought the flat of his hand down on my exposed hole. Every muscle in my body clenches and I almost have a repeat of before and come from the sharp, harsh pain. But not quite.

Moaning and writhing on the floor like a lost, feckless creature, Micah doesn't give me the chance to recover as he grabs my hips and thrusts his cock back into me. With one hand on the small of my back pushing me hard into the ground and the other digging more bruises into my hip, he pounds me brutally for a few minutes until he finally stiffens and cries out, pulsing his release deep, deep inside of me.

I clench around him, milking as much as I can. He doesn't stop there, though. As soon as he pulls out, he braces my thighs where they are, and I can feel him bring his face close to my hole.

"Push it out." His voice is dangerous.

I do as he says, and there's a soft moan while he watches his own cum seep from my hole and trail down my taint, dripping to the floor.

My hips are rocking in the air as I do it, already desperate for another release. Micah doesn't make me wait this time, though. He attacks my ass, licking and sucking his release out of me with an aggression that makes me cry out. My hips buck, but he hangs on and digs his tongue into my hole like he's desperate to excavate me.

"Oh, oh, oh, oh — Oh!" is the most articulate noise I can make.

His face is still buried in the center of me when I come again this time, spilling myself onto the floor underneath me one more time, my hips bucking into nothingness before I eventually drain myself completely and collapse in the mess.

Everything hurts. Every inch of my body is screaming, but it's a cleansing kind of pain. I've experienced so many different kinds of pain in my life, but nothing like this. I've never come this hard or this many times or even had the urge.

I'd let him do anything he wanted to me. He can rub raw any inch of my skin and tear open any hole, because the sheer, relieved bliss that's sitting at the deep, dark center of all this pain is fucking indescribable, and it's all because of him.

Micah

"How do you feel?"

Tadhg has been lying on the kitchen floor with me, covering my sticky, sweaty skin with his for a long time. We should probably get up and move, but I don't want to. I think I can see the first tendrils of dawn light creeping around the curtains, but I don't care about that either.

The only thing I care about is right in front of me. I'm scared I went too far. I'm scared about how far I wanted to go and how fucking desperate I was for it as soon as we started. Just as desperate as he seemed to be, bucking and writhing and begging for more.

Tadhg doesn't answer. I feel him shrug, but no words come out of his mouth and his face stays pressed against my skin, where he's been alternating between nosing and biting along my chest and armpit since we collapsed here. His body looks bruised and scratched, but his face is soft, at least. There's none of the blankness he gets when he's dissociating, or the maudlin weight of his depression that so often creeps in.

Just because he looks content though, doesn't mean I'm

not worried we just crossed a line. Or a thousand of them. Maybe all the lines.

"Words, doll. Use your words." I know I'm repeating myself with this, but it's become very obvious that my dearest stepbrother is a natural and seems to slip into subspace as soon as I let him.

"'M fine. Sleepy."

Close enough.

"That was okay, though? I know I can get a little carried away sometimes."

"Mmm." There's a pause, and then he finally does peek out enough to look at me. "I think I needed it. It felt... right. Good. Pure."

I blink. I wasn't expecting him to say that, but it is kind of a relief. He goes back to his work, while I trace nonsense patterns up and down all the swells of muscle on his ridiculously thick arm, and we both continue to drift back to a more normal version of reality.

Eventually, I can't keep quiet anymore. There's a question that's been burning a hole in my brain for a long time, and it seems like this soft, post-orgasmic time is as good a time to ask it as any.

"Tadhg, are you gay?"

That makes him freeze. But he looks up at me again instead of freaking out and running away, at least.

"I, um," he starts, stumbling a little over his words. "I don't know. I don't really know what that's supposed to feel like."

I have to suppress a laugh. "It feels like when you like dick. It's not that complicated." Shit. *Empathy, Micah.* Not cool. I spent so long honing my defense mechanism sass that sometimes it still comes out in really inappropriate moments, and I hate that about myself. "Sorry, it is complicated.

There's lots of places to fall on the spectrum. You don't have to give me a yes or no. There's no wrong answer. I just wanted to see how you felt."

"I never really wanted to fuck anyone, to be honest," he continues. "The whole thing seemed stressful. Like some kind of test that you can never pass. But you had to do it anyway. I don't know what that means. Like you said, I'm fucked in the head."

"I didn't say that, dick. I said you had trauma. I have trauma. *We* have trauma. It's not the same. You're allowed to not know how you really feel when it's buried under all this other shit. I shouldn't push."

For a second, I wonder if the atmosphere is about to turn. Like I managed to not cross any invisible lines with the incredibly shithot, kinky sex we just had, but I did with one dumb, insensitive question. But he keeps looking at me, and a smile steadily grows on his face.

"I like your dick, Bambi. Does that count?"

I smile back. "It's the only thing that counts, doll."

It isn't too far to stretch, so I reach down and grab a generous handful of his bare ass as it's presented up to the world. His crease is still slick with lube and cum, so I let my fingertips slip and slide as I do it. Playful, though, not to go anywhere.

Tadhg gasps anyway, his pupils dilating before my very eyes.

I lean in until I'm almost brushing up against his lips with mine, still holding eye contact even though we're too close to focus properly. While I speak, I jiggle the piece of him that I'm holding on to.

"And I love this pussy, doll. Along with everything it's connected to."

I kiss him, so he doesn't have to find words to answer

me. We'll go to bed eventually. Right now, I feel like I need more of this. I need to feel like it's solid, and no one can take it away, before I'll be ready to face the real world again.

Chapter Twenty-Three

Savage

For the next few days, everything feels frozen. I don't want to move or breathe too loudly, like it might bring more of Father's attention down on us. I'm following his orders. With the help of Colm and some of our trusted guys, we're trying to figure out just what Eamon's intentions are, and how far he's willing to fuck the Banna over to accomplish them.

But we're doing it quietly, because the last thing I want right now is a gunfight. My father favors speed over a light touch, but I'm hoping that with this one, I can get by.

Plus, the less time I spend neck-deep in Banna bullshit, the more time I have to spend with Micah. I'm still convinced that this is all going to be whipped away from me at a moment's notice. I want to take advantage of whatever time I have with him, and I'm more than happy to let him pretzel my body in any way he wants in the name of this intense new intimacy between us.

Until we inevitably get interrupted. Although tonight, of all nights, I'm happy to be interrupted, because Micah's been probing me with questions about my mental health for barely fifteen minutes and I'm ready to flee the premises.

I agreed to answer his questions because he asked, and I'm incapable of saying no to him, apparently. He asked me if I got a diagnosis, and I told him. Persistent Depressive Disorder, PTSD, and a plus-minus on something called Avoidant Personality Disorder because apparently you can't effectively apply diagnostic criteria to people who torture others under threat of their own death for a living.

My actual willingness to engage or not engage in social situations is hard to gauge, apparently.

Micah snorted when I relayed this to him, although most of it was verbatim from the shrink, apart from the torturing part. That slipped out by accident, and it's clear we're both making a very conscious effort to pretend it didn't.

He changed the subject to my meds, and when I could only remember the name of one of them, he pulled up about a thousand different pictures and names of pills on his iPad until I was able to remember the other and scrape the dosages from the recesses of my memory.

The whole conversation has been fucking exhausting, and completely pointless. It's also left me feeling more exposed in front of Micah than I would if he were literally staring at my asshole. Which isn't something I ever thought I'd have to weigh, but it's true.

"Why are we still talking about this?" I snapped at him, my anger threatening to boil over.

Micah has just looked at me, cool as ever. "Why are you so unwilling to let me help you?"

That's when the phone call came, and I've never been more grateful for an interruption in my life. Now it's four hours later, we're alone in the car again and I'm trying to think of what I want to think about less: my fucking mental health, or the shit we've just seen in Gunnar's apartment.

"How did he look?"

I don't bother to turn on the engine while I wait for Micah to answer. I think we could both stand to sit in this car in the Feral Possum parking lot for a few minutes of darkness and peace before we worry about heading home.

Not that I'm some wilting flower. I've literally eviscerated men. When I got called to my boss' apartment for a late-night 911 assist, I expected violence. When he asked me specifically to bring Micah, I expected maybe the aftermath of violence. An ER nurse is always useful in those situations.

And it was the aftermath of violence. Just not quite in the way I was expecting.

Tobias—the baby-faced Banna recruit that Eamon has been 'sticking it to', as Father put it—showed up on Gunnar's doorstep in the middle of the night, beaten half to death and showing signs of chronic physical and sexual abuse. It's not a surprise. I know Eamon, I know men like Eamon, and I saw the way he treated that kid like his personal property the one and only time we met at the bar.

The fact that Tobias had the balls to run surprises me more. Good for him. And to run to Gunnar—who actually wants to help and seems like a decent fucking human being from the limited time I've spent around him—is even more surprising. When you're beaten down for that long, it can become an instinct to run from one shitty situation into another equally shitty one. Anything else seems inconceivable, and therefore not to be trusted.

I should know. I've spent my life cowering in the belly of one monstrosity after another.

Tobias looks so small and fragile from the outside, especially right now that he's a walking bruise, but I can't imagine how he scraped together the willpower to actually do it. There's always an open window somewhere. Forcing yourself to go through it is the hard part.

Maybe that's why I'm still reeling with shock at the evidence of just how Eamon's been tearing him apart, even though I'm so accustomed to violence.

Or maybe I'm just jealous that he managed to do something I never did at his age, when Father was still laying into me regularly for failing to live up to his expectations, but I no longer had the excuse of protecting Micah to hang around for.

"Tadhg?"

Bambi's voice cuts through the thought and I turn to see him watching me from the passenger seat, his eyes shining in the soft moonlight.

"Yeah?"

"You asked how he looked, and I said I've seen worse, but he's still pretty messed up. Then you didn't reply. Where did you go just now?"

I shake my head, trying to physically banish all the memories that were threatening to creep in.

"Nowhere." There's a pause while neither of us speaks, but I still don't turn the engine over. "I feel bad. I wish we could help him more."

Micah tilts his head to the side, like he's taking me in from a different angle.

"Me too," he says, his voice gentle. After a second, he

slips his hand over the center console in the darkness and laces his fingers through mine, settling something inside me. "We'll do what we can. He'll heal on the outside. Gunnar can probably help him make a plan. I don't know him very well, but he seems like the kind of person who will immediately get over-invested in the situation. At the end of the day, he has to choose to not go back, though. That's the hard part. Especially if no one can fix whatever circumstances drove him to the Banna in the first place."

Micah's words echo what I was just thinking about, but I can't help but feel like choosing to say "the Banna" instead of "Eamon" was deliberate here. Like Micah is trying to draw parallels for me that my mind has already etched out in neon lights, thank you very much.

I'm already aware that this college-aged kid has made more significant steps toward securing his freedom than I have, with a lot less fucking help and in the face of much more intense obstacles. I get that.

Pointing out what a coward I am is redundant, at this point.

I don't say that to Micah, though. I can't find the words and the thought of fighting about it exhausts me to my core. The thought of not fighting about it and listening to him placate me with random gibberish about me being strong or good or whatever he can pull out of his ass exhausts me even more.

Instead, I grunt my acknowledgement, hoping that he'll drop it, and put my eyes on the parking lot, pulling my hand from his. If I focus on driving us home, we can cut this conversation off at the knees before it even gets started.

And if there is a god, then as soon as we get home, I'll be able to get some fucking sleep. Because right now, that's the only thing that I can think about without wanting to crawl out of my skin.

Micah's eyes are on me for the entire drive. I can feel them. This fervent gaze that's poking at me, trying to peel back the corners of my skin. But my skin is heavy, stiff with anger and hatred and misery, so he can't get any purchase on it. We continue to ride in silence, letting the inevitable misery of our future spread out in front of us like hot asphalt.

Micah

There's something wrong with Tadhg.

That seems to be how a lot of my thoughts start, these days.

Tadhg, Tadhg, Tadhg.

Maybe I should resent it for him, but I can't bring myself to. It feels too important. Like taking care of him is as much of an intrinsic part of me as his need to be taken care of is a part of him. So, I let my mind spin out the whole way home on all the different things that might be upsetting him.

Seeing Tobias was rough. He was torn up, for sure, even if he was putting on a brave face. I examine SA victims regularly as part of my job, and I've seen a wide range of hurt. Sometimes it's more obvious on the outside, sometimes the inside, sometimes both. Tobias was carrying a weight of pain, that's indisputable.

But I felt okay leaving him with Gunnar. The man has a savior-complex the size of Texas, but his heart is in the right place and frankly, my rescuing plate is full.

Because my stupid, insular brother won't tell me what's bothering him. Ever.

As soon as we get home, he mutters something at me and heads to the shower. I don't want to jump him while he's feeling off, but it seems like his walls are always down the most during sex, so I might as well try my luck and see if he's feeling it.

Sometimes he's keeping quiet because he doesn't want to talk, but most of the time it's because he wants me to drag it out of him. And the easiest way to do that seems to be with some rough touch, some gentle touch, and a lot of dirty talk.

Barely a few minutes pass between when I step into the steam-filled bathroom and when I get Tadhg facing the shower wall, leaning his face into his arms to muffle his grunts and curses as I kneel behind him and eat his ass.

With the way his body is trembling and writhing under the attention, you'd think he'd never experienced sexual pleasure before. But then again, I really don't think he had. I still don't totally understand how his brain works when it comes to attraction and how he identifies, but I'm not going to push him to figure it out. He doesn't need a label unless he wants one.

The important thing is that I'm the only one who's able to make him moan like this.

"Please, Bambi," he groans, when my hand wraps around his cock and balls.

He's mostly soft, because he struggles to get hard more often than not. But that just means I fondle him in my hand instead of stroking him. Sometimes he'll get hard later, once he's distracted enough not to overthink it. Sometimes not, but I can coax an orgasm out of him anyway, with a little patience. Orgasms and erections are on two different sets of wiring, and I have all the time in the world for both, when it comes to him.

Soft, hard, I don't give a fuck. He's still shivering and taking deep, heaving breaths like my tongue in his hole is the second coming.

"Who do you belong to?" I pause my ministrations to ask him.

"You."

His voice is so soft I can barely hear him over the water falling around us. I push two fingers into his softened hole and then join them with my tongue for a minute, enjoying the way he clenches around me.

"I'm sorry, what was that?"

"You, Bambi." He's a little louder this time.

"Perfect, doll. That's it."

Standing up, I press every inch of myself against his back. He's squirming a little, the way I've noticed he does when he gets anxious about his lack of an erection, but there's a very easy way to distract him from that.

"And what are you?"

Tadhg shivers again while I wrap one arm around him, grabbing his pec with my left hand as my right hand braces the base of my cock. I keep lube in the shower for exactly these sorts of occasions, and it's reason number one million I'm thankful I live by myself.

"Your slutty pussy," he answers.

"Mmm." I don't give him the chance to breathe before I push in, and he makes this high-pitched, squeaking sound while I quickly and relentlessly impale him on my cock. "Perfect. You don't need to worry about getting hard for me because I have this perfect pussy right here."

I don't get an answer in the form of words, but he begins to make guttural, animal noises as I fuck into him. Hard and fast, with no time to get used to the stretch. My babygirl needs to get out of his head a lot of the time, and I can help him with that.

I let myself drift, losing track of time as I continue to fuck into him over and over while telling him what a perfect slut he is for me. How tight his little snatch is. How I wish I could have my hands on him all the time.

And he moans, and begs, and comes apart in my arms.

"Do you need my cum, doll?"

"Please, Bambi." His voice is hoarse now.

"Good girls deserve to be filled up," I whisper in his ear, snapping my hips against his as I pick up the pace.

I reach around and feel that he's more than half-hard now; his cock stiffer and pointing at the ground where he's angled over at the waist.

"That's it, doll. Are you going to get the floor wet for me? Spill yourself everywhere when I fill you up?"

Tadhg doesn't answer, he just makes a raw, anguished sound as I gently shuttle my hand over his erection, pressing my fingers into all the little sensitive spots that I know make him shiver. The velvet heat of his skin is such an overwhelming sensation, it pushes me the last little bit I need until I can't hold back my own orgasm anymore.

"Fuck, you're perfect," I say in a broken whisper as I jerk my hips forward a few more times and finally spill my seed deep inside of him. I don't let my hand stop working him over, though. I'm grinding deep into him, putting as much pressure on his prostate as I can and enjoying his breathy *ah-ah*s until he finally clenches around me and seems to come with his whole fucking body.

A spray of cum hits the floor, mixing with the cooling shower water to be washed down the drain, while his cock throbs hot in my hand and his hips continue to twitch against me.

I massage his balls again with my other hand, making sure he's getting touched everywhere he needs, putting pressure against his taint until it pulls out that same little squeak from before. I have to bite the scruff of his neck to keep from laughing, because he would definitely think I'm laughing at him and get upset.

I'm not. I'm not laughing at him at all. I'm laughing because there's no way the universe made someone this fucking perfect for me and then left him sitting under my nose this whole time, under the guise of a stepbrother, so he'd be the last place I'd look.

When we finally detach from each other to get cleaned up for real this time, it's not long before Tadhg goes quiet again. And not the quiet of having his brain cells fucked out of existence. The heavy, anxious quiet he often carries with him.

Again, I don't press. We have time. We both wash and pull on some clean underwear. Then I force him to come to the kitchen with me for a snack and some water, before we both fuck ourselves into chronic dehydration.

Then, when we're finally in bed in the calm, dark silence, I decide to push my luck. I can only hope he's still fucked out enough to let me.

Savage

"What's wrong?"

The question comes out of nowhere, and I'm jolted from my initial descent into sleep.

Micah is on his side, facing me with only a few inches separating us on the bed. It's dark in here, but not so dark that I can't make out the shadow of his features. I see concern there. Real concern. It's an expression I've gotten very accustomed to seeing on my brother's face when he's around me.

"Why?"

Micah sighs a little. "I think something's wrong. There's something you've been worrying about all night, even though I'm pretty sure I just made you see god in the world's ugliest rental bathroom. You don't have to tell me, obviously. But I'd like you to. Maybe I can help."

I frown. Is there something wrong? It's hard to tease apart real problems from abstract ones from the overwhelming blanket of existential dread that can be heavier and lighter depending on the day but is always present.

I'm probably not the best person to ask if something's wrong. The answer is always going to be yes, but what's wrong is almost always not important and just a broken fragment of my brain sticking into the gears of all the other parts.

"I don't know."

I say the words slowly, like they're unfamiliar in my mouth, even though it seems like a sentence I say fucking constantly.

Now Micah's the one frowning, but his expression quickly turns to thoughtful.

"Was it Tobias? I know that was hard to see. And I know you and Eamon have this whole rivalry going on."

I don't know why I say what I say next. It's possible that his question hits a little too close to the truth and I'm deflecting. It's also possible that this has really been on my mind, and I just haven't realized it.

Either way, instead of answering him like a normal person, the words I blurt out are, "Do you wish I was a girl?"

Micah's eyes go wide. Too wide. He already has those giant Bambi eyes, now I'm worried his eyeballs are going to just roll right out of his skull.

Then he laughs a little, but it's an uncomfortable sound. "What? I don't understand. What do you mean?" He hesitates, his face scrunching up in a way that's distractingly adorable before realization begins to dawn. "Oh shit, do you mean because of the 'good girl' dirty talk stuff?"

I'm not sure what to say to that, so I just nod.

There's an uncomfortably long pause while Micah considers his words. He doesn't look uncomfortable, though. Instead, he looks like he's taking in every inch of me with searing accuracy.

Finally, he speaks. But it gives me more questions than answers.

"I'm gay, Tadhg. Sexuality is a spectrum, but I'm like… Kinsey-six gay. I don't wish you were a girl. You're perfect. That's not what it's about for me. I'm sorry, we should really have talked about this sooner. I was letting it slide because you seemed so into it, but…" He pauses, and I swear he's doing it for dramatic effect because my heart is already *thump-thumping* too hard in my chest. "Do you wish you were a girl? Or does it make you feel something about it?"

I pick through my consciousness to find whatever parts of my brain are lighting up in response to his question. It's hard. I've spent my entire life avoiding self-awareness, because it was dangerous. Secretly wanting to be a girl—or already being a girl? I don't know how people describe it— seems like exactly the kind of thing I would be dumb enough to keep secret even from myself.

It doesn't click, though. When Micah's saying those things to me as he touches me, it sets every nerve ending I have on fire. It makes my individual cells trip over themselves to be good for him. It makes me desperate and needy and basically dissolve into a wanton, slutty puddle on the floor for him.

When I think about it outside of that context, it leaves me cold. Like no part of my brain is interested.

So, I guess I don't know a lot about myself, but that much seems clear?

"No," I finally say, the word sitting heavy on my tongue. "I don't—That's just for you. I don't know why, though."

Micah nods, as if what I said made perfect sense. "Okay. It's okay either way, you know. You can always tell me how you feel."

The thought of that seems so unabatingly vast that I can't look directly at it. I shrug and avoid Micah's gaze.

He just shuffles closer, until he's inhaling the smell of me from the crook of my neck and then running the flat of his tongue over my stubble and the hinge of my jaw.

"I'm attracted to everything about you, doll," he says, his voice low and husky now. "It's like you were made just for me. And all this *maleness* is a part of that. This muscle." He squeezes my bicep, and I fail to resist the urge to flex for him. "But I've always loved having a big, strong man begging on his knees. It turns me on. I would say"—he moves down lower, sucking my nipple into his mouth and pinching it between his teeth hard enough to make my cock twitch before he finally lets it go—"that it's not about you being a '*girl*' for me. It's about you being a slut for me. And because you are always such a perfect slut, with your perfect pussy and your perfect tits, that makes you my good girl."

He takes the nipple back in between his teeth and continues to abuse it, making me hiss again. My hips rock toward them, seeking friction of their own accord even though I feel completely drained.

He pops off again to continue talking, and I want to be done with the talking portion now, so he'll keep sucking. "But mostly I just like to see you blush and squirm around until you come. And I'll say whatever you want me to say to keep that happening."

I hate that the words hit me like a spark of electricity. I hate that I can already feel a blush climbing up my cheeks, even though he can't see it. And I hate that my traitorous, unpredictable cock, which took so long to get into that action earlier, is getting hard again already.

Micah climbs up my body, both of our hands fumbling around in the dark to grab at whatever parts of each other we can reach. I roll my hips against his, feeling how hard he is in return, and he captures my mouth in a filthy kiss.

Just as I think it's worth saying *fuck sleep* to escalate this for round two of the night, Micah breaks off the kiss. He hovers in front of me, his mouth still only inches away, and our breath mingles together. It's silent for a long time while I see his gaze flicking around, like he's taking in the sight of me.

"What?" I ask, finally sick of the suspense.

"There was something else I wanted to talk to you about before you distracted me with the reminder about all your perfect, juicy little body parts I get so much pleasure out of."

His tone is light, as usual, but I can tell from his face that this is serious.

"You can tell me anything, Bambi."

It scares the shit out of me, but I mean it.

He takes in a deep breath and lets it out. Then another.

Then another. The more he seems to be working himself up to something, the more apprehensive I feel.

"Please don't kill Eamon."

Oh.

I'm not sure what to say, so I stay quiet and let him follow up with some hushed babbling.

"I know he deserves it. And you probably want to. Fuck me sideways, I want to. We all do. And there's probably an element of what he's done to embarrass the Banna or your father or blah blah fucking blah. But in the holy name of Sasha Colby, please don't do it, Tadhg. Helping Tobias get freedom or revenge or anything else can be someone else's priority right now. My priority is helping *you*. And you're never going to be free if you keep doing this shit. Do you understand?"

There's a familiar feeling of my internal organs desiccating under this kind of scrutiny so they can blow away in the wind, and it's happening right now.

I have to kill Eamon. I would anyway, just because the prick fucking deserves it, but Father will not let me live if I don't. I know that.

As much as it makes a twinge of happiness hit me that Micah cares enough about me to want me to keep my hands clean, it really just serves as a reminder that he has no idea how truly, irreversibly dirty I am. I can't escape this. Even if I can physically escape the Banna and keep Micah safe, I still can't free myself from the weight of all the violence I committed on their behalf.

One more body in the ground isn't going to make a difference, and if Micah thinks it will, it just shows how naive he is about the situation.

Numbness spreads through my chest as the reality of the situation takes hold.

"Okay, Bambi. If that's what you want," I lie.

His brow furrows, like he's not sure if he believes me, but I try to sell it with a weak smile.

When Micah leans in to kiss me, I don't let him deepen it this time. That energy from before is gone.

I just need to sleep. I need to sleep for long enough that tomorrow never comes, and then I won't have to deal with any of the problems that seem to be stacking up on my doorstep.

Micah and sleep. It's all I want.

Chapter Twenty-Four

Micah

I blame the margaritas for why I'm so fucking tactless. Tadhg may be slow when he makes them, because he's still new to having a real job, but they were fucking drunk.

Wait—that's not right. *Strong*. They were strong. I'm fucking drunk.

Or maybe I should blame the three mind-blowing orgasms I've had between the margaritas and now. Once when Tadhg blew me in the backroom of the Feral Possum after we closed down, and then two more since he carried my drunken self home. There was a pit stop in there somewhere to check on Tobias, but he was asleep on Gunnar like a spoiled kitten—Gunnar is so far gone for him, and it's barely been a week; it's both hilarious and adorable—so we decided to leave them in peace.

Either way, I know it's tactless when the words come out

of my very dry, sandy mouth. I want to shove them back in immediately, drink water, and then go to sleep because I can feel myself painfully sobering up. But it's too late for that.

"I got you meds, by the way."

That's all I say. It's enough to make Tadhg's entire face crumple and every hint of post-orgasmic bliss straight up flee the building.

"What? What meds?"

"Your psych meds. The ones you had to cold turkey from when you were dragged up here. There are a lot of online subscription providers now. I went snooping when I was getting that discreet STD panel for Tobias and I finally found one that I was able to talk into giving me the exact prescription you were on before."

"Bambi... You can't. That's the whole point, I can't have my name on stuff. It just makes me easier to find. Fuck!"

"No, no, no—I put it under my name. Don't worry, every single scrap of paperwork says 'Micah Alexander' on it. Which will hopefully not reach my bosses." I reach out to cup his face, because the panic is already rising in him, and I can see him fighting the urge to crawl out of bed and start doing something unnecessary. "I knew what to say so it sounded like I was just restarting a prescription I'd had before. Honestly, it's easy if you understand the meds. It's unethical, sure. But I think we crossed that bridge back when I was burning your fucking clothes. They won't be traced to you, doll. I promise. It's fine."

Tadhg freezes. I can see the gears working in his brain, and I suddenly get the impression he's searching for another argument against it. Which doesn't make sense.

He needed these meds so badly that he went out and got them on his own, once upon a time. He had to keep it a secret from everyone he knew, and he'd probably been told that using them made him sick or weak or something. So why is he resisting the idea now, when he has so much more support and so much less to lose?

Shaking his head, Tadhg rolls onto his back and looks away from me.

"I don't want them, Bambi. I'm fine now. I just want to focus on getting out and then everything will be fine."

Quelling the anger that statement inspires physically fucking hurts. But I do it, because this is his fucking brainwashing talking. And as much as I love to think I'm right about everything all the time, yelling at him about this is probably not going to help anyone's mental health.

I move closer to him, not letting him get away from me. Propped up on one elbow, I place my hand flat on his chest and trace a path through the faint golden hair that covers his tattoos.

"No. You're not fine. You're coasting, and that's not going to work out long term."

He doesn't pull away from me, but he does continue to look anywhere but my eyes. There's yet another long pause before he speaks, and I'm forced to go to my work-brain instead of my normal brain to find the patience to wait.

I am not, by nature, a patient person. Especially when the man I love's life is on the line.

That thought makes my brain screech to a halt, though. Is that what's happening here? Are we *in* love? I love him, of course. I've always loved him. And lusted after him, since we met as adults. But has all of that combined to being in love?

No part of my mind or body hesitates to give me the answer.

Yes.

So, I have to protect him at all costs. From himself as well as the Banna.

"Talk to me, doll." I have to prompt him when he doesn't speak for too long. "I know this is difficult, but avoiding the conversation isn't getting us anywhere."

"About what? I don't need them. I'm an adult and you're not going to force me. Just drop it."

The snap to his voice has me very fucking concerned about how I've managed to unintentionally touch a nerve.

"Oh, hell no," I say as I sit up, leaning back and pushing him until he's also scooting up to a sitting position. All that restraint I was holding on to before burns away, and I'm left with nothing but the anger and the alcohol fueling me now. "If you're going to be so defensive about this that you would rather pick a fight with me—*me*, your fucking Bambi, asshole—than talk to me about it, then we are definitely fucking talking about it. Spill. Whatever's cooking inside your head just tell me. Don't make me tie you up and edge it out of you because I am too fucking tired, and I have to work tomorrow."

I pair this rant with a little eyelash fluttering that always seems to make him melt for me, then pinch his belly when he still hesitates too long.

"Ow!"

"Speak!" I snap.

I am fresh out of fucks right now.

Tadhg rubs his belly where I pinched him, pouting at me in a way I've never seen him do before that is so fucking adorable I want to throw up. But now's not the time.

"Jesus, Micah. You're fucking savage."

I'm squinting at him to see if he meant what I think he meant, but his face is blank. No pun intended, I guess. I'll back pocket that for another time.

"Tell me the truth, Tadhg. Why don't you want the meds?"

He huffs and continues to look shifty, but now I can tell that the words are right beneath the surface. They're trying to break out, so I give him the space to let them.

"I want my dick to work, okay?"

Ah.

"Doll, that's not—"

"Save it," he interrupts. "I know my dick barely works anyway, and you like to tell me I'm perfect as part of your kinky little fetish or whatever, and that's fine. But I can't go from it working most of the time back to none of the time. Not when I have you now. It's not worth it. You make me feel ten times better than the pills ever did. Why would I risk that?"

My heart melts a little because fuck me that's sweet. Especially for someone as laconic as Tadhg. But it's not the point.

I shuffle closer, until I'm straddling his lap, and I can take his face in my hands where it belongs. He's trapped under my gaze, and I refuse to let him go anywhere.

"First of all, telling you you're perfect isn't a kink. You are perfect. Perfect for me." He blinks and tries to look away, but I hold him firm. "And second of all, nothing could happen that would fuck this up. I don't care if your cock is soft, I'll keep it warm in my wet, hot mouth all day while we watch TV. Or I'll get you a Viagra script as well, and maybe you'll get such intolerably stiff boners that I'll have to watch you fuck a fleshlight while you ride my cock. Or I'll strap you to a prostate massager and watch you come all over yourself so many times that you start getting cramps from dehydration and beg me to stop."

He's still trying not to look me in the eye, but now he's

squirming and there's a delicious pink blush painting his cheeks, telling me how much he likes the sound of all of that.

My voice softens though, because I need him to really understand. Every haze of doubt and alcohol is gone, now. I'm tired and bleary-eyed, but there's not a fucking fiber of me that doubts how I feel about him or what I want.

"Or maybe you have less interest in sex, and we find other ways to connect. I don't care. I love *you*, Tadhg. I'm *in love* with you. I think I might have been in love with you since I was eight years old. I don't care about the details, as long as we're together."

He hisses in a sharp breath, finally looking me in the eye. I know I'm squeezing his face too hard, but a sudden wave of emotion has fisted around my heart, and I can't quite control myself.

"I just need you to be alive for it, so I can keep loving you. Okay? Please?" My voice cracks on the please, and the sudden pressure behind my eyes quickly turns into tears. Only a few, though. Just enough to roll down my cheek and leave me feeling choked.

Tadhg looks whiplashed. He nods slowly before bringing his hand to my cheek to wipe the errant tear away.

"I'll be here, Bambi. I'm here to protect you, remember? I made a promise."

For whatever reason, the reminder of a pinkie promise made a million years ago sends more tears flooding up to embarrass me. I don't bother to hide it, though. I sniffle a little as my cheeks get wet and Tadhg continues to wipe them away with gentle touches.

"You better. Or I'll die too just so I can kick your ass."

The words come out all thick and wet, like they do when you're crying, but we both kind of chuckle anyway.

"I know you would. Don't worry, Bambi. I'm here."

Part of me was waiting to hear him tell me he loves me. Not that he hasn't told me a million times before, but something about this time would have felt different. If he needs more time, he needs more time, though.

I lean back a little, sniffing deeply and pressing the heel of my hand into my forehead while I try to get myself under control.

"Ugh," I say as the tears dry up. "I promise I wasn't planning on crying. This wasn't some epic emotional manipulation to get you to take the pills. I'm not even a crier, it just happened. It's your fault for giving me blowjobs and margaritas, obviously."

Tadhg lets out a soft laugh, and I latch onto it with my whole heart.

"I know, Bambi. I'm not sure you're subtle enough for emotional manipulation. You just yell at me until I do what you want."

"Damn straight." Another sniff, and then I feel more like a real person again. "Okay, well, I'm going to get the pills. I can't make you take them, but will you at least promise me you'll think about it? And I swear on Satan's ham wallet that whatever side effects you have if you take them, we will deal with them together. And it will be *fine*, as you love to say."

Tadhg mouths the words *ham wallet* at me with a furrowed brow, and I finally let out a genuine laugh of my own.

"It means vagina, Tadhg."

The scrunched up, horrified face he makes in return makes me graduate from laughing to cackling.

"You're such a baby," I say as I pull him into a tender kiss. We can revisit the medication talk again later. And again and again and again, for as long as we need, until my doll is all taken care of.

Savage

Three days after the conversation we had about meds, I'm almost convinced that the subject is dropped. I'm praying for it. Until Micah shows up to pick me up from work, looking pale and exhausted and rumpled from his shift.

I don't kiss him in the parking lot, because we're still on the DL until we can figure out how to completely get out from my father's thumb. Not that he would be caught dead here, but he has eyes everywhere. Eamon, usually, although that fucker is on his last thread of Father's patience for spending more time looking for Tobias than working. I'm pretending I don't know shit, obviously. I'm just quietly gathering information about Eamon's betrayals, like I was asked, and minding my own business otherwise.

The other issue with potentially kissing Micah in public would be explaining to the world that we're not actually brothers and never were. Especially considering how everyone keeps forgetting to use the word "step" no matter how much we remind them. But that's a problem for my future self, if he's still around.

I want to kiss him, though. Kissing Micah has become something that my body yearns for all the time, like a flower turning toward the sun. It's probably pathetic, but it's also so all-consuming that I don't care. I just want more. Letting him look at me and touch me the way that he does feels like being warm for the first time in my life, and I'll be damned if

I let anything get in the way of that. Even my own fucked-up brain.

This is what I'm thinking about when Micah starts the engine to head home, and I blame the distraction for why it takes a minute for the words to land.

"I know I promised to let you think about the meds," he says, instantly making all the muscles in my body tense. "I am. I swear. But it got me thinking about something else."

What am I supposed to say to that? Micah's gaze flits nervously to me for a second, then back to the road, before he continues.

"You keep talking about how you can't put your name in any records, and you have to lay low. That's what this is all about, right? Because Sir Shithead told you the Aryans have a bounty on your head or whatever."

The barely-restrained disdain Micah always has when he talks about Father fills me with a weird sort of warmth.

"Yeah, exactly. They could show up anytime. They won't quit until they find me, is what Father said."

Micah drums his nimble fingers on the steering wheel, chewing on the inside of his cheek for a minute while he works himself up to saying whatever he wants to say.

"Are you sure he was telling you the truth?"

I swear I bluescreen on the world for a second, because nothing he just said makes sense.

"Why the fuck would he lie about that, Bambi?"

I can't hide the irritation in my voice, but it rolls off of him. He's never been truly scared of me a day in his life, and I'm sure I'm even less intimidating now that he knows how to make me cry and beg like a little sissy for an orgasm. I don't actually want him to be scared of me, obviously, but it is annoying when that's the only way I have of getting people to do things and he's fucking immune.

Micah sighs. "Maybe he didn't lie. Maybe he thinks it's the truth, and he's just wrong. Or maybe he did lie because he wants to keep you in hiding. I don't know. I can't help but think about it, though, and no matter how I look at it, it doesn't make any sense. The Aryans and the Banna being at war—sure. But you specifically? Hunting you down and making you pay for what? Surviving their assassination attempt? You didn't even testify, which is what started this whole thing, right? But then he also said it wasn't about that; they wanted you before. This whole thing smells like bullshit."

I'm blinking and mindlessly nodding along, because for a few stuttering moments, the words don't land. They're floating around me, too intangible to take root.

The only thing I find less believable than Father lying to me is the idea that he just... Got it wrong? That doesn't happen. He has too many eyes on the world. He always knows the play. Something like this couldn't slip past someone like him.

I'm startled by warm flesh on my flesh when Micah takes my hand in his. He's still looking at the road, but the concern on his face is obvious now.

"I'm just saying, if they really wanted you that badly, don't you think they would have come for you by now? This is a small town. I know I'm not on the inside, but I've been around the Banna enough to know how things work. It's not paperwork that leads them to you; it's fucking word of mouth. You can change your name and hide out at the bar, but everyone in Possum Hollow knows who you are by now and there's no way that information hasn't made its way back to the Brotherhood. They have just as much of a foothold here as your father does."

I blink again, my thoughts drifting and too hazy to pluck out any individual ones.

"Why would he lie?"

Then Micah does turn to look at me for a few seconds, his mouth downturned.

"I don't know, doll. But I think we have to find out."

The rest of the ride back home is quiet, weighed down with the revelation that Micah just cracked open inside me. I can't stop thinking about it. Whether he lied to me or made a mistake. What he has to gain by keeping me on the sidelines, even if it's what I wanted anyway.

I've been so blinded by the distraction of this illusion of freedom, I forgot to look for all the strings that must be attached. And now not only is Father calling me back to work, but I have to figure out what pound of flesh he really wants from me.

It's too much mindfuckery to not be covering up something more sinister. But I'm used to everything he does being sinister, so I never looked more closely.

Idiot. If that man finally kills me just when I've found Micah… I won't let it happen. I know I promised Micah no more killing, even though it was always going to be a lie. But now I'm even more convinced. I'll kill whoever I need to if it carves me and Micah a path to freedom and away from all this bullshit.

Chapter Twenty-Five

Savage

Tobias is missing.

He was doing so well, and now he's gone. Right out from under Gunnar's nose. There's no evidence, but also no doubts about why that might be or who's behind it. It made me realize how selfish I've been, though.

All this time, I've been sitting around obsessing over my own shit. Did Father lie to me about the Aryans? Can I kill Eamon, and do what Father wants me to? Or do I ignore that order like Micah begged me not to? Am I so irredeemable at this point that whatever violence I continue to inflict is meaningless anyway, and only keeping Micah safe matters?

These are the thoughts that have been a maelstrom inside me, while I hide in Bambi's apartment and avoid confronting the truth.

And in the meantime, people like Tobias are suffering. Young kids who aren't so completely fucked that they can't be saved.

It's selfish. I'm selfish.

The words continue to rattle through me, vibrating my bones as I drive all the way out to the Banna farm in the search for my father. Micah is at work, thank fuck, so he doesn't know what I'm doing. He can't know.

I don't even really know what I'm doing. I still have no idea if I'm here to beg for my freedom or to tell him I'll murder Eamon for him after all, just to free the kid.

Whatever I'm doing, it has to happen now. I can't wait any longer. I can't string Micah along any longer.

The guys guarding the perimeter all look surprised to see me, but wave me in. I still belong here, after all. That won't change unless Father decides to put a bullet in me for my betrayal. I park as close to the front door as I can, as if there's any chance of me making a quick getaway if I need to. As soon as I open the door, the sound of screaming fills the air, and a dull memory slaps back into my consciousness.

Little yappy screaming fox things she sells on Facebook.

That's what Colm had said. I was so out of it with withdrawal last time I was here that I could barely process the sensory information being crammed into me, but now I remember. The cages line the wall of the house, and the stench and sound of trapped, frightened living creatures seems to take over the entire area around them.

I shiver, trying not to look too closely at them. I don't give a flying fuck about animals. But the thought of spending your life in a dirty cage so some MC club president's widow can rent out your uterus to keep her coke habit afloat really creeps me the fuck out.

"Savage? Is that you?"

I don't know who I was expecting to see in the doorway, but it wasn't Micah's mom. It occurs to me that this whole time I've been in Missouri she hasn't shown up at the apartment once. Micah briefly mentioned that they're not estranged or anything, but they're also not close.

Which tracks. He didn't say as much, but I'm assuming he's still pretty pissed about all the times she passed out or went out partying and left him alone with only me to protect him from Patrick and the elements. Congratulations on getting sober or whatever, but mortgaging someone's childhood for liquor and ice is hard to truly get over.

She looks more like him than I remembered. The same dark hair, the same skin tone. The same delicate build, only on her it looks almost frail. Bird-like, with weathered skin that's stretched too tight over bone, while Micah's body is infused with strength and vitality in every cell, even if he's not bulky like me.

"Hi, Cheryl." My voice sounds stiff and awkward as I move toward the house.

I'm not built for these kinds of social interactions; my entire body wants to flinch away from them. Or any social interactions that don't involve torture, I guess. She stands there anyway, leaning against the doorframe with her arms over her chest and a carefully neutral expression on her face.

"We weren't expecting you. Is everything okay?"

Nodding, I step into the doorway with her. The least I can do is get close enough to use my size to my advantage before she tries to intimidate me away from my own father. I really would never live that one down.

"Everything's fine. I need to speak to Father. Is he inside?"

"Cheryl? Are you okay?"

A blonde woman steps out of one of the fox cages and moves toward us, interrupting the conversation. She has the same weathered look as Micah's mom, but her skin is a deep, deep tan color that's almost tawny, her hair is bleached to be as light as Cheryl's is dark and she's plump in all the places that Cheryl looks like she's wasting away.

This must be the widow. The fox breeder. Fox-widow, I'll call her.

"It's Pat's son, Briggs. He's fine."

Fox-widow dusts off her hands, which I'm assuming are covered in fox shit, and continues moving toward us. She gives off overwhelming "fuck-off" vibes that I really don't have the energy to handle right now.

For just a second, I consider talking to them. Being rational and trying to get them on my side. They're not blocking the door or anything, they're just glaring at me like I don't belong here.

But that's the whole point, isn't it? I don't belong here. At the same time, I belong here a fuck-ton more than they do. I'm sure I've shed more blood from it, as long as we're not counting slaughtered livestock. I reach deep down inside myself and pull on the true Savage mask, letting it slide back into place with a soft *click* that settles so much of the anxiety that was churning inside me.

I don't say anything. I'm sure my demeanor changes all on its own. I don't have to move or do anything, just let the atmosphere shift until is drips with unspoken threat. These are women who've spent their lives handling violent men, but I still have to be able to scare someone, goddammit.

It's satisfying. Micah would hate me for it, but I don't care right now. I can't be so fucking worthless that even my sins have abandoned me.

The ugliest side of myself is also the most effective at getting things done. That's always been my problem.

Without any more conversation, I head into the house. Cheryl does call out after me, though.

"Tell Micah to call me, Tadhg."

I don't know if she thinks calling me by my real name is more motherly or something, but it doesn't work. Fine. I'll tell him. He won't, though.

Inside the house, there are a few guys scattered around. Mostly eating or lounging. Some of them I know, some of them I don't, but I absolutely don't care about a single one of them. I ask to be pointed in the direction of my father, and it isn't long before I end up in some room he obviously uses as a kind of office.

It's spacious, with natural light streaming in from a big bay window and a large teak desk taking up one wall. The desk is scarred up and has clearly seen better days, but it's almost regal. Like something a ship captain might have used in an old-timey boat where the furniture is all way too big for its purpose.

I'm not sure why I'm fixating on the desk instead of the man sitting behind it. I don't think I've ever seen my father sit at a desk like that before. He's normally more of a pacing and yelling kind of boss, not a sit and do paperwork one. He must have inherited all this from the MC President he took the house from, and that guy must have had real intense fucking illusions of grandeur.

His wife does not match the decor, but I'm sure he didn't either.

"Hey, Sav," Colm says, prompting me to notice him standing in the corner of the room for the first time, because apparently I'm completely oblivious today. "I wasn't expecting to see you here."

Father is still where he sits behind the desk, but he watches me with a predatory glint in his eye that I haven't seen in a long time.

"Close the door," is all he says.

I obey but can't avoid the clench of fear that hits my gut. I strode in here feeling so much like my old self. Not just myself from six months ago, but my *old*-old self. Before I allowed myself to accept how wrong this all felt. And with three words in that familiar clipped tone, all that confidence unravels within me.

"I'm assuming you're here with good news? You took care of the problem I talked to you about."

Ah. Yeah. That.

I really should have had a game plan before I marched in here, and now I feel the whole situation withering under the light.

Someone needs to help Tobias. Someone needs to keep Eamon from causing anymore destruction. I think maybe I was subconsciously planning to tell Father I would do it as long as he told me the truth about the Brotherhood and whether they really put a contract out on me or not.

Now that I'm looking at him, though, all I can picture is Micah's face when he begged me not to kill Eamon.

He wants me to keep my hands clean. He genuinely believes I'm a good enough person—or capable of becoming a good enough person—that I don't have to keep doing my father's dirty work to earn my keep.

A desperate, hopeful part of me wants to at least try to be that person for him. Even if I don't really believe it's possible.

"I'm not doing it."

It feels like someone else says the words, and I'm watching it all happen from the other side of a piece of glass.

But no—that's me. Standing there like a dumbass with no follow up while Father and Colm both stare at me.

"What?" Father snaps.

"I'm not... I'm not," I say, starting to stutter as the nerves belatedly sink in. I fight hard not to let the feeling show and keep standing tall, but I'm not sure how successful I am. This is the one person who always seems to be able to turn me into a whimpering, frightened animal if he wants to. "I'm not doing it." I shake my head. "I can't do it. I won't do it. I'm done. I'm just... I'm done. I won't."

Jesus Christ, Sav, stop fucking talking.

Father doesn't say anything, and the heat and energy of my anxiety quickly morphs into cold, slick fear dripping down my spine.

Instead, he stands, leaning over his desk with a broad stance. Colm hasn't moved. I don't even know if he's breathing. But he's watching us both intently, waiting to see how this will play out.

I think we both already know, unfortunately.

"I'm going to pretend that you just had a stroke, and everything that just came out of your mouth was a product of your brain shutting down. Because I don't remember asking you to do a goddamn thing, Savage. I told you to take care of him. You didn't do it then, and now he's running around town playing queer kidnapper and making the Banna look like a bunch of morons who can't tell their ass from a tree stump. I don't know where this new entitlement is coming from, Sav, but you'd better nip it in the bud. I did not raise you to act like a little flamer. Do your fucking job."

By the end of his speech, he's rounding the desk to move toward me.

I'm bigger than him. I'm much stronger than him now. If

it came down to a pure physical fight, I could win. But knowing that doesn't matter one little bit as he stalks closer to me, drawing himself up until he seems larger than life.

It doesn't stop me from cowering. Instinct and muscle memory squeezes my throat shut and I go silent. Words are useless at this point. He's going to do whatever he's going to do.

The first blow isn't even really a blow. He slaps me in the face. It's not that hard, but his goal here is to humiliate me rather than hurt me. It would work if my pride weren't long dead and buried. I keep my face turned at an angle, my eyes open but pointed at the ground, my expression neutral.

He slaps me again.

"Answer me."

Another one. My cheek is starting to sting as he puts more force behind it.

"You are my son, Savage. I raised you to be my legacy. Just like my father raised me. That's the point of all of this. Do you think my father and uncles let me run around doing whatever I wanted? No. The reason I'm a strong leader is because they kept me in line. Clearly, I've failed to do the same thing with you."

Another slap. This time, it's hard enough to make me inhale sharply through my nose and rock back on my feet a little.

"Maybe I should have killed the boy while I had the chance. Before he got his weakness all over you."

At that, my gaze snaps to meet his. He's working hard to look detached, but I can see the excitement in his eyes. This is what he wants. He's trying to get me to react. He's testing to see if Micah is the right button to push.

He's right, of course. There's no sense wasting time lying about it.

"Don't talk about him," I say through clenched teeth.

The old man raises his eyebrows but doesn't react in any other way.

"He's been a bad influence. He always was, but I thought you'd have outgrown being so *suggestible* by this point. I obviously overestimated you. I'll tell you what, boy."

His hand—still surprisingly strong despite the signs of age that seem more obvious in him every day—wraps around my throat and squeezes hard enough to make me sputter and suck saliva into my trachea.

"You do as you're told and take care of Eamon—and I mean right this fucking second—or I will wipe the little brat off the face of the earth and tell Cheryl it was a car accident. Or an overdose. Or he was raped to death by someone he met off one of those disgusting apps. I've tolerated him out of deference to the woman, but if he's actively interfering in my business by turning you into an even more useless lump of flesh than you were already, I don't have a choice."

I lunge toward him, but he was definitely expecting it because his grip on my throat tightens enough that black spots swim in my vision.

I've never attacked my father in my life, but right now all I can think about is how he's threatening Micah. Nothing else matters.

He fucking *laughs*, and that's enough to spur me forward. With new resolve, I bring up my forearm and smash it into him hard enough and abruptly enough to break his grip on me. I use the momentum to barrel forward, grabbing his shirt with both hands and not stopping until I have him pinned against the wall.

I'm breathing rage in a way I never have before. I'm suffused with it. But as soon as I see his placid face, still looking at me like I'm dirt and he's untouchable, I waver. I don't want to. I want to be strong for Micah, like I promised I would. But being strong for him always, always, always meant taking the beating and learning not to stand up for myself. Trying to do the opposite now is making too many pieces of me clash, until all my internal organs want to screech to a halt.

He doesn't hesitate, of course. My one moment of weakness is all the opening he needs, and apparently my show of disrespect was enough to push him over the edge and teach me the kind of lesson he hasn't needed to for a very long time.

The experience blurs together with every other time I've caught a beating in my life. It's easier that way. I hunker like a child, shielding my head and neck as he hits me with a closed fist instead of the little love taps he was giving me before. As soon as I hit the ground, his feet find my ribs as well. The pain blooms in a familiar pattern.

Short, sharp breaths. Fight the nausea. Keep your consciousness, but don't focus on what's happening. Ride it out.

Pain is temporary.

Just keep breathing until he stops.

I repeat it to myself again and again, my old mantra that lets me float on the sensations without latching onto any individual one, or trying to catalogue what he's doing to me. Or saying to me. I hear the shape of words. It's just enough to know how hateful they are, so I don't listen. He won't care either way, once he goes this far.

All I can do is wait until he tires himself out.

Which is why it's disorienting when the violence stops. Not dwindles or tapers off, just stops cold. There's more noise now, so I try to wind my brain back into human mode and lock into what's actually going on around me.

Colm has my father pinned against the wall exactly like I did a minute ago. He's the same size as me and just as strong, except there's no hesitance in his movement. There's also no rage. Or at least it's a controlled rage. He's restraining Father but not hurting him, whispering something in his ear while wearing an expression I know he's used on me a million times that I think means '*my boss is a fucking child*'.

Eventually, Father shoves Colm off, but there's a note of finality to it. He doesn't come for me again, even though I'm still cowering on the floor like a weak thing he could tear apart.

Colm stands back with his hands raised, letting Father go. But I don't miss the subtle way he angles his body in between the two of us. It's so small, I'm sure Father doesn't notice. I only do because it's something I've done for Micah a hundred thousand times.

My heart squeezes, and I feel a pressure behind my eyes.

Father looks down at me with more contempt than I've ever seen.

"Kill the queer, Savage. Today. Or I will make that boy pay the price."

Yeah, yeah, yeah. I get it. The world is an intractable fuckhole and I'm never getting off this ride. You don't need to rub it in.

"Yes, Father."

He turns to go, but I take advantage of the fact that I'm still riding the endorphin wave from my beating, and I don't really care what happens to me one way or another anymore.

"Wait. I have one question." He half-turns, one eyebrow lifted, but he doesn't leave. "Do the Aryans really have a contract for me, or was that a lie?"

Father jerks back, as if the words slapped him.

"Why would I lie about that?"

"To keep me on the sidelines. Or scared. I don't know. It just seems weird that they've had a contract on me all this time, and not one of them has even come close to tracking me down. There's Brotherhood territory all around this place. I'm not advertising my presence, but I also haven't exactly been hiding in a root cellar. I know they're dumb, but they're not that dumb. They should have found me by now if they really wanted me dead."

There's a long silence while Father mulls the information over. It's so obvious once the words are out of my mouth, though, and he clearly knows it. From the look on Colm's face, he's thinking the same thing.

"Well, it sounds like that would be something to ask Eamon about before you off the bastard."

I don't say anything, but I'm sure my question mark is written all over my face. Colm is turned away now, chewing awkwardly at his lower lip like he knows something I don't.

"He's the one who found out about the contract in the first place, Savage. If anyone is lying, it's him." Father takes a deep breath and walks a few more steps away until he's at the door. "Now go do what I trained you to do."

Chapter Twenty-Six

Savage

I don't know how long I wait for Micah to come home from work. I've spent a lot of my life in a mental state where time becomes a little abstract, and this is definitely one of those times.

At least I've showered off all the blood, unlike the last time I came home like this. The bruising on my face is even more obvious now that I'm clean, but he'll understand as soon as I tell him I saw Patrick today.

Eventually, the door cracks open and my name rings through the apartment. It immediately settles some of my nerves, but that only makes me feel guilty as hell. Why should I get to be soothed by Micah's presence when I couldn't even stand up for him?

I've never stood up for him. Not really. The only way I've protected him is by committing violence or accepting it.

All the times I've had the chance to actually tell Father to shove his hateful opinions or make it clear that Micah will be hurt over my rotten corpse, I freeze.

Because that man still has more power over me than Micah does.

Because I let him.

Of all the things I hate myself for, I think that's the one that I hate the most.

"Tadhg, what the fuck?"

He must have seen my face. I look up from where I'm sitting on the couch, trying my best to blink the world back into focus.

"It's okay, Bambi. It's just bruises."

"Yeah, but shit."

He rushes over to me, throwing his keys somewhere in the process before perching next to me on the couch. Micah grabs my face, still with the tenderness he's come to always touch me with, but also with that clinical efficiency that tells me he's still in work mode and I'm not exactly helping him relax.

My face is tilted this way and that as he examines me, stopping occasionally to prod my bruises with his fingers. It stings, but I take the pain because I definitely fucking deserve it.

I wait for the questions to come, but they don't. The first thing he says after a long silence is, "Anywhere else?"

Nodding, I take off my shirt to show him. There's no point in hiding it from him.

He makes a grumbling noise when he sees the bruising over my ribs that would be adorable under any other circumstances, then continues his exam there too. More poking and prodding. Moving my arms and checking my range of motion. At some point he pulls the stethoscope off from around his neck to listen to my lungs, muttering under his breath that if I have a punctured lung, he'll kill me himself first.

When he's finally, finally satisfied that I'm not dying he sits back to look at me, although his hand continues to rest on my knee. It's a single point of contact, but I let it tether me to the earth. It's selfish, but I need it.

"Tell me what happened. At least as much of it as you can," he says. His eyes are round and wide with some unreadable emotion, and I immediately feel yet more guilty that I'm making him feel this way.

"What happened?" I ask. *Do you mean before or after I—a grown-ass man—let my father beat the shit out of me?* "It was Patrick. You know how he gets."

Micah sighs, and it seems to sink his entire bodyweight into the couch.

"I'm sorry. Was it about us?"

"No," I lie. At least, it's not about the part of us he's asking about. "It was bullshit work stuff. He just lost his temper, and I didn't want to make it worse."

"That's it?"

He looks so open. So willing to take me as I am. I almost want to tell him the truth. The whole truth about what I did. I can't, though. He asked me for one fucking thing, and I couldn't even give him that.

Instead of pushing me to answer him, Micah takes my silence as an answer in itself.

With more patience than I knew he had in him, Micah helps pull me up and get me ready for bed. It's late. Sometime in the middle of the night, I think. At some point he shoves some toast at me, which I eat mechanically. Then water, which I drink.

By the time I'm in bed with him curled around me like a

protective buffer between me and the world, I can practically feel his concern vibrating off him. There's nothing I can do about it, though.

I can't tell him what I did. I can't tell him what's going to happen to us. And I can't even pretend that everything is going to be okay.

EAMON DOESN'T EVEN TURN AROUND WHEN I SHIMMY OPEN THE lock and let myself into the motel room I finally found him in. He's at the small Formica table next to the A/C unit, his gun spread out in front of him in pieces while he picks up each part to clean it.

This isn't a dream. Not exactly. I don't think I'm asleep enough for it to be a dream, because the details are all too sharp. It's just a fresh, raw memory playing itself in my mind over and over, refusing to let me sink any deeper than this into rest.

"It took you long enough, pet. I was beginning to think I'd have to come out and catch you again. The clock is ticking until I put your little bartender buddy in the ground, remember."

Ah. So, he's expecting Tobias back. That's why he's not on his guard.

Lucky me.

There's only six feet or so between us, and I cover the distance quickly and silently. It's been a long time since I've done this, and it feels like so much of me has changed since then that even my cells have probably shifted in how they function.

Apparently, I was wrong. Nothing's changed. My body takes over, remembering exactly what to do. Even though I'm still stiff from my own beating. Colm had picked me up and cleaned me with his sad, sympathetic eyes and surprisingly tender hands, and then I was ready to do my job.

Eamon still doesn't know what's happening when I grab the back of his skull with my hands and smash it into the table. It comes up bloody, because the trigger assembly was right under his face and cut straight through the skin of his forehead.

He normally looks slick. He's kind of pretty, but it never fits with the reptilian look in his eyes. Now, with blood rushing down over his nose and mouth, it looks more like his external self matches his internal existence.

I like it.

He's shocked for a few moments, but his training kicks in just like mine would and has him reaching for whatever other weapon he has tucked in his pants. I don't give him the chance, though. I'm operating on muscle memory. There's no hesitation in me right now. I'm a relentless, violent machine.

I kick the chair legs out from under him, sending him tumbling to the ground, and immediately step on his right wrist. The toe of my work boot grinds into his forearm hard, and I take great satisfaction in the cracking, popping sounds that I hear right before he screams.

Conveniently, he chose the best possible motel for no one giving a fuck if they hear screaming, as well as the room farthest from the office. Thanks for the assist, Eamon.

I still don't want to give him any time to regroup, because I've seen guys fight through more injuries than this. He's heaving raspy breaths while blood fills his mouth, but he's not down for the count. There's a four-inch Gerber in the side pocket of my pants.

As soon as I have it in my hand, I sink the blade into his left knee. From the side in, right in the little declivity behind the kneecap that gives me the perfect, soft entry point. He doesn't scream this time, which irritates me. I give the knife a little wiggle, seeing what I can stir up inside the joint. That pulls a much more satisfying noise out of his lying, scheming mouth.

Now that I know he's at least not running anywhere, I right the chair and then haul his quivering body into it. He slumps to the side, but when I try to pull him back up, he lunges at me with his good hand.

Asshole.

I slap him across the face. Not gently, like my father did to me, but hard enough to disorient him. I really don't have the energy to tie him up, but I also don't want to play catfight with him all night, either.

I need him to answer my questions, and then I need him dead.

"Tell me about the contract," I hiss.

Eamon blinks at me, blood running in his eyes. I give him a minute to get his bearings again, and I can tell when he really comes back to himself because the motherfucker grins.

"What contract?"

"The contract on me. The Aryan Brotherhood coming for me. Is it real? Did you make it up? Tell me the truth or I'll take your other kneecap."

Of course, Eamon has to be as obnoxious as possible, right up until the end. He laughs, like he genuinely finds this all hilarious, and I have to resist the urge to cave his fucking face in with my fist.

"I knew you were stupid, Savage. I didn't really think you were that stupid. Apparently, I overestimated you."

My eyes narrow, and I watch him take one wet, rattling breath after another while he continues to grin at me.

"You lied. Why?"

None of this makes any sense to me, but I'm not an unhinged, abusive loser with a god complex.

"You were in the way. The golden child heir, blah blah blah. I needed you gone. As soon as I realized you'd rather be spending time playing fucked-up house with your little sister," I growl and put my hand around his throat, but it doesn't stop him. "I figured it would be easy to distract you long enough to show your father how fucking worthless you are. You don't deserve the title of lieutenant, Savage. The only reason you have it is because of your blood. And if he knew who you really were, he'd have killed you himself a long time ago."

"You're such a fucking hypocrite," I whisper, tightening my grip on his throat enough to make him struggle for air.

He can sexually assault a man barely out of high school, and he thinks it makes him strong. But me loving the shit out of Micah makes me a weak little queer in his eyes.

I've hated the Banna for a long time, but I think this is the first time I truly realize how stupid we all are. It's not just a shitty lifestyle. It's fucking dumb.

Eamon gasps when I release his neck. Sudden nausea and disgust hits me that I'm even dealing with this guy. Micah was right. I shouldn't have let myself be the one to kill him. He's not worth sacrificing any more of my karma for.

It's not like I have a choice, though. I have to protect Micah, and that's more important than my own worthless, ragged morality.

Eamon keeps breathing deeply, and as soon as he licks his lips I realize he's about to start talking again. It's probably a good thing. I have other questions for him. I need to know more about the Aryans and whatever else he's fucked up for his own purposes. I should wring every last bit of information out of him that I can.

"Tell me, Savage. Does Micah's pussy taste as good as I—" His words are cut off when I pull the knife out of his kneecap and then jam it into the base of his skull.

It takes a while for him to die. I wanted it to be quiet, even though I'm confident no one here would call the cops, which is why I didn't shoot him. Or maybe I just wanted to watch the light slowly fade from his eyes.

The important thing is that he can't fucking talk. He just makes gurgling sounds and works his jaw with a blank expression, as the capillaries burst in his eyes and pink foam collects at the corner of his mouth.

When he's finally gone, the first thing I feel is a curl of satisfaction. *Bone-deep satisfaction that hasn't entered my body in a very long time. Of course, it's quickly followed by shame. This is just one more thing I did to let Micah down, and one more dirty secret I'll have to keep from him forever.*

At least it's done.

I guess.

Micah

I'm exhausted, because it was a long shift and then the forty minutes I spent taking care of Tadhg afterward was mind-numbingly draining.

I hate not being able to know what happened to him. I hate that he can't talk to me. But I know if I push him, it'll only make things worse.

Instead, I'm watching him sleep, like a lunatic stalker. I can't help it. My body won't let me rest until I've gone over all these possible scenarios a million more times. I can already feel him pulling away from me. Just tonight, he didn't look like he wanted to tell me the truth but couldn't.

He looked… blank. I hate it. It feels like looking at him through a pane of glass. It's not really him.

Maybe I underestimated how hard it would be for him to separate from the Banna. Which seems ridiculous, because I already thought of it as this insane, insurmountable task. But I think that was looking at it in the practical sense.

Getting them to let him go. Getting him safe and not being followed. That was what I was focusing on.

I never really thought about how difficult it might be for him to let it all go. Even though I know he wants out, I'm sure there are a million layers of guilt and shame and other complex emotions that I couldn't even begin to understand.

Is that what he was thinking about tonight? Or was he really hiding something from me? I trace my finger down the side of his face. Super gently, because I don't want to disturb him. Although it's clear he's not sleeping well. He's twitching and moaning a little, like he's dreaming about something that's agitating him.

If this were a movie, he'd blurt out his secret in his sleep and then all this wondering would be moot. I wait for longer than I should, but he never says anything. At least nothing intelligible. It's just soft, sad noises and more uncomfortable twitching.

Eventually I put my head back on his chest and hold him tight. It leaves me feeling useless, but I don't know what else I can do.

Chapter Twenty-Seven

Micah

I must have fallen asleep at some point, because Tadhg is looking at me when I finally open my eyes.

His expression is guarded. Unreadable, except for how obvious it is that something isn't right with him. And the fact that he's not talking to me about it makes it clear that something isn't right with *us*, either.

"Hey, doll."

My voice is low and a little hoarse from not getting enough sleep. I reach out to run my thumb over his eyebrow and then down the side of his face, and he immediately closes his eyes. All the breath leaves his lungs—not like a normal exhale, but like a balloon letting all the air escape because it's just been popped.

"How are you feeling?" I ask, but he stays still, and his eyes stay closed.

I get the impression that today isn't going to be a day with lots of communication. Part of my brain is already wide awake and scrambling to find a solution. Solving problems is what I do. Tackling a crisis. It's in my fucking bones.

But he seems more peaceful right now with my hands on him than he has in a while. I don't want to be the one to burst that bubble of tranquility. Even if it's only the illusion of tranquility.

"Tadhg?"

Again, no response. But he presses his face into my hand in a sort of nuzzling gesture, while his hands snake out under the covers to wrap around my waist and pull me closer to him. As soon as I'm near him, he's pawing at me. Every part of my body is getting tugged until there's not a single inch of space between us. I try to be mindful of his bruises, but he doesn't even wince when I touch him. I suppose this level of pain is not something that registers for him, after everything he's endured.

His eyes stay closed, but that doesn't stop his mouth from finding me. He works his way over my collarbone, up my neck, all the way to my mouth, while his hands knead and squeeze whatever soft pieces of flesh they can find. His thick thighs wrap around mine, and I can feel how hard he already is as he drags his erection up and down my quad through the thin fabric of both our boxer briefs.

I think he tries to hide it, but I hear him whimper. Not in the horny way, either. It's a desperate, desolate sound that he immediately tries to swallow before he ravages my mouth with his.

It's easy to get swept up in the moment. Everything I've been thinking about is big and difficult and scary, and the more I focus on it, the more the negative part of my brain is whispering that it doesn't see any way this situation could have a happy ending for us. I can't let that happen, though. The bad guys don't just get to win.

"What's wrong?" I try for one more question, breaking off the kiss but holding his face close to mine as I run the fingers of my right hand through his hair, scratching at his scalp.

His lip fucking quivers.

Oh, Tadhg.

"Please," he says. It's all he says.

How can I say no to that?

"Yeah, okay. Come here, doll."

He pushes his body against mine, as if we weren't already fused together. I reach down and fumble blindly under the sheets until we're both naked, and Tadhg is already panting, rocking his hips against me and leaking a trail of precum over my thigh as he dry humps me. For all the concerns filling my head with noise, I'm still fucking rock hard myself, because he never fails to get me there.

There's just something about him going from the most closed-off, tightly wound person I've ever seen to this wanton, desperate, slutty *thing* that immediately turns me all the way on. It's gorgeous. So unabashedly sexual and submissive, like he's subconsciously trying to make up for how much of his life he's spent repressed and contained.

I never want it to stop. I grab on to his ass with both hands, digging my fingers into all the muscle and flesh there and guiding him as he rocks into me. He starts making those little *ah-ah* sounds that he sometimes does before he comes, and this has got to be a record for how quickly he's gotten himself there.

He deserves this. I keep rocking him, enjoying the feel of his soft skin stretched over a flushed, stiff cockhead everywhere it touches me. Enjoying the way my own cock keeps dragging across his hipbone as he rides my leg.

And of course, I can't help but bring my mouth to his ear to whisper to him.

"So perfect for me, doll. A perfect, desperate slut with a greedy cock and a needy pussy. You look so beautiful when you ride me, I want you to make a mess all over my stomach like the hot little prize that you are. What a good girl. Rubbing off on my leg like she needs to. Perfect."

Tadhg's small gasps turn to choked, bitten-off moans and cries as his movements get faster and more uncoordinated. He's getting close, but I still have time to suck my middle finger into my mouth, getting it nice and wet, before reaching back down and slipping it into his entrance to seek out his prostate.

As soon as I stroke him inside, he loses it. With an anguished cry, he stiffens and spills thick ropes of white all over my chest, stomach, and pubes. It's everywhere. It erupts with the same level of desperation that he was humping me with.

We're both panting as he comes down from the orgasm high, and he's staring at me with those gold-tinged eyes, wide and full of wonder. Well, fear and wonder.

The fear is always there when I look at him. No matter what, it's never truly gone.

"Better?" I ask.

He pants more, his breathing not slowing down. For a second, I worry that he's about to cry or segue into a panic attack. Instead, he starts pawing at me all over again.

"More," he says, his voice cracking. "More, Bambi. Please."

I frown, because I don't know if I've ever seen him desperate in quite this way before. No matter how much begging he's done for me in the relatively short time since we started fucking.

His big, warm hand wraps around my cock and when he strokes me, his grip is tight enough to make me hiss. I can feel his intensity in every single movement, every shadow, every flicker of his expression.

He needs something from me.

I don't know what, but I can guess.

I don't waste time. I know my broth–lover better than anyone.

He whines when I lean away from him, but it's only for a second. I fish something out of the nightstand, along with the lube. When I turn back to him, he looks wrecked, like I'm about to bail. I'll show him exactly how much I'm unwilling to let him go, though.

I let myself be as rough as I need to be. I'm careful not to put pressure directly on the bruising over his ribs, but other than that I don't hold back, grabbing and pushing his larger, heavier body until he's flipped over on his belly on the bed with his legs spread wide. I pull his beautiful cheeks apart and spit onto his hole, making as much of a mess as I can, before reaching around for my toy.

"Don't worry, doll. I'm right here. I've got what you need."

By the time I finish speaking, the toy is covered in lube. I brace one hand on his ass and then, without warning and with no hesitation, I slide the entire thing into his hole.

He fucking howls. And I get it. It's a slim little toy, significantly smaller than most of the things I like to put in his ass, but with no prep whatsoever it's still going to catch him off guard. I don't relent, though. He's bucking and writhing, and I still manage to turn the fucker on to maximum vibrate where it sits snuggly against his prostate.

More animalistic noises tear out of his mouth as his hips jerk. I give his ass a sharp, hard slap for good measure. Hard enough to watch the skin pink up where I touched him. Then I slide my hand up to the back of his neck and scruff him like a lion cub.

"None of that, doll. You're getting what you need right now. You wanted my hands on you. You asked for this."

I'll cover every inch of his bruised skin with my own loving marks until he forgets his father's fucking hands have ever touched him, if that's what it takes.

I roll him onto his back again, pulling him until his head is hanging backwards off the side of the bed. The angle leaves his throat completely open and mine for the taking, and just like with the vibrator, I don't hesitate. I've been aching hard for too long, and I slide the whole, hard length of me into his throat, moaning as the muscles there flutter around me.

"Perfect."

That's all he gets before I'm too breathless to talk because I'm fucking his throat with abandon. His whole body—all 200-something pounds of muscle—rocks with each movement. His face and neck are already bright red, the flush crawling down his chest underneath all the black lines of his tattoos. And every sound that comes out of his mouth is depraved. Choking, gagging sounds that should repulse me, but actually only make me want to fill him with my cum even more.

I smother him. Not just choking him on my cock but covering his nose sometimes. Crushing his face with my pelvis. There's no reprieve, just enough of a break each time so he can suck in the air he needs to keep living and then it's back to gagging and seeing stars. I couldn't even say how long it goes on for, because I get just as lost in it as he is.

He doesn't get hard again, but I can see him chubbed a little, dark red where his cock lays against his skin and still wet from before. His hips are still jerking as the vibrator pummels his prostate relentlessly, while the rest of his body has gone limp.

When I feel my orgasm building, I pull out of his mouth. The only sounds are the wet, rattling gasps of air that he's taking, but that's quickly cut off when I start repositioning him again.

I'm almost there, but he needs to hurt more. I know it. If I don't hurt him enough now, he'll just spend the day wandering around, finding some other way to hurt himself. As long as I do it, I know it's a hurt he can quickly recover from.

It pushes me to be rougher and more aggressive than I've ever been with a partner before. Even ones who asked for it. Every touch leaves a mark. As I maneuver him, I pinch him, scratch him, bite him and slap at the most tender, exposed pieces of his flesh. Even the bruising on his ribs, I'm still careful not to press on, but I scrape the skin with my fingernails over and over, hard enough to make him wail.

Every touch makes him cry out, but his hips keep working like he's fucking the air and at some point, he starts whispering *please, please, please* whenever there's a gap between the pain.

Once he's back on his stomach, I feel for the vibrator and yank it out. He spreads his legs as wide as he can for me, his thighs already quaking so hard I'm surprised he can control them. I shouldn't lose momentum, but I can't help myself. He's so fucking beautiful here.

I let myself stroke the pads of my fingers over his hole—now bright pink and slick with lube—before dipping them inside and tugging at the rim for a minute. Just a tease. Just rubbing my finger around his rim, applying pressure as I go. That's all the prep he gets.

Once my body is braced over his, chest to back, I lean close so I can whisper in his ear one more time.

"You're getting everything you deserve, Tadhg. Never forget that."

I don't know how he'll take the words in his state of mind, but I mean them. He deserves this. He deserves to be loved unconditionally, no matter how fucked up he feels or how much his hurt makes him act out. And I'll be damned if anyone is going to stop me doing it.

I press a gentle kiss to his temple, noticing the tear tracks covering his face and nuzzling against them for just a second.

Then I lean back and push my lube-covered cock inside him. Again, he gets no respite. Just burning, stretching pain combined with the pleasure of being filled.

He doesn't scream this time. He moans, long and low, while his body trembles beneath me and his hands fist the sheet over and over in a desperate movement.

As soon as I'm seated, I start to fuck. Because as much as I love him, this isn't sex or making love. This is fucking. This is buck-nasty fucking.

The sounds we make are wet and loud, accompanied by my hoarse grunts and Tadhg's constant, feral cries. I ride his ass as hard and fast as I can, and it feels like he's squeezing around me the whole time, trying to suck me deeper, trying to keep me deep inside.

"Come again for me, doll. I know you can." I punctuate this with the hardest slap to his ass I can manage from this angle.

His cock is still soft, but his body is so responsive to

everything I don't think that will stop him. I know he has one more in him, and I want to pull it out of him.

"No, no, no, no, no," he moans, unable to articulate more than that.

"Yes." My voice is sharp and full of authority.

I jerk his hips so they're higher off the bed but put one hand on his shoulder blades, so his chest and face are still buried in the covers. With my other hand, I reach around to fondle him with the same aggressive, relentless energy I'm burying my cock inside him with, feeling him thicken a little more under my touch.

"I can't," he wails, but I only squeeze him tighter.

"Yes, you can. You're my perfect doll, and you have cum inside you that I need to fuck out. Can you get it out for me? Every last drop. Give it to me."

No more words come from Tadhg, but he starts sobbing. His hips are working though, grinding against me as I keep jerking him. I can feel the telltale pulse and twitch of his cock as he gets closer.

"That's it. Perfect. Give it all to Bambi."

Then he really does cry out. It's loud. Bother-my-neighbors loud and sounds more like an animal than a human being. But at the same time, his cock pulses and jerks in my hand; hard enough to surprise me.

There isn't a lot of cum left in him, but whatever he has left he slowly drips out of his body like it's some kind of exorcism. The sheets beneath him are wet with it, and it's all I need to push me over the edge.

With both hands on his hips, I ride him as hard as I can for a few more thrusts before burying myself as deep as I can and pulsing my own load into his tight little hole. I can practically picture it flooding his insides. Filling him up until he's soaked in all the creamy fluid I could possibly pour into him. Stretching his belly from the inside out because there's so much.

It's an exaggeration, but the thought makes me shiver all the same.

I can't help but place one hand over his belly as I pull his back to my chest. As if I could feel the head of my cock and the swell of all that cum distending him from the inside.

Tadhg is just crying now. Sobbing. It's good, though. This is what I wanted. I needed him to let go of whatever he was holding on to. I even manage to wrap my arms around his chest and then gently lower us both to the mattress on our sides without slipping out of him.

We lie like that for a very long time. I go soft eventually, but I stay inside him as long as I can, plugging my own cum in there. I keep him close, but don't say anything. I let him cry. I want it all out, and I don't want to do anything to interfere. We can talk when he's done.

He goes straight from crying to falling asleep, but that's okay. We're both disgusting and normally I'd make us clean up first, but this seems like a 'fuck it' kind of day.

So, I fall back asleep as well with him still in my arms. Both of us sticky and on filthy sheets, but with nothing left to lose.

Savage

I'm grateful that Micah still doesn't push me to talk once we wake up for the second time. I can barely get my limbs to cooperate, let alone string a sentence together, after the fucking I received.

I've seen a lot of sides to my former stepbrother. Frightened, confident, sexy as fuck, even the dominant side that surprised me so much when I first realized that was a part of him. But the kind of raw, animalistic frenzy is nothing I expected from him.

When he's broken me down before, it's been methodical. He's edged me until I cried. He never physically tried to destroy me. I'm so fucking thankful that he did, though.

I don't know how he always has this sixth sense for what I need, even when I have no clue. But that was it. That was fucking it. He nailed it.

I feel liquid now. Still exhausted at my core, and just… sad. I'm so sad about everything that's happened and everything I know is about to happen. I know that sounds childish. Adults should have more complex emotions or something.

Nope. I got nothing. Just tired and sad. I'm sad because of how much I've wasted my shitty life. I'm sad because I don't actually think I'll ever convince Father to let me leave the Banna alive, after yesterday, and I'm sad because through all of this, I couldn't even manage to do the one thing Micah asked me to and not kill Eamon.

The satisfaction of sliding my knife into his skull offset that sadness a fraction, obviously. Motherfucker deserved so much worse. But it pales in the face of how weak I feel for letting Micah down.

I should just tell him and get this over with. If he leaves me, at least it'll be done, and I can stop hovering in the in-between. Maybe he should push me.

He broke me down so systematically that I'll tell him anything he wants to know right now. All he needs to do is open his mouth and ask.

There's fuck-all food in the apartment, so Micah orders us some deli sandwiches from town. He reminds me to shower, because I'm absolutely vile, and joins me in there even though he keeps the whole thing PG. The only words we exchange are practical ones, but the whole time we move around this small space together, Micah watches me.

He watches, and watches, and watches.

I feel like a bomb is ticking somewhere. It's probably the only thing that gets my sluggish, cum-drunk body to eventually switch back on.

"Bambi, can you please say it. Whatever you're trying not to say, just say it. I can't take the suspense anymore."

Ok, so it looks like I was the one to snap.

My hands are shaking a little, and I'm staring at him from across the open living space where he's putting the sandwiches onto plates in the kitchen. At first, he gives me a wide-eyed look. Then he sighs, and his shoulder slump.

"I was trying not to pressure you, because I know how bossy I can be. Apparently, I was unsuccessful."

He wanders over to me, one plate in each hand, and places them on the little coffee table. When he gestures toward the couch, I walk over and sit. It's unnatural, though. I feel stiff and like I'm taking up too much space. Like my legs are wrong and my hands are in a weird place on my body.

This could be the last moment in my life before Micah decides he's finally done with my shit.

This could be the last moment in my life.

The thought fills me with even more exhaustion, but also a certain sense of peace. It's all out of my control, now. I can only take whatever happens and then drift away from the consequences if I can't deal with them. It makes me weak, sure, but what else is new?

"Tadhg, breathe!"

Micah's voice interrupts my thoughts, and I pull in a

breath. He moves toward me on the couch, running one hand up the back of my neck and threading the other through the fingers of my right hand.

"See, this is fucking concerning me, Tadhg. This. What is happening? Obviously giving you space isn't working, and neither is fucking some serenity into you. I'm out of ideas so I'm going back to being bossy. Tell me what's happening before I go down there and ask Patrick myself."

"No," I growl, even though I know he's bluffing.

I did all this to keep him away from Father.

Micah's eyes soften, but his mouth twists and I see so much of my sadness reflected in his face that it makes me physically ache. His thumb slides up into my hairline, and his fingers scratch hard into the skin at the base of my skull, scratching me over and over as if he can force some relaxation into me.

"Then tell me, doll. Just tell me. Whatever it is."

"Eamon's dead."

Micah frowns and looks confused for a second. Then realization dawns, and his mouth forms a small 'O'. For a second, I think he's going to ask me outright, but then he looks around his apartment as if he thinks it might be bugged.

"This is what your fight with Patrick was about, I'm guessing."

Those are the words he settles on in the end, but we both know what he means.

I nod, and he takes a long time to absorb the information. It's too quiet. I shrink further and further into myself, fighting the urge to physically curl up small and ignore all of this until it goes away.

I don't know when I stopped even being able to pretend

to be strong, but it happened. And I'm so far past caring about it.

"I'm sorry, Tadhg," Micah says at last.

Something in me cracks. Which makes something else splinter, and then crack after crack spreads through my body. I'm a salt pillar, hard on the outside but so riddled with fissures that I only need one tiny breeze to utterly collapse.

This is it. This is when he tells me to leave.

I don't feel sad anymore, though. Numbness is quickly taking over.

"I shouldn't have told you not to do it. That was dumb. It was never in your control in the first place, and I knew that. I was just being self-righteous or something."

The words come to me, but they're difficult to parse through the *whomp-whomp* of blood rushing through my ears.

"What?"

Micah's eyebrows meet in the middle, and he leans in closer to me, his hand still on my neck.

"I shouldn't be giving you ultimatums, Tadhg. It was selfish. Not while Patrick still has all the power, here. I'm sorry I made you feel like you couldn't tell me."

When I still don't answer him, blinking slowly and trying to absorb all this, Micah moves closer and ends up climbing into my lap. He wraps his legs around my waist, still gentle on the side with my bruised ribs, but his arms loop around my shoulders and squeeze me as tightly as he can.

It helps. I take a few more short, tight breaths and feel the fog lifting. He's not leaving me?

"I love you, Tadhg. I told you. I'm *in love* with you. That doesn't change because you get trapped in a shitty situation or you fuck up. I know we're both kind of used to love with strings attached so it's hard to grasp, but we can at least change that with each other, right?"

I just keep staring at him. Every word in the English language has evacuated my brain.

"Unless," he says, his brow furrowing. "You don't feel the same?"

Well, if I ever hated anything in my life, it wasn't as much as I hate the unsure look on his face right now. Not my Bambi. That's the final gut punch that gets my gears turning again and brings my tongue back to life.

"Of course I do, Bambi. You're the only person I've ever loved. I'll do anything for you. I just wish I could stop being so weak and letting you down."

"Oh, doll," he whispers, before kissing me lightly on each cheek and then my forehead. "I told you before, but I'll tell you every day if you need me to. You're so strong. You're so good. You have no idea how good you are, but I do. I promise, you could never do anything to let me down. Just keep being here and letting me love you."

I nod, choking on a lump in my throat too big to talk through.

He kisses me. Not deeply, but when he opens his mouth, I respond, and he laves his tongue lazily against mine. It goes on for a while, even though it's not headed anywhere. It feels good to have him in my hands. I want him wrapped around me forever.

When he breaks off the kiss, it's too soon and I chase him. He wants to talk, though.

"We need to deal with Patrick, though. That sadistic prick. We can't keep living in this in-between. You and me, brainstorming. Right now. We either have to find something to frighten him into letting you go, or something valuable enough to trade him so he'll let you go. So, you tell me. What's Patrick afraid of?"

I frown. I never really thought about him being afraid of anything. For my entire life, he's been a cross between a supervillain and an inhuman vigilante. Always there, always waiting, always larger than life.

Does he even feel fear?

"Come on," Micah says. "There has to be something. Spiders? Clown tchotchkes? Other gangsters? The inevitability of aging? Prison?"

I tilt my head to the side, because maybe he's onto something.

"The law, maybe. He's never been to prison, and I know he doesn't want to go now that he's getting older. He cares about his reputation and his legacy more than his money, which is why I was always so important to him, I think. I needed to carry on his name. That was what he talked about, anyway."

Micah looks thoughtful and then pecks me on the lips for good measure.

"Okay. We can work with that. Let's think."

Chapter Twenty-Eight

Savage

This is a bad plan. It had sounded so good when Bambi laid it all out. We went over it and over it and over it in minute detail. Everything made sense the way he'd explained it to me.

Now that I'm standing here, waiting for my father, it feels like a very bad plan. He won't show up. Or he will show up and he'll kill me. Or Colm won't hold up his end of the deal. Or maybe Colm will be the one to kill me.

Okay, I don't believe the last one. I've always trusted him. I shouldn't, but I do. For whatever reason, I've known he'd lay his life on the line for me since the start. He never said it because he rarely says much of anything, but it's always been true.

I can practically hear Micah's voice in my head.

"*Trust yourself, Tadhg. You're better than that worthless old fuck in every way.*"

Then he'd kissed me goodbye and said, "*Come home to me.*"

We both agreed he shouldn't be here. I was ready to fight him over it, but he didn't push the issue. I think he understood that this was something I needed to do.

I'm standing in some kind of outdoor gym behind an auto shop. I think it's the same one I visited on my whistle stop tour of the area when I was desperately searching for a job, before I ended up finding Gunnar. There's an old house a hundred feet away, but both buildings are pitch black and shut up for the night. We're surrounded by the woods apart from the two-lane road that led here, so it's *dark*-dark, and all the homemade gym equipment looms around me like sleeping monsters, or a twisted metal graveyard.

I guess there are worse places to be buried. At least I'm close to Micah here.

His friends own this place but they also have a loose association with the Banna. I didn't really understand the details when Micah explained them, because my attention was snowing in and out, but he assured me that they were connected enough that Father would trust the place to not be bugged or worry about an ambush being set up, but it was still friendly territory to us, because these guys secretly hate my father and everything he stands for.

Which I get. I might not know the details, but I understand being sucked into something you hate, so I'll take Bambi's word for it. They left for the night to avoid getting caught in the crossfire, so it's just me here. I shouldn't be nervous. I've faced worse odds with a lot less support, but still.

Father always seems to get what he wants. I don't know how to picture a world where that isn't true.

When I hear the crunch of gravel under tires, my heart rate skyrockets for a second. But then it happens. Exactly like I was hoping—my on-the-job brain takes over and I focus. My own life becomes inconsequential, and I laser in on the reason I'm here.

Protect Micah. Save myself if I can. But I'm ending tonight with no more ties to Father or his crew no matter what. Dead or alive.

Father eventually rounds the corner, accompanied by Colm, as arranged. Colm's face is tight. His hand is resting on his hip, like he's unwilling to let it stray too far from his Beretta, but I couldn't say what specific part of this is making him uneasy. All of it, I guess.

"What's the meaning of this, boy?" Father barks as soon as he gets close enough.

Deep breath in. Deep breath out. Picture Micah, alive and safe.

"I'm here to make a deal, Father."

Fuck, I hope he can't hear how my voice is wavering. He squints at me like I said something in an alien language, but he doesn't interrupt, so I guess that's a good sign.

"I want out. I'm done. I'm leaving the Banna one way or another and you're going to let me. No more crime, no more anything, and I never want to see you or speak to you ever again."

The words come out in such a rush I'm surprised he can make them all out. But by the way his eyes widen and his mouth falls open, he must. There's a long pause while he processes what I said, and I try to get the pounding of my heart under control.

"Don't be ridiculous," he says at last. "There's no out.

This is it. This is your birthright. This is everything you were meant to do."

He takes a step toward me with his hand outstretched, although I can't tell if it's in anger or supplication. I shrink back anyway, turning into myself to get away from him.

"No."

I don't follow the word with anything else, and it feels freeing. Like all the 'no's' I've never said rolled into one.

That's when his face shifts from shock to anger. I was waiting for it, but that doesn't make it any less distressing.

He moves quickly, closing the few feet of distance between us to grab me by the shirt and shake me like an unruly child. I go limp on instinct, hoping he won't escalate the situation. I can see Colm taking a half step forward, tension written throughout his body, but I shake my head at him as discreetly as I can.

"No? You don't get to say no to me. You're mine. I made you. You have a legacy to uphold, otherwise all of this was fucking pointless. Our family has run the Banna for generations and what? You're just going to be the one weak piece of shit who runs away because he feels like it? No, you're going to get your shit together, start acting like the man I raised you to be, and take over here so I can go home. And when I die, you can take over the whole thing. It's the natural fucking order."

I want to laugh, but it comes out as a sort of wet, sad sound.

"Natural order, Father?" God, I sound unhinged already, even to myself. "You want to talk about the natural order? You wanted Eamon out because he was queer, right? Well, I'm as unnatural as they get. I promise you don't want me representing your business or your family."

My stomach twists and bile climbs up the back of my

throat. This wasn't supposed to happen. We agreed I wouldn't tell him anything about me or Micah, because it would be more likely to provoke a rage. This was all supposed to be as unemotional as possible. My freedom for his.

He stares at me, his face uncomprehending once again. Then his eyes narrow, and the same fury I'm used to seeing takes over. His hand moves to my throat and squeezes. Not aggressively or in blind rage. But cold and consistent, like he's working with a purpose this time.

Fuck. This may have been a mistake.

It's barely seconds before black dots are swimming in my vision. He may be getting older, but there's still a lot of strength left in him and his hand is well on its way to crushing my throat. I try to push him off, but my movements are weak.

I'm weaker than I should be. Just like every time I go toe to toe with him, I'm holding myself back. It's pathetic, but after all this time, I still can't bring myself to fully stand up to him.

I can hear the sound of Colm rushing over, cursing as he trips on some loose piece of equipment. He pulls at Patrick, but it doesn't seem to have any effect. The dark spots get bigger and bigger, and the ground beneath me is starting to sway.

"No," I croak, barely audible through the iron grip that Patrick has on my throat.

His face is practically purple with rage, but his eyes are cold. I don't even know how much of the truth he's put together by what I just said, or if he's just so pissed that I confronted him in the first place.

It doesn't matter. I don't think I have it in me to pull away. At least like this, he'll leave Micah alone. With me alive, there would always be the chance that he could come for us. This way, Micah will always be safe.

It's the only decent thing I've ever really done for him.

The thought comforts me as a blanket of static drags me down toward the ground.

Bright lights flare, interrupting my peace and piercing my mind. The brightness hurts. I can't tell if this is a *Matrix* reborn-into-death situation or if I'm still alive and there are lights now, but I can feel Father's grip on me loosen with surprise, so my bet is on alive.

As soon as the pressure comes off my trachea, I cough, although it makes my ribs ache where they're still bruised. It's enough give for Colm to jerk him back, freeing me from him. I hit the ground immediately. My legs have no idea what to do. But no one is touching me here, which is a plus.

It is light. Or there are lights, more accurately. Big, bright halogens I didn't notice before illuminate the space.

Father shoves Colm away from him, both of them breathing hard, but he doesn't come for me again.

"What's going on?" he asks, his voice a growl.

I can hear voices from the darkness somewhere, but I can't pinpoint their location or what they're saying. We were supposed to be alone, but as soon as my brain connects the dots, I know there's only one person it can be hiding in the bushes.

That sneaky, conniving little shit.

I'm going to kill him.

Just as I realize what's happening, Micah comes crashing out of the trees at the edge of the property and runs toward me. Father has his gun in his hand, pointed at him in less than a second.

I make an animalistic noise, reaching toward him, even

though I still can't get to my feet. Everyone else is faster, though.

Colm pulls out his gun and points it at Father, barking the order to freeze. I was already impressed that he agreed to help me with this, but now he's actually turned on his boss, I know how deep his loyalty lies.

Also, behind Micah there are two more men. One is huge, with long dark hair and enough tattoos to make his otherwise pale skin blend into the darkness. I think I recognize him as the mechanic who works here. He's holding a hunting rifle pointed at my father, although I can tell from his stance that he's not happy about it.

The other man is my size, but somehow more menacing than the big guy. He's holding his weapon like it's as natural as breathing air. He follows Micah with quick, easy steps, never taking his eyes off his target, and looks more in his element here than any of the rest of us.

I'm assuming these are Micah's friends he talks about. Apparently, I even met one of them while I was unconscious and feverish, but I don't remember. All I want to know is where someone like him finds friends like this.

Micah is always brave. But he's never looked more set on anything than he is on getting to me. By the time he reaches me, kneeling in the dirt to help pull me into a sitting position, Father is surrounded and letting his gun dangle limply between his fingers.

I'm half-sitting, half-leaning in Micah's lap as he grabs my face and examines me.

"Tadhg! Can you hear me? Look at me."

He looks me over, which is something he's had to do far too many times.

"I'm okay, Bambi." My voice is barely a croak, and it hurts to push the words through, but I manage it.

"Goddamn right you are," he says, still touching me. "Idiot. Big dumb mafia idiot."

I try to speak again, but it comes out as a cough. I know what he means though. This wasn't the plan. I wasn't supposed to rile him up. I was supposed to present the terms and walk away.

Father, meanwhile, is watching us with something between awe and revulsion on his face. It's as if he can't settle on the correct emotion, so he's filtering through too many of them at once.

"Savage, what are you doing?" he asks.

"That's not his fucking name!" Micah is still holding my face as he yells at Father. He flinches away a little, because he holds the same in-built fear of the man that I do, but at least he can push past it. "He's your son. Your fucking child. You named him. You raised him. And now you want to kill him?"

Father doesn't say anything. His eyes narrow and he settles into his stance, like any trepidation he had about his own safety is gone, even though no one has stopped pointing a gun at him.

Micah leans his forehead against mine for just a second, taking a deep breath, before he lets me go. When he stands up, I feel cold and empty, but I don't try to stop him. If anyone can succeed where I failed, it's him.

"I swear to Beelzebub, I'm over this fucking cloak and dagger bullshit. I need you to focus, Patrick." The sharpness in his tone seems to take everyone aback, as well as the way he rounds on Father and draws himself up to the most intimidating version of himself. Even Father seems taken aback by the sudden shift. "Tadhg told you he's done. He's *done*. He's going to stay here and live his life, while you and all your cronies leave both of us the fuck alone. And my mom. She's out, too, whether she wants to be or not. You're going back to Oklahoma, just like you want, so none of us have to ever look at each other's faces again. And if you need that upstanding, heteronormative, well-behaved successor so badly, look behind you."

Father turns around reluctantly and eyes Colm, who is still holding a gun in his direction but with less intent, now. Colm meets his eye and shrugs, as if all this makes sense to him. Which it does, to be fair. Colm is exactly the kind of person Father should want as lieutenant. Calm, rational, and utterly dedicated to the Banna.

"It can all be very simple and painless. Eamon is gone, and he was the one causing all the drama with his fucking lies, anyway. I bet nobody else even cares if Tadhg slinks off into the night. All they care about is making their money. They'll all back Colm if you tell them to."

I can see Father's jaw clench, the muscles jumping as he internally chafes at being dictated to by someone he most likely thinks of as sub-human.

"And if I don't? Your little friends will shoot me and spend a few hours gloating until the Banna come for you all?"

The less huge one of Micah's friends waves his gun at Father like a 'hello', a wide grin on his face.

"We haven't officially met. My name's Tristan and this is Ford. Your shitty little friend blackmailed us into doing some bitch work for your organization. We thought we would help Micah and also piggy-back on the whole 'free me, free me,' situation. Like he said, Eamon's dead and he was the toxic piece of glue holding all this shit together. Time for you to go home and all of us to go back to normal."

There's no hiding the combination of sass and disdain in

his voice. He stands up to Father like he does this every day and doesn't give a shit what the man thinks.

"And if you don't," Micah says. "There's a very long, very detailed dossier of information that we've all compiled, sitting on a lawyer's desk, waiting to be sent to the feds. You'd best believe WITSEC will snap us up—all of us—with the amount of dirt we collectively know. It's extreme, sure. But I want you to know, Pat, from the bottom of my heart. If ruining my own life is what it takes to ruin yours and put you in federal prison, it's still worth it."

Micah's in his face as he says this, unblinking and undeterrable.

I expect Father to rage again. I even pull myself unsteadily to my feet to get ready for it. There's no way he won't call Micah's bluff.

Instead, my father looks around at all the men surrounding him and he literally sags.

He looks exhausted. He looks at each of them in turn before he turns his gaze to me, and this time I win the fight not to shrink under it.

"Fine."

The word echoes around the space, knocking on my skull but not able to press inside, like something I can't quite accept.

"What?" I ask, my voice more robust now.

"Fine," he says again, but he's just as stony-faced and harsh as the first time. "I'll let you live. And him." He tosses his head at Micah. "But only because I'm sick of this overgrown cornfield of a town. It stinks of shit, and I haven't found two brain cells to rub together in the whole damn place. Do whatever the fuck you want. But my name is dead to you, boy. You ruined that. Tadhg Moynihan does not exist anymore."

I open my mouth. My agreement is on the tip of my tongue, but I can't seem to force it out. I'm not hesitating. I don't give a fuck about his shitty name. I don't know why I can't make the sounds.

"Deal," Micah says for me. I sag with relief, and something deep inside me begins to accept that this might finally be over. "Now leave. Tonight. If anything happens to a single one of us, the feds are getting that dossier, remember."

For a second, I think he's going to say something to me. Some kind of goodbye, or a final insult, or a little closure. I think I want it, even if it's hateful. Even if it's acknowledgement that he couldn't love me and never will. Anything to confirm this feeling that it's all done.

He doesn't, though. I'm left hanging as Father looks at me once, opens his mouth and then shuts it again before turning to Colm.

"I guess you're proud of yourself, you little snake."

Colm takes a deep breath, looking as steady and calm as always. "I want what's best for the Banna, sir. Always. Eamon was causing problems. This feud between you and your son was causing problems. It'll be better this way, when we can focus on the real enemy. Besides, we need you at home more than we need you here, caught up in drama. Let me handle the bullshit while you go back to the big picture, and I promise this can all seem like a shitty memory."

Father doesn't say anything. Without a single backward glance or another acknowledgement of me, he sets off walking toward the car, expecting Colm to follow.

Colm comes over to me instead. I think he's going to shake my hand or something, but instead he leans in close, pulling me into a half-hug that's more intimate than any physical contact I've experienced from someone other than Micah.

"I'm proud of you," he whispers in my ear.

Then he's gone, too. Everyone else is staring at me, as if I'm supposed to do something. As if I should know what to do next, like I wasn't the only useless person during this entire situation.

I sit my ass back down on the ground, because it's the only thing I can think of.

There is not one single part of me that knows what I'm supposed to do next.

Chapter Twenty-Nine

Micah

I spent so much time emotionally preparing for the whole Western showdown situation, I forgot to plan for the aftermath. I wasn't totally convinced there would be an aftermath, to be honest. A significant, rational portion of my consciousness was convinced none of us would be walking away from tonight alive, let alone successful.

Whatever I did to have the gay gods bless this union, *thank you*. Because that was all a shot in the fucking dark.

I still have no idea if Patrick knew we were bluffing about going to the FBI. I know I sold it, and I'm a good liar when I have to be. Tadhg, bless his soul, is a terrible liar. It's one of the reasons I was always planning to crash the party. That and the fact that something like what did happened was probably inevitable.

Maybe he thought we were bluffing but didn't want to

risk it. Maybe he believed me. Maybe he just decided all this drama wasn't worth it, and he wanted to free himself of the son who had become such a burden to him as soon as it was obvious Tadhg would never be what Patrick wanted.

The real gamble was that Patrick had enough humanity in him to let Tadhg leave alive. I was always leaning toward yes, because as much as that man has terrorized our lives, he's not a Disney villain. We both know he raised us how he was raised. I was always a write-off for him, my queerness evident from the start, but I'm sure he thought he could 'fix' Tadhg's shortcomings if he just pushed him hard enough.

Unfortunately, my babygirl doesn't respond well to beatings. So buh-bye, Patrick. Whether you bought the FBI story or not, we're finally free. No more you, no more Eamon, no more Banna bullshit.

If only Tadhg seemed willing to accept this.

As soon as he hit the ground outside Ford's shop, I knew he wasn't taking this well. He's been nearly catatonic ever since. It took Ford and Tristan helping to get him into the car, and by the time we got back to the apartment he was focused enough to walk upstairs for me, but unresponsive for anything else.

He's sitting on the couch now, staring into space. I wrap a blanket around his shoulders even though it isn't cold in here, because I don't really know what else to do. I want to get him out of those stupid tactical clothes, but it would be too much of a fight. I don't expect him to be magically okay.

Sure, he got what he wanted, but he also got abandoned by someone he's spent his whole life fighting for approval from. That's tough. I get it.

But he's scaring me.

I kneel in front of him, positioned between his legs with one hand resting on each knee. My hands rub up and down his thighs over and over, gradually drawing his attention to me.

"Can you say something for me, doll? Anything. How you feel, what you want, what you're worried about?"

Tadhg frowns. "I don't... I don't know."

"Okay," I say, nodding. "That's okay. That's something to start with. Are you hungry?"

He shakes his head.

"Do you want to shower? Or sleep for a while?"

Another shake.

I study his face. He doesn't look distressed, exactly. But he didn't have to tell me he was confused for me to know; it's written in his features. His eyes dart from side to side under a furrowed brow. His hair is messy from the tussle with Patrick, and it's grown long enough that it's falling in his eyes a little.

The bruising on his neck is pretty bad and looks even worse in the light of my apartment. I really want to take him to the hospital for an actual evaluation, because strangulation can cause all sorts of terrible shit that isn't obvious right away, but I know he won't go.

Instead, I give him a little more time by doing another exam. I check him for signs of neurological deficits, or damage to the cartilage in his throat, or any kind of respiratory distress. I don't think I'm really accomplishing anything, but it makes me feel better and keeps my hands on him at the same time.

He sits quietly through it all, taking my examination as peacefully as he takes everything else I do to him.

He's still not speaking by the end of it, though, so I pull myself into his lap, bracketing his hips with my thighs and laying my arms on his broad shoulders. Normally, the closer

I get to him, the more it seems to pull him back from the brink of whatever sucks him into his own head.

I have to remind myself to be patient still, though, and ignore the flutter of panic inside my chest. I place soft kisses on his face, nuzzling into his hair and around his jaw. I scratch my nails over his scalp and dig my fingers into his tight traps.

"Come back to me, doll," I murmur in his ear.

Slowly, he stirs.

When I finally kiss him on the mouth, he responds. It's a gentle kiss. It's not going anywhere, and we're both still too drained and stressed out to be immediately popping wood, but at least he opens up for me. His warm, wet tongue responds to mine, and things start to feel a fraction more like normal.

I break off the kiss after a minute and find him looking at me with less of that vacant look in his eye.

"Talk to me."

My thumbs glide over his eyebrows and then the arch of his cheekbones, as if I can massage all the tension out of him until he talks. His mouth falls open, though, spit glistening on his pink, plush lower lip from our kiss, and there's a shudder as he inhales.

"I don't know what to say, Bambi."

His voice is so wrecked. He probably shouldn't be using it, but I need him to not go full-zombie on me until I can get a better read on where his head's at.

"We won." I arch an eyebrow at him. "I know it's kind of a hollow victory, because all we did was succeed in not getting murdered by your father, but still. We got what we wanted. You don't have to work for him anymore. He's leaving. It's over."

A long time passes before he speaks again, and it takes so much self-control not to fill that silence.

"He took my name with him," he says. Even under the hoarseness, I can hear the raw pain in his voice. "I didn't— How can he take my name?"

Tadhg shudders under my hands, so I pull him closer and rest his head against my chest for a second.

"I'm sorry, doll. He's a piece of shit." When I pull back, I look him in the eye. "You can have my name. You already belong to me a million times more than you ever belonged to him. He wants you to get a new name, I'd be fucking honored for you to share mine."

His eyebrows raise, but I can see the words land one by one, each one a hammer blow against all that misery his father has dealt him over the years.

"Really?"

"Of course. Tadhg suffered a lot of bad shit. Savage *inflicted* a lot of bad shit. You're already Sav to the guy's at the bar, and that's the start of your normal life. You can be Sav Alexander. I love you. You love me. Why can't we share a name that we're both proud of? It can be ours. Whatever that means."

His jaw tremors, but instead of tearing up, Tadhg reaches up and pulls me into a kiss. This one is more heated than the last, our mouths wide open, tongues wrestling like we're trying to climb inside each other.

It's not even sexy. It's just intense. It's exactly what we both need.

When we break apart this time, we're both panting, and I can feel my body waking up a little bit.

"I'm sorry," he says.

I can't help but scrunch up my nose at him. He apologizes for a lot of shit that isn't his fault, and I have no idea what this one is going to be.

"For what, doll?"

"I didn't tell him. I didn't tell him about us. Or me. Or anything, not really. I didn't really stand up to him. I know I was supposed to finally stand up for myself for once and end this whole big thing or get closure or be real man or whatever, and I didn't do any of it. I just let him hurt me, like always, and stayed scared. And then you had to save me."

"Oh, my love," I whisper, stroking soft fingers down his cheek and over his swollen lips. "Don't ever think that again. Promise me. You weren't weak because you didn't have some giant confrontation. If you'd made it any worse, he would have killed you. I didn't need you to tell your father anything. I don't need *anything* from that man. Not one damn thing. The only thing I needed was for you to come home to me, which you did. Letting me save you was the strongest thing you could have done."

His mouth makes a little pout at this, and it would be adorable if the context wasn't so sad. I know my words aren't landing. I know he can't wrap his head around this idea that he didn't need to be the man and stand up for himself.

He doesn't get it.

I run my nose along the bridge of his while I run my fingers through his hair and tug it hard enough to get his attention.

"I'll tell you every day if I need to, to get it through your fucking skull. Waking up, getting up, and living your life free from him. That's what makes you strong. This isn't a Hallmark movie. There's no lesson at the end. You're done. You just have to exist. And I will save you every day, over and over, as long as you need me to. You saved me enough times; I can repay the favor."

His frown deepens, but his mouth parts like he's trying to breathe my words into him and accept their meaning.

"I love you, Bambi."

I can't help but smile whenever he says that, still.

"I know, doll. And I will let you pillow princess your way right through the rest of our lives. You fucking earned it."

I don't give him the chance to object. I swallow all his words in another feverish kiss, and this time I don't let either of us come up for air. As long as he lets me, I'm going to be in charge of letting him finally get all the peace that he deserves.

Tadhg.

Sav Alexander.

None of it matters, because he'll always be my doll.

Epilogue

Three Months Later

Sav

I can tell when he walks in before I look up. I can always tell. It's like someone is smiling at me. There's a sudden warmth in the room that I only feel when he's around.

When I finish serving the drink I'm making—because Gunnar is finally letting me bartend sometimes now that he and Tobias are officially together, and he has someone else to help haul limes around—I search him out. He looks tired, because he just finished a double shift, and I know those always wreck him. I keep telling him to work less, but he's a glutton for punishment.

His scrubs are dirty, and I shudder to think what fluids are on his skin, but I don't care. Because he is smiling at me, and that warmth is the only thing in the world that matters right now.

"I told you I would make it in time to have a drink before you close," he says as he collapses onto a stool.

Time freezes for a moment. Or maybe it doesn't freeze, but it scatters in every direction, like a beam of light that's been fragmented.

I want to kiss him.

He told me I don't have to do anything that makes me uncomfortable. And even he likes to keep himself relatively buttoned up in public, because this is still a conservative area and it is what it is, as he put it. The Banna let me go like Father said they would, but the more extroverted I am with my 'perversions', the more likely rumors will get back to him and piss him off.

Not to mention, Gunnar, Tobias, and Kasia were originally introduced to Micah as my brother. I've explained the situation since then and they know we're not really related, but still living together. If the sidelong looks I get from Kasia and deliberate silence I get from Gunnar is any indicator, they might suspect there's something between us. But still, it feels awkward to just talk about myself like that and let them in on shit.

On the other hand, it's not like I'm ashamed of Micah. He's the only decent thing I've ever done.

Fuck it.

If there's anywhere I can do it, it's here. In this little pocket of safety at the Possum.

I lean over the bar, which is deep enough that I have to stand up on my toes to reach, grab Micah by the jaw and kiss him firmly on the mouth. No tongue, no lingering, but a solid enough kiss that it's unmistakably not platonic. And when I pull back, I keep my hand where it is so I can hover with our faces inches apart for a few more seconds.

Of course, Tobias wolf-whistles from somewhere behind me. The brat.

"Hi, Bambi," I murmur.

"Hi, doll."

There's a hint of flush creeping into his cheeks, and the sleepiness running through him makes him already soft in my hands.

"You want a margarita?"

His smile broadens, lovestruck and kind of dopey, and I'm still getting used to the fact that he makes that face all for me.

"Yes, please."

"Okay." I peck him on the lips one more time before I let him go, turning to get him the drink.

Everybody makes small talk for a little while. Micah fills me in on his shift, including a particularly grizzly assault victim that sounds a lot like the work of people we know, even though neither of us says that out loud. Tobias and Gunnar are disgustingly handsy with each other when they're supposed to be working, because what else is new, and I get to share exasperated looks about it with Kasia, who has sat down to drink with Micah because she's not working tonight and only came for the liquor.

It's getting closer to closing time when Micah cracks a joke that makes Kasia snort vodka out of her nose. There are only a few people left inside because it's only a Tuesday, so it's noticeable when the door opens, and a new person walks in.

Well, I don't notice right away, because I'm focusing on my work. And the constant, obsessive situational awareness I used to have has faded more quickly than I expected it to ever since I quit. The nightmares haven't faded at all. If anything, they're worse, but according to Bambi, that happens sometimes.

Either way, the only reason I take note of the new person is because Micah bristles in front of me.

I whip my head around, expecting the worst. Father, maybe. So far, it sounds like he's been keeping his word and sitting his ass in Oklahoma. He doesn't want anything to do with me, Micah, or Micah's mom, and is apparently content to pretend none of us ever existed. Of course, I'll never feel truly confident that's going to last.

Maybe it's Eamon's fucking ghost, here to haunt me along with the rest of my memories. I don't know.

It's only Colm.

He saunters in, looking as calm and subdued as ever. When he points those bright blue eyes at me, I see the same affection and loyalty in them as I always did, and it almost hurts.

I miss him, I guess. I didn't realize I would.

"Please don't tell me you're here to flee your life of crime," Gunnar says from behind the bar. "I'm out of money to hire people." He looks at Tobias and then at me, then coughs. "I mean, *alleged* life of crime."

I snort, but neither Micah or Kasia look amused. I'm expecting Tobias to protest and point out that he has his own job now and only helps out at the bar because he can, because the sass on him has become completely unmanageable now that he's not miserable and struggling to survive day to day. But when I look at him, he's silent. His eyes are dark and downcast, and his body is preternaturally still. Without a sound, he slowly slinks out of view, disappearing into the back hall, leaving Gunnar looking after him with a frown.

It makes sense. His experience of the Banna was one giant shit-fest of abuse, and it's hard to distinguish one threat from another. Colm probably looks like another Eamon in waiting to him. He looked at me the same way until I finally broke and told him what I did. He hugged me that day, which is a memory I'll hold on to for a very long time, even if I'm not quite sure what to do with it.

Colm doesn't care about the rest of us, though. He's only looking at me.

"Can I talk to you for a minute?" he asks.

"No." Micah's voice echoes through the room, much louder than the music, before I even get a chance to open my mouth. "He's closed for business. You were there, we discussed this. Now get a drink or get out."

"Calm down, Bambi," Colm says to him, still in a quiet voice, but now my blood is up, too.

"Hey," I say, but he keeps talking to Micah.

"I'm not asking him to help me assassinate the president, I just want his opinion on something."

Micah is fucking fuming. He hasn't removed Colm's eyeballs, though, which is nice. I don't want to have to pull him out of a brawl. I know from personal experience that he's a lot stronger than he looks.

"Fine. But watch your fucking mouth." I turn to Micah. "Two minutes. I'll be fine."

His eyes narrow, but he doesn't say anything. I top off his drink with a little more tequila for good measure, which makes him almost snort laugh at me, and then hustle out from behind the bar before Colm can ignite any more drama.

"I'm not going outside with you, if your plan is to jump me," I say as I drag him by the arm to the farthest corner of the room. "What do you want?"

For a second, he holds the same confident, almost-cocky expression as before, but then he softens. "Damn, Sav. Do you really think I would do that? I've always been on your side. I helped you get out and got a big fucking promotion in the process. Why would I come for you now?"

I huff, but he's not wrong.

"I miss you," he says, so quietly that I almost don't hear him. "You know you can still say hello without being asked to dig a grave or something."

I'm about to snap at him, but I stop myself. "Yeah, I know. I'm sorry. This is all new and weird."

"Is it good?" he asks. "You're happy?"

I take a deep breath and blow it out slowly, but it doesn't work so I repeat the process. "Yeah. I mean, as happy as I can be. I'm still a fucking mess. That might just be who I am, though. It's easier to deal with it when I don't have all the other shit to deal with, y'know?"

"And your little woodland creature?" he says, his mouth turning up into a smile that's just shy of salacious. "He makes you happy?"

"Fuck off." I punch him in the arm, but it barely rocks him backward. There's a twist of nerves inside me, like there always is when people finally know that Micah and I are more than whatever we were before. That we're something. That he's it. "Yes."

It's the only answer I can come up with, because talking about this with anyone, let alone a member of the Banna, makes me want to throw up. I avert my eyes, but Colm pats my arm to get my attention again.

"Good. It's good. He's a good kid." I roll my eyes a little, because he's barely a year younger than me and I think Colm is about the same age. We're all kids, really. Some of us are just also murderers. "I like how he is for you. You need someone to protect you. That was always my job, but I think he has me beat."

Colm quirks a smile, and his expression gets kind of distant. I can't read it.

"Don't worry about the guys, by the way. Patrick took most of the old timers with him when he left. I'm not saying they're progressive or anything—" He laughs. "But most of them don't seem to care enough about all this shit to go looking for trouble. The world is different now than it was for Patrick. Even our world."

I can't help but cock my head. He makes it sound simple. Father always drew this line in the sand and told me that the Banna was on one side and all the weak people of the world were on the other. There were a lot of things that were written on that line, but 'queer' was definitely one of them.

And now here's Colm, acting like it's no big deal. Like all this can eventually just drift away as people care less and less.

I can't wrap my mind around it. I don't even think I want to. It makes too much of my life a fucking waste.

"I'm sure you didn't come here to talk about my sex life," I say, before immediately regretting the ballsiness of my word choice.

Colm laughs, though. "No. Sorry. I wanted to know if you've heard of someone called 'Fallow'? No first name. I don't know if it's a title or a real name or what. People keep talking about him, and it's dark, violent shit, but it's very hush hush and I can't get a straight answer. It's like trying to ask my nan to tell me about the fair folk. Nothing but rumors and blank fucking verse."

"I'm sorry, brother. I don't know. Sounds kind of creepy, though."

"Yeah." He looks away from me, chewing on his bottom lip. "That's the problem."

There's a long silence, and once again I can't puzzle out his expression.

"Are you okay?"

Colm jumps a little, like he's snapping out of a trance, and turns his attention back to me. "Sorry. Yes. Thanks for your help, I'll leave you to your woodland creature." He smiles again, but it's weaker this time. "Come see me if you want to, okay? No strings."

When I nod and agree, I think I actually mean it. A few months ago, the idea would have crippled me with anxiety. But now that Patrick has been gone all this time and still hasn't come lurching back into our lives yet, I find it a little easier every day to convince myself he might really be letting us go free.

We exchange warm goodbyes, and it feels nice. Like the one decent part of my old, shitty life is slotting into my new one. I walk back to the bar with a small smile on my face, even if Micah is still glaring daggers at me.

"What did he want?"

My smile widens, because the vitriol in his voice could melt through the bar.

"Nothing, Bambi." I murmur the words in his ear and kiss him on the top of his head, taking the opportunity while I'm on this side of the bar. "He had a question that I couldn't answer anyway. No big deal."

"Mmm." No words follow his sound, but the distrust is written all over his face.

The last bit of my shift goes quickly. Micah is quiet, but I understand. He's probably just as freaked out at the idea of me running back to the Banna after everything we've gone through as I am at the idea of them dragging me back.

I don't poke at him, instead focusing on closing up and getting us home in one piece.

He was already tired, so the two margs I made him hit harder than normal. He's not drunk by any means, but he's a little loose and a lot sleepy by the time I drag him up to the apartment.

"Bedtime, Bambi. You look like you're about to fall asleep standing up."

I'm pulling off his shoes for him while he leans on my shoulders after we both threw our keys and phones somewhere to the side. As soon as I'm done, he pulls me up and starts to devour my face. Not even a hello kiss, this is a full-on tongue-down-my-throat kiss.

"What was that for?" I say quietly when we finally break apart. Not that I care. I'm already half hard, and his scrubs are thin enough that they're doing nothing to hide how worked up he is for me in return.

He doesn't say anything, though. He wraps his arms around my waist and rests his head on my chest, squeezing me tight. He doesn't do this very often, but whenever he does, I feel like he needs it a lot. I immediately reach out and hold him close, kissing the top of his head just like I did back at the bar.

"I'm not going anywhere, Bambi. I promise. I already spent my life savings getting my new identity, anyway. Do you have any idea how hard it is to get documents forged in the digital age? It's horseshit, I tell you. What do I need a social security number for anyway?"

That finally makes him laugh, even if the noise is muffled by my chest. Sometimes it's nice to be like this. I feel like the version of myself when we were kids, and the world was dark but simple. I knew how to protect him and that was the only thing I needed to do.

Now it's always him protecting me, and I don't know how he fucking does it because it's always so complicated I don't even know where to start. I don't understand any of it. Not the practical shit like actually learning how to become a real person, or the psychological shit like learning to live with my broken brain instead of running away from it.

He does, though. He's always there with meds or advice or sometimes just to fuck the nonsense out of me, if that's what I need in the moment. He always knows.

I lean down, wrapping my arms under his tight little ass and hitching him up until I'm carrying him. He makes a small squeak of surprise, which I file away in my memory bank with the other noises he makes for all eternity, but he only clings tighter to me as I walk us both to the shower.

"Come on. I'm sure you'd like to take out whatever these feelings you're having on my ass. Don't say I'm not here for you, Bambi."

He chuckles, but it's a maniacal sound and I know this is exactly what he was hoping would happen.

That's fine. It's exactly what I wanted as well.

We strip each other down, everything getting quicker and more frantic as the seconds pass. The water is barely warm by the time we stumble under the spray together, joined at the mouth and with Micah's hand wrapped around both our cocks.

For a while, that's enough. Grinding against each other, touching each other, tasting each other. Micah whispering, "That's it, doll," in my ear whenever we break for air.

Then he puts both his hands on the top of my head and pushes me to my knees. I buckle for him immediately, and without hesitation, he slides his hot length into my mouth.

Micah gasps when his cockhead hits the back of my throat, and I choke around it.

"Yes, fuck yeah, doll. That's it. So fucking perfect for me. You love being fed my cock, don't you?"

I can't answer, because he's holding my nose to his pubic bone and I'm busy feeling my throat spasm while spit drools down the side of my face. But yes. Yes, I do.

Just when I think I'm about to lose my vision from the oxygen deprivation, he lets up. I wait for him to do it again, but he doesn't. Instead, he starts fucking my face fast and hard, both hands still on my head to hold me steady.

It's perfect. I drift immediately, feeling like I'm being sucked into his orbit until nothing but him exists. He's making the same grunts and gasps that I adore, filling my mouth with the salt and musk of his cock, and I quickly lose the ability to think about anything else.

"Fuck your fingers while I fuck your face, slut. Show me how greedy your pussy is."

His voice is lust-soaked, and I can already see him falling apart in front of me. I do as he says, even though I'm struggling with my coordination. I fumble the shower lube, but eventually get some on my hand. It doesn't take long to work myself open, and soon I'm bouncing on my knees, rocking three fingers deeper and deeper into myself as he continues to stretch my jaw around his cock.

"Yes, yes, yes," he chants, more desperate and overwhelmed than I've seen him in a long time. "My perfect slut. She always needs her pussy filled, don't you?"

This time, he pulls out of my mouth so I can answer. My voice is so rough and desperate, so whiny, that I don't recognize it. But I recognize the feral look in Micah's eye whenever I get like this, so I don't hold back.

"Yes, Bambi. I'm a slut. My greedy pussy needs to be filled. Please give me your cum."

I buck my hips on my own fingers as I say it, because I really am desperate for him to fill me up.

"What a good girl," he says, his voice low and thick.

Instead of resuming his face fucking, Micah grabs me by the hair and jerks me up hard, making me cry out. He leans over, pulling my face until it's inches from his and my knees are beginning to lift off the ground. The pain bubbles through me, heightening everything else.

Micah tightens his grip then, looking me in the eye and saying something he's never said before, but immediately makes my cock pulse and my orgasm grow closer.

"Run."

I don't know why I instinctively know what he wants, but I want it too. He releases my hair, and I crash to my knees again, but before I even form a conscious thought, I'm up. I burst through the shower door, swinging it open so hard I'm amazed I don't break it. Out of the bathroom, down the hallway and into the apartment.

It's not a big space. There isn't far to run. But even just the few feet I've made it, wet and naked, vulnerable and desperate with my hole already stretched out for him to claim, feels insane. The drive for satisfaction is something I've never experienced before.

I hear Micah's footsteps behind me. *Slap, slap, slap* on the wood floor as he gets closer to me.

My adrenaline spikes and my cock is practically reaching backward for him, but I run.

My legs are longer, so I eat up the distance and dive for the other side of the couch. My fucking junk is loose, and it seems so unhinged, but in this moment I'm completely free. Micah is undeterred, though. He dives over the couch with a lot more grace than I managed.

His body is dripping water, his dark hair sleek and his

eyes wild. He lands practically on top of me and doesn't waste any time sweeping my legs out from under me, shoving me to the floor. My cheek hits the rug so hard I think it might bruise, but the pain explodes like another starburst of pleasure, I'm so keyed up.

He pulls my hands behind me, holding them loosely in one of his. I don't try to break his grip, because he knows I'm not going anywhere. I buck and writhe though, while he's straddling my ass. I'm not trying to get free. I just want to feel more of him and my body is operating on instinct alone. I couldn't stay still right now if you paid me, I feel like I have lightning in my veins.

"That's it, slut. You're not even pretending you don't want it. You just need my cock inside you. All my cum spilling out of that tight, wet pussy."

I fucking whine. High-pitched and long. It ends on a sob, because I need him inside me right fucking now. "Please," is the only word I can force through my lips, though. "Please" and "more." I cry them out like a prayer.

With one hand holding my wrists, Micah uses the other to guide his cock to my hole. He didn't lube himself, so there's only what's left from my fingerfucking before. I'm prepped, but it's still a burn to let him in, and I love every second of it.

It feels fucking cleansing.

"Bambi, Bambi, Bambi." My chant changes to his name as he shoves his cock inside me until he's finally seated.

As soon as he's ready, he gets that solid grip on my hair again and uses it as leverage to fuck me. It hurts everywhere. The stretch. The burn on my scalp. Every part of my body that I just scraped when I fell. The desperate ache of my cock needing release.

He fucks me relentlessly, whispering over and over that

I'm good and perfect and his slutty pussy to fill but no one else's.

Finally, Micah gasps and then cries out, burying himself deep as he pulses into me. I squeeze as hard as I can, milking him for every drop of his release and enjoying the way he shudders and kneads at the flesh of my ass while he rides out his orgasm.

For a second, I think there might be a break, but of course not. As soon as he's finished, he pulls out and roughly flips me over. His thick cock gets replaced by four fingers plunging into me, while he swallows my cock whole.

I make a strangled noise, grabbing onto his wet hair with both hands and fucking up into his mouth in desperation. He finds my prostate and works it over, and within seconds I'm spilling into his mouth, making just as much noise as he did a second ago.

I'm still blinking away the spots that were swimming in my vision during my orgasm when Micah pulls off my cock and climbs up my body to straddle my chest. He looks just as hungry and dangerous as he did before, like what we just did barely scratched the surface.

He grabs my face with his left hand, squeezing hard enough to force my jaw open. Then, with my head tilted back and my mouth open wide, he spits all the cum he just sucked out of me right into my waiting mouth. It's warm and tastes like both of us mixed together, but the utter debauchery of it is what makes me shiver.

When he shuts my mouth and nods, I swallow it down. Obedient to my core. His left hand is still on my face but immediately slaps me with the right. Not hard, but hard enough to make my entire body *zing* and feel awake again after having all my brain cells sucked out of my dick.

I gasp and look back up at him. I swear to god, my cock

is trying to get hard again faster than it ever has before. The psychotic look in his eye is only feeding it.

Micah grins at me, leaning over my face to surround me with his body, and I grin back.

I don't know who starts laughing first, but it's one of us. Soon we're both laughing hard, then kissing, then laughing in between kisses and rolling back and forth on the floor that's wet and sticky from our escapade.

Eventually, we calm down and end up lying side by side. We're still naked and damp, with our hands tangled together. Micah is playing with my fingers, and I don't have the energy to get up for a very long time.

"Well, I feel better. Do you feel better?" he asks.

I snort. "I feel like I got hit by a fucking train." I roll over, nuzzling my face into his shoulder. "But yeah, I feel better, Bambi. You always make me feel better."

More time passes, with neither of us speaking but neither of us ready to get up.

"I love you, doll," he says at last, still looking at the ceiling.

"I know," I say, and it feels like I really mean it this time. "I love you too."

"Good, because it's my fault that we need to take a whole other shower now."

I get up, groaning, and haul him to his feet as well. But we're both laughing again the whole walk there.

Medical Glossary

Tristan's notes on the medical terms, so you don't have to go look shit up:
You're welcome
-T-

Serosanguinous Fluid - When your wound gets weepy and gross, but it's not bleeding? That's serosanguinous fluid. It's the serum part of blood without the red blood cells. It has nutrients and shit in it, so when your wound is healing, especially if it's infected, your body tries to flood it with the stuff to keep it moist and well-fed. I know that's a gross way to put it, but I don't care. All wounds are going to weep, but the oozier something is, the more infected it probably is, because that's your body doing its best to fight the infection with whatever it's got.

Ceftriaxone - I called this the not-fucking-around antibiotic, and I stand by it. There are so many antibiotics, and you don't normally want to go to the big guns straight away. You save that shit for when you really need it, because of antibiotic resistance. Ceftriaxone might not be the biggest gun there is, but it's a good one. It's broad-spectrum, so it works on a bunch of shit. You might recognize it if you've ever been treated for the clap, so obviously the US Army buys it in bulk and just puts it in the water. (This is definitely a joke. But you know, not the worst idea I've ever had)

Blood Oxygen - You need oxygen in your blood. You

want that shit there. The most important thing your blood does is carry oxygen around to all your cells, so they can keep doing their little jobs and keep your body running. The whole thing is a fucking house of cards, I swear to god. Very important to keep this operation running smoothly so the cells don't die.

Lancet - Little pokey thing to get at the capillary blood in your fingertips. They make a small enough hole to basically get one drop for reading with a monitor, and then you throw each one away. If you work in a hospital on a general inpatient ward, especially med/surg, your pockets are literally always full of them.

Glucose - Sugar, basically. In medicine it's normally referring to how much sugar is your blood, because you need that to stay alive. People worry about high blood sugar and diabetics etc., and absolutely, that's a problem. I'm not underplaying it. But low blood sugar is the one that will kill you the fastest. Your brain runs almost entirely on glucose and uses a fat chunk of the glucose supply in your body. That's why you feel foggy and confused if your blood sugar tanks, because your brain is struggling. If you dip too low, it'll just give up the ghost and let you shuttle off your mortal coil. Strongly against medical advice.

Lactatometer - I promise, I don't mean a lactometer. A lactometer measures milk purity. Like *moo* milk. Or breast milk, I guess. I don't know, I don't own one, or have the ability to produce milk. Not that Ford isn't doing his level fucking best to knock me up, biology notwithstanding. A lactatometer, also called a lactate meter, measures how much lactate is in your blood. Lactate is the end product of glycolysis, and we don't have time to get into all that, but it is really fucking cool if you want to go look it up. Like Micah said before, it's basically a good ballpark gauge of how well your body is functioning. If you get someone that's a hot fucking disaster and there's a million places to start, their lactate is going to tell you if you're just starting the fuckery, and can work at a normal pace, or if you're uber quadruple fucked and racing against the reaper, so it's time to start slinging plasma and anything else you've got at it without waiting for labs.

(Not that I would do things without waiting for labs. Moi? Never. I'm a good boy, I swear.)

D5W - Saline, but with sugar added in. Two for one. I'm either giving it because your blood sugar needs a boost, or sometimes it's because the drug I'm mixing it with works better in this than plain saline.

Antibiotic Infusions - When you're getting antibiotics intravenously, they tend to be in huge volumes, so we give them over hours. Sorry, I don't have a funnier explanation for that. But if you see someone at the hospital with a big bag of fluids as well as one or two small bags, they're very possibly antibiotics that need to drip in slowly over time. Sometimes you have to change the rate during the infusion to make sure they don't have a reaction, kind of like blood, in which case there's math. So much math. If you want to go cross-eyed, try and work out the rate for doxycycline.

Pharmacology - The details on how a drug or chemical actually works, when you get down to the nitty gritty. Not for the faint-hearted. Lots of sciencey shit in there.

Cultures - This is when you swab something like a wound and then do some science shit to see exactly what bacteria, yeast, whatever is brewing in there. I think it involves petri dishes. I really don't know, can you imagine me in a lab? Hard pass. Anyway, it's a good idea to do, because then you know exactly what shit you're trying to kill with your antibiotics, and you can pick the best ones, instead of just throwing everything at the wall and seeing what sticks. Especially in the age of superbugs. But sometimes you just don't have time for that, and Micah needs to learn to be less fancy when he's triaging gangsters in his own living room.

Necrotic Tissue – Okay, I do hate lab shit, but I have a soft spot for etymology. It's my nerd weakness. Necrotic, or necrosis, means dead tissue, which comes from the latinized version of the Ancient Greek word *nekrosis*, which means - you guessed it - dead or dying. Which comes from the proto-Indo-European root *nek*, which also means death. So we've been using that sound to mean death in like a quarter of the world since the motherfucking *Bronze Age*. Isn't that dope? Also yes, I read. I can be multifaceted. Don't pigeonhole me just because I'm pretty.

Rads - X-rays. I know it doesn't make sense, but it's short for radiology. You get used to it.

Pulse Ox - Everybody learned what this was during Covid. It's a little plastic thingy that goes on the end of your finger and reads how much oxygen is in your blood. If you're still breathing, so the air is coming into your lungs, but it's not showing up in your bloodstream whose job is to carry that shit around to all your other cells, something is very, very wrong with you.

Blood Volume - Not to sound like an asshole, but it's the volume of blood in your body. You don't want to run out of that, it's important. There should be around 4-6 liters. Yes, we use the metric system in medicine because it makes sense and freedom units don't. If you start running out, your heart works overtime to keep what's left circulating, so you tend to get a racing pulse. If you don't fix the problem, you're not going to get enough oxygen to those cells, and then you're going into shock. Bad. Try to avoid. 10/10 do not recommend. That's why doctors will put fluids in you a lot of the time, to help bulk that shit out and keep it moving.

Fentanyl - I know you know what this is, you little dope fiend. It's a synthetic opiate that's supposed to be used as a hardcore painkiller in a hospital or pre-hospital setting, but really makes a killing on the recreational drug market. Oh, and it's fucking deadly. And it gets cut into all the other illegal drugs, which is why people are dying from overdoses in record numbers in America, as well as a bunch of other countries. No I will not give you a reference for that, you can google it.

Narcan - The anti-fentanyl. Narcan (naloxone is the generic name, Narcan is the brand name and also gets used as a verb now, because the opioid epidemic is so bad here we have to have a verb for this shit) reverses the effects of opioids like fentanyl, morphine, heroine, whatever. You'd use it in anything from surgery, if a patient goes too deep from their pain management while sedated, or on the street if you find someone OD'd. Frankly, everyone should carry it. It has no use other than reversing OD's. You can't get high off of it. Sling that shit everywhere. Put goody bags of it outside pharmacies for all I care.

Percocets - Yet another opioid contributing to America's soul-crushing addiction problem. This one comes in pill form and gets prescribed for serious pain. Super fucking addictive. Use with care. If you want to see exactly how much this shit fucks you up, as well as how *wildly* deliberate it was on the part of the pharmaceutical companies (allegedly) to do this to us, check out the show *Painkiller* on Netflix. I'm not kidding.

Amitriptyline - This is a very old school antidepressant. It's also prescribed for other shit sometimes, like migraines. It's been around since the fifties, and like most antidepressants it basically works by stopping the serotonin in your brain from being sucked back up so quickly, so you get more time to simmer in it. This one can have some funky side effects though and a not great detox, so it doesn't tend to be the first thing you're prescribed. Don't listen to me though, this is not my fucking area.

Emergent Paracentesis - I know it sounds obvious, but emergent is when something is an emergency. As in, it's actively in the process of becoming an emergency. Kind of. Grammar is hard. It's an adjective, anyway. Paracentesis is the act of shoving a giant horse needle in a person's abdomen to drain the fluid that's collecting there before it crushes their lungs and other organs so they can't breathe.

Centesis Kit - Centesis is any time you're puncturing a body part to drain the fluid. Anything you do a lot in medicine, the supplies tend to come prepackaged altogether in little sterile kits. You break the seal and dump it all out in your sterile field instead of having to collect each individual thing, to save time. Also, so the medical supplier can charge a bajillion dollars for them. In the case of a centesis, it's going to include a big-ass needle, among other things. I don't recommend you google this one.

Field Medicine - Officially, field medicine is a catch-all term for medicine that's performed in a non-hospital or pre-hospital setting, like what I do. Unofficially, it's a way of life. State of mind and utter badass-ness. Yes, I'm biased, but I'm the one taking the time to explain this all for you so fuck you, I'll say what I want. It's bad-fucking-ass. A lot of making it work with what you've got, making decisions on the fly, and pulling solutions out of your ass. People who are into shit like surgery might tell you pre-hospital people are just assholes who patch shit together and leave them to clean up the mess, but I say I'd like to see them practice medicine without their matching *Figs* scrub set and $12 coffee. To each their own.

(Real talk though, no shade. Surgeons & surgery staff are also badass. Just... terrifying robot people. Way too clean and more disdainful than my mother. But still badass.)

Promethazine - It's kind of like Benadryl on steroids. Not literally, but you know what I mean. You need a prescription for it though, and it has the potential for way more side effects, so I don't recommend fucking around with it. Also, like Micah said, it has a nasty habit of creating abscesses when it's injected if it's not done properly. Ouch. Professional use only. It will make a person go to sleep, though, and it's not addictive like valium etc., so in this situation it was the best I could do.

Just so everyone's clear: these are all my opinions, and I'm a fictional fucking character. Don't be a dumbass and use them as medical advice. They're not medical advice. But they are entertaining, and if you want to read up on any of it, I support you, because medicine will never not be interesting.

And when class warfare eventually descends upon us, you're going to want to know a little something about something.

Acknowledgements

I'm terrible at emoting. Everyone I have to thank knows me well enough to know that, so they'll understand my lackluster acknowledgement section stems from neurodivergence and childhood trauma rather than a lack of my appreciation for them. I would love to write a gushing essay, but just the thought of it makes me itch, so insert gushing here.

Amanda, Amy, Ash, Cara, George, Lauralee, Lauri, Rachel, and Tyla were all absolute lifesavers in the process of writing this book. Thank you for the alpha/beta reading (among other things) and answering all my meandering thoughts & questions at random times of the night.

My Street Team have also been little badasses and helped me pull this together into something resembling a professional operation.

I appreciate you all so much more than I can say.

Also, a special thank you to George for volunteering to go undercover with the Irish Mafia irl and find out just how gay they really are. How far he went through with this operation and how successful it was, I will leave to your imagination.

POSSUM HOLLOW

STUPID DIRTY
68 WHISKEY
RUNNING FERAL
HOLLOW POINT

SINS OF THE BANNA

SAVAGE
FALLOW
LUCKY
GRIEF

ERIN RUSSELL

hard love

Erin Russell is a queer author living in Los Angeles. They love to write hurt/comfort romance about neurodiverse characters. They hate writing author bios, but are extremely candid on social media.
Oh, and they love possums.

Connect with Erin on social media or check out playlists on Spotify, using the QR code below..

www.erinrussellauthor.com